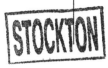

D1342681

005041186 1

A BROKEN LAND

By Jack Ludlow

THE ROADS TO WAR SERIES

The Burning Sky
A Broken Land

THE REPUBLIC SERIES

The Pillars of Rome
The Sword of Revenge
The Gods of War

THE CONQUEST SERIES

Mercenaries
Warriors
Conquest

Written as David Donachie

THE JOHN PEARCE SERIES

By the Mast Divided
A Shot Rolling Ship
An Awkward Commission
A Flag of Truce
The Admirals' Game
An Ill Wind
Blown Off Course
Enemies at Every Turn

A BROKEN LAND

JACK LUDLOW

First published in Great Britain in 2011 by
Allison & Busby Limited
13 Charlotte Mews
London W1T 4EJ
www.allisonandbusby.com

A CIP catalogue record for this book is available from
the British Library.

10 9 8 7 6 5 4 3 2 1

13-ISBN 978-0-7490-0837-6

Typeset in 11/18 pt Sabon by
Allison & Busby Ltd.

Paper used in this publication is from sustainably managed sources.
All of the wood used is procured from legal sources and is fully traceable.
The producing mill uses schemes such as ISO 14001
to monitor environmental impact.

Printed and bound by
CPI Group (UK) Ltd, Croydon, CR0 4YY

To

Eric Gleadall

A friend who experienced
everything under the sun:
good fortune as well as setbacks,
both financially and in his health.
Yet he never, whatever his condition,
let his smile slip, nor ceased to joke
and be good company.
Bravery is too shallow a word.

PROLOGUE

Cal Jardine was never himself entirely sure how he got so caught up in the counter-revolution that went on to become the Spanish Civil War. Many who knew him put it down to his inability to pass up on a scrap, but initially it was merely from being in the wrong place at the wrong time and in the company of the wrong people, like his one-time sergeant and now good friend, the boxing gym owner and anti-fascist street fighter, Vince Castellano.

His presence in Barcelona at the fateful time came about because he was doing a favour for a valued friend, one that also cocked a mighty snook at the pretensions of Nazi Germany and the stupidity of Aryan eugenics; given his openly stated antipathy to National Socialism, the idea of helping to facilitate, even on the margins, what was being called the People's Olympiad appealed to him.

The Berlin Olympics, which Adolf Hitler was using as a showcase for his absurd theories on race, were due to take place in mid August;

the idea of pre-empting that with a socialist set of competitions, as well as demonstrating there was another, saner world, had come from many sources, though it had to be admitted the organisers were no more Cal Jardine's natural bedfellows than those who claimed to be part of the master race.

Far-left socialists and intellectuals, international trade unionists, syndicalists, anarchists and communists, both Stalinist and Trotskyist in persuasion, did not easily gel with a man of independent means, who had made his way in the world for a decade by running guns and advising on the tactics of guerrilla warfare.

Asked about his own political views, Cal Jardine was inclined to reply that he generally favoured a government that had no need to incarcerate or shoot you if you disagreed with them; beyond that and a deeply honed sense of what was just and equitable, he was fairly indifferent to politics on the very good grounds that most people he had met engaged in that pursuit seemed more than a touch fraudulent.

Even then, he could have been gone a whole week before the balloon went up; the reason he was not, and this surprised no one, was a woman. Florencia Gardiola, when he sought to expound his indifference to politics, insisted he was just selfish, but then she applied that accusation to anyone who did not share her passionate belief in anarchism, the end of wage slavery and the replacement of the capitalist system with a new society based on true democracy and a state managed by the efforts of worker cooperatives; that she did this occasionally in his bed at the very superior Ritz Hotel did not seem to her – and Cal Jardine tried to make a pun out of it – an anachronism.

All he got for his poor joke was a pummelling on his naked chest which, in seeking to contain her, ended up with another bout of frantic lovemaking with the very fiery and beautiful young woman who had been assigned to him as an interpreter. His friend Sir Monty Redfern had bankrolled some of the British athletes heading to Barcelona – he had agreed to pay for their accommodation – an act the Jewish millionaire had likened, in an expression typical of a man who had hauled himself up from East End poverty, to passing a hard stool through a haemorrhoid arse. Monty's problem was that, much as he hated the far-left, he hated the Nazis more.

'But, Cal, you think I am going to just give these madmen my money?' he had cried. 'They might send it to Moscow, the crooks, or use it to buy weapons. No, I have to make sure it is spent on their hostels.'

'Hostels? I hope you don't expect me to share their accommodation, Monty.'

The response had come with a delighted hoot. 'That I should see, you in a workers' boarding house, ten to a room, with the smell of nothing but unwashed feet and garlic farts.'

That the last words had coincided with the opening of Monty's office door had made him look momentarily abashed, but not for long; as a man he was too ebullient for reserve, and probably, by now, his recently acquired assistant either had become accustomed to his vulgarity or lacked the colloquial English necessary to fully comprehend it. Elsa Ephraim was very attractive, with long black hair, alabaster skin and dark inviting eyes, and Monty, unseen by Elsa, gave a roll of the eyes that was a curse to his advanced years, not to mention a wife who would castrate him if he even looked like straying.

Cal had been gifted with a smile, having been instrumental in getting Elsa and her family out of Hamburg, crucially with a lot of their possessions, paintings and jewellery, so they had not arrived in England, like so many of their persecuted co-religionists, as paupers. Their extraction had turned out to be the last in a long line of successes; his name and activities had become known to the Gestapo, obliging him to get out of Germany himself, albeit by a different route. Not only beautiful but smart as well, Cal had brought her to the attention of Monty, who had given her a job.

'You have the draft, Elsa?' Monty had asked.

The slip of paper had been handed over, as well as a clipboard and a pen, which had made Monty frown. 'My own shekels, Cal, and I still have to sign for them.'

'Two thousand pounds is a lot of money, Mr Redfern.'

'Child, there was a time in my life when two pennies was a lot of money.'

'I should get out as quick as you can, Elsa, or the violins will start playing "Annie Laurie".'

The girl had been confused and it showed, it being English so idiomatic it taxed her still-limited knowledge of the language. She spoke it well, but tended to get her tenses mixed up.

'What this goy layabout means, Elsa, is that I am a sentimental old fool.'

Elsa had replied with a complete lack of irony, her look serious. 'My father is that too; he cries often for what we left behind in Königsberg.'

'Thank you, Elsa,' a misunderstood Monty had replied, before handing the bank draft to Cal.

'You don't want me to sign for it?' he had asked when the door closed behind her.

'Cal, I don't want anyone to know you have it, and even more I do not want anyone to know where you are taking it and why. Me paying for beds for a bunch of Bolsheviks! I like it at the synagogue when people speak to me.'

'How's Elsa doing?' Cal had asked.

'To my head she is doing things I cannot talk about, but the girl is clever and diligent. Don't fall for that sentimentality shit about her father, 'cause he's a sly old bird. Right now if he's crying, it is over the joy of buying a steel stockist on the cheap.'

'He's only been here a few months and already he's gone into business?'

'He's Jewish, Cal, it's what we do.' Monty had tapped his head. 'And it is shrewd with rearmament coming.'

'You're sure it's coming?'

'Damn sure, Cal. We are going to have to fight Hitler and you know that better than me. Now don't go losing that draft, anyone can take it to a bank and cash it.'

CHAPTER ONE

As he walked along the Strand later that day, and not for the first time in his life, Callum Jardine had been left to reflect on the effect of coming back home from an area of conflict, something he had done after the Great War and more than once since; the discomfort caused by both the experience of battle and his personal knowledge of what was happening in the Horn of Africa, set against the palpable indifference of those with whom he now mingled on one of London's busiest thoroughfares.

If the people he jostled and passed had concerns about events elsewhere in the world, it did not show; the Italians were busy annexing Ethiopia, using liberal doses of poison gas against spear-carrying tribesmen and civilians, while Nazi Germany, having torn up the Treaty of Versailles, had remilitarised the Rhineland, daring both France and Britain to react and crowing when they failed.

Having got away with that breach of their international

obligations, the Nazis were now putting the thumbscrews on Austria to join them and create a Greater German Reich, stirring up what support they had to create instability. Here at home, Britain's own fascist leader, Oswald Mosley, was ranting and raving at his blackshirts, being praised by the *Daily Mail* and becoming more like a cut-price version of Adolf Hitler every time he opened his mouth.

He could not help but wonder at what occupied the minds of those on the crowded pavements, apart from the everyday need to earn a crust. Was it sport perhaps? Fred Perry had won at Wimbledon for the third time; the Indian cricket team was struggling through a long summer of defeats, the supporters thrilled by Wally Hammond's century, showing a return to form for England's best batsman; and across the pond Max Schmeling had knocked out Joe Louis.

If the nation was still in the grip of an economic depression it hardly showed in the metropolis, especially in the short dead-end road that led to the imposing entrance of the Savoy Hotel, filled with taxis and long black limousines, all overseen by a magnificently attired doorman. The effects were being felt elsewhere, in mining villages and valleys, in the northern industrial centres and idle shipyards.

That induced a slight feeling of guilt, given his destination. Still, lunch at Simpson's was always something to look forward to: properly aged rib of beef or saddle of lamb carved at the table, though it was not a place where the matters on which he was ruminating would stir even an eyebrow. To the denizens of Simpson's the unemployed were lazy, not benighted, the dropping of mustard gas on innocents, as long as they were black or brown, more likely to lead to a degree of indifference rather than condemnation.

The spread of fascism in Europe, from the Black Sea to the Baltic, would be seen as a minor irritation in one of the great food bastions of the British upper crust; the clientele tended to be people who had a lot of admiration for anyone who made the trains run on time, added to a less than charitable attitude towards trade unions or workers demanding a decent standard of living.

Peter Lanchester was already ensconced, nursing a schooner of sherry, looking very much at home in the Grand Divan. The dark-panelled dining room was full, as usual, and there was the odd glance of recognition as the new arrival made his way to the table – London society was a touch incestuous and he was, after all, a person who carried with him a certain amount of notoriety; not many people can claim to have been acquitted of murder in an infamous *crime passionel*.

Good manners insisted he made eye contact with the one or two people who could be said to be part of his wife's social circle, as well as some of the very attractive ladies present. He was, by nature, incapable of ignoring them. In turn, they could not disregard the arrival of an extremely good-looking man, well dressed but with a hint of the rogue in him, obviously very fit and sporting a deep and even suntan of the kind hard to achieve under English skies.

'Cal, old boy! You look as if you have just come back from yachting with our besotted monarch.'

Said loud enough to be overheard at several tables, the remark was greeted with blank looks by the ignorant and a cold stare by the very few in the know. Edward, the yet-to-be-crowned King of England and Emperor of India, was sailing in the Mediterranean with his American lover, Wallis Simpson, divorced once and filing for a second, causing tongues to wag in the higher reaches of society, though the great unwashed at home were being kept in ignorance by a self-imposed news blackout. Every other national press in the world was openly speculating on how far the golden boy would go.

'The American newspapers are saying he wants to marry her,' Cal said quietly, as he slid into his seat, nodding at the invitation to join Peter in a sherry.

''Cause a hell of a stink if he tries. Anyway, how do you know what the American papers are saying?'

'Had a letter from a journalist chap I met in Ethiopia. Seems they'd rather print front-page stories about our king-emperor and his less-than-chaste mistress than anything about Italian atrocities.'

'Romance sells newspapers, poison gas dropped on fuzzy-wuzzies does not.'

That remark had got Lanchester a glare, the return look – arched eyebrows added to a cynical grin – an indication that it had been a deliberate attempt to get under Cal's skin. To his guest, Peter Lanchester had always been a mite free with his tongue when it came to the common insults, reflecting the attitudes of those with whom he mixed – members of London's clubland, the country house set and golfing bores.

Eschewing the temptation to react, he had decided to stick to the king. 'Not that one should care a fig what the booby is up to with his clapped-out paramour.'

That got an arched and cynical eyebrow. 'You call our future king a booby?'

'So would you if you'd met him.' Reacting to the enquiring look, Cal had added, 'Lizzie introduced me to him, given he moves in the same social circle as my too-easily-bored wife. As a man, he is short in the arse, vacuous in expression, vain, pig-ignorant and, for reasons best known to the gods, beloved by the great British public or the press that feed their fantasies.'

'Quite a condemnation.'

'I assume I am here for a purpose, Peter, and that has nothing to do with Edward Windsor?'

'Little bird told me you were off to Barcelona?' Cal was surprised, wondering how he knew, but he had merely nodded as a tall schooner of Manzanilla Pasada was placed before him. Lanchester had then smoothed a hand over his black swept-back hair and looked at him keenly. 'Which prompts me to ask, Cal, if you have ever heard of a body called Juan March Ordinas?'

'Hails from Majorca and has made a tremendous pile, originally from tobacco smuggling, though he was quite active during the war as well, shipping supplies of arms through the Mediterranean on the q.t. for both sides. Pals with the monarchical party, though he was threatened with choky after King Alfonso abdicated in '31 and the Republic came into being. Not fancying a prison cell, he then escaped to Gibraltar where the powers that be, namely His Majesty's Government, refused to hand him back to Spanish justice.'

'And I thought I was going to surprise you.'

'Come on, Peter, in the world in which I move Juan March is quite well known. You can't amass illegal millions through smuggling without flagging yourself up to your competitors, not to mention those who might want to avail themselves of your routes and shipping. He also dabbled in lots of other nefarious things. My guess is he did a bit of spying for us in the war and I daresay there are some skeletons in our Whitehall cupboards as far as March is concerned that no one wants made public, hence the privilege of protection.'

'He is holed up in London, Cal, and making mischief.'

'Nature of the beast.' Presented with a menu, Cal had aimed it at his host. 'I hope you are not seeking to inveigle me into risking my neck for the price of a decent luncheon, because, let me tell you, he is not a fellow to mess with, he's a killer. Quite a few who tried ended up floating face down in the Med.'

That had got a mischievous look. 'Risking your neck is something you would do whether I asked you to or not.'

Callum Jardine was unable to fault that; he had only been back in London for a few weeks and already he had felt a sense of boredom setting in, not aided by his own personal problems of a socially active wife he could neither ignore nor live with. Peter Lanchester knew him too well; they had served as soldiers together in the last months of the Great War and afterwards in seeking to contain an insurgency in Mesopotamia.

It had been a loose connection, recently strengthened by what had happened in Germany, Romania and Ethiopia, but he could not say, in any way, that he knew the man well. There had been hints of a job with British Intelligence in some capacity, but Cal had no idea if he was still employed or was, as he had hinted, on the scrap heap due to financial cutbacks brought on by government economies.

Lanchester had come to Hamburg the previous autumn to both warn and engage his old acquaintance, claiming to represent a group of wealthy or well-connected individuals who had combined to seek to put a check on the threat of fascism to Great Britain. But, apart from a couple of obvious names – and you could only speculate if he was telling the truth regarding those he had revealed – he had consistently declined to mention the identities of most of his backers.

That they had power had been proven by the way the task Peter had asked him to perform, as well as aided him to execute, had been both financed and facilitated; that it had been risky went without saying – the clandestine purchase and shipment of the weapons of war could never be anything else. In the process, Jardine's opinion of Peter Lanchester, not terribly high to begin with, had risen several notches; he was not a fellow with whom he shared much in common in the political or moral line, but he was both brave and gifted.

'So, apart from the love of my company, Peter, why this?'

'Over there in the corner,' Peter had whispered, 'those three chaps, glowering at the world in general and at each other in particular.'

That was said with a nod past his guest's shoulder; too experienced to jerk his head round, it was several moments before Cal Jardine had looked to where Lanchester indicated. The table had been as described, but there seemed to be something not quite right about the party, a stiffness that made conversation look difficult. The impression was fleeting – it had to be, because he could not stare – but it was visible that they were either earnestly engaged in serious discussion, or possibly in disagreement.

'The one with his back to you is MI6,' Lanchester had continued, idly casting his eye over the menu. 'Name of Cecil Beeb, and the grey-haired chap is Douglas Jerrold, editor of the *Catholic Review*, a nitwit who thinks the sun shines right out of Oswald Mosley's alimentary canal. He makes support of the *Mail* look tepid. Swarthy one is Luis Bolin, London correspondent of a Spanish newspaper, also, coincidentally, very anti the present Republican government.'

'And?'

'Would you not be interested in what they might be talking about, given where you are off to?'

'I'm not as nosy as you, Peter.'

'A little bird has let us know Señor March is up to no good in the Iberian Peninsula.'

Even if he had not wanted to be intrigued, Cal had been unable to help it. 'Go on.'

'We think there's going to be a military revolt in Spain, seeking to topple the Popular Front government, and Juan March is helping to finance the generals leading it. Rumour has it he has piled in over fifteen million US dollars already, with more promised when the balloon goes up.'

It had been hard not to look impressed, indeed not to emit a soft whistle, that being a very serious amount of money, but, taking into account March's background and those who constituted his enemies, the man's action made a certain sense.

'It was the Republic that sought to put him in jail,' Cal had replied, 'so he can't love democracy much, but from what I know of Juan March, which I admit is limited and second-hand, making money is his prime concern. Mind, if he pays out that much to put the soldiers in power, he can name his fee if they succeed.'

Since being apprised of the commission from Monty Redfern he had quite naturally sought to recall what he knew of present-day Spain, a seriously troubled country racked by endless political infighting, not that such a thing was new – it had been going on for years. Industrial walkouts, agrarian uprisings from peasant labourers, a full-blown revolution in the mining region of the Asturias involving a bloody military put-down, the whole mixed with various regions seeking autonomy from Madrid.

Yet when Cal had read of such things as general strikes he had to remind himself that there had been that in the United Kingdom ten years previously while he had been in the Middle East – the difference with the Iberian model being that the peasantry tended to murder the landowners and vice versa, while the industrial workers used guns and the authorities everything including tanks, artillery and bombs to put them down.

'We also have information March is shipping weapons and that he has been in contact with both Berlin and Rome about further supplies.'

'And the "we" you represent don't like it.'

'Not a bit.'

'While HMG?'

'Is either ignorant, which is doubtful, or indifferent, which is likely. We are paying the price for not stopping Hitler in the Rhineland and Mussolini in Ethiopia, we've a dictator now in Portugal, as well as a string of rightist governments throughout Central Europe, and that can only get worse if Spain goes the same way.'

There had been the temptation to press, Lanchester having connections that put him in a position to know much of what went by the name of 'official thinking', but it would have been pointless; he was close-lipped on anything like that.

'Has anyone bothered to tell Madrid of what you suspect?'

'I should think everyone has, but they either don't believe it or are very sure it is all talk and will not come to fruition. Besides which, they are always being bothered by false alarms regarding military revolts. General Sanjurjo, the chap they are talking about as being the titular leader of this one, tried it on four years ago and fell flat on his hidalgo face.'

'They did put him in jail.'

'Then let him out again!' Peter had protested. 'Why they didn't just shoot the bugger when they had the chance escapes me.'

'You must reckon this one more serious.'

'We do, because it is more comprehensive and better organised and that may have been conveyed to the Spanish government. But they are, Cal, a race not traditionally known for rapid activity or cohesive action at any time, while their army, if you exclude the chaps in Morocco, are bloody useless.'

That was an area in which Cal Jardine did possess knowledge, it being necessary to his trade. Nothing hardens and trains troops like battle, the element that also creates an *esprit de corps*. The Spanish Army of Africa, which included a unit modelled on the French Foreign Legion, had been fighting Riff tribesmen for decades. They were hard and professional; the concomitant of that was a body of experienced field officers accustomed to leading soldiers in combat right up to and including men who were now senior Spanish generals.

'They are not completely at the old siesta, mind,' Lanchester had continued, as if reading his guest's mind. 'The government have sent the dangerous brass hats off to far-flung postings to put a block on them plotting. Chap called Franco, who is army chief of staff and considered very suspect and second only to Sanjurjo, they have exiled to the Canary Islands.'

'That won't stop them,' Cal had insisted. 'Ever heard of radios?'

'Precisely.'

'So,' Cal had asked, with a very slight jerk of his head towards the trio of gloom. 'Why the interest?'

'Jerrold over there is a fanatic and has introduced Cecil Beeb to Bolin, a man funded by the money of Juan March, who, as you say, would be eager to return home and has a bottomless pit of lolly to play with. If certain key generals are going to revolt, the only way some of them can get to the mainland in time to be effective is by aeroplane – Franco particularly – which makes it doubly interesting when we see such people lunching with a chap who just happens to be both a virulent anti-communist and a qualified pilot.'

'You plan to keep an eye on Beeb?' That had got a nod, as Cal Jardine added, not without irony, 'Is it not a little bit obvious to let yourself be seen?'

'Cal, old boy, we don't have the resources to keep a clandestine eye on the bugger twenty-four hours a day, so the plan is to let him know he is under observation. Induce caution, don't you know.'

'And me?'

'Since you are off to sunny Barcelona I thought it only fair to warn you.'

Such a throwaway line had raised the suspicion that Lanchester was being disingenuous; if Cal Jardine knew all about the villainies of Juan March, it was quite possible that one or more of the people who had been pointed out to him were conscious of his name and the nature of his past activities as a gunrunner.

Indeed, that might explain the atmosphere at their table; with limited resources, Peter Lanchester was stirring the pot by letting them be seen together, creating in the mind of the trio the impression that he had lines of enquiry and sources of information that, in truth, did not exist. As Cal had already said, the clandestine movement of arms was a business where knowing what others were up to was part of the game.

'Of course,' Peter had added, 'it would also be of advantage if you were to keep an ear to the ground and let us know if anything occurs to stir the pot.' That had got a wave of the menu. 'Now we must choose some food and you must tell me about these People's Olympics of yours, which I must say sounds dire.'

That had been like a throwing down of the gauntlet, teasing Cal to enquire as to how he knew so much and even, perhaps, to seek the source of his information; he was not prepared to play.

'It could be fun,' he had responded.

'What!' Peter had exclaimed, genuinely shocked. 'All those pious lefties, Bolsheviks and anarchists?'

That had been said far too loudly and attracted looks and arched eyebrows from nearby tables that would have been less troubled, in such surroundings, if he had publicly uttered every filthy swear word in the canon.

Peter Lanchester thought he had Beeb taped, unaware that the fellow he looked to be taking on a picnic, Hugh Pollard, in the company of a couple of very attractive girls, was, as well as another MI6 operative, an aerial navigator. He had followed them to Brighton and observed the consumption of the food from their hamper and taken some pleasure in watching the females disrobe to both sunbathe and swim.

It was perfectly natural that on their way back to town from a day of sun and sea, they should pass through Croydon on the A23; what was not expected was that instead of driving straight on past the airport as they had on the way down, they should swing their open-top touring car into the avenue that led to the terminal building. Worse, they drove straight past that onto the tarmac, where a twin-engined de Havilland Dragon Rapide was already fired up, its engines warm.

If they had luggage, it was clearly already aboard, proving that their departure was a well-planned operation. Peter Lanchester did what he could to stop them, which was not much – he had no official capacity and the staff at the airport, when bearded, could only say the flight plan was one to take the aircraft to Paris, giving them no reason to block the take-off.

By the time he could get on the blower to someone with the power of prohibition, the Rapide was already airborne, the two attractive girls waving frantically from the car. On the observation deck he spotted the journalist Luis Bolin with a pair of binoculars in use. If there had been any doubt about the nature of the flight, the presence of the right-wing Spanish newspaperman laid it to rest. The flight plan was a myth and the projected revolt of the Spanish generals looked to be imminent.

The cable Peter Lanchester sent Cal Jardine was simple; it implied if he had no reason to stay, it might be time to hotfoot out. The recipient had indeed carried out the task for which he had come; the hostels and other accommodation for the Olympians had been paid for and Monty Redfern had change coming, while the opening ceremony was to take place on the morrow.

Yet, for all the febrile atmosphere of the city and the country, screaming headlines in the various journals, marches and countermarches and also a couple of high-profile political assassinations in Madrid – one of a prominent left-winger, the other, no doubt in revenge, the killing of a leading anti-socialist – the sun was shining, the food and wine were excellent and, of course, there was his interpreter, daughter of a Spanish father and an English mother, the blonde, petite and devastatingly beautiful Florencia Gardiola.

CHAPTER TWO

Cal Jardine was lying in bed, naked and sweating, with Florencia's head and messed-up hair in the crook of his arm, watching, in the first glimmer of early-morning light, a ceiling fan trying and failing to move the still, humid, midsummer air. It was a few seconds before he realised what had penetrated his slumbers, but given the sound of the yelling crowd was getting progressively louder, it did not take long to pin that down. Gently he moved Florencia's head, slipped off the bed and went to the open double window to see what the fuss was about this time.

Demonstrations were nothing unusual in Barcelona; everyone in the city, on both the right and the left, seemed to feel the only way to make a point was to take to the streets. But this was different; the wide boulevard below was jam-packed by a massive crowd moving as one, banners aloft, calling out words he could not comprehend in both Catalan and Spanish.

Their flags and raised fists left little doubt, in this case, of which side of the political divide they were on; these were workers marching in protest at what he did not know, but to that was added the crack of distant rifle shots, too many in number and from different weapons, which indicated this was no mere demonstration. The thought, an uncomfortable one, that he might have left it too late to depart, was quick to surface, but he reassured himself.

Barcelona was a port and not much more than a hundred and fifty miles from the French border. If he could not get a boat out, or a train, there was always the option of getting hold of a car, with the caveat that the Spanish roads left a lot to be desired. Then, thinking about why he was here and the fact that he might need to make a hurried exit and not on his own, he wondered if he might be required to hire a couple of buses.

The growing noise eventually penetrated the slumbers of Florencia and she stirred into her habitual groaning wakefulness, a mixture of yawning, stretching and cursing aimed at the approaching day. Normally a slow riser, she was not this time, as the import of what was happening pierced her languid brain. Leaping from the bed, she rushed to the window and out onto the balcony, pushing Cal aside, to yell in unison with the crowd as soon as she saw their banners. What came back was a cacophony of male whistles; she was, after all, stark naked.

Ignoring both her and the response, Cal made a call to the hotel reception, which did not produce much enlightenment, merely a reassurance from a silver-voiced functionary that it was a small affair of no significance. Some soldiers in Morocco had rebelled against the government and seized certain installations. It was an insurrection the man was sure would be swiftly put down.

Cal then asked for an outside line, to phone Vince Castellano at the hostel where he and his party were staying. That proved fruitless; the line was dead, which indicated to him it was serious – the first two targets for the rebellious were always the radio station and the telephone exchange.

'Get dressed.'

That her nakedness had attracted all that attention, and no doubt the anger of the marching women, did not seem to have penetrated Florencia's brain, while being of a temperament to always dispute a command, she spun round to berate her lover. At that moment came the unmistakeable rattle of a solitary machine gun, followed by a dull explosion, which stopped her protests.

'Revolution!' she hissed.

'I need to see what is going on, to find out if any of those I am responsible for are in danger.'

All he got in reply was a clenched fist, furiously shaken, which made her breasts bounce as well, rendering slightly absurd what she said. 'We must fight.'

'Not like that,' Cal replied, already in the act of putting on a shirt. He picked up the dress she had worn the night before and threw it to her. 'Not unless you're planning to shag them into surrender.'

Catching the dress, Florencia's face showed deep confusion, which Cal knew had nothing to do with his words, one of which she probably had not fully understood. Normally keen to expand her English, especially slang, she was too preoccupied now for such trifles. This was an occasion for which she had been waiting all her adult life and now it had come she had only a red silk dress he had bought her, suitable for the expensive restaurant in which they had

27

dined the night before, but hardly fitting to either support or put down an armed uprising.

'Give me a shirt and some trousers.'

'What?'

The red dress was cast aside and he was spat at. 'I cannot take part in our revolution in this.'

'Florencia, it is the generals who have revolted, not the workers.'

'You're sure?' she demanded, not without a degree of suspicion, evident in her narrowed dark-brown eyes.

Having kept from her both the contents of Peter Lanchester's telegram, and his prior warning, Cal was slightly embarrassed. 'Switch on the radio and see if there's any news.'

All that was playing on the local station was soothing music, yet oddly, for such a fiery woman, it seemed to calm her down, so that the repeated request was softly spoken. 'A shirt, please, Cal; I cannot go out into the streets to defend the city in a red silk dress.'

Already wearing the only grey shirt he possessed, the one he threw her was blue, striped and collarless, and the trousers that followed were beige, lightweight, linen and miles too big. It was an attribute to her innate sense of style that by the time she was dressed, shirt over the now rolled-up trousers, the whole fastened at the waist by a leather belt, the only thing which looked incongruous was her shoes. He had on a leather blouson she had helped him buy in a street market and they tussled over the beret that went with it. She won, leaving Cal with his fedora.

The last thing gathered was a wad of pesetas, part of Monty Redfern's contribution to the overheads, which he carried around as mad money in case the people he was funding needed anything – the unspent rest was in his money belt in the Ritz Hotel safe, a sum he kept separate from his own money. Not a man too struck by conscience, Cal was nevertheless disinclined to put the cost of his personal pleasure at the door of such a good friend, like wining and dining a beautiful woman or overstaying his time in Barcelona in a luxury hotel. The wad he stuffed into the inside pocket of his blouson, adding his own wallet.

'You have to come with me, Florencia. I have to see what I can do for the athletes and I might struggle to get to them.'

He nearly laughed at the reply, it being so serious in its delivery. 'It is my duty to come with you, *querido*. The organising committee of the Olympiad would never forgive me if I did not help you.'

Anxious groups of people, mostly Spanish and all upper-middle class, filled the lobby, probably wondering if coming on holiday or on business to the Catalan capital, at this particular time of year, had been a good idea, with the concomitant problem of how they were now going to get home.

The last place to be when the boulevard outside was full of angry workers and bullets were flying was in a hotel like the Ritz; the top hostelry in the city, it screamed luxury, and it was telling that the liveried doorman had taken refuge inside the glass doors, abandoning his customary exterior post. Cal and Florencia pushed past, getting from him, as well as the nearby concierge, a look of disdain at their clothing.

Out of the hotel and in amongst the crowds it was not only hard going, it was also impossible to get any clear news of what was happening; Florencia translated every rumour imparted to her, not one of which bore any relation to those that had gone before. Then there was the incongruity of the loudspeakers, attached to the trees that shaded the wide avenues, playing that same utterly inappropriate light music they had heard in the room.

That was backed up by the sound of shouted slogans and the singing of revolutionary songs that required no translation, creating an almost carnival atmosphere, though added to that was the sound of breaking glass as shop windows were smashed by the less politically committed who took advantage of the mayhem to loot.

Every worker in Barcelona, as well as their wives, girlfriends and daughters, seemed to be on the streets, and the way some of the well-dressed people were being harangued and harassed made Cal Jardine glad he had dressed in his leather blouson, which even if new, was still not the garb of a wealthy man.

Some of the demonstrators were armed with rifles, but that had been the case from the day Cal arrived in a country that had seemed like a tinderbox waiting for a spark. Thanks to Florencia and her local knowledge – she was Barcelona born and bred – they could use side streets, avoiding the crowded boulevards, taking alleys and cross streets to get down to the area bordering the docks, where Vince and his party were staying.

He found his one-time sergeant outside the hostel and not alone; his boys were there too – half a dozen boxers from his gym, who still, after a couple of weeks, where they were not bright red and peeling, looked pallid and underfed in a country where everyone was deeply tanned. Vince was not; with his Italian blood he had quickly gone a deep-brown colour.

There were a number of the other athletes there too, more bronzed given they trained outdoors, about fifty in number, though they were accommodated elsewhere. He recognised swimmers and runners, a long- and a high-jumper, as well as athletes of the other field events, every one of them looking very determined. With few exceptions – a couple were from universities – they were young working-class men, many funded by their trade unions, some who had come off their own bat or through Labour Party sponsors, looking forward to an opening ceremony that was supposed to take place the next day.

As soon as he saw him, Vince detached himself and came to quietly converse, cutting out Florencia in the process, which got his back an angry glare from a woman easily rendered jealous.

'Any idea what's goin' on, guv?'

'I was hoping you would tell me.'

Though a Londoner, Vince, who spoke Italian, understood a great deal of what was being said around him in Spanish. Cal spoke some, but not enough, and that was especially true when the locals spoke quickly, as they habitually did.

'If I've got it right the poxy generals have started an uprising.'

Vince being the one person he had told of the news from London, there was not much he could say. 'I told you it was possible, I just didn't think it would be this quick.'

'The bastards might have waited till we had the games.'

'I've never met a patient general, Vince, have you?'

'Never met a general at all an' I don't want to. Like as not, I'd shoot the bastard, 'cause all they ever do is get folk like me killed.'

Jardine grinned; Vince, with a few exceptions, loathed officers, whatever their rank, though his respect for the few he admired, and Cal had been one, was total. He had been a damn good soldier, if one too often in trouble with his superiors, resulting in a seesaw as far as rank was concerned; sergeant to private and back again like a jack-in-the-box.

But if Cal, as one of his company officers, had been required to discipline and demote Vince, he had also come to appreciate the feeling of having him alongside when things got sticky, because he was a real asset in a scrap, as well as a born leader in an army, like every other in the world, that could only run well by the application of its senior NCOs.

He had also been a very handy welterweight boxer, both for the regiment and after he was discharged. Such a skill made leniency when he transgressed easy to get past the colonel, an old stick-in-the-mud and martinet going nowhere, the army always being tolerant of those showing sporting prowess, especially one who could duff up the champion of a rival regiment. He was past boxing now, a trainer instead of a fighter, if you excluded going out into the streets of London to do battle with Mosley's blackshirts.

'So what do you reckon, guv?' Vince asked, turning to indicate the party of which he had obviously taken charge. 'The lads want to know.'

'Depends on how bad it gets. If it is really serious we'll need to bail out.'

'If this is what you told me it might be, an' that's what I passed on to the boys when we heard the shooting, then if there's going to be a fight, quite a few of them want to be part of it.'

'Hold on a minute, Vince, we're talking a shooting war here, not three rounds with gloves and headgear on. Besides, they're only kids.'

'What age were you when you went and joined up?'

'I'd had training.'

'I recall you saying if you'd listened to the instructors you wouldn't have lasted a bleedin' week.'

Vince had a real boxer's face: a much-broken nose and prominent bones on his cheeks and under his scarred eyebrows; now it was screwed up with what seemed to be real passion, not his normal mode of behaviour, which was generally calm and jocular. The one thing that could get him really going was anything to do with fascism.

That was why he was here with his boxers – it set him off at home and it fired him up when he talked, which he did rarely, of his political beliefs. Not in any way a joiner of parties, he was, by his very nature, a fellow who believed all men are created equal and should be treated as such.

'We came here to send a message to that shit Hitler, right?'

'Yes, but—'

'But, nothin'! If the same sort of bastards are going to try and turn Spain into another Germany or Italy, are we just goin' to scuttle off home an' let them get on with it?'

'I was going to say it's not our fight, Vince, but I suspect that might not go down too well.'

'It is, guv, and you know it,' Vince responded, deeply serious. 'It's all our fight, just as it was in Africa.'

The two locked eyes, but it was not a contest of wills, more an attempt to ascertain the next move. If anyone knew him well it was this man, and added to the mutual trust they had was the bond of recent experience; Vince had been with him all the way in the acquiring and running of guns, across Europe and into Ethiopia, sharing the risks as well as, it had to be admitted, often acting as the voice of common sense.

'What about your gym?'

'A few weeks won't make no difference, will it, and we was due to be here a fortnight in any case. Might all be over by then.'

'We don't know what is happening, Vince, or how we can help. We don't even know if we'd be welcome.'

'One way to find out.'

'March to the sound of the guns?' Cal asked, only half joking.

'That would be a start.'

'Can I talk to your boys?'

Vince nodded and Cal went towards them. He was not a total stranger, having attended the training sessions both indoors and at the track-and-field stadium, yet right at that moment it came home to him how little he really knew about them, and that extended to names. He had remained semi-detached to that in which they were involved, partly through a disassociation from their politics, added to a lack of interest, more through being too busy with his own pleasures.

'Vince tells me some of you want to get involved.' He needed to put up his hand to kill off a murmur from several dozen angry throats and the odd shaking fist. 'I can understand how you feel and I think Vince will tell you that I am experienced at this sort of thing . . .'

He had to stop then, there being nothing he could add which did not risk sounding boastful, so he turned to Florencia, who, unusually for her, had remained silent, albeit with a fixed pout, while he had talked with Vince, who was not going to be forgiven for the way he had not only ignored her, but cut her off from her man.

'Florencia, we need to find out what is really going on, not just rumours, and we will need your help if we contact anyone in authority. What I am saying is we need you.'

The pout disappeared and her eyes flashed as she responded. 'You're going to fight with us?'

'We're not going to just sit on our arse and do nowt, sweetheart,'

34

Vince growled, good-humouredly and with a smile. 'Of course we're goin' to fight.'

Cal Jardine was used to Florencia suddenly leaping to throw her arms and legs around him, then showering him with kisses; Vince was not and it showed in his rapidly reddening face, especially when the act was accompanied by a whole raft of whistles and whoops from the athletes, and more especially, his young boxers.

'Right, boys,' Cal yelled, over the din, looking at feet in an array of unsuitable footwear, in fact a lot of plimsolls. 'Get back to your billets and collect your kit and shaving gear, a change of clothes, especially spare socks and the means to wash them, a knapsack if you've got one and a blanket, even if you have to buy it. If you have boots, wear them and don't load yourself up with things you don't need. You might not be coming back to where you are now sleeping, so bring any money or valuables you have as well, and everyone has to have a hat.'

He paused, watching as that sank in, looking for signs of doubt; there was not one who did not seem still determined.

'Back here in an hour and be warned – I will inspect you and chuck in the gutter anything I think you don't need. Some of those who came to the Olympiad will want to get out, so ask them to gather here as well. This will be our rendezvous point till we find out how the land lies.'

Taking Florencia by the arm, he headed back towards the centre of the city. Vince, professional as he was, had already got together the kit he knew he needed and was on their heels.

The crowds were no longer just milling about; as an indication of how serious matters had become many were busy building barricades and doing so with an impressive professionalism. Instead of just a jumble of various artefacts hastily thrown together, they were being constructed with care, a bus or a truck the centrepiece, the paving stones ripped up from the streets not just thrown in a rising heap, but laid carefully and angled, so that any shot striking them would ricochet upwards and over instead of smashing them to pieces, with rifle slots at the crest, offset for aiming right and left to protect the men who would use them.

Florencia explained, when Cal expressed his admiration, that such skill was honed by experience, Barcelona being a city well versed in the mechanics of revolt, not least in an event they called the *Semana Trágica* – twenty-five years past but still a beacon for socialist memory – when the government, the army and the Civil Guard, using artillery, had crushed a major uprising.

The workers would not make the same mistakes of shoddy construction now as they had made then; the barricades were designed to cope with such assaults. At the same time, lorries and cars, horns blaring, flags flying, armed men on top, were racing around the city carrying food, some already with makeshift armour plating fixed to windscreens and sides.

All had big white letters painted on their bodywork to denote which of the myriad left-wing organisations they belonged to: UGT, POUM, PSOE, PCE, and the biggest and most numerous, the group of which Florencia was a member, the syndicalists and purist anarchists of the CNT-FAI, two groups who had fallen out over political purity and had recently come together again.

The Spanish left, not too dissimilar to those on the right they opposed, consisted of a plethora of shifting unions, cooperatives, labour fronts and political affiliations too confusing for a mere visitor to comprehend, despite Florencia's best efforts at enlightenment, accompanied, when not praising her own CNT-FAI colleagues, with spitting insults, the most vehement against the Popular Front government in Madrid, made up of lily-livered socialist democrats and far-left backsliders seduced by power.

They all hated each other with a passion, as groups sure their brand of socialism was the route to some political utopia, and each tried to poach members from the other, which did nothing for inter-union rivalry. The Trotskyists of the POUM saw themselves as the true heirs to Karl Marx and loathed the Stalinists and Moscow lackeys of the communist PCE. Both laughed at the far-left trade union outfit called the UGT, big in Madrid and at one time part of the government, who stood as the main rival to the equally union-based anarcho-syndicalists of the CNT.

The *Federación Anarquista Ibérica*, to which Florencia belonged through the women's organisation the *Mujeres Libres*, preached pure, unadulterated anarchism as voiced by Mikhail Bakunin: no money, no government, no police, no judges and no prisons, each person responsible for and contributing to the greater good. The POUM believed in a Spanish form of communism that had nothing to learn from Leninism or the Communist International, which gave instructions to their rivals, orders that came straight from the Kremlin.

The social democrats believed in liberal capitalism, and in amongst that and just to complicate matters, many, of whatever hue, were, in Barcelona, Catalan Nationalists seeking regional autonomy from Madrid. Yet faced with a fascist revolt, all their differences would be put aside to face what they knew to be a common enemy.

Florencia led Cal and Vince to the main meeting place of the members of both the *Confederación Nacional de Trabajo* and the *Federación Anarquista Ibérica*. Nothing could have been more inappropriately named that day than the *Café de Tranquilidad*. It wasn't tranquil now, it was like a very busy and disturbed hive, crowded, noisy and bordering on mayhem, with bees arriving to yell bits of news, or departing to carry instructions to some part of the city where their leaders expected they would need to act, and all the while, to add to the air of unreality, waiters swanned through bearing platters of food or trays of beer or coffee.

Florencia was nothing if not determined and nor, Cal later found out, was she shy in exaggeration when she got a hearing from the faction leaders. He thought he had not told her much about his past, but over two weeks of being constantly in each other's company, walking, dining and pillow talk, it amounted to more than he could recall.

She blew up what he had imparted about his military experience out of all relation to the truth, so that far from being a peripheral figure seeking information as to how he and the Olympiad athletes could help, he was soon surrounded by eager faces and, named by Florencia as a famous military genius, bombarded with questions about what these inexperienced fighters should do.

Language was a real problem, not aided by the fact that no one who posed a question was prepared to wait for an answer, and nor were their comrades, who either had contrary opinions or a query of their own. It was an uncoordinated babble of indeterminate noise in which he tried to do more listening than talking, that not easy either, as his fiery mistress was wont to interrupt any interpretation with a mouthful of Catalan abuse aimed at anyone who proposed a suggestion she disagreed with.

It was during one of these tirades that Cal tried to bring a confused and less-than-impressed Vince Castellano up to date. 'They need guns and the government won't give them any.'

'I got that much, but I'm not sure I would either, guv. This lot look like they're not sure who to shoot, an' the way they're carrying on it could be each other.'

'Did you get that a revolt started in Morocco yesterday?' Vince nodded. 'It was a bit of a mess, but the officers have risen up all over Spain and are trying to seize the main population centres.'

'Here is important to us, guv,' Vince said, as behind them a furious, passionate and utterly incomprehensible argument became, if possible, even more vicious.

'If I've got it right, so far the soldiers are still in their barracks, and it seems the Catalan government are trying a bit of negotiation.'

'A bullet in the brain works wonders,' Vince joked.

'This lot,' Cal replied, jerking his thumb, 'are sure they will fail, so the army will march out either today or tomorrow to take over the city and they have machine guns and artillery. There's a general called Goded flying in from Majorca to take command. The real question is what the armed police will do, the Civil and Assault Guards, and right now that is an unknown quantity.'

Vince was confused and he was not alone; the Civil Guard they both knew as the everyday near-military coppers, with their funny black hats, green uniforms and miserable expressions – they acted as if smiling was a punishable offence. Neither were certain about the latter group called the Assault Guards, which had been set up fairly recently to police the towns and cities, the places most likely to explode into organised revolt. But, in truth, names made no difference; both were fully armed and trained, while the workers who might have to oppose them were not.

'So weapons are the priority.'

'Guv, if the government knows what's coming, then they should know how to put the mockers on it.'

'They probably do, but they are not talking to the people who can stop it physically, the various far-left organisations like this lot. They are just as frightened of them as they are of the generals.'

Just then a messenger rushed in, spouted some news, and set off another loud and incomprehensible argument, full of waving fists and triumphant cries, which at least indicated the proffered information was positive.

'Good news,' Florencia explained, having detached herself from the ballyhoo. 'The Assault Guard are handing out weapons to the workers and we have certain armouries we are sure we can capture with their guns. News has come from the dock workers' union as well. There is a ship in the harbour carrying explosives and I have volunteered us to help capture it.'

'With what?' Cal demanded, making the sign of a pistol.

That got another flash of those dark eyes, attached to a look of determination. 'If we have weapons, good; if not, we will take the ship with our bare hands.'

Grabbing her shoulders Cal looked right into those lovely liquid pools. 'Go back into that mob and tell them, from me: no weapons, no help.'

'I have told them how brave you are!'

'Tell them how stupid I'm not and also tell them all Vince and I have is a bunch of untrained amateurs, some of whom might be able to swim, others who can box, many who can run a mile in not much over four minutes and none who know how to use a gun, which they must have, just as we must show them how to employ them before they go anywhere near a fight.'

There was a crestfallen air about Florencia as he spoke those words, as if he had gone down miles in her estimation, the rate marked by the spirit of her deflation.

'Look, we are willing, but we must have weapons.'

'I cannot deal with this,' she cried, with a toss of her blonde curls. 'I will get Juan Luis Laporta. He speaks French and so do you.'

'And who is he?'

Florencia managed to give Cal Jardine the kind of look that implied he must have spent the last ten years on the moon. 'Juan Luis is a senior military commander of the CNT-FAI and a true and experienced revolutionary. Surely you have read about him?'

Then she was gone.

'Fancy you not knowin' that, guv, eh?' said Vince, dryly.

CHAPTER THREE

Dragging her man away from the heated discussions took time; it was clear he was important, a person whose views counted in the mass of conflicting arguments. In order that they could talk in relative peace, Cal and Vince moved to a corner window that looked out onto the wide and crowded pavement to wait. Coming towards them, edging past people in the bustling café, exchanging words with some and looks with others, allowed Cal to examine Laporta more closely.

'He looks a bit useful,' Vince said, before he got close, as a boxer, well used to observing a potential opponent.

Broad-faced and stocky of build, clad in a worn leather coat and a battered forage cap of the same material, with a pistol worn on his hip, he looked like a fighter – and not just with a gun. The way he held his hands indicated he was prepared to use his fists too, while the hunch on the shoulders pointed to a degree of power to back those up. But most of all, the steady gaze, once he had fixed on Cal Jardine, indicated a man who was confident in his own ability.

For all his physicality, the thing that impressed Cal most about Juan Luis Laporta, once they had started to converse in French, was his lack of excitability. Unlike many in the room he was calm and controlled, a man who could listen as well as talk, while it was obvious that, if he knew these two strangers were assessing him, he was doing the same to them.

It is little things that tell you a man is an experienced fighter, especially if you have been round the block a few times yourself. The scars he has and where they are located are the same ones you see in the shaving mirror or when you are washing your hands; another indicator the wary way they carry themselves, as if trouble is a constant possibility.

'Monsieur,' he said, once Cal had outlined the operation they had been volunteered for, as well as his objections. 'None of the people you see in this room have such training.'

There was an obvious truth in that; those present were workers, but Cal was instinctively aware the man he was talking to knew his business, though his fighting was likely, given his politics, to be of the unconventional kind.

'They are not only untrained, but unarmed.'

'Matters are in hand to secure a supply of weapons.'

'I suspected they must be.'

The silence in such close proximity was highlighted by the surrounding noise, and it lasted for several seconds. 'Florencia tells me you are an ex-soldier.'

'As is my friend.'

Laporta flicked a smile at Vince, before casting a long up-and-down stare at Cal, seemingly taken by his looks – the cut of his clothing, blouson aside, and his shoes, which were handmade and recognisably so in a country where people knew about footwear. They also had a patina of age that only came from being well looked after over decades.

'You were an officer, I suspect.'

'That, monsieur, is not a crime.'

'Why are you in Barcelona?'

'Has Florencia not said?'

'She has,' Laporta replied, his eyes hardening. 'But a room in the Ritz Hotel is not the place for those who I expect to share our political beliefs, or of the class that have come here to take part in the People's Olympiad.'

'I don't share your political beliefs, Señor Laporta, in fact I think they are foolish.'

'It would be interesting to know, monsieur, what you do believe in?'

Cal jerked his head to include Vince. 'I think you will find that my friend and I have a certain type of adversary, one we might share with many people, and not just the Spanish. Plus, if you have not been told already, we are here representing many who are sympathetic to your cause.'

'Your athletes want to fight the generals?'

'I think it might be a bit broader in purpose, more they want to fight fascism, something they intended to demonstrate through their athletic prowess. They just happen to be here, now, when events are unfolding. I daresay there are young men from every represented nationality at the games who feel the same and are willing to take up arms in the cause you all share.'

'Right now, monsieur, I am not sure what I would do with them.'

'Is he givin' us the elbow, guv?' Vince asked.

Vince had picked up the odd word and had not mistaken the tone, as well as the cynical look in the Spaniard's eyes. His intervention caused Laporta to look at him again, but it was brief, his attention turning back to Cal.

'Your athletes, if they want to be of use, need to be trained, as do many of the workers. You, as an officer at one time, are used to training soldiers, no? But are you a good officer or a bad one? There are many of those, too many, in the Spanish army.'

And, Cal thought, you would struggle to trust them. The man was suspicious of him too, and right to be so; no offence need be taken regarding such an attitude, for if, as suspected, he had participated in insurrection before, there would be within that a memory of both betrayal and incompetence, expensive in terms of plans unsuccessfully executed and lives lost.

'Maybe it would be best if I was shown what you can do.'

The steady look had within an implication of a test, and Cal Jardine was too long in the war-fighting tooth to allow anyone to examine his ability. 'I have no objection to being active, but I will only do what I think is both wise and achievable.'

'And I, monsieur, would only ask you to do what I would also ask of my own comrades.'

'You may be the kind of man who asks too much.'

'I may.'

'So?'

'There is a small armoury at the *Capitanía Marítima*, the naval headquarters. We need to take the weapons and distribute them, perhaps to your athletes.'

'Defended?'

'Of course, by naval officers and probably cadets, though I doubt there are any sailors, since they, almost to a man, sympathise with us.'

'When do you intend to attack?'

'After I have eaten and after they have eaten,' he said. 'To disturb, perhaps, their siesta. You will eat with me and tell me things that perhaps I do not know.'

'I've got about fifty athletes waiting to fight and even more, I suspect, wondering how to get home.'

The Spanish was rapid, and clearly what he issued was a command, received by Florencia with a composure she had never demonstrated to anyone else, Cal Jardine included. Her chest came out and, on a very warm day, lacking a bra, while in a shirt far too big and loose for her, it gave Laporta, judging by his dropping and reacting eyes, an obvious and entertaining eyeful.

Cal was both amused and pleased; he hated the idea of being involved with some revolutionary zealot with no human emotions, and it was even more satisfying to observe the Spaniard's eyes as they followed her swaying hips as she departed.

'I have sent her to tell your men to wait, to say we are making plans and to eat. Come.'

The place was crowded, but it was a testimony to Laporta's standing that a table was quickly procured, as was a bottle of wine and oil, salt, garlic and bread, then last, a bowl of superbly ripe tomatoes, which Laporta proceeded to combine and eat, indicating that his companions should do likewise.

'Vince,' Cal said in English, to a man whose mouth was already full, careful as he did so to smile at Laporta. 'If he speaks in Spanish to anyone, work out what he's on about.'

'So, British officer, we have a fight on our hands, how would you suggest we act?'

'Not the way you are carrying on now,' Cal replied, throwing a less than flattering glance at the continuing and seemingly irresolvable arguments Laporta had left. 'You need a proper structure of command, preferably one leader.'

'That is not the anarchist way.'

Cal made no attempt to soften his sarcastic response; what was happening was too serious. 'That sounds like a good way to get beaten, but if you can't have one leader and must have several, define the areas of responsibility, defence, recruitment, training, supply. You should have a room in which only those people with responsibility have the right to speak, with maps of your dispositions and accurate intelligence on what your opponents are up to.'

'We have that already.'

Responding to obvious curiosity, Laporta gave what Cal suspected was a highly edited account of what he knew of the intention of the Spanish army. Basically it came down to their preparations to leave their various barracks, once the General Goded arrived, to take control of the city, spilling as much blood as necessary in the process. There were two cavalry regiments and a light-artillery unit, as well as a battalion of infantry in the main Parque Barracks.

The Assault Guards were mostly already on the side of the workers, but it was interesting Laporta made no mention of the more important, as well as more numerous, Civil Guard, which indicated they were still an unknown quantity. Dipping his finger in his wine, the Spaniard made a very rough map on the table showing how the various opposition forces were presently disposed.

'If they are coming from separate locations,' Cal pointed out, 'it would be wise to so dispose your men to stop them combining, the whole being greater than the sum of its parts. There have to be locations you feel best placed to defend, and if you direct the flow of your enemy to those, you have the advantage. The biggest problem is they are soldiers – they are trained and they have artillery.'

'How little you know of the Spanish metropolitan army, monsieur,' Laporta replied, with a sympathetic grin.

'I take it you know more.'

'I have made it my duty as a revolutionary to study my enemy, men whom I have already fought against many, many times.'

'Very wise.'

'The soldiers are badly paid and led by either fools or thieves. Their equipment is poor and their training in combat is zero. Many will have rarely fired off their rifles even once. The officers are fools and, worse, they are scum, more likely to sell their men's rations than distribute them, that is when they are not hiring them out as labourers to anyone who will pay for their work, or using them to tend their own gardens.'

'You talk of the metropolitan army, you do not mention the colonial troops.'

'They are in Morocco and, if they are kept there, not a concern.'

'But if they were brought to the mainland?' The look answered the question; they would be a handful. 'A fact, surely, known to the generals who have begun the uprising, some of whom may not be fools.'

'Right now, monsieur,' Laporta said, standing up, clearly slightly irritated by what he saw as close to an interrogation, 'my immediate concern is Barcelona. Let Madrid worry about the Army of Africa.'

Then he was gone, leaving Cal to explain what they had been talking about to Vince.

'What do you know about anarchists?' When Vince looked surprised at the question, Cal added, 'I was hoping it was more than me.'

'It's the big thing here, guv.'

'That I do know. I have my ear bashed by Florencia.'

'Just your ear?'

'Don't tell me you've been idle.'

'They all hate each other,' Vince responded, not very helpfully and utterly declining to comment about what he had been up to in his leisure time.

'Anarchism sounds like a recipe for chaos to me. No government, no money, just everyone contributing to the common good and taking responsibility for their own actions.'

'The word you're looking for is "bollocks".'

Vince, looking sideways, caught sight of Laporta coming back to the table with two rifles under his arm and used his head to indicate that to Cal. The rifles were laid on the edge of the table, the bullets to load them, plus extra rounds, extracted from the pocket of his leather coat rolled onto the table.

Cal reached out and picked one up, a Mauser of a fairly old pattern, and here he was at home. This was a business he knew about, like the fact that the weapon was of German design, was made under licence in Spain and was standard issue for their forces. He had shipped some of these to South America.

Quickly he worked the bolt a couple of times, then nodded. 'Well maintained.'

'They need to keep them well oiled in case they need to shoot the workers. Come.'

Both Cal and Vince were on their feet immediately, and by the time they had pocketed the ammo, Laporta was out on the pavement shouting to a group of armed men lounging in the shade of the trees. They rose with no great haste to fall in behind him, which at least allowed the two Brits to get alongside their leader.

'Any idea of numbers?' Cal asked in French.

Laporta just shrugged. 'However many there are, we will kill them.'

'They might surrender.'

Another shrug and an enigmatic smile, which left Cal wondering what would happen if they gave in. If there was one thing he recalled from South America it was the Spanish propensity for violence and cruelty, an attitude not aided by the nihilism of the indigenous Amerindians. The Chaco War, in which he had first been an arms supplier and then a participant, had shown that mercy was not an Iberian quality.

That trait was something anyone who read about the conquistadors could not fail to realise. Cal Jardine was not in any way squeamish, but shooting innocents or surrendering soldiers, which he had witnessed too many times in his life, was not an activity in which he wanted to be involved.

The heat of the city was stifling, the breeze off the Mediterranean so hot it failed to mitigate the temperature of a relentless sun, the only relief coming from staying under the shade of the myriad trees or using the cover of the high buildings. Even in revolt, Barcelona seemed somnolent at this time of day, the hours of the mid afternoon being the time for siesta, which, as Florencia had demonstrated, was not solely for sleeping. More people were awake than normal, but they were still, and on the barricades they circumvented, even the defenders were taking turns to doze out of the sun's rays.

There were already worker-fighters outside the *Capitanía Marítima*, undisciplined and milling around, but by their presence blocking any escape from the naval HQ, and Laporta immediately went to try to get them into some sort of order while his own party took up firing positions. Cal, who was certain he was about to be asked to aid the assault, indicated silently to Vince and they began to reconnoitre a place well known to the locals, but a mystery to them.

It was a six-storey stone building, classically fronted, not triangular but narrower at the entrance than the back, occupying a site on a U-shaped bend in the tree-lined road. There was a large open space to the rear, too exposed to be of any use in an assault and leading, in any case, only to heavy doorways that they had, as far as they knew, no explosives to breach; the front presented a better prospect, if not an easy one.

The numerous trees allowed for a comprehensive reconnaissance, as well as the chance of getting close, but that only underlined that, possessing dozens of windows, and with a roof topped by a balustrade, the points of any defence were numerous and left no arc of fire uncovered, while whoever controlled the building was keeping his powder very dry. No rifles appeared from any of the windows and no shots were fired to deter the observations that Cal and Vince made as they dodged around from cover to cover.

Like a lot of local buildings the ground floor windows were barred, and added to that were what looked like stout internal shutters. Even the classical Palladian portico was defensible, being deep and shaded at the base entrance, while above that there was a balcony with thick stone columns, wide enough to hide a shooter, backed by an array of french windows. For observation there was what looked like a high cupola on the roof, probably a water cistern, from which snipers could dominate the further approaches.

'Well, Vince?' Cal asked finally, as they got back to their start point, looking at the triple-arched front.

'A mortar would be handy for that roof, guv, to keep any buggers up there honest.'

'As would a bit of field artillery to blow in the front doors, which we don't have either.'

Looking over to where the main party had gathered, Cal could see they had been joined by a steady stream of other fighters, men and women, a few armed, most not, no doubt the locals who had joined what was already being called the counter-revolution. To both men watching it seemed they were gathering for an assault, finger-pointing mixed with much of the sort of chest-beating folk use to bolster their resolve. Certainly Laporta was haranguing them in what Cal suspected was a bout of revolutionary fervour.

'Bad place to try and rush,' Vince said.

'Especially if they have any machine pistols and grenades.'

It took no great imagination for Cal Jardine to put himself in the mind of the person organising the defence. He would be aware those trying to assault the place had neither the right weaponry, infantry training or much more than their own fervour as a spur, nor any real knowledge of the dangers of fighting in what constituted, for war purposes, one of the deadliest arenas for combat – a stout building with clear approaches and killing zones provided by the intervening roadway and the tree-dotted esplanade before the entrance.

Below that balcony the main triple-arched entrance was the most obvious place to make inroads against a resistance expected to be weak. A good tactician would first let any skirmishers get close, thus encouraging the main assault to come on, with a few rifle shots to indicate some level of resistance. Once crowded in that deep doorway, it would be child's play to drop a few grenades over the balcony; the trapped attackers would be shredded and lose their momentum. Then put all your available firepower into killing those panicked into retreat.

'So?' Vince asked, having had that elaborated and gloomily agreed.

'If I was in charge of taking the place, I'd be looking for the water and electricity supplies. Cut them off and wait, unless we can get hold of a cannon big enough to blow the front in.'

'They might have enough food and water for a month.'

'They might have enough firepower for a massacre.'

'Chum's coming.'

Dodging from tree to tree, Laporta was crossing the ground between where he had been giving his lecture and the line of tree trunks his men, Cal and Vince included, were using as cover. As soon as he was kneeling beside Cal he asked him for an opinion, which induced a look of despondency as he listened to the response and the recommendation.

'We do not have time for such manoeuvres, monsieur.'

'That was the one thing I hoped you would not say,' Cal replied, doing a quick count of the number of available rifles and then the number of windows. 'In that case we have to draw some fire to see what they have got.'

'Monsieur, we have to attack.'

'Without knowing what you face, it will be bloody.'

The response was almost a snarl. 'That is the difference between soldiers and revolutionary workers, monsieur, we are prepared to die for what we believe in.' With that he called to his men, to follow him to a point right before the front of the naval headquarters to join what was now a milling mass of volunteers, his final words to Cal, but aimed at both he and Vince: 'You are free to join us.'

Cal actually laughed. 'We are also free to decline. I have told you what I think. If you have any men who are good shots leave them with us and we will seek to subdue the defence. That, at least, might save a few lives.'

Laporta thought for a long time, before nodding. He then reeled off several names, calling half a dozen men over and giving them rapid instructions.

'He's telling 'em to take orders from you, guv.'

'Any idea of the Spanish words for window and balcony?'

'Not a clue, Guv.'

CHAPTER FOUR

Not knowing the words in either Spanish or Catalan meant a great deal of finger-pointing, as each rifleman was allotted a target he thought might be the spot from which fire would come – the smaller windows to the side of the classical portico and the parapet on the roof. Just as troubling was the level of noise coming from those preparing to rush forward, a ringing howl of determination mixed with what had to be cursing; they might as well have sent a telegram to say they were about to attack.

Oddly, it was that noise which brought the first shots from the building, caused by either indiscipline or the mere fact of the defenders being unnerved by the rising crescendo of screeching. Judging by the cry that went up, at least one of the bullets found flesh, but instead of dispersing the attackers it galvanised them – or was it Laporta? They rushed out from what little cover they had, those with weapons firing them off with wild abandon, those without brandishing bits of wood or metal or nothing but their fists.

The result was immediate: controlled fire from the front windows, which sliced into the mob and took out at least a dozen people, two of them middle-aged women. Vince's orders, which he only hoped were fully understood, had been to follow Cal's lead. When he fired, they should all let off a couple of bullets at their chosen targets, then pause to spot which areas showed the smoke from the defenders' rifles, the idea to immediately switch to the one nearest each rifleman's original window and fire off single shots aimed at the spot. To kill anyone would be luck, given their level of cover; the idea was to get them to keep their heads down.

Four of the six men allotted to him did as they were bid; the other two, in their fury at seeing their comrades dropping as volley followed volley, stood up, stepped forward and emptied their five-round magazines without selecting anything. Stone chips flying off the building might look impressive but they achieved very little, except that some of the defenders, no more disciplined than their opponents, turned their fire towards these useless assailants, now standing exposed as they sought to reload.

If suicidal bravery was a virtue – and to Cal Jardine it was the opposite – these Catalan workers had it in spades. So fired up were they that they ignored their casualties, only a few of them stopping to aid the wounded or examine those who might already be dead. Sheer numbers overwhelmed the attempt to stop them getting to the triple-arched doorway, and inside that was cover into which they huddled in what was effectively, as Cal had already surmised, a trap; they had no means to batter down the door and to withdraw promised more death.

When the firing died away, Cal was pleased to see the more astute were following him and Vince in making sure they had a full magazine ready. Within seconds all were aimed at those columns and the row of french windows, Cal fully expecting his pre-imagined grenade-throwers would show.

What did appear, and this shocked him even more than the desperate attack, was a body flying from the roof, a man in a dark-blue uniform, alive, flaying and screaming as he fell, till he splattered into a bloody pulp on the flagstone of the esplanade, that immediately followed by a furiously waving white flag.

The sound of shots did not cease, only now they were muffled, confined within the building, with Cal examining several possibilities on how to gain access and join what was obviously a fight between two factions of the Spanish navy, none of which he could execute. The bars on the lower windows were too thick, the distance to the next level too high without ladders, and all the while that white flag was waving, the man moving it not prepared to stand up, a wise precaution when facing people lacking any notion of restraint.

The solution arrived as a truck came slowly grinding up the road, covered in plating that had to weigh several tons, one great piece with horizontal slits across the windscreen, other plates down the sides with vertical firing slots. More important was the height of its plated roof, and shouting to Vince, Cal ran out, frantically waving that it should get alongside the building so that it could be used as a means of gaining entry.

It was a good job the men Laporta had left with him followed; dressed as he was and waving a rifle, he could have been anyone, but they had on their sleeves the red and black armbands of the

CNT-FAI, which ensured the rifle muzzles which came out of the side of the truck held their fire. From then on it was sign language and yelling, which led Cal Jardine to the absurd thought, at this time and in this situation, that he was behaving, in dealing with the locals, like the typical Briton abroad.

Whatever, it worked; the driver turned his wheel and ran the truck down the side of the building. Cal, followed by Vince, was already clambering up the side, and once on top he yelled that the man on the wheel should stop, this as he used his rifle butt to break one of the panes that made up a casement window, reaching through to search for the catch that would keep the frame shut. Vince just pushed; it wasn't locked.

Through, with his feet scrunching on broken glass, Cal looked back to ensure his party had followed, as well as the occupants of the truck, before he examined the first floor room, not well lit given the windows were small. Unadorned desks, chairs, no quality to either, lots of filing cabinets, a closed door to the rest of the building, an office for no one important, while two floors up were what had looked like more spacious rooms with balconies of their own, no doubt the preserve of senior officers.

He opened the door to the landing cautiously, hearing shots, but not close, echoing in what was a substantial and open staircase – they were fighting on the upper floors. That body coming off the roof indicated that those sent up there to defend the place from that location had decided they were on the wrong side. Guess number two was that they were fighting those who had been on the lower floors who disagreed, probably officers who had chosen to fight in the shade, versus lower ranks ordered to stay out in the midday sun – reason enough in itself for antagonism.

'Main doors, guv, it's got to be.'

The signs Cal used, two silent fingers to him, two repeated to Vince, were those he would have made with trained fighters, yet so obvious the men with him nodded that they understood. Vince's duo, following him to the staircase going up, knelt and aimed their rifles to take on anyone descending, this while Cal was already slipping downstairs.

Slowly and silently, his pair following, he edged round a staircase bend that revealed a large hallway. At the very bottom of the stairway sat two men, in white naval hats and blue shirts, on a light machine gun aimed at the great double doors which shut off the outside world.

The right thing to do was shoot them without warning; that machine gun was no weight and could be swung round quickly if these two were determined to resist, but it is hard to put a bullet in another human being's back if there is any chance they might surrender. The tap on the shoulder and the look he observed in the eye of the man who had made it, as well as his jabbing muzzle, told him that he, at least, did not share his scruples, but it was good that he was asking permission to shoot, not just doing as he pleased.

The shot Cal loosed off went right by the ear of the man on the right, hit the marble floor, then slammed into the bare stone wall of the main hall, the noise reverberating round the whole chamber. Ducking initially, the two sailors looked over their shoulder, but as they did so the one on the left was already lifting the weapon to swing it round, and as it had to be, given their situation, the safety catch was set to off.

Time has a separate dimension in such situations: it seems to slow, so that a second takes on the appearance of an age. There were those naval caps flying off as the two sailors spun, the realisation that their faces were very young, probably those of cadets, that one was very blond like Florencia in a country where so many had hair of the deepest black.

In their eyes was a mixture of terror and resolve and it was the latter which proved fatal, though it was moot whose bullets killed them, for all three rifles fired at once, sending them spinning away, the muzzles following as shot after shot tore into their bodies. Then, there was silence.

Cal reloaded while his two companions rushed down to open the double doors, one aiming an unnecessary kick at the twitching body of a youth who was almost certainly doomed. There was no time to look further; having slipped down to pick up the machine gun, automatically seeking out and clicking on the safety, Cal then rushed up the stairs to join Vince, while behind him the roar of the crowd as they stormed into the building grew to drown out every other sound, including the upstairs shooting, which meant they must have heard it too.

Some sense prevailed; there was a stream of shouted commands to the mob to stay on the ground floor and a minute later Laporta and the rest of his riflemen joined him and Vince on the first landing. Now, behind them and below, they could hear things being broken: wood and glass. The machine gun was handed over, with Cal showing the set safety catch to the man who took it, as well as ensuring he was holding it properly in a way it could be used without a tripod.

He got a nod from the leader, but if it was thanks it was not heartfelt, more one that implied Laporta had expected no less. Ascending the stair, pistol out and rifles behind him, the Spaniard showed some skill: there was no rush this time, he kept his back to the wall to give himself maximum vision and slid upwards, his balance so precise that he could dive back down if threatened. At a corner, he waved up the fellow with the machine gun, with a sharp hand signal for the other riflemen to kneel and cover, all this while gunshots still echoed throughout the higher parts of the stairwell.

'Shall we leave this to them, guv?' Vince asked.

Cal replied, with a wry grin, 'Might not be a good idea to steal all the glory.'

Remembering that twitching cadet, Cal indicated to Vince and went down the stairs; the kid might still be alive – he had known people survive multiple shot wounds too many times to assume automatic death.

The young cadet might have lived through those, he could not have lived through what the fired-up crowd had done. The uniforms of the two cadets had been ripped off and they were bloodily naked, their faces unrecognisable, their bodies broken so badly that their bones, all at impossible angles, were showing as people stepped over them, taking from the building anything they thought of value.

Pushing through them to go out onto the esplanade and the roadway, now covered by that armour-plated truck, they were confronted by women keening over bodies of both sexes. It was not just hindsight that underlined the stupidity of what they had done, it was the fact that those still trying to hold the building were now facing fire from their own; all that had been needed was a demonstration of intent. Once the riflemen on the roof turned their guns against their comrades they could have walked out of the cover of the trees without losing a soul.

At least some of those shot were surviving, being borne away on makeshift stretchers. Sitting down, Vince pulled out a packet of cigarettes and lit up, puffing away and ignoring the waving hand of his companion trying to keep the smoke from blowing in his face, this while he reprised in his mind what had just happened, those ruminations distracted by the rattle of the machine gun. When silence followed, and was maintained, Cal and Vince exchanged glances; the job was done.

The so-called magazine yielded little more than what had been used in the defence, but the building served up a line of sorry-looking prisoners who were marched out through two lines of locals spitting at them, their hands on their heads, their uniforms bloody and filthy, and their faces showing the capture had not been gentle.

Jeers and spittle turned to cheers as the sailors who had rebelled, obviously lower deck by their uniforms, came out to handshakes and female kisses, a beaming Laporta behind them, who immediately climbed onto the truck and began to make a rousing speech.

The gist was easy to follow; even without a smattering of Spanish you just had to watch his eyes and the reactions of his audience. He was, Cal was certain, telling them they were brave and wonderful instead of excited and imprudent, praising what they had achieved and ignoring the cost in lives lost to their revolutionary fervour.

The whole farce ended up with a raised fist and a huge oratorical cry of 'Revolution!', taken up and raised to an echoing yell. Then, once he had pointed back to the centre of the city, sending his unruly cohorts on their way, Laporta jumped down and came to rejoin his own fighters.

'Well, Englishman?' he said as he approached Cal, still sitting, back to a tree by a smoking Vince.

'*Escocés!*' Cal replied sharply; he was not a rabid Scot, but enough of one to want to be properly identified.

'We had success.'

'You had luck.'

Laporta's face changed as soon as Cal uttered the words *la chance*, and the man he was addressing knew why. He was full of his own rhetoric, still in the warm mood of his victory speech, and he was talking to a realist, not a follower, and one speaking in a voice deliberately devoid of emotion.

'The mode of your attack was not just foolish, my friend, it bordered on the stupid! The building is now yours because the ordinary sailors turned their guns on their officers and we were lucky an armoured truck happened by. Had those two events not occurred you might have lost everyone you led. If you continue to treat your enemies like that, they will beat you every time.'

Even if they could not comprehend what was said, Laporta's men picked up the tone and it showed on their faces; they too were basking in the glow of victory. Vince had come to the same conclusion through observing those same faces, not least that of their leader, which was bordering on thunderous.

'This might not be the moment to tell him he's a stupid bastard, guv.'

'I can think of no better time, Vince. We might just save a few lives, yours and mine included, if we are going to stay with this.'

'And you would have done it without loss?' Laporta demanded.

Reverting to French, Cal replied. 'I will tell you now that if I was leading any men in this anti-fascist fight and you ordered that kind of assault, I would not allow them to take part.'

A shrug. 'If they do not want to fight—'

That got a response which cut right across the Spaniard, and one which had Vince dropping the muzzle of his rifle, not threateningly, but enough to cause a few eyes to flicker towards him, given it was pointed at their leader's heart.

'They do want to fight, friend, but they do not want to die as uselessly as the poor souls who are still waiting to be carried away from here. There are ways to kill your enemies without dying yourself and that is called good soldiering. It is possible to admire your zeal and still be unhappy with your method. Now, tell me if you want the Olympiad volunteers or not, tell me you will listen to sense, or I will go back to the hostel and tell them they would be best going home.'

Laporta flicked a hand to indicate his men. 'Perhaps it is you who is being foolish.'

'Look, Laporta, you are a revolutionary, yes?' That got a nod. 'How many real battles have you been in?' Cal had to hold up his hand then and speak quickly, his passion obvious. 'I don't mean demonstrations, I don't mean workers' uprisings, I mean real battle, fighting trained soldiers who know what they are doing.'

That got a dismissive wave, replicated in the tone of the voice. 'Where are they, these soldiers?'

'On the way, I should think. Rule number one is never underestimate your enemy. I've told you, if you know the metropolitan army is useless, so do the generals who began this revolt, which means they also know, if they are to have any chance of success, they must get the only proper soldiers they have across the Gibraltar Straits. That means they would not have fired the starting pistol until they were sure that was possible.'

It was Cal's turn to flick a hand at Laporta's men. 'Now tell me, these fellows of yours, who are brave, certainly, and some of them are steady, can they stand up against soldiers, half of whom are not Spanish and a fair number of whom are criminals on the run or out-and-out adventurers, men who have spent years fighting Riff tribesmen in the mountains of Morocco?'

The sun was dipping in the sky, less fierce than it had been but still emitting heat, and Cal Jardine's voice was dropping too, the passion cooling enough for him to smile.

'That, my friend, can be changed, it *has* to be changed, but it will take time. As you so rightly said, in the coming days the job now is to hold on to Barcelona.' Cal stood up and went right up to a still-irritated Juan Luis Laporta. 'And that we will help you do, but after that, we will see. Now, I believe there is a job to do, some ship in the harbour that needs to be captured.'

The response was not warm; the man was still smarting from the lecture. 'You take risks, my friend. For a moment I was tempted to have you killed, and if my men had understood a word you said I think one of them might have shot you.'

It was superfluous to point out he would not have survived either; he had not missed the line of Vince's rifle and neither had Cal Jardine.

'If I thought your men understood I would not have uttered them publicly. As for risks, they are part of war-fighting, the trick is to know which ones to take.' The smile he used now was aimed at everyone, their eyes then drawn to the wad of pesetas he produced from his inside pocket. 'Now, even if you are anarchists, I suggest we go back to the *Café de Tranquilidad,* where I can buy us all a drink.'

For a group that, politically, were supposed to hate the mere thought of money in any form as a means to corrupt society, the result was surprisingly convivial. Only Laporta seemed to disapprove, but that Cal put down to the wigging he had just administered.

In the end both he and Vince were shoreside observers to the taking of the explosive-carrying cargo ship, as well as an old hulk – a former cruiser being used as a prison – a target because the warders were armed. The vessel carrying the explosives was hauled into the quayside by tug and quickly unloaded, the job now to turn the raw dynamite into weapons they could use to stop the army when they debouched from their barracks.

Every hand was employed, socialist athletes from every nation had now gathered in the city centre, lashing together sticks of dynamite and attaching detonators to some for static use, and lines of fuses to others for use as makeshift grenades, these sent out with an instructor to the various barricades.

No one slept, there was too much to do; a watch had to be kept on the various military installations to prevent a surprise – including the as-yet-uncommitted Civil Guard. Every defensive location designed to canalise them when they did emerge must be supplied with ammunition, runners selected to take and deliver messages as well as locating stocks of food and water, enough so that those facing the generals' uprising could fight all day in the heat.

Vince was engaged in basic training, showing his young athletes how to grip, aim and fire a rifle, while Cal Jardine was one of those tasked, in moonlight and aided by Florencia, to identify the best rooftop location from which rifle fire could enfilade the soldiers as they marched out to do battle with their enemies; what machine guns they had captured were kept for use on the barricades.

And there were the conferences, of which they were thankfully not a part, though what was discussed was disseminated; the officials of the Catalan government wanted to be in control, the various left factions equally determined they should not be bound by the politicians, especially the anarchists, who held as a principle the need for individual responsibility and the right to choose.

The small communist party, the PCE, backed the government on the grounds of the need for central political control of the forthcoming fight; the Trotskyists of the POUM faction opposed that motion just because the lackeys of Moscow insisted it was essential.

As reported, they talked and argued and shouted and stormed out, only to be dragged back to the negotiating table – sometimes, apparently, too willingly for their objections to be taken seriously, but eventually a consensus emerged: there would be a general plan, an outline, but each faction would control its own fighters in an agreed tactical area; basically they would take on the army unit by unit and try to keep them from coming together, not an outstanding strategic goal, but a workable one.

As the sky to the east was tinged with the first hint of light, the sun was about to arise on a huge city in which nothing was moving in the streets, though tongues were still furiously wagging in the various outposts, given agreement was never arrived at. Vince led his boys to the agreed location, now with rifles and sporting black and red armbands, to the place they had been allotted to fight, overlooking the gates of the massive Parque Barracks.

In there, as well as in the other military locations, the soldiers were being fed enough rum to give them the courage their officers did not think they would need; how could mere workers and peasants stand up to the regular soldiers of the Spanish army?

CHAPTER FIVE

Laporta and his fellow leaders were not behind barricades as the troops prepared to emerge; they were observing the great double gates of the barracks as the lead units of the infantry regiments appeared, proud officers first on tall gleaming mounts, unsheathed swords at their shoulders, the troops marching behind them in column, wearing forage caps instead of steel helmets, in between each company the carts carrying their ammunition and the equipment for the machine gun and mortar sections.

'Pigs!' Florencia yelled, shaking her fist, from the position that had been selected on the rooftops.

'That'll scare them, luv.'

Vince had responded with deep irony, pleased that he got a glare no less ferocious than that aimed at the army. She looked at Cal to put him in his place, getting in response only a grim smile through stubble and tired eyes; his old army chum was not a man you easily put down.

Her anger and a pout made her look damned alluring and rendered it doubly galling he had not been able to get back to the Ritz; quite apart from his present thoughts, a clean shirt and a shave would have been welcome. Time to concentrate on examining the enemy, which he did through a pair of binoculars she had acquired.

From a distance they looked impressive in their grey-green uniforms and the initially tidy formations of four-abreast columns; eyed through magnification it was a different story. Cal Jardine saw neither of the two attributes which might induce caution, if not downright apprehension: either the steady gaze of the professional warrior at ease with the prospect of battle or the fiery glare of the right-wing zealot.

Such an attitude was palpably present in the group that brought up the rear, individuals in dark-blue shirts, young and steely-eyed, staring straight ahead with a look of grim determination, the lead cohort carrying a flag with the yoke and arrows device of Spain's only openly fascist movement, the Falange.

Made up of mostly young middle-class men, as soon as the insurrection was announced, they had rushed to support the army, or, as Florencia had it, scurried like mice into the safety of the barracks to avoid being strung up to a lamppost.

Apart from their numbers, they could be discounted; such youths were irregulars and, if by reputation murderous, no more to be feared in close combat than any other untrained body. The soldiers before them held the key to what was about to occur and they, in the main, were surreptitiously glancing right and left in a manner that implied trepidation, while the lack of a high standard of discipline was soon apparent as their ranks lost a fair amount of cohesion.

Like most military establishments there was a lot of clear ground in front of the barrack gates, not just for pageantry but a must in any country with a history of revolt. In this case it was a parade ground forming one part of a spacious plaza. There was no attempt to immediately deploy; it was clear the officers were heading with determination straight for the city centre.

The small band of anarchist skirmishers placed close to the walls sought to make their exit as uncomfortable as possible, seeking to pick off the odd target, especially those mounted fools too arrogant to foot-slog with their men. That they succeeded twice, and that those they missed refused to dismount, pointed to a conceit bordering on folly.

There was no wisdom in what was happening; the man in command must have known their opponents were waiting for them and that their march to the centre would not happen unopposed, which must entail street fighting. If an army is poorly trained to fight a conventional war, it is doubly at a disadvantage when it comes to combat in a built-up area, which would become obvious once they sought to exit the open ground.

Such fighting requires tight battlefield control, a clear understanding between leaders and the led, more individual initiative and a high degree of application in tactical and weapon skills. It was obvious the men in command were hoping – or were they even convinced? – that numbers alone, the mere sight of marching troops, would overawe the workers of Barcelona, which fitted exactly Cal's nostrum delivered to Laporta the day before about not underestimating your enemy.

There had been no overnight reconnaissance, no probing of possible resistance to test the workers' strength, which would then allow for the use of alternatives, like moves to outwit those waiting to engage them in battle by the use of small mobile teams. There had to be more than one entrance to such an extensive barracks complex, yet they were massed and coming out of the main gate! Runners were already out, sent to the far-off barricades to denude the positions of most of their men so that they could be concentrated to meet the soldiers head-on.

Cal had elected to keep Vince and all of his athletes on the rooftops; without both training and Spanish they were as likely to be shot by their friends as their enemies. They had carried up a sack full of dynamite, sticks that, once fused, had been kept in a cool cellar to avoid them sweating their nitroglycerine. They were being kept in the shade on the roofs for the same reason, for the sun would soon be full up and handling such unstable objects was fraught with risk.

From such a vantage point Cal had a panoramic view of the military stupidity unfolding before him, and it was on both sides. The workers' militias, at a rush, emerged far too quickly, attacking the marching column with neither order nor fear, bringing them to a halt certainly, before they were forced to fall back from a badly coordinated fusillade, which nevertheless left the plaza dotted with bodies, some writhing, most still.

The infantry then began to manoeuvre, with no shortage of confusion, from column to line, fixing bayonets for an attack, every shouted order floating up in the warm air. Cal was shaking his head in disbelief. Surely, even the most dense military brain must first look to secure the integrity of the plaza.

It was essential to observe the high surrounding buildings and assume the rooftops would have riflemen, the answer to take them first while holding off the ground assault. With the advantage gained, the soldiers would be able to enfilade the area and seriously disrupt any further attacks from the workers' militias.

Like most spacious plazas it had, leading off it, a number of streets, some wide and sunlit, others narrow and dark. Strong parties should have been detached to secure those and close them off to guarantee the integrity of the position before any advance, making sure the flanks were secure by sealing off all the exits except the one by which they wished to move towards the city centre! Failing that, they should have at least set up machine guns or mortars to turn every avenue and alleyway into a potential death trap for any forces concentrated there who might try to get behind them.

'Not too good,' Vince whispered in Cal's ear as they observed the endless attempts of the Spanish NCOs to properly dress the untidy line. 'I don't think we're going to see Trooping the Colour, guv.'

'It's a mess, Vince, but have a gander at the bloke in command.'

Cal passed over the binoculars and watched as Vince focused in on the fat sod he had indicated, sat on his charger, huffing and puffing in frustration, his sword twitching as though he was dying to run through one of his own men as an example. Red-faced and with bulbous eyes, he reminded Cal Jardine of the military donkeys he had met too often in the British army, aged majors and colonels full of grub and port, erroneously too sure of their own military genius to be left in charge of a pisspot, never mind a company or regiment.

Their sole function in life, when not making the life of their juniors a misery, seemed set on blocking any chance of promotion for anyone with half an unaddled brain. He had often said that his leaving of the army was due to such idiots and there was some truth in the level of frustration he had felt, but the final straw that had him sending in his papers had been the indiscriminate bombing of Iraqi villages and the killing of women and children under the banner of putting down an Arab insurrection.

He had been part of an army with tanks, trucks and artillery, plus a vast advantage in firepower, facing committed insurgents with rifles, and still they could not prevail, for their enemies had possessed a willingness to die for that in which they believed. The Arabs felt betrayed by a combination of powers, French and British, who had promised them full self-determination when seeking their aid in throwing off their Turkish overlords, only to find they had a new oppressor when the Great War guns fell silent.

The excuses to mask what was naked greed were not long in coming. The locals were no good at governance; left alone the area would descend into chaos. In truth, the sandy desert was rich in oil. His had been a lone voice in the mess when it came to condemnation of both the enforcement of the League of Nations mandate, something to which the unrepresented Arabs had not been allowed to object, and of the methods of control, most tellingly the bombing – to most of his fellow soldiers, officers and other ranks, airmen included, it had been the proper way to make war on folk they saw as lesser mortals.

The overweight bugger Vince was examining had, no doubt, exactly the same attitude: the men and women opposing him were scum; he was an officer, a gentleman and he had a God-given right to both his position and the blood he was sure he was about to spill. Maybe if he had had good troops under him he might have succeeded; he did not, he had command of what was now, clearly, a uniformed rabble.

'They're getting ready to move,' Vince said, passing the binoculars back.

'At least set up your machine guns,' Cal spat, exasperated.

'You sound as if you want them to win.'

'You know me, Vince, I'm all heart.'

As in all fights, the people who did battle on the side of the Republican government only saw the action before their eyes, and for what happened elsewhere that Sunday a severe filter to boasting was required to sort fact from fiction, yet the nature of this fight seemed to have been replicated throughout. Released from any other care, the workers of Barcelona, both sexes, in their hundreds outside the Parque Barracks, in their thousands throughout the city, inflicted total defeat on the army over a long and sultry day of continuous combat.

Every military column was halted and very often quickly thrown back. Others were forced to seek shelter themselves by throwing up hasty barricades or retreating into buildings in which they became besieged. On the ground, it was the sheer fury of the counter-attacks; from the rooftops the riflemen could pick their targets early and thin the advancing units, while others rained down on them home-made bombs that caused numerous casualties as they pressed forward.

In the plaza below the Olympians, once the soldiers eventually began a slow advance, they marched into a maelstrom. Having driven off the initial assault, their officers no doubt thought progress would be easy. They had no idea of the numbers they now faced or the arms they possessed and, having made no attempt to find out, they, as well as the men they led, paid a prohibitive price.

Vince had the discus thrower from the Olympiad hurling the dynamite sticks on which he had trimmed and lit the fuses, causing more confusion than casualties given the distance from landing to flesh, but once the massed workers had debouched from the various side streets, they had to desist, for they risked killing their own, now a dense and screaming mass hurling themselves forward.

The infantry were first checked by that, then driven into a disordered retreat, many throwing down their weapons – those, and this was risible in the midst of a bloody battle, to be embraced by folk who had been intent on killing them a few seconds before, while another comrade snatched up their weapon and turned it on their fellows.

No such leniency was afforded the Falange blueshirts, exposed by the break-up of the rankers who had shielded them. It had to be admitted they sought no mercy, fighting with as much fervour as those they faced, killing many, but eventually either forced to retreat or die. The Spanish officers were glad of their horses, which gave them the speed to escape certain slaughter, and if it shamed them to abandon their men, there was little evidence of it.

Those that did stay loyal to their commanders retreated back towards the barrack gate slowly, and in many cases bravely and in reasonable order, downing their opponents as they went, while the more intelligent had secured and withdrawn the carts carrying the machine guns and mortars.

From being dotted with bodies the plaza was now full of the wounded and the slain, while before the barrack gates they lay in a mass, the price of facing bayonets with nothing but naked flesh and empty weapons, as well as the sustained fire of those not willing to surrender, men who knew how to reload on the move.

'You must come, you are needed elsewhere.'

Florencia, having received the message from a runner, had been required to tug hard at his sleeve to get his attention – with so many weapons being discharged the air was full of noise, but there was another reason he was concentrating; from this vantage point Cal could see that a pair of machine guns were being set up on the walls of the barracks on either side of the gates – there had to be a proper parapet there – and they would sweep the plaza and make it a killing zone as deadly as any wartime no man's land.

'Vince,' he shouted, shrugging her off.

Carrying his rifle, Vince was with him in seconds, taking the proffered binoculars, through which it took only a couple more for him to see the problem. Without another word both men set themselves to steady their aim, taking as a target one machine gun each. There was no blasting off, it was one round at a time, with tiny adjustments made for a fresh aim as stone chips began to fly around the gunners, who were just getting ready to fire.

The reaction was immediate; the weapons swung to aim at them, not an easy shot, but given the rate of fire and the range of under a thousand yards, potentially deadly. Vince rolled behind a chimney, Cal had to grab a half-standing Florencia and drag her down as the air cracked with passing shot. Now it was their turn to be splattered with dislodged stone as, crouched down, they quickly reloaded, shouting for others to be ready to join them, waiting for the belt of both machine guns to run through.

A trained man can change an ammunition belt in under half a minute, but that is an eternity if you are faced with accurate and quick rifle fire. If the Spaniards had been sensible they would have employed one machine gun at a time so as not to be caught exposed, but, smarting from the drubbing they had just received, they had run the belts right through and were cack-handed in replacing them, there being a very strong possibility that it was not the usual gunners manning the weapons, indeed a couple seemed to be blueshirts.

They got five rounds rapid from two Mausers, then more from the loaded weapons handed to Vince and Cal by the athletes, which first disrupted the reloading, then drove them away from the weapons in a continuous hail of bullets, two of them clearly taking lead and spinning away, certainly wounded, possibly on the way to being dead.

Whatever else happened, the guns had not been used on the crowds in the plaza. They were now thinning as their leaders exercised late control and sought to get them under cover, safe from the remains of those they had chased, now behind stout walls, closed gates and regrouping.

'Vince, you stay here and keep those bastards honest.'

'We'll need more ammo, guv.'

'I'll get it sent up.'

'See if any bugger has a sniper rifle too,' Vince croaked. 'In fact, a proper sniper would be ace.'

Cal called to the youngsters, not easy with Florencia seeking to drag him away again. 'Stay with him and make sure he has a loaded rifle at all times. Anything else, Vince?'

'Order me up a pint of draught bitter, guv, I'm sick of bleedin' wine.'

It was a relief to get off the roof – the temperature was now in the nineties – and into the shade of the stairway; only then did Cal realise how dry was his own throat, but a mouth turning to something like leather is the first thing that happens in combat and he was quick to put his whole head under a landing tap.

Once he reached the doorway to the plaza, he was wise enough to stop and have a good look before proceeding, though he had to drag Florencia back from just exposing herself; the gates and walls of the barracks were in range and plain sight.

'Why worry? They are beaten.'

'They are behind stone walls, the best soldiers have survived and you don't take chances, ever.' The air expelled from her heaving chest was immediate and derogatory, as was his anger, manifested in him grabbing and shaking her. 'Why is it all you Spaniards want to martyr yourselves? I'm sick of it. Now, do as I do or as I say, or go and find someone else to bury you.'

'*Querido.*'

The Spanish word for 'darling' he knew only too well; it was the one Florencia always employed when patently in the wrong and always expressed with warmth. She then smiled and gave him a kiss on the cheek, before walking right out of the door and into the exposed plaza without looking.

The battle, as recounted later in all its confusion, soon became fluid and not always decisive; the army had a plan to seize strategic buildings as well as dominate the streets and wide avenues, before taking control of the city centre, and that made things harder as it began to take proper shape.

While they succeeded in some of the former – they held the captain general's headquarters and the area surrounding it – the latter was proving difficult and that led to them being trapped in places like the main telephone exchange, previously occupied and closed down by the government. Unbeknown to Cal, they were also cooped up in some of the big luxury hotels, like the Ritz and the nearby Colón.

Everywhere he went, trailing Juan Luis Laporta, loudspeakers were blaring out news of the progress of the battle, or relaying messages for those not already engaged in a fight where to find one. They rushed from position to position, in one of which Cal witnessed a sight that was doubly cheering, the scattering of the Santiago Cavalry

Regiment, one of the elite mounted units of Spain, by the men of the POUM, armed workers all shouting out, he was told, in Catalan and in shades of 1917, that it was time to kill the Cossacks.

At another barricade, the newspaper workers – printers, typesetters, electricians and even some journalists, members of the UGT – had driven out of their buildings the lorries carrying the huge rolls of newsprint required to produce the paper and set them up across a wide boulevard, creating a defence so solid it was impervious even to artillery fire. The workers had another weapon: a fellow feeling for those soldiers reluctant in their efforts, fighting from fear of their officers, not from conviction.

If they could get to them, and they often did, brave women especially, persuading men from their own social class to down their weapons and join the Republican cause was not only successful, it was often decisive. It one case a group of anarchists even persuaded the artillerymen in charge of two 75 mm Schneider cannon to turn their fire on their own comrades.

Finally the commanders of the Civil Guard, no doubt with an eye on the way matters were progressing, threw in their lot with the workers, emerging from their barracks to parade down the wide avenue of Las Ramblas, before a cheering crowd, as well as Lluís Companys, the head of the regional Catalan government, before proceeding to become engaged in the actual fighting.

News also arrived that at the Castle of Montjuïc, a formidable mediaeval stronghold which overlooked the city, the soldiers had refused to obey their officers; instead they had shot them and armed the workers. At the airport, an officer sympathetic to the Republic had refused to join the uprising and instead sent his planes to bomb the rebels.

Now it was the turn of the workers to go on the outright offensive and attack the military barricades with that same suicidal bravery – or was it foolhardiness? – Cal had witnessed the day before at the *Capitanía Marítima*.

But it was not just bare flesh they employed; those armoured trucks, ungainly as they looked in their newly acquired sheet plating, were sent towards the hastily erected obstacles, crashing through them, driven by men who did not care if they survived the assault, and many did not.

By the end of the day, the battle, while not over, was well on the way to being won, with the various flags of the numerous workers' organisations flying all over the city centre, while at the same time some of the good news began to be disseminated to back up the action of the eight-hundred-strong and highly professional Civil Guard.

Now the fight was on to take the buildings into which the rebellious soldiers and their Falangist allies, unable to get back to their now-besieged barracks, had taken refuge.

CHAPTER SIX

One very important building was the telephone exchange, and taking that, delegated to Laporta, was to be an operation wholly carried out by the anarchists of the CNT-FAI, though he accepted Cal, Vince and their party, now back together as one unit, as honorary members; after all, each had been issued with a black and red armband to confirm their status.

Offered aid from the Civil Guard, including trained marksmen, he declined; let them do their work elsewhere. Whatever the man's faults, an inability to learn was not apparently amongst them. Without any acknowledgement to the man who had berated him the day before, he vetoed any attempt by his followers for an immediate mass charge on the place.

Instead, he elected to wait until the artillery taken earlier in the day became available to subdue the defence in what was another formidable stone building – weapons presently being deployed against the army headquarters, seeking to get General Goded to surrender. Added to that, the exchange was held in the most part by the zealots of the Falange; they would not sell their lives cheaply, and knowing the fate that most likely awaited them, surrender was out of the question.

The event was not without comedy: first, Laporta had been required to see off the consul of the USA, who insisted that damage to the building was out of the question; it was American property, belonging to the communications giant, ITT, who had bought the Spanish telephone system from a previous government. Pompous and emotional, he was seen off with a waved pistol and much jeering.

The besiegers were then free to turn their minds to the problem of capture, though they were required to do so from a distance and good cover, given the sporadic shots coming from the exchange. Square and massive, it had narrow alleyways to either side separating it from other buildings.

These, unfortunately, had lower roofs which were easily dominated from the higher elevation of the exchange, and that was a place with few windows, none at ground level, while it also had, as seemed to be ubiquitous in Spain, both a low parapet wall on the roof and a large open concourse to the front, dotted with trees for shade, and in this case a narrow entrance with two massive metal doors.

Briefly Laporta had suggested trying to use the alleyways to get to the rear of the building, but it was plain to Cal that the defenders had good observation from the roof as well as, very likely, a supply of grenades, either manufactured or makeshift, in the same manner as those Vince had employed earlier. In such confined space as an alleyway between high walls, such a weapon, dropped from above, would be extremely effective. It had to be a frontal assault, and even with cannon, that was going to be gory.

Patience, for all the talk of *mañana,* is not a truly Spanish virtue and certainly not one to which the Catalans of Barcelona subscribed; argument is, however, a national pastime and, being anarchists, as usual everyone was convinced that their opinion had as much validity as any other being voiced.

For all his evident authority Laporta had a great deal of trouble in stopping a rush on the building, finding himself in the end shouted down by a series of arguments that, translated, both Cal and Vince knew to be insane. One group was particularly troublesome. Florencia explained they were ex-miners from the coal-mining region of the Asturias, pure anarchists to a man and from an occupation internationally famous for its industrial militancy.

'They fought the army two years ago in their uprising. There is a bastard general called Franco Bahamonde they would love to cut into little pieces. He dropped bombs on them and had a cruiser shell the coastal towns from the sea. Many women and children died as well as miners.'

To the observation that Laporta was in charge, all the two Brits got was a shrug; the miners, added to their natural radicalism, came from an extreme political sect. You did not have to be around the workers' militias for long to find out that a common agenda was missing. Purists like these mining men thought their anarcho-syndicalist allies were backsliders, that left socialists were class traitors, communists of whatever hue were not only wrong but could not be trusted, and social democrats purblind fools.

The present Popular Front government, as well as its Catalan equivalent the Generalitat, was nothing more than a corrupt compromise manned by men who could never be relied on to follow the proper course necessary to bring about a just society. Naturally, everyone else viewed these political Jesuits with equal suspicion.

Cal did not bother to point out, as Florencia explained their various travails, that their actions in 1934 had not been an uprising so much as a full-blown attempt at revolution, the aim to overthrow a democratically elected government, albeit more to the right than the present one. It was no different from the coup they were seeking to contain now.

Armed to the teeth, the miners had taken control of their region of north-west Spain, even capturing the major city of Oviedo, beating a military garrison of over a thousand men. It had taken units brought in from the Army of Africa, and every modern weapon in their armoury, naval and air included, to subdue them and, as was only to be expected, the reprisals had been horrific, given what the insurgents had done when they rebelled.

Neither side had shown an ounce of mercy; at the outbreak, if you were rich – a landowner or an unsympathetic manager, even a priest – the miners were likely to shoot you out of hand. When the army recaptured territory they took a like revenge.

Quite apart from bombing and shelling, if you were poor or had skin ingrained with coal, had served as a mayor or a provincial councillor, or had held any kind of union office, you stood a very high risk of becoming a victim of the reprisals, leaving the region soaked in blood.

Now these miners, forced with their families to come to Barcelona to find work, wanted revenge and that desire was crowding out any common sense they might have possessed. Worse was the support they were receiving from others around them, buoyed up by the successes of the day and now sure they were invincible.

Sometimes a person will do something so brave or unexpected that it will entirely colour the way you see them and even radically affect a previously held view; Juan Luis Laporta did that now. Pulling out his pistol, he walked up to the most vociferous of the ex-miners, a tall, loud-mouthed fellow called Xavier, and put the muzzle to his head.

The reaction was swift: each of the threatened fellow's companions was armed and their weapons were levelled at Laporta, the bolts snapped to put a bullet in the chamber. It made no difference that the anarchist leader's men responded in kind; this was a showdown he could not survive if it went wrong. Cal, with Florencia whispering in his ear, was treated to a simultaneous translation.

'The only way you can mount an attack,' Laporta said, with an air of remarkable calm, 'is to kill me, comrade, but I shall see you in hell with me.'

'Hell?' Cal asked in a soft voice. 'I thought you lot didn't believe in God?'

'Every Spaniard believes in God, *querido*. It is priests and the church they don't believe in.'

'We are here to kill fascists, brother,' the miner replied, his eyes swivelling to try and see the muzzle of the gun, 'not each other.'

'The Commission of Public Order—'

That was interrupted by a low growl; the aforesaid committee, hastily set up to seek to coordinate local resistance to the coup, contained politicians of every hue, including social democrats and Catalan Nationalists, as well as the regional government – naturally it was treated with deep suspicion.

'The committee has given me the task of taking this building, which we will do, but when and how it will be done is a decision I will make. So, friend, you obey me or we will both die.'

'If you pray, Cal,' Florencia said, when she had completed her translation, 'do it now.'

Pride makes fools of us all and it was obvious Xavier was unwilling to lose face by a quick submission, so it was a tense several seconds till he allowed himself the very slightest of nods. Of course, when he spoke, he took care to include a caveat designed to protect his honour, one that barely required conversion to English.

'Let us beat the fascists, brother,' Florencia whispered, as Xavier spoke. 'Then perhaps you and I may have a talk alone.'

'Can't beat brotherly love, can you, guv?'

Said really loudly and not understood by the majority, it still turned every eye on Vince, which gave Laporta a chance to lower his pistol and take a step backwards. Try as he might, the miner could not help but release the pent-up breath from his body.

'Good thinking, Vince,' Cal said softly, knowing what his friend had done to be deliberate, a way to break down the tension.

'Any idea how many fights I've had to break up in my time?'

Several shots from the exchange broke what stress remained and had everyone hunching their shoulders and making sure they were behind cover again; the dispute had broken up that concern. They were not aimed at the assault group, but at a messenger dodging from doorway to doorway and heading in their direction.

His final dash brought him to Laporta, who passed on the message that the army HQ had surrendered and General Goded had been taken into custody, the radio station was firmly in Republican hands and the cannon were on the way.

The continuing bulletins from loudspeakers had been like a background buzz throughout all that had previously occurred, and now, if you listened hard, the name of Goded was just audible. News of his surrender was being broadcast and it had to be the case that those defending the telephone exchange had a radio and thus knowledge of that fact.

Would they believe it to be true, would they realise their position was hopeless and ask for safe passage; would Laporta grant that to save lives? No one was crazy enough to walk out into the open with a white flag and ask, which was just as well; waved from behind a thick tree trunk and in full view of the building, it was shredded by rifle fire within seconds. It was going to be a fight to the finish and it seemed the defenders had ammunition to spare!

The two 75 mm Schneiders arrived, drawn by horse teams now under the control of local carters. The man in charge of loading and firing them, a dock worker by trade, had been an artilleryman at one time, so he knew not to bring them too close, to a point where the gunners would be at risk from concentrated rifle fire, just as he knew to warn those along the avenue to get out of the way. Given the angle from which he was required to fire, shells could very well ricochet off the stone frontage and bring more destruction further on.

The first target was the parapet, yet even blasted – and some of the shot went right over – it was impossible to utterly destroy that, which still left good fire positions for the men occupying the roof, who, under bombardment, had been safe from anything other than flying stone by a mere withdrawal, protected by an angle of fire that could not directly do them harm.

Next it was the nearest set of windows, a row rising to the sixth storey; a shell entering through one of those would do massive interior damage, both in terms of destruction and noise, but his first efforts proved the wisdom of his earlier precautions. Hitting the front of the building the shell bounced off and within seconds had reduced to splinters one of the large trees a good hundred yards further on. Aim adjusted, the next shell hit the joint between the window and the surround, smashing through in a cacophony of tearing wood and shattering glass, followed by audible screams.

Laporta had been standing by, or to be more precise, reinforcing his restraint, given the mere sound of the shot and the long-flamed muzzle flashes were acting on his already excited cohorts to make the task ten times harder. The safe option was to fire at the rooftop and windows from cover, to keep the heads of the defenders down while not exposing yourself. It was a testimony to the level of excitement that both Vince and Cal had to yell at their own party of eager young athletes to stay still and not do as was being demonstrated to them by the others – stepping out into the open to blast off full magazines.

Even with shellfire hitting the building, and at least half the shot doing serious internal and external damage, the amount of returned fire was lethal, and several of the workers paid the price, this just as the cannon fire shifted to the main target, the double doors, which were well pounded. Yet they, being bronze, seemed like a sort of malleable armour plate, buckling but not cracking, despite taking several hits. It became increasingly clear they would need to be blown; from the angle at which the shells were striking they could not break open the part that mattered, the point at which the doors joined.

Charges were sent for while the windows of the telephone exchange building were systematically blown in until not one remained intact. Parts of the frontage, knocked off, now sat as a layer of disordered rubble before the building, yet still the defenders returned fire and inflicted casualties on anyone foolish enough to overexpose themselves, which they did regularly, leading to a steady stream of wounded and dying being borne away to the hospitals under covering fire.

When the dynamite did arrive, brought by a runner, Vince nearly had a fit as he saw the amount it had sweated. Like a father with a new baby, he held it and wiped each stick clean, careful with the cloth as well, so unstable was the nitroglycerine, before he bound the sticks into one tenfold charge, inserting a short length of fuse, while others were made ready singly and with even less fuse, to be thrown through the now-destroyed first-storey windows.

The problem, exacerbated by the fact that they were still being observed from the rooftop, was now twofold: the charge had to be laid by the doors and that meant crossing open ground under the eyes of the men on the roof; even coming from the sides, if they exposed themselves for short periods, those defenders could see what was being executed. Then, with the possibility of dropping grenades, the fuses had to be lit, and the man doing that, who must be the last to run and therefore a lone target, had to get far enough away to be safe.

Again, Cal experienced a sea change in attitude; Xavier, hitherto seen as a noisy and argumentative pest, was now transformed into a hero who would not countenance that anyone else but a miner should undertake the task, not that he had too much opposition to that stand. Laporta, who had barely spoken to Cal since the confrontation with Xavier, called to him and, with the aid of Florencia, sought his views. They were given freely, but the primary recommendation was to take time and to comprehensively explain to each person taking part, in proper detail, their individual task.

'Otherwise, monsieur, you will have confusion, and if you have that, it will fail.'

Dusk was close by the time that task was completed, the front of the east-facing building now in deep and useful shadow. The attack was split into three parts, four if the cannon were included. Vince, with his single sticks of dynamite, took one party down the avenue well away from the exchange; Cal took another in the opposite direction and that included Xavier, both sets of attackers obliged to dodge from doorway to doorway until they were far enough off to cross the road. They would come at the exchange from the sides, using their proximity to the front of those adjoining buildings, as well as their doorways and moulded parapets, to provide some protection.

Laporta had his riflemen aiming at what remained of the roof, to keep down the heads of those watching the attackers' movements. Any sight of one popping up resulted in a fusillade; that such action presaged an assault just had to be accepted. At the signal, the artillery would take over that task while the rifles were trained on the windows, their orders, which only existed as a hope, being that they would put a series of single shots through each one to suppress the defence enough to provide the time needed to place the charge.

At Laporta's signal Cal and Vince led their groups forward, backs pressed into stone as the docker-artilleryman aimed the shot, falling masonry another risk that just had to be accepted. The defenders knew what was coming and the first grenade, a proper one, popped out to bounce on the rubble-strewn pavement, really too far off to do serious damage.

As soon as that emerged, Vince's men went into a huddle in

which matches were set to lengths of fuse, the explosion acting as the signal to rush forward and for the riflemen to commence their suppression fire. There was no way to throw those individual sticks through the destroyed windows without stepping back to do so, and that created another risk.

Anyone shot dropping a lit fuse would endanger his own, something which happened immediately. This was an occasion when suicidal courage was admirable: the man shot did not let his dropped stick injure his fellows; twisting, he flung his body on top of the charge, bouncing in the air, his guts blown apart as it detonated.

The other sticks made their targets, exploding inside and below the level of the sills under which the attackers were now crouched, protecting their heads from both the blast which emerged and the bits of stone crashing down from above, some of them big enough to kill. Steady gunfire was coming from the main position as Xavier flung himself into the doorway and with great care lit the fuse. Just as he did so, a second grenade dropped no more than ten feet away from him.

Cal Jardine dashed forward and just kicked it, sending it spinning away before he flung his body into the doorway to huddle beside the miner, who had used his own bulk to shield the charge, cheek pressed against the cold bronze and arm up to cover his face, aware that time was limited; that fuse was fizzing. Thankfully, exploding in the open, the blast of the grenade, now too far away to wound, was dispersed and, as soon as that dissipated, Cal grabbed Xavier and dragged him away.

There was no time left to get clear, the only security lay in using the corner of the building. Dodging into the narrow alleyway, both men hunched down, hands pressed over their ears as the charge went off with an almighty drum-splitting boom. Cal was unable to observe the result, not that he was looking, but when he did open his eyes and look out it was to see a mass of workers, led by Laporta, rushing across the intervening ground, yelling and firing their weapons, to rush through the blasted and now-gaping doorway and into the building. Once inside, there could only be one outcome.

Darkness was upon them by the time the exchange was fully secured, every defender either killed or taken prisoner, mostly the former. The telephonic systems, the stacks of switching gear, housed in the basement, were intact, thus restoring communication not only with Madrid, but also with the rest of the world. It was a dust-covered Cal Jardine that joined an equally mucky and weary Vince Castellano and a delighted, if grubby, Florencia, who gave him a hug.

'That,' Cal sighed, 'has got to be enough for one day. Time to go back to the hotel and clean up.'

It was the look on Florencia's face that provided the first hint, the words that followed the facts.

'*Querido*, some of the soldiers have taken refuge in the hotels. The Colón and the Ritz are under siege.'

'You did not think to tell me this before?' As usual, when challenged, Florencia did not look abashed, but defiant, as though it was he, not she, who might be in the wrong. 'What did you think I was going to do, rush back and see if my luggage was safe?'

'I told you, guv,' Vince said. 'You should have stayed in the hostel with us, not some swanky hotel.'

CHAPTER SEVEN

This time Cal Jardine was a spectator to a siege, and for once he was watching professionals at work. The Civil Guards were the body attacking the Ritz and doing so with some skill; it being dark, they had brought up searchlights and aimed them at the hotel front to blind the opposition and cover their own manoeuvres. No one moved without an order, no order was executed that did not come with a corresponding distraction to confuse the defence.

This was an organisation, near-military in its set-up, accustomed to dealing with civil unrest, and they were trained in the necessary tactics of fire and movement as well as those required to take a static obstacle. The only drawback to the man watching was the fact that one of the windows they were firing at was the corner room he had left in such haste twenty hours previously.

The rest of the city was far from quiet, but all the indications now pointed to it being mopping up rather than pitched battles against the insurgents. With the telephone exchange working again, news was coming in from all over the country as well as abroad, though it was probably being managed to sustain morale. Most important was that Madrid seemed to be safe for the Republic; if the capital had fallen to rebels, it would have been fairly certain the coup had succeeded. As it was, there was some hope it could be suppressed.

Sitting on a wall behind those searchlights, far enough away from the fighting to feel reasonably safe, and after a short but restorative nap, time for reflection was possible, aided by bread, cured ham and a bottle of wine, interrupted only occasionally by the distant blast of a grenade. Vince had taken his party back to the hostel to eat and sleep, while Florencia had gone to her own home to clean up and acquire a change of clothes more suitable for the counter-revolution.

There had been no end to the desire of the various factions to show their colours, usually huge flags on trucks full of armed men roaring around the city to no seeming purpose, which did lead Cal to wonder if the present alliance would hold. The mistrust was not hidden; it was out in the open whenever the various groupings came across each other viz. those Asturian miners.

'Florencia told me I would find you here.'

It took a moment to realise he was being addressed, and another to turn from English thoughts to spoken French, but no time at all to recognise the voice. Almost immediately Juan Luis Laporta was sitting beside him, looking right ahead at the starkly illuminated Ritz Hotel, this as an explosion erupted.

'It is like a film, no? Eisenstein.'

'Does the hero die or survive?' Cal replied, while he wondered at the reason for the visit. The anarchist leader was an important person and should surely be busy, too occupied certainly for an evening stroll and a leisurely chat.

'There are heroes dying all over Spain, my friend, but more are still living.'

The appellation was interesting; even if the relationship throughout the day had moved from downright abrasive to a degree of mutual respect and cooperation, it had certainly never been friendly. Tempted to push as to why it should be so now, Cal nevertheless hesitated, and asked how matters were progressing elsewhere in the country, only to be given a taste of how confused was the whole situation.

Seville was very much in the hands of the insurgents, the whole of Morocco too, with, it was reported, a quick bullet for any officers who hinted that they might stay loyal to the Republic. Burgos and Valladolid had declared for the uprising – not surprising given the old heartlands of Castile and León had always been rightist in their politics – while the central Pyrenean foothills were a stronghold of the deeply religious and conservative Carlist movement and thus natural allies to the generals.

Elsewhere it was confusion, with no way of knowing whose side anyone in authority was on; before them the Civil Guard were supporting the workers, elsewhere they were in the opposite camp, the Assault Guards the same. Some regional authorities were still refusing to arm the workers, too fearful to give guns to those they trusted just as little as they trusted the army, while in separatist regions like the Basque country, support for the Republic was more an opportunistic grab at regional autonomy than driven by conviction.

Worryingly, the insurgents seemingly held the major military port of Cádiz and the narrows at Gibraltar, though Valencia was an unknown quantity. Most of the navy was loyal – the lower deck had been very organised – yet there existed ships where the officers had prevailed, and it was suspected such vessels would be heading for the Straits to help the Army of Africa get troops and heavy equipment to the mainland.

A depressing rumour was circulating that two large German warships were also actively screening such a crossing from interference, which removed the doubt – if there ever had been any – that this was a fascist coup welcomed in both Berlin and Rome, who had already, it was fairly obvious, supplied weapons like rifles and machine guns.

Unclear was what the democracies would do in response, for neither France nor Britain would be happy to see Spain go into the dictators' camp, the latter especially, with the route to India to protect. Yet just as telling was the fact that there was no mention of the Royal Navy in what Laporta was telling him; a mere gesture from the fleet based at Gibraltar and Valletta, which included several battleships, would send those two German warships packing.

Tempted to mention the fact, Cal kept silent; from what he knew of the British officer class, naval or otherwise, sympathy for Republican ideals was not a common thread. They would only act if instructed to do so and, quite inadvertently, he was back in Simpson's, looking into the faces of the kind of folk who constituted what really passed for public opinion in good old Blighty – if they had no sympathy for the dispossessed in their own country, it was highly likely they would have even less for foreign workers.

'How soon will this end?' the Spaniard asked, waving a lazy hand at the besieged hotel, as a sudden burst of fire chopped bits of stone from the frontage.

'It will end as soon as whoever is leading the defence realises they cannot win. It's a choice, really: die in the hotel, or come out and hope the treatment you receive is better than that being meted out by your confrères.'

Cal waited, not with much in the way of hope, to see if Laporta would condemn some of the excesses being reported from around the city, albeit mostly by rumour; little mercy was being shown to those who failed to quickly surrender, and not much to those who did. A tale was circulating that some priests had been shot, accused by a party of workers of firing at them from their steeples, and in many places it seemed summary executions were taking place as old scores were settled with ruthless employers or outright class and political enemies.

Such acts were troubling but not unexpected; revolutions were always bloody affairs and luck played as much a part in survival as any other factor. Able to intervene, Cal Jardine would have stopped such activities, yet he knew that even if the desire to do so was strong, leaders like Laporta risked a bullet themselves if they interfered with passions let loose after decades of resentment. Turning a blind eye was often necessary, regardless of personal feelings.

That he, himself, had a streak of callousness Jardine did not doubt; how could it be otherwise after the experiences he had endured in the last six months of the Great War? When you have seen your friends die, led men in a battle knowing many will not survive, witnessed mass slaughter and inflicted death on enemies yourself, life loses some of its value. When you have, in cold blood, shot your wife's lover in the marital bed you shared, it is hypocrisy to expect morality in conflict from others.

'I would just bring up the Schneider cannon and blast them to hell,' Laporta said, breaking too long a silence.

'I wouldn't. My luggage is in there.'

'Why did you come to Spain, monsieur, at such a time?'

Implicit in the question was the intimation that he had some prior knowledge of the coup, which was true, not that he was about to say so. 'The People's Olympiad.'

'You are not a socialist.'

'I am not anything. I was in London, I was asked to do something as a favour and I agreed.'

'London I do not know, Paris yes, but I think they must be the same, full of rich fascists and oppressed workers.'

'You lived there?'

'When I fled Spain, yes.'

'I won't ask why you had to get out.'

'I have spent my life fighting the oppressors,' Laporta responded, though not with any hint of fire. 'Even those in France.'

The man was weary, leading Cal to wonder if he had managed even a short nap, something the low wall on which he was sitting had provided during a lull in the fighting. As if in answer to the question not posed, Laporta gave a huge yawn.

'And at times it seems I wonder if I will ever reach my goal.'

Tempted to enquire about that, Cal hesitated again; the last thing he could face was a lecture on the ambitions of anarchism. Instead he asked Laporta about how he came to be where he was, a leader obviously, and a man deferred to as a fighter of long experience. It was the tale of a poor upbringing for a bright boy, and the struggle to make his way in a world pitted against his class, of fights for his elders and parents with miserly employers who did not hesitate to hire assassins to shoot those who dared to lead strikes demanding better pay and conditions.

The bitter boy had grown into a man determined to effect change, and if those he fought used murder as a weapon, then so must he. He and his colleagues had formed a tight cell dedicated to assassination, even at one time trying to kill King Alfonso. Naturally, those in power had struck back hard and forced flight.

Laporta had fought just as hard in France for those things in which he believed. There was a strong Spanish community in Paris, as well as left-leaning thinkers from all over Europe, many of them exiles rather than living there from choice, and if Spain was a troubled country politically, so was France, with its right-wing madmen, members of organisations like the *Croix de Feu* and *Action Française*.

In his time with Florencia, the limited knowledge he had of the Iberian Peninsula had been fleshed out, albeit from her point of view, and even allowing for her bias it was a tale of terrible poverty, haughty aristocrats unwilling to surrender an ounce of their prerogatives, intransigent land and factory owners and particularly pernicious mine managers, of a country mired in the trap of a post-imperial legacy and centuries of an obscurantist Catholic religion, which made the British Isles, for all its manifest faults and problems, sound like a haven of peace and harmony.

'But I have not come to talk of such things, monsieur.'

'I didn't think you had.'

There was a very lengthy pause before Laporta continued; it was as if he was looking for certain words and those that emerged seemed to Cal to be somehow amiss. 'Once we have secured the city, which will be soon, we must seek to aid our comrades elsewhere.'

'Which ones?'

'Saragossa first – it is under threat; in fact, it might have already fallen to the generals.' There was reflected light enough for Laporta to see that the name, even if he knew it to be a large city, did not register in any other way. 'It is the capital of Aragón and an anarchist stronghold, a place we cannot allow to remain in the hands of the generals and their lackeys, who will shoot anyone who opposes them. The CNT leadership are forming a flying column to bring relief to the city.'

Another pause accompanied by a sigh. 'Florencia has told me things about you, as you already know.' Which I now regret telling her, Cal thought. 'I must go to what I hope will be a final conference—'

'*Another* one?' Cal interrupted, which brought a rare smile to the lips of a man not much given to such expressions.

'A necessary curse, monsieur; everyone must have their say, even in the highest councils of Catalonia. I have come from the first and I must return soon for a second.'

The conferences were being held at the Generalitat, the seat of the regional government. It seemed all the time Callum Jardine had spent snoozing and as a spectator, Laporta had spent arguing about what course to take next to defeat the insurgency, without a final decision being made. As related, it did not sound like fun, but was Laporta seeking advice or maybe just a disinterested sounding board?

'You asked me a question before, and I think you will know my opinion of your conferences by what I said then.'

'We have agreed not to send thousands of men into Aragón without the leadership of an appointed commander; in this case the committee has put forward Colonel Villabova, who has stayed loyal to the Republic.'

'That is good, surely?'

'Is it? Villabova is sure he is another Cortez, but he is an arrogant fool who has no idea of how useless he is, and neither do those proposing him.'

'He will be appointed by vote?' Laporta nodded. 'Not yours, then?'

The response was spat out. 'No!'

Why was Laporta telling him this? Indeed, with so much going on, why had he sought him out? Was he looking for help? If he was, the man was too proud to say the words and Cal would have to think about that. Any decision would have much to do with what Vince and his boys intended and, as well as those committed to the fight, the majority of the People's Olympians had to be accounted for. Most would want to get out of the country, and he had as much responsibility for that as anything else, given it would be a proper use of what remained of the funds entrusted to him.

A ship was the most obvious, but even if the Spanish navy was mostly on the side of the elected government, that was not wholly the case and rebel warships might intercept vessels sailing for other Mediterranean ports. The land route, provided it was not blocked, or a zone of battle, was the safest, quickest and, no small consideration, the cheapest way out, but only if he could find them transport to the French border and that was going to be hard; a lot of the Barcelona buses had been used as barricades, and if the anarchists were off to Saragossa they would need what was left for transport.

'My men,' Laporta continued, after a very long silence, 'those I commanded today, are not soldiers.'

Cal Jardine had to stop himself from too hearty an agreement, while at the same time thinking that the Spaniard was beginning to rise another notch in his estimation, because nothing so far had intimated anything other than a blind faith in the power of political belief to overcome any difficulty. It took courage, of a sort, to admit it was insufficient.

'Here,' the Spaniard waved, to encompass the city, 'they are effective, for they are people of the city, but once we are out in open country they will not have the skills needed to fight, and if they do not have these things they will suffer.'

If you want to ask for help, do so, Cal thought, knowing he was damned if he was going to volunteer. The question that followed only hinted at the possibility.

'Will you stay and fight?'

'I have other responsibilities.'

'Florencia has told me of these.' Laporta stood up; he was clearly not going to beg but he did point out that the shooting was dying down and that a contingent of Civil Guards was now making for the entrance to the Ritz Hotel. 'If you do not decide to stay on, then I must thank you and your people for what you have already done this day.'

With hand held out to shake, Cal was obliged to stand up and take it, then, with a nod, Laporta departed.

The hotel guests, those who had not already fled and who had taken refuge in the basement with the staff, were being led out of the Ritz as he made his way towards the entrance. With his black and red CNT armband and a rifle sling on his shoulder, he was stopped by a grime-covered Civil Guard who demanded in Spanish where he thought he was going; getting over that took some doing – it was not easy for anyone to either understand him or believe that someone staying in a luxury hotel would be on the side of the government and filthy from a day's fighting.

It required that he be vouched for by the hotel manager, a seriously harassed individual, aided by the receptionist – both of whom clearly disapproved of the connection – to identify him as a proper guest so he could go to his room, passing, in the lobby before the lifts, those who had defended the place and survived, sat in dejected rows, hands over their heads and eyes cast down.

The staff had clearly not taken part in the fighting. They were now working hard to get the public spaces back to rights so it could function again as a proper hotel, and once you got away from the parts adjoining the frontage it was hard to match up the deep-piled carpets and the walls lined with pastoral pictures and silk wallpaper as anything to do with what he had witnessed out front.

Reality bit as soon as he opened his own door without the need for his key. The room was a mess, the plaster to rear and side blasted off the walls by bullets, one or two of which had taken splinters out of the door, though Cal was grateful there was no sign of blood, despite the high number of spent shell casings by the window. His luggage had been ransacked and was strewn all over the floor, while the mattress was full of holes, having been used as a shield, but it was still likely to be more comfortable than any alternative, and bliss for a very weary man, so he heaved it back onto the bed frame.

Running the taps in the bathroom, he was grateful the water had been kept piping hot, and within minutes he was stripped off and soaping, before enjoying a good long soak, listening to the popping sounds of distant gunfire and the odd explosion through windows entirely lacking in glass. Dry, aching to sleep and fearing to be disturbed by an overzealous maid wanting to tidy the place, while enjoying the delicious irony, he hung the 'do not disturb' sign on his door handle, not forgetting to put out his shoes to be cleaned and polished, before jamming a chair under the handle of the door.

Florencia had to bang on that for an age before he opened it the next morning; he had been having another luxurious soak and was wrapped in a towel, she in a fetching pair of blue overalls, a pistol at her waist and one in a holster for him. Whatever they had been when first acquired, the garment was now tailored to her enticing figure, with the top buttons undone enough to show a decent amount of cleavage, this while his towel failed in any way to hide his quickening interest.

Not much later, languishing in post-carnal relaxation, he found he was required to respond to a lover desperate to ensure his continued assistance, without being aware if Laporta had asked her to apply pressure. Any resistance to the idea of taking part in the move on Saragossa was sapped as quickly as had been his sexual energy, though he did manage the caveat that he would have to talk to Vince Castellano before making any decision.

If he had hoped that would be an end to Florencia's attempts at persuasion he was disappointed; if a female anarchist was anything, she was persistent.

CHAPTER EIGHT

Throughout the barrage of passionately delivered arguments, Cal Jardine had to consider what he might be joining, never mind any commitment to back up Vince. To his mind, the principles of the group to which Florencia belonged had within them all the ingredients that could create a recipe for disaster, one policy crossing with another to produce mostly confusion; if everyone had a right to an opinion, as well as the entitlement to express it, who made the decisions – a committee, a show of hands?

The notion of any form of organised government was anathema, as were courts, the law, a police force and prison for offenders against the commonwealth. Taxation was transgression; a way of taking from the productive to feather the nest of the idle, indeed money itself was nothing but the primary step to the corruption of the ideal of an economy based on trust – he had observed some anarchists lighting their cigars with high-denomination peseta notes, fortunately not his – which might be all very well in ordered times; these were far from that.

But now it appeared the CNT-FAI had a real problem, for they had to accept that not only was government necessary for Catalonia, but they had to be part of it. The streets had to be policed, the distribution of food and the provision of medical care supervised, while the not-so-minor problem of mistrust meant an organised military force needed to be maintained to ensure that crime was held in check, and also that no one body could exercise control. The Civil and Assault Guards had to be watched as well, to protect against any backsliding – for all their recent support, such one-time state entities were not to be trusted.

Observation over the last forty-eight hours had been confused, but for all the flag-flying and display it was obvious to even the most inattentive mind that the CNT-FAI activists were the party that had done most to save Barcelona, hardly surprising given they were by far the most numerous and committed. On barricades, and in those flying columns of truck-borne fighters, the red and black colours had been the most prominent by a factor of five to one. They were in a position to control what happened next, yet it was those very same principles Florencia espoused that prevented them for exercising that power.

To force others to accept their governance flew in the face of their core ideology; they did not believe in dictatorship, not even their own, which meant cooperation with other political organisations was inevitable, while at this moment, such consideration had to take a back seat to the primary task, the defeat of the revolt. Into that mix was thrown the endemic desire of the various factions who constituted the regional government that Catalonia should be an autonomous federated province of Spain, if not an outright independent state, which put the whole state on a collision course with Madrid.

Laporta, apparently, had spent half the night arguing the toss with the other faction leaders and Catalonian separatists about how to proceed, both in governance and in pursuance of the conflict. The CNT was desperate and determined to go to the relief of Saragossa; everyone else, even if they had conceded the point, was concerned about the security of what they already held, fearful that a city denuded of so many fighters might be vulnerable to attack in what was a very confused picture about what was happening throughout the Peninsula.

'Does the man ever sleep?' Cal asked this while once more drying himself, after a second and shared bath. The saucy look he got in response made him grab for his clothes and answer with some haste. 'We must go to Vince, who will be wondering what's happening.'

The streets were quieter than the day before, but nothing like as settled as they had been prior to the uprising. Still lorries roared around, but the barricades had been opened and normality was in full swing: mothers pushing babies in prams, shopkeepers laying out their wares or patching damaged windows, even sweepers cleaning up the debris of the street battles. Tellingly there were no bodies – they had been removed – though the smell of their one-time presence had not faded in a sun-drenched city.

On street corners and outside important buildings, unshaven men in blue overalls and varied armbands, rifles slung over the shoulders, muzzles pointing down in the manner of the classic revolutionary, eyed passers-by with looks that would not have disgraced the most cheerless Civil Guard, who, tellingly, were not to be seen. Passing damaged buildings, pocked with bullet marks, Cal was struck by one wall, where the indentations were mixed with the black stains of sun-dried blood.

Pointed out to Florencia as an obvious place of execution, he was struck by her indifference and wondered how it was that a woman so passionate in person, and one whom he had witnessed being kind and considerate over the time they had spent together, could now be so unfeeling. The spilling of blood did that, of course, the sight of bodies and the witnessing of killing hardening the senses until such a sight seemed normal, not softened by a sense of righteousness no less deep than the kind that had supported the Spanish Inquisition.

On arrival at the hostel, they found Vince giving his boys training in the very basics, lecturing them on how to strip, oil and reassemble their rifles, which, Cal knew from experience, he would keep at them to do until it was a task that could be carried out in the dark; rumours had abounded about the planned move on Saragossa, and looking into their faces, and watching Vince acting as an instructor, Cal was taken back to a time when he too had trained youngsters to be soldiers.

For all his misgivings about the British army and the way it was led and directed, he could recall the satisfaction that came from turning raw recruits into effective soldiers, as well as the pleasure of leading them in combat and watching them grow from boys into men. Would that happen now, would he feel the same with these kids? In the end it was the attitude of them and Vince that forced a decision; he was not prepared to leave these inexperienced boys to do what they intended without his help, which meant Cal, already swayed by Florencia, felt he had no option but to do likewise.

He and she left them at their training and went to find out

what the rest of the British party were up to, only to discover, as they toured their various places of accommodation, that they had already voted with their feet. By their very nature a spirited bunch of individuals, the athletes had, with a few exceptions, upped sticks and made some form of exit, many it seemed just deciding to hitchhike north to the French border. Those few he found still present he gave some money and told them to make their way home too, taking care to settle any outstanding bills due to their Spanish hosts.

Returning, they found Vince and his boys lined up on parade, weapons reassembled, looking smart, each with a blanket round their shoulders, a beret on their heads and a knapsack on their backs, leaving Cal to wonder if they had looted a store or paid for items that created a kind of uniform. He instituted a final equipment check, pleased that so little needed to be discarded.

Within the hour they set off for the assembly point, the park that surrounded the home of the Catalan parliament, becoming part of a stream that turned into a river of men, women, cars and trucks, not all armed, but all heading in the same direction, singing revolutionary songs with the light of battle in their eyes and bearing. Cynical as he was, it was hard for Cal Jardine not to be impressed.

Juan Luis Laporta greeted them, but not with much in the way of grace, which Cal put down to lack of sleep and being harassed by the need to get away his flying column of five hundred men, who would be the first to depart, with instruction to see how far forward lay the enemy. Allocated three trucks of their own and a motorcyclist to act as messenger, what Cal had taken to calling the Olympians were not at the head of the column, but they were close, not that it was moving at any great speed; that was dictated by a van laden with armour plating, naturally slow.

Excited, cheerful, making jokes, they shouted happily and incomprehensibly at any human or animal presence they encountered, travelling, once they were past the outskirts of the city, on an uneven road that ran up from the coastal plain through the high hills and beyond into open country dotted with dwellings but few large settlements. Pretty soon the clouds of dust thrown up by those ahead calmed the enthusiasm; a shut and covered mouth became the norm.

Yet they could not help but be like the kids they were, eager to drink in the details of a strange landscape, earth that alternated from being baked dry, with red rock-filled fields, then, in more hilly country, changing to deep-green and abundant grasslands, with thick, small, but well-watered forest and grand if rather faded manor houses.

A few miles further on, the trees were sparse and isolated, under which goats used the shade to stay cool, grubbing at earth that would provide little sustenance, while water came from deep-sunk wells and was obviously a precious commodity.

Cal and Vince were looking at the country with equal concentration but with a different level of interest. Wells could mean a water shortage and that would have a bearing on what was militarily possible, especially as they were easy to corrupt. They were high above sea level, but it was no plateau; too many high hills made sure that movement would be observed and at a good distance, allowing any enemy to set up their defences in plenty of time.

Fertile or near-barren, the crop fields, pasture and olive groves were small and enclosed by drystone walls, another fact immediately noted by a pair looking out for the conditions under which they might have to fight, such structures presenting excellent cover when attacking, while being perfect for defence in what Cal Jardine suspected would be small-unit engagements.

With a keen sense of history, he could not help but also imagine the other warriors who had passed this way over the centuries, fighting in these very hills and valleys: Iberian aborigines facing migrating Celtic tribesmen, they in turn battling the Carthaginians, who in time fell to the highly disciplined Roman legionaries. After several centuries those same Romans lost the provinces to the flaxen-haired Visigoth invaders, the whole mix progenitors of the present population.

There would be Moorish blood too, for the warriors of Islam would have come this way as they conquered in the name of Allah, an incursion from Africa that took them all the way, before they were checked, to the middle of modern France. They were passing through the same landscape as eleventh-century knights like El Cid, advancing to throw the Moors back under a papal banner in that great crusade called the *Reconquista*, an event that still seemed to define Spain as much as their American empire and the horrors of the Inquisition.

In the beginning they were in territory that was friendly and untouched by conflict, cheered and showered with flowers by the peasants in the hamlets they passed through as much for being Catalan as being Republican supporters of the government, which made the shock of their first encounter with the presence of an enemy all the greater, signalled at a distance by a column of smoke, slowly rising into a clear blue sky, the whole image distorted by waves of hot air.

The small town, not much more really than an extended village, sat in a fertile plain. Beyond that the road they had travelled split in two, one wide and the main road to Saragossa, the other nearer to a track. All around, though distant, lay higher ground, the source of the water that fed their trees and crops, though in late July it was beginning to show signs of baking from the relentless summer heat, while not far off a high and deep pine-forested mound overlooked the place, a huddle of buildings bisected by the road, with a small square dominated in normal times by the church; not now.

First they had seen the burning buildings; what took the eye now was the row of bodies, some shot, some strung up to trees, the latter having been tortured as well, the naked flesh already black from being exposed to the unrelenting sun. There were, too, in a couple of the untorched houses, young women, lying in positions and a state of undress which left no doubt about what they had suffered before they had been killed, while over it all there was the smell of smoke, burnt and rotting flesh; many of the youths they led could not avoid the need to vomit, which led to them being laughed at by their less squeamish Spanish companions.

Not everyone was dead or mutilated; as in most scenes like this there were those who had survived, either by hiding or not being a target of the killers, soon identified as members of the Falange, well-heeled youths who had been aided by the local Civil Guard in ridding the nation of people they saw as their class enemies. Those who came upon this did not at the time know this to be a scene being replicated all over the Peninsula, and it was not confined to one side or the other, especially given the desire for revenge for years of oppression or bloody peasant and worker uprisings.

Although he had watched these boys train for their various events, Cal hardly knew them, even Vince's boxers, something which he would have to redress if he was to lead them properly. There was a downside to that, of course: faces became names and names became personalities, and when they were wounded or killed, which was unavoidable once the bullets stared flying, it made it that much harder to be indifferent. Now both he and Vince were busy, reassuring those throwing up, telling them to ignore the Spanish taunts, insisting, not without a degree of despondency, that they would get used to it.

'Takes you back, guv,' Vince said, once they were out of earshot.

Both had seen too many scenes like this, as serving soldiers in what had been Mesopotamia and was now Iraq, a part of the world more soaked in blood over time than even this. Vince had many times reflected that you could not walk a yard in that benighted part of the world without treading on the bones of the dead – Arabs, Armenians, Kurds, and even Turks, and it was made no better by the presence of Europeans – the killing just became industrial.

'The mayor, a left socialist, was the first to die,' said Florencia, who had been part of the questioning of the survivors, that carried out as the bodies were cut down and laid out with those shot or bayoneted. 'Followed by anyone who had served on the local committees.'

She pointed to the other ubiquitous feature found in a Spanish village square, the *taberna*. 'Once they had strung up the owner they drank his wine, every drop, and then the spirits.'

There was no need to say that fired up by that, the men who had done this would then have gone on the rampage – that was how it went, first the settling of perceived scores, followed by a celebration and inebriation, leading to outright sack, the fate of captured towns and villages since time immemorial; knowledge did not, however, make it acceptable.

'They came from Barcelona, the pigs,' she spat, 'running away like the dogs they are.'

Cal was used to such mixed metaphors from Florencia, but he was tempted to say you could not fault them for that, and the evidence was on that wall they had passed this very morning; the anarchists were likewise shooting the Falangists out of hand, and not just them, if they were rooted out in Barcelona.

Cal asked instead, 'Do they know where they went?'

'West, towards Lérida.'

Cal nodded and they went over to Vince. 'It'll be dark soon and I expect we will bivvy here for the night.' He looked at the sky, now clouding over, with an even darker mass coming in from the east, promising rain; warm as it was, the boys would need to be under cover. 'I'm going to talk to Juan Luis.'

'Burial party, guv?'

Cal pulled a face, coupled with a sharp indrawn breath. 'Best leave that to their own, Vince.'

'They don't seem in much of a hurry.'

'We have sent for a priest from one of the villages we passed through,' Florencia replied, in a manner that implied such an action was obvious. 'The relatives have requested it.'

'There must have been a priest here, girl,' Vince growled, pointing to the church.

'There was,' she replied sadly, 'but it was he who first identified those to be killed.'

'It's dirty this, Vince,' Cal said, 'and I would think it's about to get dirtier.'

His friend looked at the bodies, now in a line and covered over, his voice sad. 'Can't see how.'

Cal tapped him on the back. 'Get the lads settled and fed if you can. Florencia, has Juan Luis asked about the strength of the people who did this?' She shrugged, which left the possibility that such a basic set of questions had not been posed. 'We need to question the survivors about more than victims. How many men came here, how were they armed, and more important, if the local Civil Guard joined them, what are their numbers and weapon strength now?'

The information that came back to him, an hour later, pointed to a potential total strength of eighty men, the majority blueshirts in the kind of cars the middle-class youths who made up the bulk of the Falange would own – fast and open-topped – their weapons rifles and pistols. The Civil Guard was more worrying, being more a military than a police force. They had both trucks and he knew from Barcelona they possessed automatic weapons including light machine guns.

The real question for the column was simple. Where were they now?

'Don't like that hilly forest,' Vince said, when Cal discussed it with him.

'Nor do I.'

'It is not necessary,' Laporta insisted, waving a hand at a sun that, in dying, rendered black and even more menacing the east side of the hill Vince had alluded to. 'The swine are cowards who have run away. They could be in Lérida by now.'

Upset by the suggestion they needed to protect themselves, Laporta had been even more dismissive of the notion of digging a foxhole by the side of the road west and manning it with the sole machine gun he possessed, while covering the other exits with rifles and sentries.

Also, they had explosives, wire and the ability to make charges; they could cover the areas of dead ground with booby traps, and tripwires that would set them off and alert the defence.

That too was dismissed as unnecessary, with Cal's impression of the man sinking as quickly as it had previously risen outside the telephone exchange; especially galling was the way he had obviously translated the concerns Cal expressed to those men who surrounded him, his senior lieutenants, seeking their approval for his negative responses, which was readily given. Never mind what was right and what was wrong; it was as if he needed to reassure himself he was popular.

'And,' Cal said, 'they could be sitting up a tree watching us through binoculars. If you don't put out guards they might come back.'

'My men are tired,' he snapped. 'They will not be happy to stay up all night and they are far too weary to dig. Besides, it is not the Spanish way to fight from a hole in the ground.'

'They will be a damned sight less happy if some of them die from a slit throat.'

Said with venom, it brought a predictable response. 'I command here.'

'Then I ask permission to do with my men what I deem prudent.'

That was greeted with an expressive shrug. The slow salute with which Cal responded was as much an insult as a mark of respect and was taken as the former, but by the time Laporta could react he was looking at the man's back. It was only in walking away that Cal realised it was he who had been foolish, and it was far from pleasant to acknowledge the fact.

He had approached Laporta when men whose good opinion he craved surrounded him. As at the *Capitanía Marítima*, he took umbrage automatically at what looked like a challenge to his authority when in their presence. Laporta alone, as they had been outside the besieged Ritz, had seemed a different fellow, and Cal was sure he had come to seek his help. He promised himself never again to make any suggestions unless they were out of both view and earshot.

'I've told the boys we will sleep in the church,' Vince said, 'though there are a couple with Irish parents who have refused.'

'Give them a week and they'll sleep on the altar and drink the communion wine,' Cal snapped, still angry with himself. 'But we are going to have to take turns with them guarding the roads in. Our Spanish friends don't think we need to.'

Vince looked at the cloud-covered sky. 'There will be no moon, and they won't fancy being stuck out in the pitch dark, so young and all.'

The implication was obvious; night guard duty with no moon was bad enough for the experienced soldier – you heard and saw things that were not there, but knew not to just shout or shoot. These keen but inexperienced boys would likely be trigger-happy and blasting off at threats more imagined than real. Being out in the open was a task for either himself or Vince, and much as he disliked the idea, Cal knew he would have to go out on his own.

'A gunshot will do the trick.' Cal jerked his head towards a group of Spaniards sitting outside the *taberna*, Florencia laughing and joking with them. 'Even this lot will wake up to that.'

'And shoot anything that moves,' Vince growled. 'So don't you go rushing about or you'll be their target.'

'What I wouldn't give for a box of flares.'

He got the eye from those worker-fighters as he went to talk to Florencia, not friendly either, with quiet ribald comments and stifled laughter. It was, he suspected, no more than a demonstration of stupid male pride, the same kind of thing he had experienced before in too many locations. It seemed the hotter the country, the more the menfolk felt the need to look and act with bravado, and that was doubled by what they had achieved so far in fighting the army.

He wanted to say to them that a healthy dose of fear and a bucketload of caution would serve them better, but he lacked both the language and the desire. At least Florencia rose and smiled at him, moving to take his arm, which did nothing to soften the looks he was getting, jealousy now thrown into the mix as, heads close, he explained his concerns.

'We don't want to give these poor village people any more grief, so it would be better if they moved to the centre of the village where they will be safer.'

As the last of the light was fading, Cal Jardine was out on the western edge of the village, a full water canteen over his shoulder, looking at the ground, eyeing those places where lay the kind of dead spaces into which a crawling man could move unseen, as well as the walled-off areas of planted crops, vines, olive trees and vegetable plots, which would help to cover a discreet approach. He used the remaining light to pick out a line of approach to the village, one he would use himself to get close unseen, then he selected a spot from which he could cover it.

That was a gnarled old olive tree, on a slight mound, that had probably been there since the Romans ruled. Being above ground was not comfortable – quite the reverse – but it gave him a better view if the cloud should break, and he knew from experience a crawling intruder rarely looked skywards, too intent on avoiding noise by taking care with what lay in front of him. Clambering up and lodging himself between two branches, his mood, a far from happy one, was not improved as the first heavy drops of rain began to fall.

Even with eyes well accustomed to the dark there was nothing to be seen; it was all about listening, getting accustomed to the sounds that occurred naturally – croaking frogs, barking dogs, as well as raindrops hitting leaves and the chirping insects hiding under them – making sure his thoughts, which were unavoidable, did not distract him from his purpose.

CHAPTER NINE

The looks he got when he came back in the morning were close to sneers; nothing had happened, no threat had appeared and every one of the Spaniards had enjoyed a good night's sleep. Nor had any orders come to move on and by which route, which surprised him, given the supposed need to get to Saragossa quickly. Still, it was their fight, not his – the man in command, this Colonel Villabova, might have information not vouchsafed to Laporta; and if it was military incompetence, that was not something to which he was unaccustomed.

Years of training allowed Cal Jardine to get by on catnaps, one of which he took after a less-than-sustaining breakfast of unleavened bread and a fruit compote washed down with water; if there had been coffee, which he and his men had become accustomed to in Barcelona, the Falangists had pinched it. Then he spent twenty minutes lying dead flat on a warm stone, his hat pulled down to keep the sun out of his eyes and out to the world.

By the time he came round, Vince had drawn from the well and heated some water, insisting that the boys should wash and shave, even if some of them barely had the necessary growth; it paid to stay clean when you could because, when it came to a fight, you could spend a long time between opportunities.

He had also been at them before they went to sleep, insisting they washed their socks and inspected their feet and also showing them that a properly stuffed knapsack made a good pillow. Then he had ensured that, while their rifles were loaded, the safety catches were set to off.

Next they were lined up in singlets and shorts for exercises, which actually produced outright laughter from the anarchist contingent, but there were no complaints from the boys doing the leaps, squats and press-ups; they all took their own fitness seriously, and one, called Bernard, a marathon runner, had actually set off to do his usual long wake-up jog before breakfast, heading, as advised by Vince, due east. After exercises, given there were still no orders to move, Cal got them dressed and took them out into the open for training in fire and movement, the former in dumbshow.

'My friends think you are a mad Englishman,' Florencia said, as she joined Cal, with an air that half indicated she agreed with them.

'I hope you told them I am not either.'

'They wonder how can a man spend the night lying in a ditch when he has a woman to keep him warm.'

'I was up a tree, actually,' Cal replied, rubbing an ache that came from the position he had been obliged to adopt and maintain, while wondering if the complaint was her own.

'And now you want these boys to run around and play at soldiers?'

'Before you become a soldier it helps to play, Florencia. You learn how to stay alive. Shall I explain what we are trying to do?'

She shrugged. 'If you like.'

'We have a body of young men who, in the parlance of the British army, do not know their arse from their elbow.' There was a pause while Florencia filed that away; she was a keen collector of idioms in English, and in the past had made Cal write them down for her. 'Now, when it comes to tactics, some of them will be clever and some of them will be idiots, and the first trick is to make sure in a battle it is the clever leading the idiots and not the other way round.'

He nearly added that in most armies, not least the one he had served in, you found out, especially after a long period of peace, that the reverse was generally the case, viz. that pompous idiot who had led his men out of the Parque Barracks. Putting that thought aside he pointed to a party moving along a drystone wall at a crouch.

'What we are trying to do is to spot the natural leaders.'

'You lead them, and your Vince.'

'We can't be everywhere, so we will break our group into five units of ten men, four of which will be rifle squads, each with a leader and an assistant, the rest we will use as a reserve under my personal supervision, also as messengers, medics and reinforcements. If we get machine guns, and I hope we do, each rifle squad will have a two-man gun team.'

The one leading the squad being put through its paces had reached a corner and peered round, his hand held up to stop his companions. They obeyed, but one of the lads could not resist raising his own head to look, which occasioned a furious bark from Vince, who then walked over to the leader and spoke quietly.

'Vince will be telling him that in such a situation he should have added a gesture to keep their heads down, not just signal to stay still. Come on, let's get closer and listen in.'

'OK,' Vince said, loud enough to be heard even before they got close. 'All have a shufti and tell me, once you leave the protection of this wall, where would you go?'

Cal pointed to the low rise on which he had spent the previous night, talking quietly. 'For the purposes of this, we have said that is where the enemy is and the task is to take possession of it. That's part of the basics whichever side you're on, always seek to dominate the ground.'

Ask a question of those without experience, as Vince was doing now, and not everyone will answer. The ones who do, at the most basic level, are the lads you want to sort out, as long as their answer isn't downright stupid, which is what came from one of Vince's boxers, a spotty-faced kid called Sid, who picked out an area of sparse trees with gnarled but thin trunks in an open field. The response took Cal back to his own basic training.

'A million sperm,' Vince sighed, with a shake of the head, 'and the egg got you.'

'What aboot that wee gully o'er there?' suggested a youngster who had been sent to the Olympiad by his local East Lothian mining branch.

Vince nodded. 'And how, Jock, would you get from where you are to where you need to be?'

'Am' no sure, Vince, 'cause I think if we just rushed we aw' get shot.'

'You're right, so let's sort out how to do it.'

Vince got them back behind the wall, with the kid called Jock at the apex, where he crouched down himself to speak to him. 'What you do, as the squad leader, is stay still and select the pair you're goin' to send ahead first. The squad will go two at a time. The rest you tell to give covering fire, but you must say where the target is and how many rounds to fire, understand?'

Young Jock nodded nervously as Vince demonstrated the necessary hand signals and verbal commands, adding, 'Look, son, this is an exercise, not the real thing. Nobody gets killed if you get it wrong. OK?' Another nervous nod followed. 'You send two men at a run, with four selected to give covering fire. Nobody moves till everybody knows what's happenin' and has made it plain they understand. On your command they move and at speed. Now, who would you select to go first?'

There was a pause, before Jock replied, 'Tommy and Ed are hundred-yard sprinters.'

That got an upraised thumb. 'Covering fire?'

That occasioned another pause before he tapped the last line of stones and Vince was patient. 'The last four in the group, 'cause the buggers will be watching the corner.'

A nod. 'Then let's try it.'

'How many rounds, Vince?'

'Three rapid, but you have to tell them the target and where it is.'

Vince addressed them all, his hand, jabbing like an axe, pointing in the direction of the mound, with Jock watching him intently.

'It's a small hill and you've got to keep the heads down of anybody up there; a kill is a bonus, so you're aimin' for the line where the earth joins the sky. Furthest left takes furthest left and so on across to the right, which falls to the last man. Tommy, Ed, once you are in position stay in sight of your squad leader if possible, and when he signals the movement of the next pair of runners, your task is to split the defensive fire. Everybody clear?'

The nodding was less than hearty, and if what followed in dumbshow looked impressive to Florencia – especially the speed at which the boys moved over about twenty-five yards of ground – it was less so to Cal and Vince, who knew that much of what they were saying and seeking to impart was massively oversimplified.

Tactics were things you worked on again and again, not once or twice. It took months to properly train an infantryman, not a morning or a few days, and then they had to learn to work as part of a single unit, before combining to become an element of an effective company, going through the various stages of dumbshow – firing blanks and harmless explosions – to the actual experience of the sound of live fire. This lot would have, he suspected, to learn on the job, but at least they were fit, which was not the case with any new recruit he had ever encountered.

Young Jock did a reasonable job of orchestrating the supposed firefight, a bit messy but promising. He had to be told to order an immediate reload, never just leave it, never to assume, to always give the necessary orders even to trained men, to keep a check on your ammunition levels because the worst thing you can do is to get into a situation where you find you are in peril and running low.

'Right,' Vince called to the other groups of ten, who had been watching. 'Let's see how you do.'

The next sermon, given by Cal, was about the need when moving forward to use cover, and if that was sparse, to seek to avoid standing upright, making a particular point about the excellent protection afforded by the seemingly ubiquitous drystone walls. Using them was not always possible, nor was it always the case that you knew you had an enemy to root out, so it was essential if you had to move quickly over open ground not to bunch up, but to advance in extended order.

In another situation – broken ground, woods or approaching a building – two men should scout forward covered by their mates. If a threat developed, think about what support you can call on, like heavier weaponry, before advancing. Was it essential that the position be taken? What about going round, which could be as good as going through?

Sat in a circle they listened as it was drummed home that a good squad commander never left anything to chance, supervised every move and issued continuous hand and verbal instructions, while always looking for ways to use his men to maximum effect, as well as seeking to minimise casualties when attempting to take an enemy position. Cal did not say that sometimes it was not possible; you don't.

Regardless of what he had said to Florencia, still watching and listening, he had no intention of letting these kids operate on their own in squads – in time, yes, if they were granted that and it was necessary, but not immediately; yet the purpose of the training was the hope that it might produce leaders who would grow quickly into the role and to minimise losses from any sudden contact. More importantly, and the key to effectiveness, was to accustom the boys they led to obey orders unquestioningly.

'Right,' he said finally, looking skywards at the sun, now well risen and approaching its zenith. 'Time to get in the shade.'

'And eat,' Vince added. 'Can we use some of the rations we brought with us, guv? There's not much spare left in the town.'

As they made their way back to the main square, the truth of Vince's words was on the faces of those whom they passed, the folk who had survived the recent terror; true, the approach of the anarchist column had driven the murderers away and saved the town from further torture and death, but now they were finding that their liberators, not having moved on and needing to be fed, watered and accommodated, were as much of a burden as the fascists.

Their attitude did not help either: Laporta's men had a swagger about them, the confidence of the victors of Barcelona. Added to that they were urban workers, atheists to a man, many of them seriously uncouth, now occupying a rural settlement where their city manners, political beliefs and their disdain for religion were anathema. Also, if the area surrounding was well watered and fertile, following on from the previous depredations and the subsequent loss of livestock and grain, it was not so blessed as to accommodate the needs of five hundred hungry souls.

Cal Jardine was awoken from another snooze by the sound of roaring engines, opening his eyes to observe a new unit arriving in a quartet of trucks and a cloud of road dust. The bright-red flags, above the cabs, with the hammer and sickle, identified them as members of the *Partido Comunista de España*. As they swung to in front of the church, and for all his dislike of Bolsheviks – which was nothing as compared to the way they were viewed by the anarchists – Cal was impressed by their discipline, as well as the fact that each vehicle carried drums of precious fuel, enough for the whole column, without which they would struggle to continue the advance.

Ten men to a truck, clean-shaven and dressed in the same garb of black – jackets, berets, trousers and high boots, each with a bandolier of bullets over their shoulder – they sat upright with their rifles between their knees and did not disembark until ordered to do so. When on the ground they immediately formed up in a proper military fashion, dressing their lines, all eyes turned to the man who had emerged from the lead truck and barked the requisite commands.

Tall, unsmiling and hard-looking, with a tight belt around his waist and a pistol at his hip, a machine pistol in his hand, he was dressed in the same clothing as his men, except, instead of a beret, he wore a short-brimmed cap with a red star at the front over blond hair cut very short. Three others, obviously section leaders, had already emerged from the other cabs carrying rifles, which they slung over the shoulder as they took up station before their squads. There was no noise, no talking and no looking about; with the exception of their leader it was all eyes front.

They paid no attention to the shuffling mass of Laporta's men made curious by their arrival, who came to look them over, or to the remarks being made, which Cal suspected to be well-worn insults, every one of which the communists had heard before. They had no effect on the commander either, who, satisfied that his men were behaving properly, gave a sharp order that saw them fall out and begin to unload their personal kit, before lighting a excessively long cigarette, which he held in a curious fashion between his second and third fingers.

Juan Luis emerged from the crowd to talk to this new arrival, and feeling he had the right, Cal went to join them, aware as he did so that the communist leader was looking around him with disdain, as if he had descended to this place from a higher political plane, that underscored by the way he held his smoking hand, high, almost as an affectation, so it was level with his chin. Certainly there was no order in the contingent that filled the square; those who had not come to rib the new arrivals were lounging about in the shade.

'Laporta,' the communist leader said with a sharp nod; he obviously knew Juan Luis.

'Drecker.'

The name interested Cal, as had the guttural way he had pronounced the Spaniard's name, as well as his appearance; was he German? As he began to converse it certainly seemed so, and it was also apparent he was passing on instructions. When he finished, Laporta turned to Cal and spoke in French.

'Orders from Villabova. Instead of heading straight for Lérida we are to move forward along the southern fork up ahead.' The flick of the finger, aimed at the communist, was disdainful. 'Our German friend, Manfred Drecker, is to come with us, while the main road is to be left free for Villabova's main force. He is sure Lérida is too big a nut for the insurgents to swallow, but we are to act as flank guards and make sure nothing comes at the main body from the south.'

Drecker was examining Cal as Laporta spoke, and in a seriously unfriendly way, not that such a thing bothered him; first impressions of this fellow, his unsmiling face and haughty demeanour, fag included, pointed to that being habitual. What troubled him was the difficulty presented by the addition of a third commander, one who would see to the needs of his own men first, added to the fact that he did not speak Spanish.

He had Florencia, and Laporta spoke French; this Drecker, judging by his look of incomprehension, did not, but he was German, a language in which Cal was fluent. The potential for operational confusion was obvious.

'I take it you are still in command?'

'I have the most men,' Laporta replied, though he looked away from Drecker as he added, 'but I have never met a communist yet who would take orders from anyone but their own.'

'When do we move?'

That brought on a long pause, before he spoke. 'We will stay here today and move out at dawn.'

'Not immediately?'

'We are not ready,' Laporta snapped.

'I was just thinking the people of this place would be glad to see us go. Another day of feeding so many men will leave them to starve in the months to come.'

'Let their God send them loaves and fishes.'

The sun was dipping now, throwing the base of the hill to the west into shadow. The route they had been ordered to take, unlike the main road, was seriously narrow, barely wide enough for a single vehicle. It ran right through a deep belt of pine trees which, from what Cal could see, hemmed the road in and formed an overhead canopy that cut out sunlight, a perfect place for an ambush if the Falangists and their Civil Guard allies were inclined to set one.

'How deep is that forest?'

'How would I know?' Laporta replied, as if the question was inappropriate.

'Surely you have a map that tells you?'

'Map?' Laporta laughed. 'We are going west to Saragossa, who needs a map?'

'Herr Drecker, *haben Sie eine Karte, bitte?*'

Drecker spun on his heel and shouted, which, after a few seconds, brought one of his men running, he having fetched the necessary from the cab of the lead truck. Cal's hopes sank as soon as it was handed over, it being no more than a very basic road map, of the kind you might get in the UK from the Automobile Association, while at the same time he suppressed the desire to curse himself, not that he felt entirely guilty.

He had spent half the day saying to his boys that you must never leave anything to chance, which was precisely what he had done; the Barcelona military, now overthrown and everything in their barracks available to be used, had to have regional maps of the kind they needed, the sort any army used, showing features, elevations related to sea level, significant landmarks, watercourses and all the things a soldier needs to make their way through unfamiliar terrain.

A good map was like a safety blanket – with that, a compass and visibility, getting lost for a good map-reader was impossible and Cal had always prided himself on his ability in that area. No map was a prelude to a fog and he had just assumed Laporta would have what was required. He was about to ask if the Spaniard had a compass but, certain he would reply in the negative, he just left it. More worrying was Laporta's next remark, that with them all being in trucks, and if they set off at first light, they might get to Lérida before nightfall.

'Do you intend to just drive on without a reconnaissance?' Cal asked, 'through a forest?'

'Why would I not?'

Cal looked around him, aware that many of Laporta's lieutenants were once more within earshot. The absurdity of what he then asked did not escape him – they did not speak French – but it was the man's face he was worried about and his inability to keep hidden his pride when challenged. He waved a hand towards the entrance to the church and the darkened interior.

'Can I talk to you in private?'

'This is not?'

'Not for what I want to say.'

Laporta did not look at Manfred Decker, but he did appear cautious if not downright suspicious. 'Without our friend?'

Cal nodded, then sauntered off, leaving Laporta to decide how to follow him without causing Drecker offence. The communist, having finished one cigarette – it was the long Russian variety with a tube – immediately lit another.

CHAPTER TEN

'I have decided to take my athletes back to Barcelona.'

Seeing the Spaniard stiffen, he carried on before he could interrupt, struggling to keep any hint of anger out of his voice.

'And I will tell you why; it is because I fear they will die to no purpose under your leadership. You intend to advance without knowing what is ahead – and I say you cannot just barge on as if there is no force opposing you and, even worse, you have no idea where they are.'

'The Falangists do not frighten me and they are cowards.'

'They are eighty strong and stiffened by Civil Guards.'

'We are over five hundred, six now that Drecker has joined us.'

'Advancing along a single-track road.'

'One they have no idea we will take,' Laporta snapped. 'They will expect us to continue on the main road to Lérida.'

That was true, but to Cal it did not obviate the need to reconnoitre any road before they passed through.

'If I were your enemy, I would be making preparations whichever route you took, and you would find, halfway through on either road, enough trees blocking it to make forward movement impossible.'

'We have an armour-plated van.'

'I have seen proper tanks destroyed by men with grenades.'

'They would die trying.'

'Perhaps, like you, they are prepared for that.'

'Then we will fight and kill them.'

'They may kill you.'

'So, my men will avenge me.'

'Will they? Other trees would then be felled behind them to block any retreat, and the enemy have a machine gun.'

'They cannot kill us all.'

'No, but they can kill many and then just disappear, leaving you to clear the road. Somewhere up ahead of that I would have already picked the next place to make you pay in blood for your progress.'

'This is no more than a dream.'

'Look, my friend, you are a good leader of your men, they respect you, but this is my profession. I don't say there is an ambush waiting for us, only there might be and the proper course of action is to find out. Let us advance like soldiers and not a rabble.'

The silence was as long as the stare that accompanied it, before the Spaniard spoke. 'I think we should rejoin Drecker or he will think we are plotting against him.'

'Why would he think that?'

Laporta laughed out loud, albeit low and hoarse. 'My friend, he is a communist. They are convinced everyone is plotting against them.'

'And the road ahead?' The nod was slow, but positive, so Cal asked, 'Sentries?'

That killed off any humour and Laporta once more looked grim.

'Look, if your men are going to behave like soldiers, that is the best place to start.'

The answer did not come immediately; it was the same as sitting on that wall outside the Ritz Hotel. The anarchist suspected he was out of his depth and in need of advice, but he was too proud to ask, yet hanging in the air was Cal's threat to take himself and his men away.

'Tonight, they will be my men,' Laporta said, finally and with confidence.

Later on, when the time came to execute such a promise, it turned out to be a lot less simple, only solved after a noisy discussion, which seemed again to involve every one of the Barcelona anarchists who had an opinion and the conviction of their right to air it. Cal stayed well out of it, but he did observe that Laporta finally began to lay down the law, in essence to begin to act like a proper commander and not the chairman of some revolutionary committee.

Not that his orders were accepted with grace; it was a sullen bunch of anarchists who went out into the gathering gloom, while their leader continued to argue with his senior underlings as to whose job it was to ensure both that the necessary changes were made and who should be responsible.

Vince summed it up in one well-worn phrase. 'Fred Karno's Circus, guv.'

'It's a new tactic, Vince, you make so much noise arguing the toss you frighten away your enemy.'

* * *

Another salient fact was the way the atmosphere was noticeably changed by the arrival of the chain-smoking Drecker and his men; they kept themselves separate in a way that did not apply to the British contingent, made up of youngsters who had a sunny disposition on life, took the ribbing they had received earlier in good humour and generally showed their Spanish compatriots a comradely attitude.

The communists were not given to smiling at anyone, not even each other, seeming like a particularly committed set of monks in their sense of purpose. They had appropriated one corner of the square and they stayed there, being subjected, after eating, to what looked like lectures that had to be about politics, given by their squad leaders, and Cal, seeing Laporta was still with Drecker, wandered over to listen, though it was more the tone than the words, given he could not understand them; he could tell by the gestures it was all about purpose.

So intent were they that no attention was paid to him, which allowed him to look over their stacked equipment. With the eye of a professional he did not have to get too close to their rifles to recognise them as Mosin-Nagants, the standard rifle of the Russians since czarist times; bolt action and magazine fed, they were a pretty useful weapon.

Idling on, he walked behind their trucks, and with the rear flaps down he could see they had ample ammunition and what he thought were boxes of grenades, all with Cyrillic script lettering to denote their Soviet provenance. It was not too surprising that communists looked to Russia for their weaponry, but it was just another indication of the state of the nation; how easy it had been over the years for such a group as the PCE to smuggle in their own armoury.

Back out in the open, Cal, in reacting to a shout, was dragged into having dinner with Drecker and Laporta – he half suspected the Spaniard could not abide that he should eat with the German alone. That was a sore trial; if the anarchist was given to an excess of pride in the company of his lieutenants, he was positively barbed by the new arrival. Not that he was alone in that. Both were eager to air their differences in a dialectical debate on competing principles, and the German bugger smoked incessantly, holding his cigarette in that affected manner.

What it came down to, as far as Cal could make out – not easy in a three-way language discussion – was the difference between the communist ideal of central control and the anarchist view, which was the precise opposite. For Juan Luis Laporta, centralism was an abomination and he made no attempt to keep hidden his repugnance of the notion, the idea that the leadership was not only always right, but that it had no need to explain itself to those who followed.

Listening to them argue, it was worrying how this would play out in action, and not only in the tripartite relaying of orders; Laporta, by dint of his numbers, was the leader, and if Cal Jardine was determined to educate him he must seek to do nothing to openly undermine his position in the process.

Less certain in that regard, and it was only an impression, was Drecker, a humourless prig who also had, as well as his beliefs, an air of arrogance recognisably German and of the most intolerant Prussian hue, which went against his rough Ruhr accent. He created the feeling that he might question every instruction given, which would be fatal in an engagement.

It was a relief to get away and meet up with Florencia, who had found an abandoned house into which she was eager to drag him, though he was obliged to keep her waiting while he checked on his charges, making sure they were ready for the morning, pleased that they seemed eager to undertake the task outlined, for, given a chance to engage in some on-the-job basic training for the Olympians, there was not even a suggestion that any of the Spaniards should undertake the reconnaissance.

Rejoining Florencia, and she linking her arm with his as they began to move, Cal was very aware of Drecker. He was smoking another of his long cigarettes and watching them from the communist section of the square with what looked, in the torchlight, like narrowed eyes; so was Florencia and her response was typical.

'He is like,' she said, with a slight giggle, relishing the chance to use an idiom that Cal had applied to one of the Ritz receptionists, 'a man with a broom up his arse, that is what you English say, yes?'

'Not in polite company.'

'Is he polite company?'

'No.'

Taking a puff in the strange manner in which he smoked, Cal saw that the flaring cigarette end lit up the red star on his cap.

Vince had his boys kitted up and ready to move in the hour before dawn and they were out of the built-up area before the sky turned grey, where they waited till there was enough light to move. Nor did they just march out of the town and straight down the road to be taken by the main body, to the point at which it forked south. They moved at an angle, as previously lectured, in extended order, five staggered squads deep, well apart, weapons ready, that took them towards the treeline, now bathed in low sunlight.

Aware of the power of imagination and approaching a forest that rose before them, dark-green and menacing, the notion that this might be something other than an exercise was not mentioned, but it was drummed in that coming out of a low sun and advancing on a forest edge illuminated by the same strong backlight created the best conditions for the approach. The sunlight rendered them indistinct, while any movement in the trees should be obvious.

Once in the shade, Cal explained what they must look for and where, outlining the same scenario as that with which he had regaled Laporta. 'We will move on both sides of the roadway. There was rain the night before last, so look for disturbed ground at the edges, the same, as well as cuts, at the base of the bigger trees, wood chippings or sawdust, then wires leading to hidden explosives, but if you find any don't touch.'

As he was talking Cal realised he was probably addressing a load of townies – there was not a country boy amongst them; the best he could hope for was the likes of Jock, from a small mining village.

'Anybody keep pigeons?'

Two lads from Tyneside put up their hands, shipyard workers, he recalled. Even in what was close to the most depressed part of the country they still kept up their hobbies.

'Well, Jack,' Cal said, hoping he had the name right, 'you know the noise a bird makes when disturbed, and that could signal an enemy moving if they fly towards you. Anything suspicious, it is hand up by the lead men and everyone else crouch down. Have your rifles at the ready but do not turn them inwards to the road. Remember who is on the other side – your own mates.'

'What aboot the Spaniards, like, Mr Jardine?' asked one of the Geordies.

'They are coming behind us, when they have got themselves organised.'

'Organised?' came the heavily accented Geordie response. 'Ha'way, man, they divn't ken the meaning o' the word.'

'Right,' Vince called, 'let's get moving and no more talking.'

You cannot blame young and inexperienced lads for being excitable and a lot of the time was spent hushing them up, but once more, in such a situation, you can observe those who take the whole thing seriously, not joking with each other, but keeping themselves alert to possible dangers, and they are the ones you want to give responsibility. When the chance presented itself, both the pros took the time to show individuals where to look for tree-felling charges, first the larger one that would blast open the trunk, then the secondary explosion which, going off a fraction later, would ensure the tree fell the right way towards the road.

Not that there were any, nor, for a long time, was there evidence that the men fleeing the town had come this way. It was one of the two lads on point, in this case Jock, holding up his hand and immediately crouching down, who first indicated some kind of threat, which led Cal and Vince to move forward from the position further to the rear where they were seeking to contain the exuberance of some of their charges – an inability to avoid whispered banter – all now silent and on their haunches. Once they joined the signaller they could see clearly the four large lengths of mature pine that lay across the road.

The first thing Cal looked for was the stumps from which they had been felled, even in the gloom of the deep forest a stark white, the angle of the face showing they had been brought down by axes, not explosives; not surprising, for that would have been heard in the town where they had bivouacked.

Given there had been no evidence of any laid charges through the parts they had already traversed it seemed unlikely they faced any threat from the rear, quite apart from the fact they were on foot; if there was a trap set it was for the motorised column, not those who could just leave the road and retreat through the trees.

'Just a hold-up to help them get clear?' Vince suggested.

'Probably. They had no idea Laporta would stop.'

'How do we check it out?'

The question implicit in that was about the rawness of their recruits and whether the possibility of real danger existed, not a thing you could ever be a hundred per cent sure about. For them to lead a recce into the depth of the trees carried a risk, but here again was a chance to engage in a practical exercise. If he had been up against a wholly professional foe, one who could not only conceal themselves but also stay still and hidden, it would have been out of the question. But he was not; even the Civil Guard would not have been trained in the requisite tactics for this kind of scenario.

'Bring up the rifle squads one at a time.'

That took a while and was achieved in silence with finger and hand signals – each squad was now numbered – and if there had been any temptation to banter it was suppressed by their uncertainty about what was about to be asked of them, this while Jardine, just in case, ranged his eyes over the forest ahead looking for tiny signs of movement, a branch being twitched, a rifle muzzle jerking; even for highly trained troops it was hard for a large party of men to stay absolutely still. The more he looked, the more he was convinced there was no danger.

When Vince had them gathered, Cal dropped back slightly to a point where they could observe the obstacle but be in a position to quickly fall back, and explained quietly what they faced, having first pointed out those starkly white tree stumps and what could be read from them. With the ground rising to one side, that was the most likely spot to set your shooters, given it gave dominance over the killing zone and slowed any counter-attacking force obliged to move uphill.

Not that you could assume – that was stupid, he continued. Both sides had to be checked but any ambush could only be set to one side of the road; not to do so was to risk killing your own men once the bullets started flying. The way to check it out was simple – three squads would be left as support, while the others would be led into the woods at a right angle, then forward in extended order moving from tree to tree.

Selecting the two who would play out what had been proposed presented a problem; he needed to leave Vince in charge of the main body, just in case his assumptions proved false. So he took one squad on the left-hand route and gave young Jock from the Broxburn mines charge of the other, on balance the less likely to pose a risk. When they moved out there was no joshing; they took it seriously, moving in near-silence, careful where they placed their feet.

The sudden sound of breaking undergrowth was instructive; every one of Cal's party immediately sought cover and aimed their weapons towards the source of the noise, for there was nothing to see until the wild boar showed itself between two patches of thick bush. That was enough for Cal, who already had his rifle at his cheek, the muzzle moving slightly ahead of the rushing game, habit for a man who had shot pheasant and grouse, as well as been taken stag hunting by his father in the Highlands.

The single shot took the animal in the head and dropped it, the sound echoing through the forest. Slowly he moved forward, another bullet in the chamber, for a boar was a dangerous animal and not always alone, followed by his extremely curious squad of lads, to stand over the twitching body of the wild pig.

'That's dinner taken care of,' Cal said, well aware that the presence of the beast was a sure sign there were no other humans present. 'We need a runner to go back and bring on the others.

Bernard the marathon man was only too keen to volunteer.

By the time the first trucks arrived, the slow armour-plated van first, the animal had been gutted and tied onto a pole, the sight enough to give Laporta another discipline problem: half his men wanted to go hunting for what was a highly appreciated local dish. Cal did not bother to explain that them blundering about in the woods would drive every boar into hiding, and if they got close, especially if there were piglets around, it might be them that suffered and not the animals.

Using ropes, the route was cleared and within an hour they were on their way, soon once more in open rolling country following a depressing route of destruction as, in farmhouse after farmhouse and village after village, they found houses destroyed and people either shot or hung from trees, with the mood of the column getting increasingly gloomy and resentful, the desire for bloody revenge building at every incident, even if they were unsure which side had done the individual deeds – some of those farmhouses might have been gutted by peasants.

The bigger landowners in every case, and the priests in most, had fled with the Falange and, when survivors were questioned, it was clear that to the present squad of Civil Guards had been added others, though not all. In one small town they found that the local semi-military policemen, having sided with those they lived amongst, had been the victims, not the perpetrators.

Nothing signified more the confusion that was to become commonplace than their half-dozen uniformed bodies crumpled against the wall where they had been shot. They, at least, had been given the last rites by a priest who, Cal was told, having tried to protect his flock, was lucky to survive.

Little time was spent in such places by the main body – enough to establish the strength of the fleeing enemy and to issue a few consoling words. Then they were back on the road and making good progress.

CHAPTER ELEVEN

The first real obstacle to progress came at a town called Albatàrrec, marginally larger than the others they had passed through. It lay on a narrow canal close to the provincial border of Catalonia-Aragón, the water barrier providing a natural obstacle lending itself to defence, given the crossing was by way of a single bridge. Had a proper soldier been at the head of the column he would have stopped the convoy and sent forward a party on foot to assess the level of risk.

That was not the Republican way. In every town or village so far, the Falange had just pillaged the place, spread terror and passed through. Here, their enemies had determined to make a stand and, as they approached the first buildings, a blast of machine gun fire tore into the lead vehicles, first shredding the tyres on the armoured van and bringing it to a halt. It then set about those following, in one of which was Laporta.

Ten trucks to the rear, Cal Jardine, jumping out of his own cab, saw the fighters ahead of him abandoning their vehicles, as well as ground being torn up by bullets. Surrounded by ploughed fields, there was little cover, and given the road was bounded by deep ditches, which acted as storm drains, the only protection enjoyed by his own truck was the presence of those in front. Being within range, albeit near the limit for a light machine gun, he needed to get his men off, while the drivers reversed to get their vehicles out of harm's way.

He got his own truckload, Florencia included, into one of the deep ditches, bone dry at this time of year and giving good shelter, the others behind taking that cue, till they were all safe, while on the road, with a mayhem of shouting, arguing, arm-waving and the odd sound of metal on metal, the trucks were grinding backwards.

Telling them all to stay down, Cal went forward at a crouch to find out what was happening. At the head of the ditch, where it joined a culvert that dropped to the waters of the canal, it was full of fighters, their leader amongst them, he having escaped from the cab of the second truck. On the road lay the cost of not being either vigilant or a professional, several bodies, while the vehicles in which they had travelled were now ablaze from end to end. The flames reached the fuel tank of one, creating a boom that made everyone duck their heads into their shoulders, as well as sending up a sheet of bright-orange flame.

Laporta was swearing, a continuous stream of Spanish invective that was as useless as his military prowess, and the look he gave Cal Jardine dared him to even think of alluding to that lack of foresight, but he did agree that it was nonsense to just stay pinned down in the ditch; something had to be done to silence that machine gun and it could not be done from where they were cowering. When

Cal indicated he would seek its precise location, the anarchist leader nodded with real gratitude.

In short controlled bursts, bullets were now pinging off the plate armour of the van, making noise, but posing little real threat, while the smoke from the burning trucks was blowing across their front to obscure the location from which the enemy fire was coming. The only person in that makeshift tank was the driver and he had changed places with another several times; no one wanted to travel on a July day in what was close to an oven, and that included the riflemen allotted to it.

If that meant no return fire, its bulk, added to the billowing black smoke, allowed Cal to get forward to the rear of the van and, between bursts, get a snatched view of what lay ahead – a kind of big barn to one side of the road, probably the place where the crops from the surrounding fields were stored after harvest. In construction, it conformed to a type of which the convoy had seen hundreds on their travels: probably two-storey, with rough-hewn sandstone blocks held together by untidy layers of mortar.

Rectangular, it sat right by the edge of the road and it should, Cal thought, be a single layer of wall surrounding an interior open area, which triggered a possible solution, if not an easy one to execute. But first it was necessary to think through the portents of what had just happened. As far as he could make out it was a single weapon, probably operated by two men, so where were the rest of the party they had been pursuing and why had it been employed? To keep them away from the bridge perhaps?

With enough ammo that machine gun could keep them here until the light faded, and if it was speculation to assume the hold-up was a deliberate tactic, that perhaps even less charming surprises requiring time to be completed were being prepared on the other side of the canal, then that was what war-fighting was like; you had to use what knowledge you had, add it to experience, then make assumptions on which you could act.

Sporadic fire was being returned from the ditches, but a few single rifles were not having much impact on a well-concealed machine-gunner, firing from an elevated position. Crawling under the truck, closer to the ground than normal on its flat front tyres, Cal managed to get a look at what lay ahead: more red sandstone buildings on the other side of a narrow bridge, then a road that went straight on into the town, though from such a low point he could see nothing more that looked like a threat.

Getting across that bridge, if the rest of the Falange decided to contest it, would be tough and it could be mined. A fair amount of dynamite would be needed to blow the thing when the first vehicle was halfway over, though he doubted they had the means, doubly so because only a fool would start a fight on the far side of the bridge with that killer option up their sleeve.

Yet it would make sense if you were waiting for explosives, or you had them but not the time to set both charges and the means to fire them; hold up the enemy till it gets dark, deploy enough firepower to keep them to the east of the canal and use the night to mine the bridge. Dodging back to Laporta he gave his opinion, glad that the anarchist leader did not seek to challenge what could only be assumptions; there could be another case to make: that their enemies were as militarily naive as the man to whom he was talking.

'I need an interpreter and that has to be you.' Laporta nodded: fiery as she was, what was proposed was no task for Florencia. 'Send someone back to Drecker; I think he has grenades and I need them.'

'He might not give them up, my friend,' came the reply. 'The communists like to keep their own weapons for their own use, and not just that – this morning, after you were gone, I had to threaten to take fuel for our trucks by force if he did not give it up.'

There was no time to be shocked or surprised at that, no time to ask for an explanation either. 'Then tell him he will have to sacrifice some men if he does not want to give up the weapons I need. His choice!'

The Spanish was rattled off quickly and Cal followed a crouching runner down the ditch to where Vince sat, his back propped up against the side, smoking a fag, eyes closed and his face turned to the sky. One of his lads nudged him to say Cal was approaching.

'This is no time for forty winks, Vince,' Cal joked; if anything he was pleased with Vince setting such an example of sangfroid.

'Just working on a suntan, guv.'

'Where's Florencia?'

'She's gone back to the trucks to set up a field kitchen, in case we're stuck here for a while.'

'And we might be unless we give that machine gun Johnny ahead something to think about.'

Cal looked over the rim of the ditch, first to where the transport had withdrawn, well out of range, then at the field on the right-hand side of the road, seemingly recently ploughed, a fact he pointed out to Vince.

'The furrows will give some protection at long range, so let's get a squad across and deployed in extended order and looking as if they are there to advance. It will split his attention and, if he fires, I think he will be lucky at the distance to do much damage.'

'You?'

'I've got to try to get inside and silence the bugger.' Vince was then given the same assessment as he had passed to Laporta, the notion he had formed lying under the armoured van. 'I have a suspicion we have to get across that bridge as quickly as we can.'

'You need two at least for a job like that, guv.'

He was right, and by the look on his face, Vince was suggesting that he be the second person. 'But can we leave the lads to work on their own?'

'They have to start sometime, and provided they don't get too pushy this is as good as any.' Responding to the enquiring look, Vince added, 'I'd put that kid Jock in charge, he comes across like a natural and I think the lads respect him.'

'I never asked what he did.'

'Field sports he was, pole vault.' That occasioned a grin. 'Come in handy if they do blow the bleedin' bridge, eh!'

'So will the swimmers.'

'Here comes the Happy Hun.'

Drecker arrived at a crouch, machine pistol in hand, one of his squad leaders behind him, and Cal was glad to see his pockets were bulging.

'Laporta,' he demanded.

Cal jerked a thumb. 'I'll go forward with him, Vince; you come too once you've sorted out the lads.'

Getting in front of Drecker, Cal was struck by the fact that the communist commander was only heading forward now, once he had been asked for something, whereas he had done what would have been expected from a subordinate commander, gone forward immediately. There was no point in dwelling on that; it was necessary to deal with what they faced now. Over his shoulder, he explained what they faced and how he intended to go about neutralising it.

'Before I give you what you have asked for I must see for myself if it is a good use of such scarce and valuable weapons and that you will not just waste them.'

There was a great temptation to tell him he was 'a cheeky bugger'; he was a military ignoramus as far as Cal could tell, but the need for diplomacy won out. Getting the grenades was more important than telling this sod he knew what he was doing. What Drecker's response did tell him, though, was that the limited cooperation from the communists, which he had up till now only speculated on, looked as if it might be real.

When they joined Juan Luis, Drecker's parsimony was not greeted by any Spanish restraint or diplomacy; indeed there was a loud and fractious argument, which only stopped when Cal interrupted in German to find out what was going on.

'This man does not command me or my cadres,' Drecker shouted.

Proving to Cal he was not the only one who could work by tone alone, Laporta addressed him in French. 'This communist pig will wait till there is easy glory to be had, when half my men are dead, then he might do something.'

The use of the word 'cochon' was unfortunate – Drecker knew what it meant and the two began spitting at each other in Spanish, this reaching a crescendo as Vince joined his guv'nor, which was just as well, given he could translate most of what was passing between them, imparted with his usual laconic manner.

'Seems, guv, that while both their mothers were no better than they should be, neither of 'em has a dad. 'Part from that there's a load of guff about politics.'

'Have you seen Decker's oppo?' Cal whispered. The squad leader had his hand on his pistol, the flap on the holster was open and his gaze was fixed on Laporta. 'Now, has he been told to do that or is he just nervous?'

'It's me that's nervous, guv, but I think they've agreed that we can have a couple of grenades.'

Still furious from his dispute with Laporta, Drecker pulled the grenades from his pocket and handed them over, his expression turning haughty as he indicated he would show Cal how to use them. So intent was he – or was it arrogance? – that he did not see the look aimed at Vince, which was one of frustrated impatience at his pedantic tone.

'Tell him, guv, it's only a bleedin' F1 and Christ knows you've seen enough of them in your time.'

'It would spoil his day, Vince,' Cal replied, before adding, with Drecker still talking, 'four-second fuses, he says.'

'Just the job, then.'

The covering fire was no more than a distraction to draw a response, with the trio of Cal, Laporta and Vince racing for the back of the armoured van, then diving underneath, before crawling forward, the Spaniard to the front, his hand reaching out and up to bang on the cab door on the non-threatened side, an act he had to repeat three time before the driver responded and opened it. His unshaven face and half a naked body appeared right on top of that of his leader and some sharp words were exchanged.

'Driver says his tyres are in shreds,' Vince said quietly to Cal. 'Golden boy is telling him to just do as he's told.'

That was not the end of it, but Vince did not bother to say any more, it was just variations, it seemed, on the same points. Eventually the face disappeared and Laporta, as previously arranged, slid his rifle onto the floor and hauled himself up into the cab in a snake-like motion, the engine bursting into life as soon as the door slammed. By that time Vince and Cal were standing at the back, weapons ready.

'If this don't work, we are going to be in trouble gettin' back to cover.'

'Vince,' Cal replied, with fitting irony. 'When have you ever known my ideas not to work?'

The sound of the van moving forward was horrible, the shredded tyres soon flaying and exposing the wheel rims to the hard road surface. Never a speedy vehicle, due to the excess weight, it struggled to get up to the kind of pace necessary, with Cal and Vince not required to follow at more than a fast walking pace, bodies low to ensure that as it got closer to the building the angle of fire did not expose them, with yet more shots coming from the ditch and the popping sound of Laporta firing his own weapon through the cab slit.

The metal plating that protected the engine hit the corner of the barn with a thud and the van stopped dead, though the cloud of dust that came billowing up was reassuring. Gears crunching, it began to reverse, with Cal peering round from the back to see if it had achieved the effect he hoped. There was damage, but not enough, and he could imagine the anarchist leader cursing and urging a repeat. Because of the need to do that, Cal had a grenade in one hand and a finger of the other through the pin.

It took three hits to dislodge enough of the stonework and, not surprisingly, when the base blocks were removed, a good number of what they were supporting came down too, creating a cloud of choking dust and a fall that would have crushed the van had it not been plated in thick metal. As it was, reversing, because of the rubble created, took several jarring attempts.

The gap left when it did get clear was just a narrow and dark dust-filled hole with no way of knowing what was concealed behind it, and it was into that Cal tossed his grenade, on the assumption that whoever was on that machine gun, and there might be more than two, could not fail to figure out what they were trying to do, not knowing that once they were inside it was a very different kind of fight.

The two men were on the points of their feet waiting for the blast, which when it came pushed the heavy van into their backs. There was no time to even think on that; Cal spun out from behind, pistol raised, and fired off three rounds, before rushing for the hole, stumbling over the rubble, aware that Laporta was likewise firing into the gap, also that Vince was coming behind him.

Once through he went left and dived for the floor, Vince going right and doing the same. Neither stopped for more than a split second; both were up, hunched and moving in opposite directions, weapons out, knowing that, with eyes unaccustomed to the gloom, if there was an enemy close he could see them more clearly than they could see him. Cal found some stacked bales of hay as protection and stopped, breathing heavily and seeking clarity of vision.

The body lay against the opposite wall, nearer to where Vince was moving, his aim to get behind a long cart, loaded with sapling-type poles for making frames; that would give him some cover. As soon as he was there, Cal gave him the signs for one man down and his location and got a nod in return. Then, with his eyes adjusting to the gloom, Cal held up a trio of fingers, the sign that as soon as they disappeared he would move on three, that also acknowledged as Vince would move immediately after, his rifle ready to use.

When Cal came out from behind the hay it was as a dive into a forward roll in which he spun up onto one knee, pistol out and moving in search of a target. The bullet aimed at him passed his ear with a crack and he began to squeeze on his trigger, aiming at the hatless man in Civil Guard uniform on the open staircase, only to hear another shot and see him jerk backwards. Naturally he looked to Vince; he just twitched his head back and chopped to the rear with his hand.

Looking over his shoulder, Cal saw Laporta standing in the gap created by the armoured van, silhouetted against the sunlight at his back, a sitting duck of a target for anyone who wanted to shoot him. The shout, in French, which included the words that told him he was a stupid arse, at least moved him till his back was against stone. By that time Cal and Vince were moving rapidly for the stairs and, once there, taking them three at a time, though there was a slight pause to make sure the man Laporta had shot was no longer capable of being active.

At the top of the staircase there was just an open floor space, better lit than the ground floor, below which they stopped. With Cal crouching and aiming, Vince laid aside his rifle, pulled the pin on his grenade and tossed it in the general direction of where he thought the machine gun might be, before they both dropped several steps and covered their ears, the thud of the thing landing and rolling audible.

The blast passed overhead, but no other sound came, and with great care Cal lifted his head to the point where his eyes were level with the floor, his pistol horizontal to it and ready for use. In air full of dust he took his time but it was soon clear there had been more than two men on a weapon; number three lay against the outside wall, just below the window from which he had been firing, his face covered in blood, with more, from some other wound, seeping from his body.

Even so, it was with some caution that Cal and Vince moved upwards and onto the first-floor planking, eyes searching in case there was an unknown threat. Not Juan Luis Laporta; he had followed them up, having stopped only to strip the man on the stairs of his weapons: a rifle and a pistol on a leather belt.

He came right up as if he were in his own home and marched noisily over to where the other body lay, looked at Cal and Vince, nodded, then went to the window, holding up the pistol belt to show his comrades. The second he came into view, stone chips began to fly, as did he as he dived back into safety, screaming curses at his own men, who could not hear him, damn them, for nearly killing him.

CHAPTER TWELVE

Taking the machine gun out of the equation did not solve the problem completely; that bridge still had to be crossed and it was very quickly obvious, indicated by the level of movement, that whoever was in command over the other side had decided to hold his position. Shadowy figures carrying weapons, scurrying about, seeking cover and good fire positions were not about to withdraw. The light was going too; it would be dark soon and the decision had to be made whether to try a crossing immediately or wait until dawn.

Canals throw up different military problems to rivers, which, when not in spate, usually present crossing points, fords or flood plains where the water level is low. Add to that the banks are slopes, not walls. A lack of maps had been bad enough before; now it was crippling, because no one knew if there was another bridge within marching distance – there was certainly on this side no lateral road they could use – by which they could outflank the defenders, and nor did they have boats; if those had existed, owned by the locals, they had either been sunk or removed.

The answer lay in a forced crossing at another point, but for people who lived in a port it was shocking how few of them could swim, and in truth, to get them across the canal would require they march to a point out of sight of the town without alerting the opposition – not something Cal Jardine thought the anarchists capable of; moving in formation on foot was no more their forte than silence. Also, they would have to get across without mishap and that too, given the aversion to discipline, seemed unlikely.

They would have to fight their way to the bridge and help to secure it intact, because without the vehicles they would be moribund and on foot: any notion of going on to Saragossa hinged on the column remaining fully mobile. The option of moving back to find another route and another bridge foundered on the same problem; they could travel miles and find the road just petering out, and it had been obvious from the outset that few of the people they could question knew anything beyond the confines of their own village and their nearest neighbours.

Task number one was to repair the armoured van, which, naturally, had only one spare wheel, and on the face of it that meant cannibalising another one from a second lorry and it had to be an exact match, not easy given the vehicles in the convoy consisted of every kind of commercial transport in existence, a lot of them French, a few Italian or American and none of them with common features.

In fact it was worse; driving on the rims to take out that stonework had deformed them, and it was only by a stroke of sheer luck that some of Laporta's men, mechanics and those from engineering factories, had the ability to undertake the required repairs. That, of necessity, took time and as the light faded it was necessary to bring forward other trucks and use their headlights so that work could continue in darkness. It was telling that, even at long rifle range, the insurgents made no attempt to impede the repair.

A conference was convened, lit by oil lamps, with Florencia on hand to translate for Cal if Spanish was employed; when it came to attendance, Manfred Drecker was much more willing than he had been to bring forward and risk his men or offer material support. Asked his opinion, his sole idea, made with his fastidious cigarette hand, was that Laporta and his fighters should just charge the bridge at dawn, using the repaired armoured van, and blast their way on to the other side.

Tellingly, and once more, worryingly, the man to whom he addressed this madcap idea did not demur, so it was left to Cal Jardine to point out the inherent flaws: the notion that a strong party could just advance behind the van was nonsense. The bullets they faced would come from up and down the canal banks, reducing the level of protection the further forward they went. And what if the armoured van lost its tyres again, all four this time, and was rendered immobile ? – that would block the bridge completely.

'He is asking if you suggest doing nothing,' Florencia said when Drecker barked Spanish at him.

'For such an assault you must split their defence. If you just rush the bridge, whoever you send will just walk into a hail of concentrated fire, and for all we know that machine gun we took out was not the only one.'

'And where,' Drecker demanded, reverting to German, 'is this machine gun?'

'It might be more than one and they will be where we can't see them, just like the weapon that opened up earlier. If you think it's such a good idea to force a crossing by rushing the bridge, use your own men.'

That induced a look of cold fury but no spoken response, and to Cal it sent a clear message, one that intimated that the loss of life, as long as it was anarchists dying, or even the youngsters he led, was something to be welcomed for its own sake, but Drecker would keep what he called his cadres away from risk.

'They will not attack,' Cal said to Juan Luis. 'The choice of what we do rests with us.'

'We risk losing valuable time,' he responded.

That was imparted with an unhappy look that had within it an unspoken desire that Cal Jardine, or even Drecker, should come up with a solution. Yet again, he was not prepared to openly ask for help.

'We must give it more thought.'

Drecker, asking what was said in French be explained, just looked at the Spaniard as if he was something untoward on his shoe when told, then turned on his heel and went back to his own encampment.

'I will get my men across,' Cal said softly, as soon as the German was out of earshot.

The question in Laporta's expression was unspoken but plain: why wait till the communist had left? But that did not last long as Cal explained, with a heavy dose of diplomacy. He could hardly elaborate on his previous thoughts about the inability of Laporta's men to undertake what was required, but he did point out that his Olympians were young, fit and willing, in unspoken contrast to Juan Luis's anarchists.

What was required needed experience of things the anarchist leader would know nothing about; night operations were ten times more difficult than movements undertaken during the day. For Laporta it was enough that he offered a solution and took responsibility for implementing it, though he was careful to salvage some pride by asking several pointed questions, until Cal reminded him he was not proposing to act alone; the Spaniards needed to do their bit.

'Your men need to be ready for a dawn attack across the bridge, to fix the attention of the defenders, but I want two other things. Work should continue on the armoured van even if it is finished, with lots of banging and crashing of metal on metal to convince them that the assault they expect will take place. Secondly, I want you to position a party of riflemen to keep a careful watch on the underside of the bridge and to shoot if they see movement.'

The notion of it being wired with explosives was still a possibility, but not one easy to carry out under observation and, potentially, a hail of bullets.

'Now I must go and get my lads ready. I need to brief them on what to do.'

Florencia patted her pistol. 'I will come too.'

The 'no' in reply was firm and taken badly.

The Spaniards had laughed at the lads doing their exercises but they missed the point: these youngsters were competition-fit and committed to staying that way. If the insurrection had not broken out they would have been doing their bit on track and field by now, so when it came to a two-mile night march it was a piece of cake.

They set out with mud-blackened faces and lightened knapsacks, one squad with spades, under a star-filled sky and a crescent moon, another squad carrying half a dozen long frame poles, those taken from the barn, and a heavy towing rope, on an eastern detour until they could turn south well out of sight from the enemy.

At the canal side, the first task was to make sure the opposite bank was unoccupied, with patrols being sent in both directions to check, making no attempt, albeit they were cautious, to hide their presence, this to flush out anyone posted to counter such a manoeuvre, perhaps with a flare or just a loosed-off shot. The supposition being the far side was clear, they all gathered at the chosen crossing point.

Vince repeated his joke about pole-vaulting and that had everyone laughing except Jock, but in truth the canal was too wide for that, so two of what the others called 'water babies' stripped off, and naked, made sure Vince got over – he being an indifferent swimmer. They then came back for the rope and a trio of sapling poles of the kind farmers use to make growing frames, which they floated to the far bank, this while a series of foxholes were being dug by one squad, another standing guard.

Try as they might, what was required could not be done quietly and on a still night the sound had to carry a long way. It was only guesswork that the distance was great enough not to alert the men defending the bridge, just as it had been guesswork that they would not have sentinels out down the western edge to look out for what was a fairly obvious ploy.

The whole operation was predicated on two assumptions: first, that the lack of military appreciation or imagination existed on both sides – the insurgents would focus on a forced bridge crossing, especially with all those headlights illuminating the repairs taking place in plain view to them, now a dim glow in the distance to the assault group. Then there was numbers; from what he knew, even with the extra Civil Guards and others they had picked up on the way, the Barcelona column faced no more than a hundred and twenty to thirty opponents.

If the insurgents feared a separate crossing, that could happen anywhere north or south as far as several miles, meaning they would have to be spread very thin to guard against it and they should not expect it so soon, certainly not before a rush on the bridge failed. Therefore, while no one would take off their boots, he hoped they would try to rotate sleep so as to be fresh to face the battle they anticipated.

Cal set about making a tripod, which Vince would be replicating on the far bank, lashing the tops together. A sharp whistle told him it was time to tighten the rope, which involved both men erecting, then securing, what they had constructed; this lifted the rope clear of the water, which was then anchored to the ground with a stake driven into the hard earth to act as a guy. This gave the crossing party, four-squads strong, a way over the water that would keep their bodies dry; their feet would get wet but that was unavoidable.

They went across hand over hand; each checked to ensure they had secured their weapons in the right way, straps spread over their necks so that the whole lay atop their knapsacks, the weight spread evenly across their shoulders. Also sent over was a thinner line, so that ammo, water and food could be hauled across, as well as the rolled-up kit of the swimmers.

While that was happening Cal was repeating the briefing he had given those chosen as the rearguard. They would use the shallow foxholes they had dug to the right of the crossing point to hold the eastern bank so that if it all went wrong there was a defence sufficient to slow and possibly deter any pursuit.

'Password, Bernard?' he asked of the man in command.

'Barcelona.'

'If we are being chased we will be coming at a run, but regardless of what you think you see, do not open fire until you hear a shout of "Barcelona" from those seeking to get back across, or you will risk killing your own. We will be engaged in a fighting retreat and at best I think we will have parity because the defenders cannot denude the main crossing. Lanterns?'

These were produced and held up, two oil lamps that would denote in the dark the limits of the line of defence, to be lit if they heard gunfire, those seeking to escape having been briefed to stay south of the one to their right. Also, Bernard, and he alone, would have to make a judgement if anyone came wandering along while Cal and the rest were out of sight: to shoot or stay doggo, the only clear instruction being to maintain the integrity of the rope crossing at all costs.

'Everybody clear?' The response was a low murmur. 'Good. Now remember, try to stay still and silent. No talking.'

The agreement was the same and had as much chance of being held to as pigs flying. They would talk to each other, but it would be no more than reassuring whispers.

Cal Jardine was the last rifleman to cross, it having taken a couple of hours to get everything sorted, that added to the time it had taken to get to the crossing point, but that was no problem; one bonus of this part of the world was you got regular hours of darkness, even in high summer.

After an equipment check was carried out, those who had crossed set off, moving away from the bank at a right angle through ploughed fields and growing crops. Cal led one squad ahead as a screen, counting off the yardage, which he hoped would take him beyond Albatàrrec. After an hour he called a halt and checked his figure with Vince to about a mile, then made sure the squad leaders knew the distance already travelled and the location of the North Star, triangulating that with the glow still faintly visible from the east of the bridge.

Soon they were marching due north, footwear claggy from gathered mud, aiming to meet the road that continued west, the distance again counted off. The whole movement, as it had been previously, carried out in silence; even the daft ones were careful not to make a sound, though there was something like a collective sigh as they reached the deep ditch that lined the road.

The same as that on the other side of the canal, it was as dry as a bone, perfect to keep them out of sight, with just enough overhead light to make progress reasonably quick, but the primary act was to call another period of rest and to tell his lads to take on some water. Before they moved again it was necessary to make sure the squad leaders knew the number of paces to get back to the turning point, as well as those needed to get back to the canal. If anything happened to Cal and Vince they might need to get out on their own.

They moved out in single file and, as they got closer to the town, dogs began barking. That forced a halt till they calmed down, but it indicated the proximity of habitation and the fact they were making too much noise in the ditch. Not that there was an alternative, like using the roadway level with their heads; the only security lay in taking time.

Cal was seeking out the first line of buildings, which would be silhouetted against the starlit sky, but before that they passed the plots where the folk who lived on the western edge of the town grew vegetables and raised animals, and that made any movement even more circumspect. The worry then was not the hen coops, or the rabbit hutches, not the tethered goat or the snuffling pig; it was geese, who were noisy buggers at the best of times and, ahead of dogs, the most potent guards in creation. If they were around, they would raise Cain.

Having reached the end of the ditch, Cal clambered up onto the road and, sweating profusely, darted towards the first building to get his back against a wall; the night was hot and the stones themselves still seemed to have in them the warmth of the day, so glaring had been the sun. Vince came to join him and engage in a whispered conversation.

'No guards, guv?'

'Doesn't seem so.'

'Piss poor, that.'

Cal looked at the luminous dial on his watch; it was still two hours to dawn. 'Might be some further in, but I reckon we have enough time for a good look to see what's what.'

'You and me?'

'Only if the boys are all right.'

'The only thing botherin' them is biting insects and you've told them what you want them to do.'

That had been part of his initial briefing, predicated on getting this far: he and Vince would do a recce of the town. If the lads heard shots they were to withdraw to the canal on the same dog-leg that had got them here. If that proved impossible, the squad leaders had been told to take over the first set of houses they could find and be prepared to defend the position till they were relieved, but to stay doggo and hope they were not spotted, which meant locking up the owners to keep them quiet.

'I gave them another instruction if they do take a building,' Vince added, 'to keep an eye out for you an' me runnin' like buggery and to open the door and give us a shout.'

The laugh was as soft as it needed to be.

'Ready?'

Vince eased himself upright and darted across to the other side of the road, before edging along level, Cal doing the same. The place was seemingly asleep, but they had to reckon that behind the walls along which they crept there must be frightened people who knew that some kind of battle was imminent. Perhaps, inside the closed window shutters, there were locals praying to be spared, and there might well be homes already in mourning; there was every reason to assume that the Falangists, who had been here for at least a day, had treated this town as they had every other along their route.

The street began to narrow the closer they got to the town centre until they were no more than the width of a single truck apart. It was Vince who first heard the voices, and even in the deep shadow Cal saw his hand move, giving the flat palm sign to halt and, after a short pause, he slid across to join him, feeling the hot breath on his ear.

'Talking up ahead, so more than one, but not a group.'

'Go round?'

No discussion followed, they just retreated slowly to the first side street they had passed, really an alleyway, and moved down it, counting paces, till another way of moving forward opened up before them. Cal took a long look before he signalled it was safe for Vince to cross, he following into the doorway where they could keep out of sight.

Peering out, it was obvious, once they had a good view, that this street, at the end and like the one they had just left, opened out into the town's Plaza Mayor, and that was lit, at the far side, by rows of flickering torches. In between, in shadow on the left of the square, stood a line of cars and trucks, the transport the insurgents had used to stay ahead of the Barcelona column. But it was what those torches illuminated which caused concern: the unmistakeable shape of a field cannon and a sizeable group of men around it.

CHAPTER THIRTEEN

'Where the hell has that come from?' Vince whispered.

'Who cares, it's here and it changes everything.'

What followed was a period of several seconds while both men made separate appreciations of what lay before them.

'It's a fair guess,' Vince responded, eventually, 'that the exit from the square opposite leads to the canal.'

Cal was thinking his original plan was dead and it was time to formulate another. There was no point now bringing his lads forward to launch any attack from the rear or a flank and throw the defenders into a panic. That cannon, which looked to be another 75 mm Schneider, would not be visible from the other side of the bridge, but wheeled, it would take seconds to alter that. As much to clarify his own thinking as to inform Vince, he explained the way the road on this side came arrow straight into the town.

'So, shunt the sod out as Laporta begins to cross, and – splat.'

A shell fired over open sights and at point-blank range would demolish that armoured van and probably kill anyone advancing behind it. Had it only just arrived? Was the anticipation of that the reason they had sacrificed three men and a machine gun to keep the column away from the bridge until dark? It made no odds; it was here, and with enough shells, they could make that crossing impossible.

'Let's go,' Cal hissed.

They moved back across the road and down the alley, careful as they exited into the street by which they had entered the town, then moving as swiftly as they could back to where the lads had gathered at the end of the storm ditch, with Cal making plans on the hoof. There was no time for a lengthy briefing; that cannon either had to be taken, rendered useless, or prevented from firing before the sun rose.

When he outlined what each squad would do, not everyone was happy; half of his boys would have to stay still, a strong group in the storm ditch acting as a backstop just as there was one at the canal crossing. That was in itself tactically sound, but in part the real reason for taking less than the total number forward was the problem of control.

His original plan had not been rigid, based on the very sound principle outlined by Carl von Clausewitz, the man who wrote the tactical bible, that no plan ever survived contact with the enemy. Once the recce was complete and he and Vince had some idea of what they faced and where they could best do damage, he had envisaged them taking two squads each into the town to attack as Laporta began to move, the noise of that advance the signal to proceed.

He had then anticipated they would very likely be required to withdraw, possibly run, maybe fighting as they went, but at the very least drawing off some of the defence and easing the numbers facing the Barcelona column. The objective was to sow uncertainty, not to win any outright victory, while making the best of what chances presented themselves; if the Falangists abandoned the bridge, the column could move again.

Now he envisaged a firefight in an open square, in which he and Vince could handle only so many problems, and those in an engagement where improvisation was a must – actions that the Olympians did not have either the skill or experience to know how to react to. Using the whole group as one unit would be too unwieldy and lead to more potential casualties, not fewer.

'Look, son,' Vince said, cutting across Cal Jardine as he addressed the men who would be left behind, four of whom were his boxers, and using language he knew they would understand. 'Our arse could be up in the air if this all goes to shit, so we will need you lot to rescue us.'

'And,' Cal added, 'we have only a guess at the numbers we will face. If they can bring up a cannon, they can also bring up more men. This is a smash-and-grab job and if anyone wants to pull out this is the time to speak up.'

That got a series of negative growls. 'Good! Now, we have no more time to talk, so let's get moving.'

If the sky had the first hint of daylight inasmuch as the stars had lost some distinction, it seemed even darker in the streets now, Stygian in the alleys. Cal tried to imagine what was happening over the bridge, for that had a massive bearing on what could be achieved and when. Would Laporta move as soon as the sun rose or would that famous

Spanish laxity regarding time surface to delay the assault, exposing his lads to action in full sunlight?

He stayed on the main road while Vince took another squad down the alley they had used previously, both aware that there was no way to coordinate what they would do. They would have to act on an individual appreciation of what they could see, but they had posited various scenarios and agreed that if the Barcelona column did not move at the right time, they would have to think about an immediate withdrawal.

Looking skywards it had begun to go grey, the deep blue of night now fading to the west, the stars no longer visible. Crawling forward and using what shadow remained, Cal tried to get a sight of the cannon, thinking any sign of it moving would be a signal that Laporta was on his way. The first indication lay in the number of men around the gun – he counted a dozen, and he could see one fellow at the corner of the building, an officer of some sort, he suspected, his hand held up to halt any movement, while at the same time looking down the roadway to the bridge. Behind the men set to manhandle the cannon, along the base of the wall, shells stood like a row of sentinels, enough ammunition to turn that bridge into a charnel house.

In the still morning air, the sound of the Republican motor engines starting up and revving carried, not loudly, but with a deep soft beat that seemed to move the warm dawn air, for which Cal was grateful; this was a bonus on which he could not have calculated, nor could he have wished for more from that watching officer, required to pump his halting hand to stop those on the cannon who had set their shoulders to the wheels, obviously eager to push.

Creeping back, he issued his orders in a soft voice, then led his squad along the wall of the last building to the point at which the road joined the square, his eyes naturally drawn first to the line of vehicles, then to the tower of the church, a spot from which he and his men could be easily seen, his hope that, if there was a spotter up there, and there should be, his attention was on what was coming from the east.

On the cannon, no one was looking anywhere except at the man in command, still with his hand held up and palm flat. He obviously had a very good idea of how long he needed to deploy the Schneider, which, no doubt, already had its first shell loaded, while to aim it was simple, the barrel being at a very low elevation. All that was needed was to push the gun into place in the middle of the road.

The sound of motors had increased – the column was moving, but no shots were fired. Cal was watching a classic ploy to draw your enemy on, but nothing could be done. He needed the defenders to be engaged; the last thing he could cope with, and that had applied from the outset, was that they should know about the presence of his boys until they were committed to the forward battle.

The hand was now doing a sort of bouncing movement, clearly he was eager, which was the point at which Cal motioned for his lads to spread out across the roadway, his admonition, with a finger at his lips for silence, received with nods. There was enough light now to just see the faces of these youngsters and it took him back years to observe no fear, just determination. It was the same look he had seen on the faces of the men he had led into battle in 1918 and it had not lasted long.

He had five kneeling, five standing, Cal to one side with his rifle raised. He held his aim on that observer, and as soon as his hand moved from stop to go, Cal pulled the trigger and dropped him. The sound of his shot had no sooner filled the square, oddly sending aloft a flock of flapping pigeons, than the front rank of his Olympians followed, their target the bunched figures around the cannon wheels, their instructions five rounds rapid. As their standing oppos opened fire, they were busy reloading.

Vince and his lads emerged from the left to rush into the square even before Cal's squad had got off one mag apiece, yelling like banshees as they attacked what remained of the men set to push the gun – not many, for they had suffered badly. Those remaining were trying to spin the light field gun round, one man on the lanyard that would set off the charge; he was Cal's next victim, taking a bullet in the chest that sent him flying back, the rope still clasped in his hand.

The cannon went off and the shell tore uselessly into the front of the church, doing, at such short range, massive damage. But there would be no reloading; Vince and his lads were too close and those still standing abandoned the cannon and ran, this while Cal brought his squad out into the square, eye ranging over the tops of the buildings, the church in particular.

He shouted to them to get forward and grab the line of artillery shells while he put a full magazine into the bell tower as a precaution, the ring of the cast metal adding a mournful cadence to what was now a cacophony of noisy gunfire, which included at least one machine gun, as the defenders attempted to stop the Republican advance without the use of the weapon on which they had been relying.

Vince's lads had tipped the wheeled cannon on its side and his boys were running back to where Cal stood, rifles now slung, with the artillery shells cradled like babes in arms, so far without anyone taking a hit. Broxburn Jock yelled at him, his face alight, asking to disable the vehicles by taking out their tyres, but Cal shook his head and indicated it was time to withdraw.

With no trucks or cars the Falangists would be forced to stand and fight, but that might mean him having to take on a number of them in a fight he could not control, which in a maze of buildings and alleyways was inevitable. Better to get out of the way of an enemy who would probably take the chance to retreat, some of them highly capable Civil Guards. There was also the problem of some very fired-up Republican fighters whom, when they got inside the town, he did not trust not to kill their own.

Vince was with him and, as was right and proper, he made no attempt to question Cal's orders, he merely formed his boys up in a way that allowed them to fall back in good order and act as a rearguard for the squad in front, loaded with shells, forming a line of five, then a second the first could retreat through, always with a set of rifles ready to shoot anyone who showed their face, until they were back at the ditch.

'Dump the shells,' Cal shouted, before he began to organise the whole party for what he expected was about to happen, lining them along the ditch in squads so as to concentrate their fire, Vince taking up position at the mid-point. He was shouting orders; there was no need for quiet now.

'If they are pushed back they are going to bugger off out of here in their trucks and maybe we can give them a fright.' The cheers that got annoyed him. 'But only fire when ordered, and that might mean letting some of the bastards through.'

Tempting as it was to ambush the whole lot, it would be too much to expect that he could so decimate them that he would have greater numbers than they. He would have instead what he had already avoided, a battle with people who were desperate and motivated, who probably outnumbered him, were probably better armed than his lads and who, even if he beat them, would kill or maim a number of the boys he led.

Cal knew better than most that you could not fight without the risk of casualties and he had often said he had seen too many in his time. Yet he had a bunch of untrained enthusiasts under his care and it was more important to him to keep up the spirits of these young Olympians, rather than have them ruined by seeing their mates die. They had done really well on this mission, their morale was high and that was the way he wanted it kept for now.

The sounds of battle were still audible, including the boom of explosions that indicated grenades were being employed, but by whom there was no way of telling. The fight at the bridge was continuing, but if Laporta pressed home his attack, and everything Cal had seen up until now indicated he would, there could only be one outcome. The sound of the first car, an open-topped Hispano Suiza packed with blueshirts with weapons held aloft, some sitting on the body, had been masked by the noise of gunfire, but it burst out from the last of the houses at speed, well ahead of anyone following.

There was no way the lads in the first squad, who had been obliged to sit it out in this ditch while their mates had disabled that cannon, could resist such a tempting target. On top of that frustration, they knew only too well what these fascists had done, had seen the results of torture, murder and rape, and had they not come to Spain and the People's Olympics to send them and their ilk a message?

They let fly without any command being given, and if the volley that raked the car was ragged and did not much more than pepper the bodywork with holes, it was only the first, and those that followed, with a fraction more time to aim, were deadly and directed at the passengers, not the car. The driver was a clear casualty as his windscreen was shattered before his amazed and frightened eyes, then the car steered away and into the opposite ditch, throwing into the air, as it shot to the far side, all of those who had been extra passengers.

Cal had his pistol out and was running up from his ditch, half an eye on the road from the town. He raced across the road and stood arms outstretched looking for movement, barely aware that Vince was beside him, his rifle aimed into the field where lay the twitching bodies of those who had been tossed clear. They fired simultaneously, Cal at a passenger moving in the car, Vince at one of those figures who had got up and was staggering trying to run, this being no time for mercy.

'Leave the rest,' Cal shouted as he heard a truck engine, amplified by being in the narrow confines of the buildings that enclosed the street, and as he ran back his shout had both anger and volume. 'Hold your bloody fire and get your heads down.'

The truck roared into view and Cal had a fleeting glimpse that told him it was a Civil Guard wagon, open-topped and packed. He knew he and Vince must have been seen by the driver and whoever else was either in the cab or on top of it, just as they would see the back of the Hispano Suiza sticking up out of the ditch. Would they stop, that was the question, and if they did how many men were they carrying and of what calibre would they be?

His entry into the ditch was an ignominious dive, Vince using more of a slither but both were close-run affairs as the ground behind them began to spurt up great chunks of earth. All Cal could think about at first was the noise of the roaring engine, but then he was listening for the sound of brakes, praying it was one he would not hear, but he had to be prepared.

'Everybody ready?' he yelled, spinning upright, his pistol poised.

Vince's shout melded into his own. 'Keep your heads down.'

Now the bullets were ripping into the back of the ditch, uselessly in terms of hitting flesh but a first real taste for these boys of what it was like to be under sustained fire, and damned unpleasant it was; nothing ever inures you to the crack of a bullet passing close and for them this was their baptism. The breath he had been holding left Cal Jardine's body as the truck roared on; either they did not care about the blueshirts or they saw they were beyond salvation. Added to that, their fusillade had ceased; it was time to give them a little present.

'Squad four,' he shouted, raising his head just enough to see the cloud of receding dust, sure in his heart that they would not stop now, his instructions backed up by his hands. 'Truck at ten o'clock, fire at will.'

The lads scrambled up the bank, too high in truth, showing too much upper body, but they did a good job of delivery in the parting shot, steady, trying to aim as well as fire, sending enough shots in through the truck tailgate to do damage, one clever enough to take out a rear tyre. Too keen to see how they had done, one or two then raised themselves, and it took a sharp command to seek to get them to take cover again.

Vince, in giving that, was a fraction too late. The return fire might have been from the back of a moving bucking vehicle but it was concentrated and probably came from highly trained men. One of the squad took a bullet in the shoulder, judging by the way he jerked sideways, then he tumbled back to lay inert at the ditch bottom, his mates crowding round him.

'Leave him,' Cal yelled. 'Reload.'

Vince was on his way to provide first aid, and just before he blocked his view, Cal saw the look of shock on those young faces at the idea that one of their comrades should be left to suffer – but this was a battle, and how serious a one was yet to be made plain. Vince must have quietly backed up that command, given they attended to their empty rifles while Cal, looking back into the town, was aware that one thing that needed to be done to create a functioning fighting unit had not been fulfilled – the selection of who would act as medics.

A trio of cars were on their way, large, black and hardtops, nose to tail, not only packed inside but with blueshirts hanging on to the door rims, their feet on the running boards. His policy remained the same: do not stop them before they reached his position, let them pass, then put a fusillade into them to speed their flight, hopefully giving them wounded with whom they would be required to deal.

His hope played out well, his notion that people already in flight and past the real centre of resistance would not stop and retrace their route to engage, so a procession of cars, a few trucks and a couple of motorcycles with sidecars were afforded the same treatment, the second of the latter taking such deadly fire that it went over on its side spilling rider, pillion passenger and the two who had crammed into the sidecar.

Cal had the pleasure then of yelling to hold fire; the next vehicle through was carrying a great black and red flag and was crowded with Laporta's men, the driver skidding to a halt as the fighters tumbled out to make sure that anyone wounded from both the overturned car and motorcycle combination were killed off.

Only then could Cal Jardine relax enough to go and see how the wounded man was faring.

CHAPTER FOURTEEN

Perhaps the greatest gift in taking the town so suddenly was the restoration of the ability to communicate with Barcelona; any telephone equipment in previous locations had either been ripped out and removed by the Falangists or destroyed. Somewhere behind the Barcelona column repairs to damaged wires had been undertaken so that, albeit with difficulty, much switching and a very crackling line, Juan Luis Laporta was able to contact Colonel Villabova to find out the progress of the main body advancing on Lérida, as well as report his own successes.

Expecting praise for his rapid progress and recent victory, Laporta was infuriated by the tone of complaint in the response of the titular commander. The list of towns and villages from which the enemy had been ejected was, it seemed, not just insignificant, the whole strategy of the column was mistaken, racing ahead with no thought to their flanks or the taking and securing of territory for the Republic.

Not a witness to this exchange – he would not have understood it anyway – Cal Jardine had got his wounded boy into the home of the local doctor who, if he had fled, being no supporter of Republicanism, had at least left in his surgery the means to deal with a bullet wound.

There were many other casualties and a row of sheet-covered bodies by the bridge, evidence that taking it had extracted a high price in blood. Those of the enemy dead, and there were no wounded, were thrown into the canal to float south as a warning to other places tempted to support the generals.

Florencia, interrogating the jubilant survivors of Albatàrrec – it had suffered death and torture as had everywhere else and its inhabitants were now busy feeding and fêting their saviours – had found a woman who used to act as the doctor's nurse and she was fetched into the surgery to take charge. Competent, she knew how to stem the flow of blood as well as cleanse the wound, though it was soon apparent the bullet was still lodged in the left shoulder and would need to be removed, an operation better carried out back in the city. The lad, named Stanley, would be sent to Barcelona with the anarchist wounded.

As soon as he was sure Stanley was in good hands he left to make sure that the rest of his boys were being cared for – the rearguard having been fetched in from their foxholes – that they had food and drink as well as the means to clean both themselves and their equipment, both adequately dealt with by Vince Castellano, now sorting them out a billet so they could get some much sought-after sleep. He also felt the need to give them a lecture and, of course, to praise them.

'I couldn't have asked for more. For men who are raw you

performed splendidly.' Though these youngsters were pleased and knew they had every right to be, the rearguard less than the others, Cal could sense a residual layer of resentment, exemplified by the looks on their faces when Broxburn Jock spoke, his face tired and pinched, his voice cracked.

'How's wee Stan farin'?'

'He's in good hands, Jock, comfortable and asleep. The wound is clean and he will be evacuated to a proper hospital for an operation to remove a bullet.' The pause was brief, the tone Cal employed turning quite hard. 'I know you are not chuffed with the order I gave to leave Stan when he took his wound, but we were in the middle of a fight.'

One or two nodded, others did not. Tempted, as he was, to admit he had failed to designate anyone to deal with casualties, Cal felt it would come across as false. He had to be hard of heart and that was something they needed to learn, and he glanced at Vince, who had returned from his search and was looking at him, unseen by the lads, with an amused expression on his face as if to imply he knew what was coming.

'That's the way it is, and you'd best get used to it. In a battle, the effectives come before everyone else, and most important, you lot forgot to reload, which should be automatic. How would that have played out if one of those trucks full of Civil Guards had decided to stop and make a fight of it and you with empty weapons? It would not just be wee Stan in the surgery. You're all volunteers, so if you don't like it you can ship out anytime and I won't seek to keep you, but know this. If I'm here and Vince is here, we tell you what to do and you do it without question. It has to be that way to keep you alive.'

They were not all abashed by his tone; the best of them held their cold stares and Cal would not have had it any other way. While he could not abide the way the anarchists behaved, neither did he want to lead men who were incapable of individual thoughts or were too frightened to express them. The best soldiers had a combination of both, as well as the initiative to act without orders.

'Now, for the future, if any of you know first aid, give your names to Vince, and I will see about getting the kind of kit you need to be effective as medics.'

'Right, you lot,' Vince called. 'I got us a billet in the schoolhouse, so let's get some rest.'

Crossing the main square, now full of the column's trucks, as well as the now-upright cannon and an abandoned fuel bowser, Cal and Florencia passed the communists, as before in a separate section by the steps to the church, their equipment neatly arranged and looking as smart as they had the first time he had seen them. Florencia took pleasure in telling Cal, in a voice loud enough for them to overhear, that 'the cowards took no part in the battle, but stayed to the rear where they were safe'.

The only reaction she got was from one of the squad leaders, who looked at her with the same level of hate as she was displaying, then snapped his upraised thumb through his teeth, which meant Cal had to drag his woman away from what would have been a futile dispute.

'Come on, let's find out what your leader has in mind.'

They found Juan Luis in the office of the town mayor, sitting behind his desk: he, a left socialist, had been found hanging from the wide archway of the door that led to the courtyard of his house, with a notice saying he was a traitor pinned to his chest. Inside, his family – a wife and two daughters – had been raped and mutilated, then finished off with gunshots to the head.

In total, the insurgents had murdered some thirty-four of the town's inhabitants before fleeing, taking with them those sympathisers who had not already fled to safety, the locals who supported their aims and had helped their 'cleansing'. It had to be hoped that in raking those fleeing vehicles, some of those who had betrayed their fellow citizens to the Falange had been killed along with the blueshirts.

Having not long come off the phone to Villabova, Laporta was in a mood of quiet fury, and in reacting to Cal Jardine he showed scant gratitude for the fact that his bacon had been saved by the actions of the Olympians. A question as to the removal of the wounded got a very brusque response, almost a dismissive wave of the hand. About to remonstrate with him, Florencia beat Cal to it; she launched into a furious burst of Spanish invective, halfway through which Laporta started to laugh, his shoulders shaking.

'My friend, she has just told me I am an ingrate.' Then his hand went up to protect his face as Florencia, still yelling at him in Spanish, picked up the late mayor's ashtray and made to throw it at his head; he was saved by Cal grabbing it out of her hand. 'If she is like this in bed I wonder you have the energy to fight.'

'I think you owe my boys a vote of thanks,' Cal said, not in the least amused, now actually restraining Florencia with one arm round her waist, seeking to avoid her kicking legs and now suffering an equal number of insults as the man behind the desk.

The look on Laporta's face changed immediately, and the laughter ceased. 'Which I will do in person, my friend, but right now I am suffering from being told by Villabova, our little Cortez, that everything we have done is an error.'

'What?' Cal enquired, before snapping at Florencia to calm down, which she did as Laporta talked; his tone was enough to tell her that the matter was serious.

'He has told me we need to secure the whole region through which we have passed, not just the road to Saragossa, and he listed a whole number of places I have never heard of that we have failed to occupy and cleanse of fascists. Clearly he had a map which tells him this, but one fact is obvious: he has been so busy taking other areas he has not yet reached Lérida, this while our friends are being executed by the hundred further west.'

'But you all agreed back in Barcelona that taking back Saragossa is vital—'

'My friend,' Laporta interrupted, 'Villabova is not of the CNT or FAI. He is a soldier and I am not, something of which he was keen to remind me.'

'But I am.'

'Yes, you are, so I now ask you, as a soldier, what should I do?'

Cal pointed to a sulking Florencia and said, 'I think you best tell her what you have just told me.'

The explanation did nothing to lessen her fury but it did redirect it and the name Villabova, mixed with a few choice insults, was the result. It served the purpose, giving Cal time to think and to reflect that Laporta was, at last, open about the need for military advice. He was, of course, not in the presence of his lieutenants, so it might be a one-off.

'What is happening elsewhere in the Peninsula?'

The list that followed took some getting hold of, but thankfully every time Laporta included Florencia, Cal had time to absorb it, well aware, and the anarchist had added the caveat, that much of what he said was less than hard, incontestable fact; the situation was still fluid, the only certainty being that in the territory they controlled, the fascists were not only shooting people by the hundreds, they were boasting about it on the radio, especially one of the senior generals in Seville, who was daily listing the details of his operation to cleanse 'sacred Spain' of the disease of socialism.

Enough ships had stayed loyal to their officers to get the first elements of the Army of Africa, especially their heavy equipment, over the Straits to the mainland, and they were being shielded from Republican destroyers by two German pocket battleships, while the man who had taken command in Morocco, General Franco, lacking enough vessels to move his men in time, had sent a message to Rome and Berlin requesting aircraft to provide transport.

'Have they agreed?' Cal asked.

'No one knows yet. Our government have appealed for aid to London and Paris.'

Cal was tempted to tell Laporta not to hold his breath on that one; if Peter Lanchester was right, the British government would want to stay well out of it. Paris, with a Popular Front government of its own, could be more sympathetic to the Republic, and so was a better bet. There was good news from Valencia, the vital port for agricultural exports and thus the flow of much needed currency: it had been saved, while the leader of the revolt, that serial rebel General Sanjurjo, had died in a plane crash.

'So who will take over?'

Laporta shrugged. 'Let us hope they all kill each other trying.'

Confused as it was, it became apparent to Cal, as Juan Luis talked, that the population centres, the bigger cities, seemed to be the key; it was those the insurgent generals were seeking to take and it had to be a strategy designed to suit their purpose, so it was axiomatic that the best course of action was to deny them their aim.

Great swathes of land did not matter to them because they had seen clearly a fact still obscure to the likes of Villabova: this was not conventional warfare, in which one army manoeuvred to defeat another and took ground; it was a series of disjointed regional actions in which the Republic was reacting to events, not imposing its will.

The army knew they could occupy the hinterland once they had control of the provincial centres, and one of those was Saragossa. Whatever happened elsewhere, and that could have no bearing on the present conversation, Laporta should continue to head for his objective; this Villabova character was dead wrong.

'Do we know the level of the enemy forces in Saragossa?'

'Madrid say it is being held by disloyal army units, with a force of Carlists on the way from Navarre to help them hold it.'

Fired by religion, which was what bound them to both the cause of the generals and, historically, that of Don Carlos, a junior member of the monarchical House of Bourbon, the Carlists would be as fanatical as the Falange. The people of Navarre had fought two full and bloody wars against the Spanish government, and launched several insurrections that had lasted over forty years. Whatever else they were militarily, they were not quitters.

'Then the best thing you can do is get there as quickly as possible, that is, before they do.'

'Disobey him?'

'Has he ordered you to stop and consolidate?'

'No.'

'Then I have given you my advice. You can also demand that Villabova support you.'

Laporta got up from the desk, came round, and embraced Cal. That was acceptable; the great smacking kiss on the cheek was not and the Spaniard was forcibly pushed away, Cal sitting down to avoid repetition.

'But for the love of God, before we move any further, get hold of some maps.'

While they continued talking, neither had noticed that Florencia had edged towards the door – she had heard a voice they had not – opening it a fraction and putting her ear to the crack. After a few moments, she waved an impatient hand at Cal and gestured that he should come to join her; his lifted eyebrows and glance at Laporta only made her cross, so he nodded to Juan Luis and slipped out of his chair. Invited to put his ear to the door, he could hear what he thought was Manfred Drecker's voice, but it was incomprehensible.

'*Querido*,' Florencia whispered, pushing the door till the crack disappeared. 'That bastard Drecker is on the phone to one of his slimy friends and he is telling him how he and his communists took the town by crossing the canal downstream and attacking it from the rear.'

'What?'

That got him a finger to her lips and the door was opened a crack again, ear to it, her face screwed up, but Cal had heard enough. He grabbed the handle and pulled it open, seeing Drecker with his back to him talking on the phone, fag in the air, his voice emphatic and before him some kind of map-like drawing, obviously so engrossed he had not heard. Florencia had come to join him and then Laporta appeared in the open doorway, and now it was Cal's turn to call for silence.

It could only have been the feeling of eyes on his back that made the communist turn round, the look he gave the trio one of unadulterated loathing. Quickly he spoke into the phone, Cal surmised to say he would call back, then slowly put it down, picking up and folding the paper he had laid on the table.

'Herr Drecker, can I ask you what that call was about?'

'Why would it be any of your business, Herr Jardine?'

'Florencia tells me that you are claiming to have undertaken the task carried out by the men I led, that you are in fact claiming to have taken the town.'

If it was true, and Cal thought it very much so – for why would Florencia lie? – Drecker seemed unabashed. 'I am engaged, Herr Jardine, in the very necessary task of giving the people the news of the victory of the forces of the left over the fascists.'

'*My* victory,' Cal snapped, then jerked his head, 'as well as that of Juan Luis, his men and mine. From what I saw of your men on the way here, they do not look as if they have been fighting at all.'

'They were held in reserve.'

'Far enough back, I suppose, not to even get dust on their boots, while others died.'

'That is of no importance. What is important is that the people read that the forces opposing the general and their lackeys have gained an important success.'

'Read? You were talking to a newspaper?'

'I was talking to the organ of my party and they will spread the news.'

'That will spread a lie.'

Drecker smiled, a cold thin-lipped expression that reminded Cal of a particularly supercilious schoolmaster he had endured, one who never ever accepted he could be in the wrong, then spun on his heel to leave, his words delivered over one shoulder.

'The cause for which we fight does not need truth, Herr Jardine, what it requires is the right propaganda targeted at the *needs* of the cause, words that will make the proletariat rise up and fight.'

Complaining to Laporta did not achieve much, he just shrugged and suggested you could expect no less from such a *canaille*; it was months before Cal Jardine found out that he had done exactly the same as Drecker, phoning in to the anarchist newspapers in Barcelona an account of the column's progress and the battle for Albatàrrec which made no mention of foreign Olympians, but extolled the furious bravery of his own men and their indifference to losses. Communists were likewise not mentioned.

The column pulled out as the heat went out of the sun in the late afternoon, this time at least aware of both the name and distance to their next stopping point, a village where they found that, unlike previous encounters, their enemy had not stopped to exact a blood price, but had driven straight through without halting. During the night, a motorcycle messenger arrived with a set of maps, querulous because, as Florencia explained, he had not thought he would have to come so far.

Under lantern light Cal studied the maps, seeking to establish the places where between their present position and Saragossa the Falangists could stop to make a stand, none of which, unless they were reinforced, he thought they could hold. Not that he discounted the possibility of meeting stronger opposition – where had the cannon the column now possessed come from?

Speed was the key, giving them no time to settle and build defences, and if they could get to Saragossa and it was lightly held, the city might be taken back by a quick coup. The same map showed why such a recapture was important: Saragossa stood on the Ebro, the largest river in Spain, and it served as an important rail and road communication centre in all directions, especially north and south. It was thus a vital artery for the lateral movement of troops.

It was also a vital connection for the Republic to the north-west of Spain, to the provinces of Cantábrica, the Asturias, as well as the Basque region and Galicia; held, and the corridor extended to the Atlantic Coast, it would also cut off the Carlists of Navarre from the Nationalist centres of Burgos and Valladolid. More importantly, it blocked the road south to Madrid.

The next few days took on the nature of a race, with constant reports sent back to Colonel Villabova naming the places taken and bypassed, with requests that he support the Barcelona column. Finally they arrived before the walls of Saragossa, to find it held by a force strong enough to repulse their first feeble attack; how could it be anything else with nothing but waves of human bodies to throw at the defences and only one piece of artillery?

Worse, there was no sign of any support, and by the time Villabova was persuaded of his error in taking territory instead of towns, it was too late to effect even a siege that stood any chance of success. Worse, the defenders, reinforced, were not content to stay within the confines of the city; they came out to fight and in numbers that drove the Republican forces back until the battle lines sank into a rigidity that lasted weeks, while around the country things went from bad to worse for the Republican cause. Communications, being in touch with the rear areas and news of what was happening elsewhere, turned into a mixed blessing.

The advantage, as it had from the outset, lay with the rebellious generals, the only hope of an immediate collapse the possibility of a divided army command – that the generals would fall out amongst themselves. Such a possibility was dashed when it seemed they had settled on the former army chief of staff, General Francisco Franco, to lead them.

As the man who commanded the colonial forces, as well as, it transpired, the backing of Berlin and Rome, he emerged as the most potent voice in the Nationalist cause and he came to prominence with the Republic in chaos, struggling in the north-west provinces, bogged down in Aragón, with an ineffectual navy lacking in officers so that no blockade could be enforced, and the capital city incapable of defending itself from a determined thrust.

His Army of Africa columns swung up from Seville to attack the old fortress town of Badajoz, taken, but at a high cost in experienced troops. For all the losses of trained men, that capture linked the two halves of the Nationalist forces and cut the Republicans off from their confrères in the west. It also gave Franco the Portuguese border, over which the Nationalists were able to receive support from the openly fascist dictator, António Salazar.

Following the Badajoz assault Franco should have headed straight for Madrid, it was there for the taking, but instead he turned aside to lift a siege of the huge barracks and magazine known as the Alcázar, in the strategic as well as emotionally vital city of Toledo, more to cement his position than for any real strategic gain, thus allowing time for the defences of the capital to be strengthened.

Throughout August and into September other important centres fell to bloody reprisals, the Nationalists using every weapon in the modern armoury, including naval bombardment and massed artillery, to take the cities. But the key to their rapid success lay in what came to them from abroad. German bombers to terrorise civilians and pulverise troop concentrations, and fighters to strafe their fleeing enemies.

For the first time, the names of German pilots crept into news reports, the fiction that the planes supplied by Hitler were being flown by Spaniards the same kind of lie as that propagated by Manfred Drecker; the war in Spain was moving from a purely native fight between two political ideologies to become a cockpit for an international war by proxy.

CHAPTER FIFTEEN

The arrival of the main body of militias outside Saragossa, nearly three thousand strong and made up of members of the POUM as well as the CNT-FAI, had severely diminished the position of Juan Luis Laporta, who now found himself relegated to being one of a number of leaders instead of in sole control of his men. It did not, however, improve matters in the military sphere.

None of the new arrivals seemed capable of the kind of agreement that would enhance the needs of the Republic, which demanded a rapid advance into the Nationalist heartlands in order to force them to divert their efforts from elsewhere. Comfortably headquartered in an abandoned monastery by the River Ebro, the military hierarchy seemed like the *Café de Tranquilidad* all over again: endless argument which led to bad compromises, ineffective tactics, and futile mass assaults which burdened the militias with serious casualties.

As before, the need to dig in was scoffed at, which led to an even greater loss when the enemy counter-attacked, the only sector not to suffer the one held by the fully entrenched Olympians, simply because, wisely, the Nationalists, having carried out a thorough recce, came nowhere near it. Yet that secure position had to be abandoned due to the retreat of the main body.

It was obvious that on the Saragossa Front things were going nowhere, so Cal Jardine was not sorry when it came to his attention that time had run out for many of those he led. The young athletes had come to Spain for a period of three weeks – two to train and one to compete – and were now approaching a third month.

As aware as the men who led them of the faults of the Republican leadership, they now found a pressing need to get home to jobs and, in one or two cases, families of their own. Those who elected to stay, twelve in number, would mostly only be returning to the dole queue, but it was obvious that, numerically, they were too small to be useful.

The news that the Republic was forming International Brigades from foreign volunteers provided a solution for them, and Cal agreed to take them to the city of Albacete, where the brigades were being assembled, before determining what to do himself. Vince, funded by the last of Monty Redfern's money, would see the others home.

Yet detaching the returnees was not easy; their departure was fought tooth and nail by Manfred Drecker, who maintained that no one had the right to desert the cause and anyone who even implied such a thing deserved to be shot; Laporta backed the athletes and took pleasure in doing so.

The antipathy between the men, political and personal, had

not improved on the move into Aragón. Laporta took pleasure in pointing out what the Olympians had achieved, as opposed to Drecker's communist cadres, which led to a blazing row in which accusations of backsliding, cowardice and chicanery were liberally thrown about.

The other anarchist leaders backed Laporta, as did the Trotskyists of the POUM, leaving Drecker isolated and fuming, the clinching argument being that they had joined with Laporta's column, so any decision on their future was his to make. Cal backed that up; he was more concerned with the outcome than any claim of rights but he knew, from the looks thrown his way, that as far as Manfred Drecker was concerned he had joined the ranks of his enemies.

The day the main party left for Barcelona was a sad one; even prior to fighting, these lads had bonded together merely through their political outlook and shared stories. Yet combat, even the limited amount they had experienced, cemented that even more, while they had a fully justified pride in what they had achieved. It was handshakes and clasping all round, with many not afraid to show a tear as they clambered into the trucks that would take them to the docks and a ship to Marseilles. For Vince and Cal Jardine, this was just one more parting in a life of many.

'See you in London, guv. Maybe we can go out an' have a drink.'

'Only if you promise not to belt anyone.'

Vince threw back his head and laughed. 'I've mellowed.'

That got a disbelieving look; the last time Cal had taken Vince out, the mistake had been to take him first to a pub in Chelsea full of what Vince called 'chinless wonders', then to a late-night drinking club in Soho much frequented by what his one-time sergeant described to the police as 'toffee-nosed ponces and poufs'. Cal was an amiable drunk, Vince a bellicose one, so the night had ended with a brawl, a visit to the cells and a fine from a morning magistrate.

Vince nodded towards Florencia, saying her own goodbyes. 'How special is that one?'

'Good question.'

'You might have trouble getting away.'

'I might not want to, Vince.'

The tone of the response was not jocular, the indication that his old friend was risking overstepping the mark obvious, but Vince had something to say and, typical of the man, he was going to say it regardless.

'I wouldn't hitch myself to this lot if I were you.' He was not talking about Florencia, but the Barcelona militia. 'The way they are now, they're on a hiding to nothing and if our lot and the Frogs don't help I can't see how they can win.'

'It's early days. It might pan out.'

'I hope you're right,' Vince replied as the first of the truck engines began to throb into life. 'I'd hate to have to come back and rescue you.'

'Take care, Vince,' Cal said, hand held out to be grasped and shaken. 'And don't forget to send those trucks back. I'm stuck here with the rest of the lads until you do.'

'Give you a chance to learn some more Spanish.'

'*Hasta la vista, compadre.*'

Vince nodded and climbed into the cab of the lead truck, Florencia coming to join Cal as they disappeared in a cloud of dust. What was cheering was the way the road was lined with the men alongside whom they had fought – communists apart – not ribbing them now, but all smiling and yelling encouragement, with their right hands raised, their fists tight in salute.

It was impossible to miss the increasingly febrile atmosphere in the Republican lines; necessity made comrades of the various factions only up to a point. This was especially apparent at the point where the CNT and POUM sectors met that of the communists, now reinforced so that Drecker had under his command a couple of hundred men.

Every time the cadres were subjected to lectures on dialectic materialism and other Marxist nostrums, the anarchist militiamen would gather to jeer, loud enough to make difficult what those lecturing were trying to impart, and no one in authority sought to interfere.

Had he been in command, Cal would have stopped it and quickly, not in support of communism but with the aim of improving the fighting ability of the whole; if the two factions went into action they would not support one another, hardly a sound military policy. Yet even as he registered the mutual dislike, he did not pick up on the increasing tensions behind it, and if it had not been for Florencia, he would have had no idea what was really going on.

When she cursed the *Partido Comunista de España* he took it as just her usual railing against her political rivals. Certainly, he recorded her fears that they were poaching members from the CNT, as well as her assertion that some hypocrites were joining the PCE as a way of ensuring they were not seen as class enemies, but it did not penetrate deeply and he knew the CNT to be just as guilty when it came to recruitment; it was a game they all played.

The mutual antagonism deepened seriously when Vince's truck

drivers returned with the news that the first Soviet ships had arrived, bringing in fresh arms, including tanks and aircraft. The information lifted everyone's spirits until it was clear neither of those were going to be seen in Aragón; they were sent straight to bolster the defence of Madrid, in essence a sound policy given that was where the danger to the Republic was most severe.

Yet as another set of trucks arrived, it was very soon obvious that the drivers were communists and what they carried was a cargo exclusively for Drecker's cadres, who received weapons of a quality and modernity that surpassed that with which they had been supplied before, just as it was clear none of these were being passed to anyone else. There was no attempt at discretion, obvious as the communists paraded to show off their equipment.

Drecker and his squad leaders carried PPD-40 machine pistols, which as far as Cal was aware – and it was his business to know these things – had only recently been supplied to the forces of the Soviet Interior Ministry. Enough Degtyarov light machine guns had been supplied to set up gun teams within every platoon-sized section, while Drecker's command, now more than company strength, also had possession of two 50 mm mortars.

'These weapons, *mon ami*,' Juan Luis Laporta asked, as they were paraded under the eyes of their supposed anarchist comrades-in-arms. 'Are they any good?'

On home turf, Cal rattled off their capabilities, ranges and rates of fire, summing it up thus: 'Let's put it this way, Juan Luis, if you can get hold of any, do so.'

'We cannot,' Laporta replied, his face showing both regret and, under that, a hint of fury. 'And believe me, I have tried.'

* * *

It took several days to get to Albacete, a medium-sized town on the road from Valencia to Madrid, and what Cal found there was less than impressive, though in fairness he knew that to criticise was far from wholly just; the Spanish Republic had very few of the systems required to deal with an influx of volunteers, a fact much exacerbated by the nature of the recruits, who had come from all over the continent of Europe.

The sheer number of spoken languages would have defeated even the best-intentioned and most professional army command, while the quality of those who had come to the aid of the cause was so variable as to impose even more strain, many having near-starved to get this far. The only way to organise such mayhem was by nationality, easier with the large French contingent, to whom could be added the Belgians, as well as Germans who had fled over the Rhine from Hitler.

The British were bolstered by volunteers from the various ex-colonies, not that there was much love lost, but that looked like comradeship compared to the Italians and Austrians, while the Russians and Ukrainians – in the main, exiles from Soviet Russia looking for a way home by proving their communist credentials – seemed more likely to turn their weapons on each other than the enemy.

That was if they could first of all find a gun that fired, then locate the ammunition it required to function; the armament was a mess of conflicting patterns and differing calibres, many from well before the Great War, and the bullets were not sorted, even by box – it was necessary to rummage and select the right projectile for the weapon with which you had been issued.

Cal Jardine was not impressed enough to offer his own services, especially given the command was held by an internationally famous communist called André Marty, the man who claimed to have been instrumental in the mutiny of the French Black Seas Fleet in 1919. He was a member, too, of the Communist International, run from Moscow and dedicated to the spread of Marxism-Leninism.

Whatever else he was, Marty was no soldier, which underlined the nature of the brigades; even if he had experienced commanders at unit level, they too seemed to be communists, so the whole would be driven by ideology, not sound military principles, and that was not something he could be part of.

He hung around long enough to get his lads equipped with a combination of rifles and bullets that would at least mean that, should they get into a fight, they could function, and showed them how to scrounge the things they needed – uniforms, rations and some grenades – well aware that there was disappointment he would not be leading them into the coming battle.

'You cannae be persuaded tae stay, Mr Jardine?' asked Broxburn Jock, who had assumed the leadership of the dozen brigaders.

Cal shook his head. 'No, I'll be more use in Aragón, I think, trying to sort out some of those militias.'

That was a lie and there was no doubt that, in the young Scotsman's face, he knew it to be so. It had been natural in the few days Cal had been in Albacete that he and his boys should gravitate towards their fellow countrymen, just as it was hardly surprising that many, though not all, were card-carrying members of the British Communist Party or at the very least to the far left of Labour.

In the main, when they were workers, miners, dockers and factory men from the devastated industrial areas of the UK, that was understandable; even if he did not share their politics, he could appreciate the reasons for their allegiance to the cause. Had he shared their life – surrounded by poverty, put upon by rapacious employers, or on the dole, as well as being citizens of an indifferent state – he might also have shared their views.

It was the university and middle-class types that got up Cal's nose, too many of them from comfortable backgrounds, romantics with no grasp whatsoever of the lives of the poor and certainly not a clue about the nature of life in Soviet Russia, which, when he talked with them, was something they saw through spectacles that were more blacked out than rose-tinted.

A gentle hint that life might not be so sweet east of Poland, that it might be as bad as Nazi Germany, led to a tirade of abuse, well argued and articulate, but utterly wrong, this before he was treated to a quasi-religious attempt to point out that the way he lived his life was to fly in the face of what they called 'historical determinism'; only good manners inculcated into him from birth stopped him from telling these intellectual idiots to get stuffed.

'The bodies that have been gi'en officer's rank are no a bit like you or Vince,' Jock added. 'Some 'o them seem right mental.'

'And the rest of your brigade is not like you, Jock. It will be you teaching them how to fire a rifle now, and if they've got any sense they will promote you.'

'Fat bloody chance.'

Politics apart, that was another reason to leave, albeit there was an element of guilt at abandoning what he saw as 'his boys'. The command structure was chaotic, and from what he had observed, as had Jock, the senior positions in the brigades went to only two types: megalomaniacs and high-ranking communists – sometimes they were both – and what he had observed of the standard of training, if it could even be graced with such a term, was pandemonium, which was worrying given that they might be pitched into battle before they were ready, as the Republic was still losing on all fronts.

'I might not even stay in Spain, Jock.'

'Away, yer lassie will'na let ye go.'

'Another reason for going back to Aragón, yes?'

'No a bad yin, aw the same.'

'Take care of the rest of the boys, Jock; you are the best soldier, you know that, and they look up to you.'

That produced a blush on the square face, highlighting, as it flared, his heavy acne, the smile that followed showing his uneven teeth. Then it was time to shake the others by the hand and depart, with a silent hope that whatever they faced they would survive.

He never returned to the Saragossa Front, finding, when he stopped off in Barcelona, as he had said he would, not just Florencia in the city but Juan Luis Laporta as well. As soon as he checked back into the Ritz – they had stored his luggage – both, alerted by some member of the hotel staff, arrived to see him, she very welcome, he much less so.

It was soon made obvious they had left the monastery headquarters seething with tension: the anarchists were furious at being denied the better weapons distributed to Drecker's cadres, despite repeated requests, and it was the same for the other political groups, including those in Barcelona and Madrid.

The *Partido Comunista* controlled the distribution of Soviet equipment, and even the non-fighting communists in the rear areas were better armed than their rivals on the fighting fronts, while what had come in with the weaponry was even less welcome to the likes of Laporta: Soviet advisors who behaved as if they were dealing with idiots.

When that was advanced Cal could not but agree with the assessment, even if he could accept such condescension was unwelcome, for, if such advisors were anything like the ones he had met in Albacete, they would not, as he had tried to do since his first dust-up with Laporta, temper their advice with a sugar coating.

He had heard counterclaims in Albacete for the communists, incensed about the way they claimed the anarchists, who controlled the border with France, were denying entry to any party member trying to cross into Spain to join the International Brigades; it was all part of the fabric of endemic mistrust which permeated the Republican cause.

At the same time, it seemed to Cal, no one was doing much to fight the real enemy. When he enquired about the progress in Aragón it transpired there had been none – the Barcelona militias were still stuck outside Saragossa, the only thing of significance being that Drecker and his men, with their superior equipment, had left for Madrid, now threatened with four columns advancing on the city from Burgos, Toledo and two from Badajoz.

Try as he might, Cal could not shift the conversation to the state of the Republican forces and the manifest threats they faced, which made the conversation surreal; there was, to him, in the political bickering, an element that he mentally likened to fiddling while Rome burnt.

'As long as the communist pigs control the supply of weapons,' Laporta insisted, banging on, sticking to the same topic, 'they will use them to strengthen their position.'

As would you, thought Cal, as he yawned, having had a long day of travelling. He was also wondering when they could stop all this, if he could eat with Florencia and if Juan Luis would ever tire of the subject and disappear so they could be alone.

'And they will do so completely now the government has sent most of our gold reserves to Moscow.'

'What!' Weary as he was, when Laporta said that it woke him up. 'Why in God's name did they do that?'

It was Florencia who replied, 'Who else will sell us the guns we need?'

'France will not, as we had hoped,' Laporta added, once she had explained to him what she had just said. 'And as for you British . . .'

'Don't blame me, my friend.'

It came to Cal later that in the pause that followed, and with the looks the pair exchanged, the conversation had come to the real reason they were here, and it was Florencia who first dipped her toe.

'You know about these things, *querido*, you have told me. Where else could we buy weapons that we can control?'

Just then the phone rang and Cal went to pick it up, listened for a second, then said, 'I'm not expecting anyone.'

'Yes you are,' Florencia snapped, rushing over to take it out of his hand and spouting fast and furious Spanish. Having learnt quite a bit in the last weeks, Cal understood 'send him up'.

'Send whom up?'

'Andreu Nin,' she replied, putting the phone down, as if it was the most natural thing in the world. 'The leader of the Workers' Party of Marxist Unification.'

'We have invited him to meet with you,' Laporta added. 'On a matter of grave concern.'

'Get back on the phone,' Cal said wearily; this was not going to end soon, for when this lot started talking, never mind arguing, time lost all meaning. 'Order up some food.'

CHAPTER SIXTEEN

'I'm not sure I can do what you want.' Cal said that while aiming a jaundiced look at Florencia, who was too prone to putting him forward for things, albeit he knew it was his own fault for telling her too much about his past. 'And I certainly could not do it without money, and lot's of it.'

'And if you had money?' asked Florencia.

'Let me explain to you about what you have to do to buy weapons.'

Cal had to pause then for a knock at the door, which he opened to find a waiter and a trolley with food for everyone, as well as beers and bottles of wine, a sight so redolent of peacetime it was hard to think there was a war going on, that there were armed men on every Barcelona corner and he went nowhere himself without his pistol. Having wheeled the trolley in, the waiter began to lay things out until Florencia, rudely, told him to leave it and depart.

'He's only doing his job,' Cal said as the door shut behind him.

'No man should be a lackey to another,' she snapped.

'I'll remember that when we're in bed.'

She began to go red, until she recalled that the other two men present did not understand English. Florencia then proceeded to deny her own words by doing for the trio of menfolk the task the waiter had been about to carry out, setting the plates, distributing food and pouring wine and beer, translating as Cal talked; her mother would have been proud of her.

'First you have to find somebody willing to sell, and that is not easy. Then, if it's a government, you need from them an End User Certificate to say where the weapons are going and to what purpose they will be put.'

He had to pause and explain that further, which took time with Florencia translating. Then there was the fact that the certificate could, in some circumstances, be circumvented by bribery. Some countries were more interested in the money than any morality. By all means kill your own citizens, even fight people we call allies, as long as we get the gold and they do not find out.

'And when you buy on what is a black market, the price reflects that, to the tune of maybe paying a high premium on the normal cost.'

Seeing he was making the Spaniards glum, he apologised, but he also knew there was no point in gilding the lily; they had to know it was a murky world and a dirty game, and it was also one in which it was very easy to become the victim of what you were seeking to buy if anything went wrong.

Andreu Nin began to talk, Cal listening with concentration as Florencia turned his words into English. Not the histrionic type, he spoke carefully and dispassionately, which accorded with his schoolmasterly appearance and donnish manner, a round, rather inexpressive face, serious glasses and black curly hair, using an unlit pipe to make his points.

Basically, and Juan Luis Laporta nodded along in agreement, he outlined the fact that they must do something to check the communists before they became too strong. Cal, thinking he was exaggerating the perceived threat, was treated to more background about Spanish and Catalan politics than he cared to hear, but what it came down to he already knew: it was a bear pit.

The POUM was adamant the Workers' Party was, only a few months into the struggle, weakening while the communists were getting stronger and that, if it continued, portended disaster. To prove that led Nin into a long aside regarding the crimes of Josef Stalin and the Comintern – not least the four million reckoned to have died in the Ukrainian famine – with, of course, much reference to the purity of his brand of Marxism. Yet for all his seeming paranoia, he did know how his enemies worked.

They would manoeuvre behind the scenes, steering clear of taking positions, because by doing so they could avoid blame for mistakes while openly criticising and diminishing their more politically active rivals. Yet at the same time they would continue to gather into their hands the levers of power, for example the control of weapons supply and military advice, the keys to the pursuance of the conflict.

Already, on the Madrid Front, no weapons could be committed without their approval; fighter planes would not fly and tanks would not be sent into battle because the pilots were Soviets, and so were the armoured-unit commanders, and they would obey an order only when it came from one of their own generals.

In the purely political sphere the communists were bringing in their secret police – Nin was certain a squad of the Soviet Secret Police, the NKVD, had arrived with the first shipment of weapons. Not one of the leaders, of whatever nationality, Spanish and Catalan included, did anything without a direct order from the Communist International in Moscow.

The Comintern took its instructions directly from Stalin, and those who were actual members and deeply experienced in political subversion were already present: the likes of Marty, who was not the only leading French communist to have come from Paris. Palmiro Togliatti, known to be the Comintern representative for all Spain, was already present from his Italian exile.

Stalin would want to control everything in Spain as he had in Russia – he could not brook dissent, Nin insisted, referring to the show trials in which he was disposing of his old comrades who might be rivals. The Comintern was committed to worldwide revolution, the enforcement of a system based on lies and a bullet for rebellion, real or imagined. Once they had enough influence, they would set out to undermine their political enemies in Spain too.

This they would do one by one, targeting the leaders of the other factions, until they had them so cornered as to be able to safely eliminate them, and if it could not be achieved by devious process they would resort to assassination. They had a willingness to kill outside Soviet borders, if necessary using foreign surrogates.

'In Barcelona,' Nin continued, 'first it will be the POUM, for we are weaker than the CNT, but they will suffer too and I will tell you how. If you want to eat, if you want a good weapon, if you want to fight, they will say join the communists. Then, once they have begun to eliminate us, it will be known to all, so they will say join us, or you might be the next victim. First control, then power, and finally terror.'

'Only with our own supply of weapons can we prevent this,' Laporta said, having been silent for a longer time than Cal had ever known him to be; for all their political differences, he clearly respected Andreu Nin. 'Without that we will be powerless.'

'I come back to my point about money,' Cal said to him in French.

'And I, my friend, say to you that we will find whatever funds you need.'

'Where?'

'Not all of the gold has gone to Moscow. The government must be persuaded to give us the use of what is left.'

It took no great imagination to guess at the mayhem that would cause and it was hard to believe it could be done secretly; the communists were bound to find out.

'Juan Luis, you cannot beat the Nationalists if you are openly fighting each other in government.'

'You did not like the notion of a fascist Spain, my friend.'

'No, I did not.'

'Would you prefer a Stalinist one?' asked Laporta, doing an immediate translation for the POUM leader.

Even if the answer was a heartfelt negative, the question was not one to reply to in haste. In his time, mostly in situations of some comfort and detachment from reality, Cal had met too many people who looked at the Soviet Union with blinkered stupidity. For all the opaque nature of the world in which he had moved over many years, there was a clarity about certain areas that never reached the ears of those outside it, and one of those was the truth about life in Stalinist Russia.

The people who lived on its borders had no illusions, those who had escaped its clutches even less, all the way back to the White Russians who had fled in 1917. Many of both types, forced onto the margins of society by their exile and required to exist in clandestine trades, nevertheless had contacts inside the communist state. One voice spouting outright condemnation could be put down to personal prejudice; a chorus as loud as that which had assailed his ears spoke the truth: if anything, Soviet Russia was worse than Nazi Germany.

'All I can do is put out some feelers,' he said, after a long pause.

'Will you do that, *querido*?'

'Not tonight, I need some rest.'

The expression on Florencia's face then told Cal Jardine that was a forlorn hope.

The cable he sent to Monaco the next morning had to be extremely circumspect; Cal could mention no names, not even his own, and for a location he used his room number. But it was coded in such a way that it would have taken more than a cryptographer to unravel it, given it was between two people who knew each other enough to reference things known only to them. It also went to a nominated address and box number in which the recipient was not named.

The reply he received came within a day and not from the principal to whom it had been sent, albeit Cal was assured he was aware of the contents of both the message and the reply. It had been sent by his private secretary, whom Cal Jardine had met before, this referenced by the date of that meeting without using his name.

Drouhin told him that his master was unwell, and given he was about to celebrate his birthday – no number was used but Cal reckoned he would be eighty-seven – that was a concern. However, should his old friend care to visit, he would seek to find out beforehand where the kind of consignment hinted at could be both located and purchased, though the market was at the moment very difficult.

His suggestion that Florencia should accompany him – Monte Carlo being an enticing place to visit and one which would be made even better in her company – was turned down flat. How could she leave Spain in the midst of what was a fight to the death with the fascist pigs, now intent on taking the capital? There was a question about whether he should leave; the news that came in over the next days was alarming, but rationally, what could he, one man, do? Best to act as requested and go.

The problem did exist of getting across the French border and he worried about the land route, even though Juan Luis assured him the crossing was controlled by the CNT – with the communists complaining about their fighters being blocked from crossing into Spain. That was still a place where the communists were bound to have a presence, and how comprehensive that could be he did not know; they might well check the names on every passport by bribing the French border guards, just to ensure they knew who was coming and going.

The look in the anarchist's eye that implied he was taking caution too far he declined to respond to – it was his habit to always overdo safety where possible – but there was another consideration: going out would be easy, the French would be lax about that, coming back would not. Besides, the land route was long and would involve several changes of train once in France.

The solution was a boat, one of the many abandoned in the

harbour by the owners who had fled Barcelona and scooted to the Nationalist side of the divide. They had not been left to rust but had provided an opportunity for the kind of men who may well have made their living smuggling before the war in less salubrious craft – he did not enquire.

All Cal needed to do was to get to a landfall close to Marseilles, and without any details as to who he was and why, with people who had already paid the necessary *douceurs* to the overburdened French customs men to be allowed to trade – not a problem on a long coastline dotted with tiny fishing ports near-impossible to police. These were places that had been involved in smuggling ever since tariffs were invented, close to a city in which he had spent some of his formative years, and known to be the crime capital of France.

Once there, it was a simple train journey to his destination, much of it spent in the dining car.

His first impression of Monaco was that it was beginning to recover some of its gloss, which, like the whole of the Riviera, had been knocked by the Great Depression. At one time the winter watering hole of the British upper crust and American millionaires, they had found their pounds and dollars, of which they had less to disburse, insufficient to spend several months avoiding the weather back home, gambling merrily away at the casino.

The man he had come to see had saved that establishment from bankruptcy and it was possible he still owned it, though he never went there or gambled at the tables. No one knew for certain; Sir Basil Zaharoff's dealings were always clouded in secrecy whatever activity he engaged in.

Drouhin's face was grave as he came to greet Cal, nodding to the rather burly servant who had stood by him that it was safe to depart; in the house of a man who, for all that he was long retired, had dealt in arms for decades and was known by the soubriquet of 'The Merchant of Death', while searching a visitor for the means to assassinate the owner would not do, no one was trusted to be left alone.

'Monsieur Jardine.' Cal shook his hand; he did not really know the man, having met him only briefly on a previous visit, but he knew that Sir Basil trusted him absolutely, so he could do so too. 'My patron is sleeping at the moment, but if you will, we can take a drink on the terrace and you can outline your needs to me.'

'How ill is he?'

'It is serious, monsieur,' Drouhin replied, his face sad, his eyes quickly turning lachrymose, while he rather embarrassingly crossed himself; that, however, told Cal Jardine that whatever assailed the old man was likely to be terminal. 'He is still lucid when awake and has particularly made a point of his desire to see you.'

'I'm grateful.'

'My patron has a high regard for you, monsieur,' Drouhin replied, as they exited onto a terrace with a magnificent view of the harbour, with Cal wondering why that should be. 'He is most anxious that, if we can assist you, we should.'

There were courtesies to get out of the way while they waited for a servant to bring a tray of coffee – how was your journey, the weather, etc, which, contrary to the British view, is an international obsession, not just one on which Albion is fixated. Once the coffee was served and the manservant gone, it was time for *affaires*. Little explanation was required given from where he had come.

It was immediately obvious, though, in Drouhin's expression, that his view of what was possible tended to the pessimistic, not that his visitor was surprised. The general sentiment amongst those who might be able to provide a supply of weapons – and for what was required they would need to be governments – was unlikely to be sympathetic to the cause of the Republicans in Spain, and even if they were, such states bordered on and were fearful of the major dictators.

Belgium clung to its neutrality in desperation, to avoid a repeat of 1914, Holland was not a major manufacturer, though well disposed to the Republic, while Czechoslovakia, by many miles the place with the required levels of production and quality of arms, would show extreme caution with Hitler's Germany on its western border.

'Has Poland rearmed?'

'Not as much as it should and, as you must know, monsieur, they have a military government, so would incline more towards the Spanish Nationalists than the Republicans. There are, we are informed, people in certain sections of the Ministry of War in Warsaw who are open to bribery, so it may be an avenue to pursue.'

As information this was touched with gold; even inactive for years, Sir Basil Zaharoff had maintained a private intelligence network that would have shamed most national governments – he called it 'keeping his hand in', but really it was a game the old man played because he could afford it, having amassed a vast fortune, said to be the largest in Europe, over many decades of trading arms, making investments and buying and selling businesses.

He also traded on the romance of his nickname; many was the minor functionary in a state enterprise who did not require a cash payment for small amounts of information, people who were content to know in their own hearts, and possibly to let on with a nod and a wink to their friends or mistresses, that they were a friend of such a man. When all these snippets were added together, what looked pretty innocuous in isolation gave the old spider at the centre of the web a comprehensive picture.

'Would that run to names?'

'Only if my patron sanctions it, but added to that I will put out enquiries in Sweden and various contacts in South America.' Drouhin gave a thin smile then. 'Some of whom you know. But those who supply government to government are not numerous and are scrutinising very hard the End User Certificates, so even if you used a country like Argentina or Uruguay you would have difficulty in explaining the quantity you require.'

'And one sniff of Spain?'

'Exactly. In some sense it is a pity that Mexico backed the Republican side so quickly – they would have been perfect.'

The servant reappeared with the news that the master was awake and eager to see his visitor. Admonished not to overtire him, Cal was shown into a large bedroom, lit only by what sunshine came through slatted blinds, with Sir Basil propped up on pillows. Even in the gloom, Cal could see his skin was translucent and he could hear his somewhat laboured breathing. Not without a sense of drama himself, he guessed he was witnessing the end of an era.

'My good friend, come and sit close by the bed so I do not have to do more than whisper.'

As soon as he obliged, he explained to the old man what he had just told his private secretary. The response was the same, followed by a bout of coughing which had Cal grasping his skeletal hand, surprised at the strength still evident in the grip.

'You must tell me why you have become involved in this.'

There was no gilding it, he gave it to Sir Basil as it was, well aware that he too would not be sympathetic to anarchists and the like; luckily he had a visceral hatred of communists and through husky breath he rehearsed some of the crimes of the Soviets in much the same manner as Cal already knew, but with more accuracy, given his sources, his conclusion that unpalatable as it was to support far-left socialists, such criminals as existed in Moscow should be stopped.

'But how?' Cal asked. 'Drouhin was not encouraging.'

'Many times in my life I have been told that this and that was impossible, only to find a way, and I think now there must be a route to solving this.' The old man coughed again, gripping even tighter Cal's hand. 'You have no idea how it cheers me you have come, Callum – you do not mind me calling you that?'

'I was not aware you knew it to be my name.'

The frail chest heaved as he laughed. 'Now you are being disingenuous, for the only other possibility is that you are foolish and I know that not to be true. So, you must leave this with me. You have given me a project and to find a solution will fill my last days on this earth.'

'Sir,' Cal protested, only to be tutted into silence.

'You will go back to Barcelona?'

'I will, to tell them what is possible, or in this case, unlikely to be so.'

'Then it is also possible you will not see me again, and before you protest once more, death comes to us all, and if you mourn there are many who will not. They will hope that Satan, having got me into his clutches, is making me pay for the crimes and sins I am accused of.' Another hacking laugh followed as it took several seconds for him to get his breath. 'Not a few of which I am proud to have committed.'

For all he had protested, Cal had seen too much death in his time to be in any other mind than that the old man was right; it could not be long, even if he had, which he would, the best medical care going.

'You know, Callum, I will not apologise if I do meet my maker. I will say to him, as I have often said to my accusers, it takes two to make a bargain. If you wish to call it a sin to sell weapons of death, then is it not also a sin to buy them and use them, which I never did?'

'You may find, when you get to the Pearly Gates, he's looking for some Maxim guns to keep his angels in line.'

A bony finger went up. 'A good point, but I shall make him pay a high price if he does.'

The head went back onto the pillows, he was tiring, and Cal made the noises to leave, but the old man was not finished.

'I am not sorry to be leaving now, for it is going to be bad, the future, Callum, very bad. In my lifetime the ways we have found to kill our fellow humans have increased so much, until we had slaughter on an industrial scale in the Great War. But I fear it will be worse than even that. There is an evil abroad I do not think was on this earth when I first walked upon it.' The last grip was the hardest. 'Stalin and Hitler are a different breed of monster.'

'Mussolini?'

'Is a fat fool running a bankrupt nation of soldiers who do not want to fight, and who can blame them? For all his boasting he is as nothing – but the others, take care, my young friend, not to be consumed by them and their schemes. Now, ask Drouhin to come and see me.'

* * *

221

The arrangement was that whatever was found out would be delivered to the Ritz Hotel in Barcelona with the coded name, Mr Maxim. Cal did not enquire as to how it would be sent; he trusted both the old man and his assistant to secure the secrecy of the communication. As Drouhin imparted this to him he could tell by his tone that he was wondering if the named address would still be in Republican hands. Cal did not bother to suggest anything different – if it was not, then what was delivered would be redundant.

After a night alone in Monte Carlo, where he ate well and visited the casino, he was glad of two things. First, that he did not lose much at baccarat; second, that he managed to avoid the looks of the women who sought to catch his eye, not one of whom was younger than fifty years and a good many of whom, even under pancake make-up, were a good deal older. Anyway, there were enough glossily attired and barbered young men around to drool over them and their money.

The next morning, the mere delivery of his newspaper was enough to galvanise him; he was done here in any case but there would be no leisurely return to Barcelona. The screaming headline in *Le Temps* told the whole of France that one of the Spanish Nationalist columns had reached and actually breached the outskirts of the capital. Franco was about to launch an all-out assault on Madrid.

CHAPTER SEVENTEEN

There was no time to wait for a smuggler's boat – the arrangement had been a loose one and might mean waiting several days or even a week. Cal sent a cable to Florencia at CNT headquarters, bought a car in Marseilles and made straight for the main eastern crossing of the Franco-Spanish border at Le Perthus, where he found a town in some ways like those Wild West frontier settlements so beloved of American film-makers, the only thing missing being ten-gallon hats and shoot-outs.

Thanks to the war, the place was booming, bursting at the seams with those seeking to profit from Spain's misery, the road to the border post lined with endless overstocked shops, and where there was a gap traders had set up stalls overcharging for everything, especially gasoline. Somewhere among them he knew there would be those tasked to get fighters over the border, if necessary by taking them through the surrounding high Pyrenees on foot.

He had less trouble than he suspected; international communists and Republican sympathisers did not, it seemed, arrive on four wheels, but on foot, though the car was searched to ensure it was not carrying contraband. Besides, he had a British passport and was assumed to be just one of those mad Englishmen so beloved of European caricaturists; if he wanted to go into a war zone and get himself killed, why should a French customs officer stop him?

What news he had garnered from the newspapers indicated that the battles to the west and south of Madrid were bloody and favoured the Nationalists, with the Republicans launching furious counter-attacks only to have them broken up by air and artillery attacks. The French press reported aerial battles as well as those on the ground, and high casualties on both sides.

This did raise the question of the wisdom of his actions – might it not be better to wait until he saw which way the battle went? But then there was Florencia – if the city was lost he would take her out of the country, regardless of any protests; if Madrid fell so would the Republic, and someone like her, taken by the Nationalists, would suffer more than just a summary execution.

When he got to Barcelona, it was to find a woman even more fired up than she had been when he departed, sure that Madrid would hold and even more determined that the political fight should be carried to the communists; there was even talk of the anarchists, pressed by their more pragmatic syndicalist allies, joining the National government on the grounds that they suffered from being outside a leadership in which the communists were exercising influence.

The first thing to do was get travel papers from the Catalan government and that took an age, given there was a long queue at the Generalitat of people needing the same thing. The time taken, nearly a whole day, had to be accepted – it was going to be too dangerous to travel anywhere in Spain without documentation; there were too many armed men out in the country just itching to shoot anyone they suspected of not being for the Republic.

The next morning Cal, dressed once more for fighting, was back on the road, Florencia by his side, speeding towards Madrid, where Andreu Nin had gone to seek allies and to plead with the government for the funds Cal Jardine might need. Juan Luis Laporta had gone back to the Saragossa Front.

There was no doubt many were fleeing the city, already subjected to air attack, and it was not surprising to find that in the streaming refugee column there were poor people from the provinces to the west pushing carts or leading donkeys carrying everything they possessed, fighting for road space with those wealthy enough to afford motor transport, as well as armaments and truck convoys seeking to go in the opposite direction. Progress was slow and a night spent sleeping in the car was necessary.

The city, when they reached it, had a strange air – sandbags in the streets, signs for air raid shelters posted over the entrances to the metro, armed men, rifles slung barrel down, on street corners, who, to Cal's mind, would have been more use at the front – yet still a bustle that went with its station as the nation's main metropolis, though many an eye was cast skywards, this being the first European capital city to face aerial bombing.

It was still the seat of government, with the ministries working flat-out, full of the functionaries necessary to support the work of those and the parliament, diplomats who had yet to abandon the capital and, of course, those men from the worldwide press covering the front line.

Many hotels had been taken over by workers' organisations as well as the extra official bodies needed to fight a war, and even with wealthy clients scarce, getting accommodation was difficult. Luckily they got a room in the Hotel Florida, set aside for the foreign press; with its Edwardian luxury, it seemed to be something that might be taking place on another planet.

After lunch, Florencia wanted to sleep; not being Spanish, Cal went to the bar, which was quite busy and noisier than the numbers would indicate, making for a quiet corner well away from the hubbub of the raucous conversation of the journalists, which ebbed and flowed as they came and went.

'You know, they say there is no such thing as a bad penny, but looking at you, Callum Jardine, well, I ain't so sure that's true.'

Alverson's deep, slow, West Coast drawl was instantly recognisable, so smiling, Cal put down his whisky and turned to face him. Dressed in a slightly crumpled pale linen suit, his panama hat in his hand and a small camera over his shoulder, Cal's first thought was that he had not changed, but then why should he, it being only months since they had last parted?

'Hey, Tyler, you drinking?' a basso profundo American voice called from the other end of the bar, a big fellow with thick black hair and a heavy moustache.

'I just met an old friend, Ernie, be with you later.'

The American's eyes turned back to Cal and looked over his clothing, his now slightly battered leather blouson, scuffed twill trousers and sturdy boots, which was of the kind that, prior to the present conflict, would have got him stopped at the front door of a place like the Florida Hotel. They then dropped to the belt at Cal's waist and the very obvious holster.

'Since I see you're packing a gun, I can guess your presence in Madrid is not purely social.'

'I know yours won't be.'

'I'm a reporter, Cal, it's my job to be where the trouble is.'

'Right now I'm told that's on the other side of the river.'

'I'll leave the front line to those crazy photographers.'

Cal indicated the knot of his fellow reporters at the other end of the bar. 'Same go for them?'

'Some, not all.'

'Drink?'

'Bourbon.'

Cal signalled to the barman and ordered that and another whisky for himself, while Tyler Alverson's head rotated slightly to acknowledge their surroundings, all dark wood, leather and comfort, with a white-coated barman fronting gleaming glasses and bottles.

'You staying here, Cal?'

'The fellow at reception was happy to see us, not too many people are checking in right now.'

'Us?'

'Florencia.' Cal grinned. 'My Spanish interpreter.'

That got a raised and amused eyebrow. 'Interprets dreams, does she, brother?'

'Disrupts them, more like. Right now she's having her siesta but I'm sure she'll be down in a bit and that will cause you to have dreams, Tyler.'

'A looker is she?'

'And some!' Cal nodded to a set of leather banquettes. 'Let's sit, shall we?'

Comfortably accommodated, though slightly too close to the loud journalistic banter, Alverson examined his companion with a languid eye. That and the habitual half smile, if anything, made Cal more guarded, he being well aware that the American possessed a razor-sharp mind and a manner that invited unwitting disclosure.

'So, brother, are you goin' to fill me in on what you've been up to since our last little adventure?'

'You first, Tyler.'

There was calculation in that; given his reasons for being in Madrid, he was not sure whether to be open or keep matters to himself. Tyler Alverson was close to a friend – they had shared much danger in each other's company – but he was a newspaperman first and foremost, and there was no knowing where disclosure would lead. Thankfully, he seemed happy to oblige.

'What's to tell? When we parted company in Aden I went back home, told my Abyssinian stories in great depth and waited for the nation to rise up in disgust at the horror of Italian atrocities there. Sad to say, I'm still waiting.'

'London's no better. My people seem more interested in keeping Mussolini happy than the gassing of the African natives.'

'Then this little brouhaha blew up and the agency asked me to cover it.'

Cal Jardine had first met the American in Somaliland when in the process of seeking to smuggle guns into Ethiopia. Keen to get to a battle zone barred to journalists, Alverson had hitched a ride with him and over the weeks that followed there had grown a degree of mutual respect. Only months past, it seemed like years, but Cal was happy to indulge in a bit of reminiscence about dodging not only Italian bullets, but also clouds of air-delivered poison gas, until inevitably the conversation moved on to where they were now.

'So, come clean, are you involved in this war too, Cal?'

'Might be.'

The pistol holster got anther meaningful look. 'I'm not sure you'll like it much here.'

'Why not?'

'I know you and the way you like to do things, but you'll find yourself dealing with a bunch of military misfits as well as a whole heap of Russian so-called advisors.'

The look Cal gave was meant to imply this was news to him. 'So-called?'

'From what I can see they are running the show, with the Spanish commanders acting as nothing but a fig leaf. Not that it's admitted, of course, but a guy I spoke to a bit lower down the command structure says the locals can't get a tank or a plane to move without Ivan's say-so.'

'That doesn't sound good,' Cal replied, his face decidedly bland.

Right then the other American, who had called to Tyler, raised his voice to finish off a particularly noisy anecdote to do with the price of a whore, which gave Cal an excuse to seek to change the subject.

'Seems quite a character, your friend.'

'That's Ernie Hemingway.'

'*The* Hemingway?'

'Yep, and he's not a friend, but a rival, reporting for the *New York Times* and a total pain in the ass, but he does love to be where the bullets fly. Never mind Ernie, are you goin' to tell me how you come to be in Spain?'

'Maybe I love the climate and the food.' Alverson's eyes were not languid now, they had a distinct glint; with his hound's nose he was beginning to smell something. 'I was in Barcelona the day the balloon went up and sort of stayed. Helping hand, you know.'

'See much?'

'More than I bargained for, Tyler, like the fight for the Parque Barracks and the main telephone exchange.'

'Care to tell me the story?'

'It's old hat, months ago now.'

Alverson eased out a notebook, though Cal noticed he took care to keep it on his lap, hidden from the knot of fellow reporters. 'Never turn down a first-hand account from a trusted source. You have no idea how much bullshit we hacks get fed in our honest endeavours.'

Loud laughter came with the finish of the tale, which seemed to involve Hemingway in chastising some Spanish pimp with fists he was now waving around; it sounded remarkably like boasting to Cal.

'Seems you can dish it out as well.'

'I take it you were in Barcelona because of this dame.'

'Not really, I had a brief to look out for the British athletes attending the People's Olympiad and needed an interpreter. The anarchists supplied one and she just happened to be irresistible, so I stayed a bit longer than I should.'

'You will forgive me if I say the People's Olympiad and anarchists do not sound like "your cup of tea".' The last three words were delivered in a faux snooty accent.

'I've got hidden depths and they're good boys. A lot of them volunteered when the trouble started. A few of them stayed and are still fighting.'

'Tell me more.'

Willing to talk about them, he needed to keep Monty Redfern out of it; the last thing he would want was to be identified in a newspaper, especially an American one, given he was always trying to get from the wealthy Jews of New York donations to help his and their co-religionists out of Nazi Germany. Vince was different; Alverson knew him from Ethiopia, so explaining his presence presented no problem.

'He brought over some of his young boxers but he's gone home now.'

'So,' Alverson said, sitting forward and over his notebook. 'Tell me what you two witnessed.'

The pencil raced as Cal talked, with Alverson posing apposite questions to get a picture of what Cal and Vince had both seen and participated in, the Olympians as well.

'That makes a good story. Plucky Brits taking on the forces of evil.'

Naturally, the name of Juan Luis Laporta was mentioned more than once and it was clear Alverson found him interesting too, so he built the man up a bit to keep the talk going and promised an introduction.

'So what happened after you and Vince saved Barcelona?'

'Aragón happened.'

That story ended with the disappointment of being stuck in front of Saragossa, the command problems and infighting not helped by the ineffectiveness of the militias and the deviousness of people like Drecker, which had inevitable led to the break up of his unit. Alverson related what he had witnessed and already investigated, written up and cabled back to his agency. In essence, Madrid was as confused as anywhere else, just more so, the fight for control more vicious given the city's strategic importance.

'The communists are the best equipped and organised here too.'

'And the most miserable bunch of shits I have ever met, Drecker especially.'

Alverson laughed. 'Marx banned smiling as well as capitalism.'

'What's the latest on this front?'

'It's not going well for your side.'

'Not our side, Tyler?'

'Regardless of where my natural sympathies lie, Cal, it's my job to send my editor all the news fit to print, without bias, which is damned hard 'cause every bastard I talk to tells me lies.'

'Do your bosses have a reporter on the Nationalist side?'

'Naturally, everybody does, and before you ask, that guy Franco is not telling him any more truths than Largo Caballero is telling people like me.'

'You met the prime minister?'

'Power of the press, brother.'

'What's he like?'

The way Alverson paused for a second told Cal he had asked that question too eagerly. Largo Caballero held the purse strings and was, according to Florencia, one of the people he might be required to meet.

'He's pretty smart, a politician to his toes, who wants help from the USA.' He nodded towards those at the bar. 'And talking to me and other Americans he hopes will aid that. It won't, any more than talking to the London *Times* or *Le Temps* will get anything from London or Paris.'

It was time for Cal to change the subject again and that comment of Alverson's gave him an outlet. 'That Anthony Eden sounds like a real slippery bastard.'

'Unlike Fatso and Adolf.'

Cal lifted his glass. 'To hell with the lot of them.'

'Amen,' Alverson said, downing his drink. 'Another?'

'My shout.'

'Hey, brother,' Tyler said, raising his empty glass to the barman, 'I'm on expenses.'

'So no chance of aid for the Republic from the democracies?'

'Can't see it.'

Cal steered the conversation on to that subject. With total cynicism the British government – worried about upsetting Mussolini and Hitler – had made pious noises about non-intervention in what they called a purely national dispute, ignoring the obvious evidence of what those same dictators were up to, plumping instead for an international discussion forum called the Non-Intervention Committee while refusing arms to both sides – in effect, given Franco was getting everything he needed, denying the Republic vital support.

The French, fearful of acting on their own, as well as under pressure from their own right-wing zealots, having offered to supply arms to Madrid and sending a few obsolete planes, had supinely withdrawn that after political protests and street demonstrations and the lack of British support, while the USA was staying strictly neutral.

'Yep, thanks to our so-called democracies Franco could be sitting in this bar in a week.'

'It won't be pretty if he does.'

'And some.'

That provided another diversion; you could not have a conversation about the conflict without talking about the killing taking place, and often being boasted about in some kind of Spanish love of blood and death in a heated propaganda war in which it was increasingly hard to tell the truth from the exaggerations.

It was bad in the cities, but there was little doubt in areas where the peasantry had risen up – long the victims of rapacious landlord power – death and destruction were particularly acute, with manor houses torched and their owners and families butchered. The priests who had supported them were victims too, often locked inside burning churches with those of their flock considered class enemies, while the Nationalists claimed nuns were being raped and mutilated all over the country, stories vehemently denied by the Republican press.

Yet it was hard to believe even a ferocious, long-downtrodden and exploited peasantry and angry workers could outdo the forces of reaction who, if reports were true, were killing on an industrial scale, while allowing their Foreign Legion troops a free hand in how they terrorised the places they captured, leading to mass rapes and summary executions. It was said that the Nationalist commander who took Badajoz had ordered shot a couple of thousand people before he headed for Madrid.

'Holy Shamolly.'

That emphatic and utterly incomprehensible outburst, given they were discussing murder and mayhem, made Cal Jardine spin round. He had failed to notice that the babble at the bar had seriously diminished; all eyes were on their banquette.

'*Querido.*'

Tyler Alverson did not quite whistle, but judging by the look he gave Florencia as both men stood he might as well have. She was dressed in close-fitting jodhpurs and riding boots, while her leather coat was folded over her arm so that the silk shirt she had on showed her figure to perfection, and she was returning the look, waiting for an introduction, which was quickly supplied.

'Tyler, you sly old dog,' Hemingway hooted.

Alverson called back. 'You can't have all the ladies, Ernie, stick to Martha.'

A glass was raised and Hemingway was not looking at Alverson, but then neither was anyone else in a group which, with his size and bulk, he dominated, his response another call. 'When the cat's away . . .'

'Cal tells me you're an anarchist?' Alverson said, his attention back on Florencia, with a look that implied disbelief.

'*Si.*'

'Tell me, honey, how do I join?'

There is a fine line between flattering someone and patronising them, added to which there was Florencia's ability to see a slight where there was none intended and she had a temperament to match. Seeing her eyes narrow, Cal had to intervene quickly.

'Tyler helped me get guns into Ethiopia.' That gave her pause. 'You should read some of his reports on Italian atrocities. He hates Mussolini.'

As a way of saying 'he's one of us' it was perfect and the look on her face changed from impending anger to a dazzling smile. Quite out of character, because he was not the type for gallantry, Tyler leant over, lifted her hand and kissed it, then smiled.

'I would be happy to read them to you.'

'As bedtime stories?' Cal interjected, not without irony.

'Can I buy you guys dinner later?'

'We'll see,' was the reply from Callum Jardine.

The look on Tyler Alverson's face then was a curious one, almost wolfish. 'We're bound to run into each other; after all, I'm staying in this joint too.'

'I'm sure we will.'

'And then, Callum Jardine, you can tell what it is you are being so secretive about.'

Cal tried bluff. 'Who says I am being secretive?'

Tyler Alverson tapped his nose. 'This old buddy of mine, and it's never wrong.'

CHAPTER EIGHTEEN

Prime Minister Largo Caballero was not a man who could be called upon in secret; in the atmosphere prevailing inside his government, which, with much manoeuvring and abandonment of principle the anarchists were preparing to join, suspicion was the watchword. Trust no one, watch everyone and keep a keen nose twitching for betrayal, so arrangements had been made to meet him away from the parliament building, *El Congreso de los Diputados*.

But first Cal had to be introduced to the politician who would represent the CNT-FAI, Juan García Oliver, a man about the same age and, according to Florencia, as much of a long-time firebrand as Laporta, with whom he had planned and carried out assassinations. He looked very much less of a fighter, being slim and handsome, with a high forehead, though he shared a countenance not much given to smiling.

He certainly did not favour the foreigner with one, and though it was clear that he and Andreu Nin, now a full member of the Catalan regional government, had already agreed a common position, it was also obvious, from the looks thrown in his direction, that García Oliver questioned the need for Cal to be present. Nin had to take him aside and engage in a whispered discussion to put his mind at rest.

That over, the quartet – it included Florencia – proceeded to their destination. The meeting took place at the home of a trusted political ally of Caballero, a house in a quiet cul-de-sac where Cal came face-to-face with a man whom he knew from the reports he had boned up on had, as much as any other, inflamed the politics of elections during the Republic.

A fiery orator in the tradition of men obliged by internal competition to ratchet up the rhetoric of blood-filled gutters should his opponents get back into power, it was Caballero who had threatened mayhem should the parties of the centre and right triumph in the last elections, he who had possibly created in the generals, now fighting, the feeling that Spain was about to sink into anarchy.

Yet for someone supposed to be a demagogue, Largo Caballero looked remarkably ordinary, more like a career bureaucrat than a budding Lenin: silver-haired, well barbered, bland-faced and very polite, with a calm manner of speaking much at odds with the passionate arguments to which he was obliged to listen.

Cal could only be partly involved; his improved Spanish was insufficient to follow more than the drift of what was a circumlocutory conversation between the male trio, in which little would be openly stated, this not aided by the loathing each had for the other, while Florencia was too intent on what was being said to do much translating.

It was more by watching her face that he followed the drift of the conversation, which appeared to be positive, indicated more by half-smiles and semi-nods from Caballero than any outright declaration. The meeting broke up with handshakes, and only when they were away from the house, in the open, did Florencia fully enlighten him.

'Caballero agrees that the possibilities should be investigated.'

'No more than that?'

'No.'

'Money,' Cal said as a weary reminder.

She nodded to include Nin and Oliver and, preparatory to telling him, she first advised them as to what she was about to say, before reverting to Englsih.

'The POUM have agreed to provide funds from their party coffers to begin the investigation in to making a purchase of arms, though apart from Andreu they have no knowledge of you. Likewise, García Oliver and Juan Luis will be the only anarchists who know of your identity and purpose.'

The use of the names had both men looking at him keenly.

'No one else must know. Caballero dare not be found undermining his cabinet, for if he is it will fall apart, nor can he seek to apportion what is needed for purchase until matters are close to a conclusion, since he will have to sneak the payment past the communists, but he is sure it can be shipped, as and when needed, at a few days' notice.'

'That will not do, Florencia.' Unfazed by her flash of anger, picked up by the two men, Cal continued, 'The money has to be there before the deal is done. It is a transfer that has to be simultaneous. This is a business in which there is no such thing as trust.'

That was followed by a rapid burst of explanation. Nin, who responded after a brief word with Oliver, which was followed by a handshake and his departure, was thankfully more calm and measured than her.

'Andreu says one step at a time,' Florencia said, with none of the tone in which it had been imparted to her.

'I gathered that.'

They were now near the main boulevard, and worried about being observed in Nin's company, Cal had a look around. Tyler Alverson was easy to spot, mainly because he was making no attempt to disguise himself or hide; he was, after all, dressed in a near-white suit. Cheekily, the American touched the rim of his panama, then immediately spun round and departed.

Annoying as it was, there being nothing he could do to change that Cal concentrated on finalising the arrangements to transfer funds into the account that he had opened with Monty Redfern's bank draft, which was obviously a speculative amount and he was careful to ensure there could be more if needed.

There was no way of knowing if and what Drouhin would send him and what would be required to be expended, so he was obliged to play safe and request a hefty sum of money that made Nin think hard before agreeing, with the caveat that approval for such a large amount would have to be sought from his committee.

That engendered a discussion of keeping the information secure; if infiltration was a communist tactic, Cal insisted, it would be naive to assume that spies had not penetrated both the POUM and the CNT. That was when it ceased to be a dialogue and became a row, Nin and Florencia displeased with the notion that their close comrades would betray them.

Agreement was reached eventually that the money would be earmarked for foreign propaganda purposes – no mention would be made of armaments to anyone who did not already know of the plans – and finally Cal and Florencia parted company and made their way back to the Florida Hotel as night began to fall. Tyler Alverson was in the lobby.

'Bit early to eat, Cal,' he boomed, 'but just the time for the first drink of the evening.'

The American was too shrewd to enquire what Cal was up to while Florencia was present, instead he kept the conversation genial and general about the places he had been and the things he had seen – and often wished he had not – in the trouble spots of the world. A natural topic was his and Cal's shared adventure in Abyssinia; the one subject he tried to stay off was the present civil war.

If he was aware that Cal was watching him the way a tabby cat eyes a mouse, and he had to be, Tyler Alverson ignored it, moving on to talk about President Roosevelt and the proposed Second New Deal, the '36 election just having been decided, only referring to what was happening in Madrid in his explanation of why America would not support the Republic with weapons and credits.

'I don't know if Franco and his guys figured on this, but they kicked off right in the middle of an election campaign and nobody could have predicted that the Democrats would win by a landslide. Roosevelt had to promise to stay out of European affairs to get the votes he needed.'

'But now?' Florencia asked, her face eager. 'Perhaps he will help now.'

'Honey,' Alverson intoned, that alone enough to dampen any

enthusiasm, 'I don't think you know how bad things are in the USA. If you ain't got your own house in order, you can't go getting involved in saving the abode of anyone else. I think we will be sorry one day, and a lot of other folk do too, but them and I don't run things.' He looked at his watch. 'Is it time for dinner yet? I can't wait till ten, when you guys eat.'

Florencia stood. 'I will go and change.'

'Nice dame,' Alverson said as she walked away, his eyes not the only ones following her. 'And I mean as a person too.'

'She has her moments.'

'I bet.'

'You know, I don't take to being tailed.'

'Who says me seeing you was not just a coincidence?'

'I do.'

'So, I followed you. I figured you were up to something and it's my job to find out stuff like that.'

'You could have just asked.'

Alverson produced a lazy grin. 'And you would do what you are about to do now, tell me to mind my own business.'

'Yes.'

'So let's see what my nose tells me. You are caught in Spain because you are tied up with Florencia which, I have to admit, is a damn good reason. Maybe because of her, but more likely for all the right reasons, you get involved in a couple of shoot-outs—'

'They were a bit more than that.'

'Battles, then – but you're not battling now, Cal, you are visiting a discreet location in the company of a couple of guys called Andreu Nin and García Oliver, who, I hear, is being touted to join the government.'

242

'You're so sure you know their identities?'

'Cal, it's my job to know. I have a photograph of every serious player on both sides in my suitcase.'

'Go on.'

'Now, when I first met you, what were you doing?' There was no need to answer. 'And what does the Republic need right now?'

'A bit tenuous, Tyler.'

'Is it, Cal? You're a gunrunner and they need weapons, and my guess is that they worry about depending on Stalin for everything. I know the guys I've met in Madrid don't like taking orders from the Russians, just as I know how much those communist bastards like giving them out.'

'They're not short on arrogance.'

'So now that I have said all that, you have a choice. You can either let me speculate in print – in short, tell the American public what I suspect is going on – or you can tell me the story and ask me to sit on it.'

'How do I know you would be satisfied with that?'

'You don't, and it won't be friendship that decides, it will be what I consider best for the papers that pay my wages and are waiting for an explanation of what is going on in this benighted part of the globe. So it's half a story now, cobbled together out of speculation and observation, or the full shebang later on.'

Cal stood up and rubbed his chin. 'I need to change for dinner too.'

Alverson's look was salacious enough to explain his reply. 'Don't you go getting distracted up there in that bedroom, my stomach is already rumbling.'

* * *

243

As he scraped his chin, in a mirror steamed up by his bathwater, listening to Florencia singing softly in the bedroom as she dressed, Cal was aware that he had to open up to Alverson. Whether, come the endgame – always supposing there was one – he would tell all, was another matter. What he needed now was secrecy – any hint that an international gunrunner was seeking weapons would be fatal.

He trusted the American would not use his actual name, but nor would he just settle for the nebulous story so far. He would be on his tail, asking questions at every stage of any deal, and if he was, he would be hard to fool. There was a moment, when he dipped his face to wash off the last of the shaving foam, when he wondered whether to pack the whole thing in, but Florencia had reached a high note in her song and he knew he was committed, and why.

With Florencia a late riser, Cal met Tyler Alverson over breakfast, taking a table as far away as possible from any other journalists, the first bit of the tale his trip to Monaco and what had transpired.

'So old Zaharoff is on the way out?'

'Sadly, yes.'

'Not many would share that sentiment.'

'Because people like you have demonised him.'

'Hey, buddy, hold on. Zaharoff is not only a crook, he admits he's one and takes pride in telling the world of his scams.'

'You don't know the gunrunning business, Tyler; it's full of crooks, and when it comes to governments it is a case of dealing with charlatans.'

'I'll leave it to you to tell me which one of those you are, Cal.' That was responded to with a jaundiced look, as Alverson added,

'But if you don't mind I will alert the rag. Zaharoff is news and they will want someone there when he pops his clogs.'

'Can't see it makes any difference.'

'So how can he help you if he is so ill?'

The name Drouhin was kept back and Alverson did not push for it, though Cal knew he might at a later stage. He explained the arrangement, as well as the reasons, glad that the American was not taking notes. As he suspected, the reporter was not satisfied with just that.

'For me to get this right, I need to know where you're going, when you are there and who you are dealing with.'

'You can't use names, Tyler, especially not mine.'

'I can use hints, brother. I will give you a cable address in the States. I will be like you, moving around, but Scripps Howard always know where I am and you can use that to tell me where you are, then I can keep in touch.'

'Why don't you just wait till it's all done and dusted?'

'Because, Cal, I am not a dummy. If I wait, you will have all the information and the decision to give or withhold it. This way you don't.'

'I will not put myself in danger to keep you posted, that you have to know.'

'I can live with that.'

'I wouldn't live without it – I'd end up face down in a river, if I'm lucky.'

'Now, how would you come to a fate like that, friend?'

Concentrating, neither had seen Hemingway approach and both were obliged to look up at him, the first thing to notice the fact that he looked pretty bleary in the eye. There was also a more gravelly quality to the voice, which indicated a heavy night.

'You look well, Ernie.'

'Tyler, I feel like shit,' he croaked. 'I woke up on a table in Chicote's Bar. Is there any coffee in that pot?'

'Sure.' Alverson pushed his empty cup across the table and Hemingway filled it and drank deeply, just before sitting down. 'Do join us.'

'You goin' to introduce me, Tyler?'

'Why not? Ernie Hemingway, meet Callum Thomas.'

Cal just held out his hand, not in the least fazed by the false name, paying no attention to the way that the American squeezed it far too hard, just as he ignored the look in those reddened eyes that went with it. As he had observed before, this was a man who liked to dominate.

'So, Mr Thomas, how does someone like you end up face down in a river?'

'Drinking too much, maybe,' Cal replied, holding the stare.

'I'd take that as a warning, Ernie.'

'Was it meant as that, Mr Thomas?'

Cal smiled, but there was no humour in his voice. 'It has been my practice in life, Mr Hemingway, never to warn people.'

The decision that he was dealing with a possible bully was quickly arrived at and there was only one way to counter that: make it known right away that you are up for a scrap. The mutual stare, still in place, lasted only a few more seconds. Then Hemingway laughed, a booming sound that filled the room and turned heads.

'Maybe, Mr Thomas, we'll have a drink sometime.'

'If you wish.'

'Hey there,' Alverson cried, looking towards the door to the lobby. 'Here comes the lovely Florencia, and at a run.'

Cal could see her hair was still tousled from sleep and what clothes she was wearing had been flung on; whatever it was she was coming to say had to be important and he stood to go and meet her halfway, only to be given the news with a shout.

'The Nationalist pigs will attack Madrid in two days.'

That got Alverson and Hemingway to their feet as well, but it was Tyler who spoke. 'How do you know?'

'Some comrades have found the plans in an Italian tank,' she answered, breathlessly, grabbing a roll from the bowl on the table. 'I must go to the front.'

'You can't print that, Tyler, it will tell Franco his plans are no longer secret.'

The American looked at the other occupants, all of whom were staring at Florencia, now munching away. 'Can't see why not, brother, it's not much of a secret.'

That was when it became easy to tell the journalists from the rest of the hotel guests: they were the ones running off to the phones, and it had to be said that Hemingway, hung-over as he was, led the pack and showed that elbows made good weapons.

In the end, it was not a scoop, it was common knowledge; Largo Caballero came on the radio to announce to the world the impending attack, and worse, as far as Cal Jardine was concerned, he told the enemy just how and where they were going to be repulsed, naming by number and strength the newly formed brigades that had been cobbled together in an attempt to impose some order on the militias who still constituted the majority of fighters.

Trying to calm an excited Florencia, he knew he had to go back to Barcelona, first to arrange to see if any package had arrived for Mr Maxim, and suggested she come with him, an offer that she would not accept, but she was not about to say goodbye to Callum Jardine without a proper parting, albeit a very quick one; the situation did not allow for languorous carnality.

They found Tyler Alverson in the hotel lobby, camera over his shoulder and dressed in the kind of garments that suggested, despite his protestations, he was going to look for a story where the bullets flew. The look he gave Cal when he said he had to make a quick trip to Barcelona, while Florencia was staying in Madrid, was one designed to take the rise out of him.

'Don't you worry, Cal, I will take care of your gal.'

'That's what worries me, Tyler.'

In truth, it was not the American who worried him but Florencia herself; she thought herself immune from harm and she would, regardless of what he said, want to be in the forefront of the fighting, doing battle alongside her comrades, many of whom, as he had seen in Barcelona, were like her, young women. He had tried to lecture her upstairs about taking care and she had responded with her customary dismissals and a confidence not in the least dented by what she had experienced up till now.

'We will beat them into the dust, *querido*!'

It had been impossible not to laugh, and there was no derision in it either. She just looked so damned beautiful in her fighting overalls, with the heavy pistol at her hip; blonde hair, golden olive skin, dark-brown eyes and that smile to melt his heart. If he had ever wondered why he was proposing to do what he was about to try and achieve, standing before him was the answer.

He paid for the room for another week, then departed to the sound of air raid sirens and the citizens rushing for the shelters, which was followed by a snowstorm of leaflets which filled the sky. He only had to open a window to catch one and his schoolboy Latin aided him in reading the warning message to the people of Madrid, telling them to surrender or the Nationalist aviators would wipe them off the face of the earth.

CHAPTER NINETEEN

Caballero's stupid radio announcement of both the forthcoming assault and the intended response had made the road situation ten times worse; anyone who had hung on in the hope that things would improve was on the road, as well as a suspicious number of armed men of fighting age who seemed to be more concerned with directing traffic out of the city than helping in the forthcoming battle.

It took three days to get to Barcelona and when he arrived he found the lower parts of the Ritz had been turned into some kind of workers' canteen, which made the juxtaposition of those who ran the hotel with the stream of armed and hungry men who used the dining room a sight to see. The reception was still functioning as it had previously, as were most of the upper floors, and he had no trouble in either retrieving his luggage or getting a room.

As soon as he picked up a newspaper, it was obvious the Nationalist attack had pressed even further from the western suburbs towards the centre of Madrid, which made him worry – something to which he was not generally prone. He had been troubled during the Great War about a Zeppelin bomb dropping on his wife, but that had been a long time ago and as a proportion of risk it was small. Likewise he always carried concerns about any men he commanded, with the caveat that they were soldiers and knew the risks of combat.

Florencia was different; she would be in the anarchist front line wherever that was, and she was part of a force that lacked both the weapons and the knowledge to take on those they were fighting. Would the Russians support the anarchists? They might if the whole Madrid position was threatened but he would not put it past the communists to sacrifice their political rivals in the same way Manfred Decker had done to Laporta's men on the borders of Aragón.

He had to put that aside, for gnawing on his concerns for her would serve no purpose, yet he found himself praying to any God that would listen to keep her safe, and he made a call to her family home, where at least he could converse with her mother and father, both naturally worried, to reassure them she was safe, even if he was far from certain he was right.

There was no news from Monaco, hardly surprising given the limited time since his return, which meant he would have to endure an agonising wait while events unfolded to the west. Having told the reception desk prior to leaving for Madrid that anything for Mr Maxim was for him, he did consider having a word with the concierge – a fellow accustomed to meeting the requests, however strange, of the hotel guests – to forward anything so addressed to the Florida Hotel.

That had to be put aside, given he could not risk it being sent on to a Madrid under what amounted to a siege. Quite apart from the difficulties of delivery, he had no idea if any kind of postal censorship was in place, nor of the nature of what he was going to receive, but he had to find out what was going on and he was not prepared to just rely on the Republican press.

His lifeline became the expensive radio he bought and sneaked into the hotel, as well as a map and the telephone. With his own set, albeit he kept the sound level low, he was able to listen to both sides as well as the BBC Empire Service. Their reporting of Spain was slim but it was good on the international ramifications, which amounted, it seemed, to who could outfib whom.

With the Spanish stations it was necessary to listen to repeat bulletins to make sure he was hearing it right, and naturally the news from the capital was mixed, being tinged with the needs of propaganda, but with difficult filtering it seemed there were limited gains for the insurgents.

But it was not all one-sided; cheering news came of dogfights over the city as Russian fighters, put up for the first time, surprised the Italian and German bombers – now dropping high explosives, not leaflets – though the figures for what they were reported to have shot down were not to be taken literally, and surely such biplanes had faced opposition from the faster Italian Fiats; certainly the Nationalists claimed so.

But, of course, there was a high degree of boasting on both sides – the Nationalists insisted they would celebrate some national saint's day in Madrid, but that looked unlikely. The militias claimed they were more than a match for the Army of Africa and that was not possible. Exaggerated casualty figures he would expect as the norm and he made no suppositions on his map until he was sure of the truth. Yet what he saw was plain: the Republic was losing ground, even if there had been no collapse.

It came as a shock to hear that Caballero and his government had abandoned Madrid and fled to Valencia, a junta being appointed to defend the city, with names he had never heard of, and that made little impression as to them being good or bad appointments. Difficult as it was, the telephone brought some clarity, as he was able to have brief and shouted conversations with Alverson, who retired after each day's fighting to the Florida Hotel.

As far as the American knew, over a crackly line, Florencia was alive. 'But they are being beaten back time after time, Cal. Those poor bastards out there are fighting tanks with nothing but rifles and petrol bombs.'

'What the hell is that?'

'Something our kids learnt from the Moroccan Regulares. You fill a bottle with petrol, jam in a rag that soaks up enough to be flammable, and when a tank comes along you light the cloth and throw it, that is if a machine gun has not cut you down in the process. Damned effective, though, if you can hit your target.'

'Do you know where Florencia is?'

'On the western edge of the Casa de Campo the last time I saw her. Now I've got to go, there's a queue for this phone line.'

'I'll try to call you tomorrow. Good luck.'

Cal went back to the maps; the Casa de Campo was an old royal hunting ground as big as Richmond Park, forming a buffer for the city as well as a lung, but being open country it would be hard to defend and, he suddenly realised, a place as dangerous for Alverson as it would be for any militia defender.

He was also wondering at the tactics. The desire to hold ground was understandable, especially since the main working-class district lay to the west of the River Manzanares right in the path of the Nationalists, and therefore the place where the majority of those defending the capital lived; they would not want to give up their homes.

Yet the way to beat Franco was to bleed him – it took not great genius to work out he only had a finite number of regular colonial troops, backed by his highly effective Moroccan levies, and over open parkland like the Casa de Campo trained soldiers had to have the advantage, never mind that they also had superior weaponry; they would impose losses rather than suffer them.

Ground could be as much of a trap as a symbol, especially if you possessed limited firepower, thus it made sound tactical sense to draw your enemy into concentrating on an objective you could defend, like a bridge, with the added bonus that it could be blown if it looked like being lost.

That might force an attempt at a boat crossing, which, if undertaken against entrenched opposition on the far bank, was bound to result in heavy casualties, and, in the first place, did the Nationalists have the necessary craft to transport fighting troops over water with enough equipment to give battle?

Endless speculation can drive you mad, but it was unavoidable given he had nothing else to do, apart from eat, have an occasional drink, and, with his black and red CNT armband once more on his arm, pound the streets of Barcelona, walking past other luxury hotels that had been turned into political headquarters, or down the wide tree-lined boulevards past knots of armed men.

Surprisingly, the message from Drouhin, when it came, was verbal; he had expected it to be in writing, yet there was sense in the method when he considered it – anything committed to paper could be read by eyes other than those you knew you could trust. When the phone rang in his room the desk told him that there was a gentleman to see him, and Cal went down to the lobby to find, waiting, being passed by streams of scruffy workers, what could only be described as a dandy.

A gentleman of advanced years and slim build, he was clad in beautifully cut clothes, set off by a yellow silk waistcoat, a four-in-hand tie, and spats over highly polished shoes, while in his gloved hand was a silver-topped malacca cane. He had a narrow, high-boned face and a set of grey, waxed and well-tended moustaches over a trimmed goatee beard. It came as no surprise to Cal Jardine when he addressed him in French.

'Monsieur Maxim?' As soon as Cal nodded, the man rose, his fine nose twitching as if picking up an untoward smell. 'I cannot believe it is safe to talk in this place.'

'Then we shall walk, monsieur.'

The elderly dandy nodded and looked Cal up and down, sniffed disapprovingly at his clothing – he was in blouson and twills – picked up the homburg hat which lay on the seat beside him and placed it with some care on his head. The cane then flicked towards the now unmanned door and he waited till Cal moved, following in his wake.

Out on the street, the malacca cane was elegantly used, its ferrule striking a steady tattoo as they made their way along busy pavements and streets rendered noisy by passing traffic. He said nothing until they were out onto the wide plaza where, separated from road noise and able to ensure he was not overheard, he passed on what he had been sent to impart.

To a man not easy to shock, what he said was startling, so much so that Cal could not believe he was telling the truth as relayed to him by Drouhin – had there been some leak? Could this dandy really be saying to him that the best place to buy what was needed was from Nazi Germany?

They traversed the plaza three times with much repetition, so that the unnamed dandy was sure Monsieur Maxim had all the names and contact details memorised – not easy, as one, a German-speaking Greek, went by the name of Manousos Constantou-Georgiadis. He owned an Athens company whose main shareholder was Rheinmetall-Borsig, and that German enterprise, which made armaments, was controlled by none other than the deputy Führer, Hermann Göring.

'The old gentleman of Monaco assures you that should you contact the Greek gentleman and make known what it is you need, he will take the matter to Göring, where he is sure you will receive a positive response, though he also advises the price you will be charged will be painful.'

'He did not propose any alternative?'

'Only some countries who might seek to take your money and avoid delivery.'

'And the Germans will not?' Cal asked, making no attempt to disguise the irony.

'Greed will ensure they do not. Now, if you are clear in the details I have given you, I will depart.'

Cal said goodbye to the old fellow, wondering if he should pinch himself, yet there was one task he had to carry out very quickly. In a code only he would understand he had to get down on paper the details he had been given before they slipped entirely from his mind. He would need to get to Valencia and see if he could convince the people with whom he was dealing that this was on the up and not some fiddle.

But before that he was determined to go to Madrid and find Florencia.

Miles away it was clear much of the city was ablaze, or had been; Madrid was covered in a blanket of smoke, with black plumes rising from places still on fire and, closer, the crump of artillery shells registered faintly for the first time, along with that strange feeling of the air around you moving. The only blessing was that the jams had ceased; everyone who was going had gone and what little traffic there was flowed freely in one direction: towards the battle.

He was stopped on the outskirts by militiamen checking his papers, with deep suspicion very evident, which did not surprise him; one of the things he had heard on the radio was an early claim from General Mola, who was in command of the assault on the capital, that, as well as the four columns which had advanced on Madrid, he had what he called a 'fifth column' inside the city, creating a scare in which innocents risked being shot as suspected spies.

Once in the city the noise of battle was constant, and as well as the whining sound of shells coming in, then the boom of them exploding, there was the distant rattle of gunnery, volley fire from small arms and the occasional staccato sound of a machine gun.

Planes were in the air, but not many, and they were mostly Russian biplanes on patrol, but he had passed several bombed buildings and one street closed off, in which a downed Italian bomber lay wrecked and twisted. He could feel on his tongue the dust that permeated everything in an urban battle area and see in the faces of those he drove past that etched look of fear which comes from not knowing if the next bullet, shell or bomb is meant for you.

With lots of time to think there was one thing Cal Jardine knew: if he was about to get involved in the fighting – very likely, given Florencia – he did not want to be part of anything structured, a member of a militia or some International Brigade. All he wanted was to find out where the anarchist forces were fighting, which was where she would be, and get alongside her.

That way he might be able to keep her alive, for try as he had, he could think of no way to detach her from her cause; she had grown up with it and it had formed a large part of her life. In his heart he knew that as long as the battle went on she would want to be in the thick of it, and by extension, so would he. Buying arms, even if he doubted it was truly possible, could wait till the fate of Madrid was decided.

With darkness falling he made straight for the Hotel Florida on the very good grounds that she might well be using it as a base. Besides that, if she was not, the war reporters would know as much about what was going on as anyone, and he trusted Tyler Alverson, as he had already, to keep tabs on her location if he could.

Not that it was easy: he kept getting stopped at checkpoints and his papers were getting tattered from being so often examined. As well as that, many of the streets were being used as sheep and cattle pens and those he suspected owned the animals had set up shelters in which to live. By the time he got to the hotel it was clear, by the diminishing noise level, that, as darkness fell, the fighting was slacking off.

The room, when he got to it, was empty, with no evidence that she had been back since he left, and that was a worry, yet he had to avoid the temptation to just go looking. With his limited Spanish and obvious foreignness, even if he did have papers, he was safer at the Florida until he knew what was going on. Albeit under a fine layer of dust and a skeleton staff, the hotel was still functioning, but there was scant evidence of any of the reporters.

Yet there was food in the kitchens, no doubt bought from the streets he had passed through, and, of course, wine in the cellars. He treated himself to some Castilian lamb and a good bottle from the best Spanish region and bodega he knew, a Vega Sicilia Unico from Ribera del Duero. If he was going to get involved in this war it would be a long time before he would get anything as good.

He was in the bar when the first of the reporters began to troop back in from a day of observation, which got him many a dusty look from grimy hacks who were both hungry and thirsty, one of whom was Tyler Alverson who, grubby as he was, shouted for a beer and flopped down on a chair next to Cal.

'Don't ask till I've had a drink.'

'Bad?'

Alverson just shook his head and picked up the cold beer, drinking deeply, paused for one breath, then emptied the glass. Cal immediately ordered another.

'The Foreign Legion took the San Fernando Bridge this morning and got into the University district, though by Christ it cost them plenty.'

'Worth it,' Cal replied, his heart sinking; he was wondering how, when the commanders must have known the river bridges had to be held whatever the cost, they had allowed one to be lost. 'Florencia?'

'She's some dame,' Alverson added. 'A *dinamitera*.'

'We had those in Barcelona.'

'She throws a mean grenade.'

'I need to get to her, Tyler. Is she still in the Casa de Campo?'

'The bit they still hold, which ain't going to be much. That's the other place the Regulares attacked. I'll take you there in the morning.'

'Not now?'

Alverson shook his head as though the suggestion was absurd. 'You don't go far after dark, and certainly not towards the front. There are too many trigger-happy guys out there just itching to shoot at anything that moves.' He looked at Jardine keenly. 'You haven't heard about the Model Prison?'

'No. I've been out of touch with news, on the road.'

'This one won't be on the radio, unless the Nationalists get hold of it. Some of our finest went to the Model Prison, evacuated the inmates to some place further east and massacred them as potential spies. They say there are hundreds of bodies in a mass grave.'

'How could they be spies when they were in prison?'

'Blame that stupid bastard Mola, him and his goddam fifth column.' Alverson called for another beer. 'He's got everybody looking at everybody else like they're traitors.'

'He has to have some friends in the city.'

'They've either gone or are in hiding. I gotta eat something. You?'

'Been there, but I'll join you and you can bring me up to date.'

What Cal Jardine heard was a sorry tale; the militias were suffering badly and, as he suspected, tanks, artillery and heavy weapons were often not committed, though Alverson insisted it was because of scarcity more than politics.

'No, brother, the soldiers and airmen are doing their best. The politics are here in the city centre and it runs right to the top. Caballero tried to get the POUM into his government after the anarchists joined, but the Soviet ambassador vetoed that idea, no doubt on orders from Moscow. If Joe Stalin hates anything it's a Trotskyite, so it was no POUM or no more weapons.'

Talking as he ate, it did not get any better; the communists had taken over security, the Civil Guard had been purged and the Assault Guard sent to Valencia, while suspected opponents were being rounded up by NKVD-led patrols. Yet in amongst the gloom, Alverson had positives, not least the way the *madrileños* had responded to the threat to their city.

'Every hand was put to the pump, Cal – women and kids carrying rocks for barricades, men digging trenches, not a factory that did not have its own militia unit. The pity is they do not have enough weapons, and then only small arms. But they don't hold back, they attack even when they know they can't win.'

'That I have seen before.'

'I don't know whether to pity them or just admire them.'

'Can they hold, Tyler?'

'I'm no military man, Cal, but unless they get reinforcements I think it might be time to light out.'

'Not without Florencia.'

'That struck, eh? I wish you luck, brother.' Just then there was a bellow, another American voice shouting for food and drink, which brought one unnecessary word from Alverson. 'Ernie.' Surprisingly he waved Hemingway over, then reacted to the look he got from his companion. 'He might be a pain in the ass but he's one hell of a reporter. Ask him if they can hold.'

The man's dark hair and moustache seemed full of the same kind of dust that lay everywhere, and when he sat down it was clear he was weary, and there was silence until he had a tall glass in front of him, whisky of some kind mixed with water, which he drank from deeply. Then he nodded to Cal.

'You came back? Not many doin' that.'

'Not many stayed either, Ernie.'

'Nope. As soon as the shit started flying most of our brave colleagues upped and left for safer climes, afraid of taking a dying, I reckon.'

'And you're not?'

'I've faced my demons in Italy in '18.'

'And,' Tyler Alverson said, with heavy emphasis, 'you have been trying to get yourself killed ever since.'

'Charmed life, Tyler.'

'Cal wants to know if the place will hold.'

Hemingway sat forward then, in a way so forceful a lesser man might have felt threatened.

'If it does not, there won't be many of Franco's boys still standing. These *madrileños* will fight for every stone. I have never met folk so fearless. It's like they welcome death.'

There was a look in the American's eye then, and it was remarkably like envy. Draining his glass, he hauled himself to his feet, waved a big hand, and left.

Cal Jardine was about to ask Hemingway why someone so successful was here in a war zone, but it died in his throat – it was a question he could have posed to himself. But the subject did surface later as they had a drink in a nearby bar called Chicote's, where what journos were left in Madrid went to do what they did everywhere in the world, get plastered.

Big Ernie was a topic of conversation it was hard to avoid, so telling was his presence, and, it had to be admitted, there was a degree of envy for his success and reputation, though not from Tyler Alverson. He had come to Spain as soon as the war began with his latest woman and not his wife, another reporter called Martha, who was filing for *Collier's Weekly*, though by all accounts it was a pretty stormy relationship in which they competed more than cooperated.

'So where is she, this Martha?' Cal asked, as the press corps started singing a filthy drinking song that would see one of them having to down something disgusting as a forfeit.

'Time to go, Cal, this can only get worse. And Martha – covering somewhere else, which is what she does after every screaming match.'

CHAPTER TWENTY

Having brought his map with him, Cal was able to bring it up to date, and it was not looking good despite Hemingway's confidence. To the north, the Nationalists, having in fact secured two bridges, should have been able to push deep into the University Quarter, a place of little domestic occupation, large buildings and lots of wide open spaces, sweeping grassy areas, plazas and wide boulevards, perfect for an army intent on avoiding the heavily built-up areas.

The key now was to first contain them there and hold the rest of the bridges to the south, then to counter-attack, though he had no idea if the Republic had the means – it would not have done his thought process much good to have known neither did the Madrid military commanders. He had no concept of the depth of the fog surrounding operations but it took little time to find out.

Alverson took him out just before dawn, the time when any

assaults planned overnight would be launched, and they joined a stream of fighters crossing the wide Segovia Bridge, passing through sandbagged emplacements equipped with heavy machine guns and mortars and, only just visible, a pair of heavily camouflaged T26 Russian tanks. Cal was very tempted to look them over out of professional interest, they being some of the best of their kind in the world and reputedly more than a match for the German Panzers, but there was no time.

The signs of actual battle were not long in showing: trees shattered by artillery fire, shell craters and even deeper, wider depressions where the Casa de Campo had been heavily bombed, and, incongruously, little bunches of flowers, no doubt marking where some relative had fallen, their bodies carried back into the city along with those merely wounded. Then there was the smell, of burning and cordite mixed with the gassy odour of churned-up ground, the only one seemingly out of place the strong stink of petrol.

Florencia, when they found her, looked haggard, her face not only grubby but having lost its total fullness, and with bags formed under her eyes. Nor did she possess her usual fountain of energy; the kiss she gave Cal Jardine was as weary as the clasp she managed with her arms, and that was not easy, she being festooned with grenades attached to her overalls with sewn-on thread. Tyler Alverson merely got a nod.

'Who's in command?'

She just shrugged and waved a lazy arm, this as the first distinctive phut came of a discharged mortar. Habit made Jardine duck low, which got him a look of disdain from those around Florencia; he would find out later they had endured days of this. The shell passed overhead to land with a crump on the road that led to the bridge;

hitting the metalled surface the explosion was made more deadly by the lack of absorption in the solid roadway.

The screams that arose were mixed; some from those caught in the blast, others shouting to get into the trees. Several more landed with a small radius behind them and Cal knew instinctively what was coming. The mortar team were isolating those in the front line preparatory to an infantry assault, and overhead they could hear, too, the drones of approaching bombers. Reassuringly the higher pitch of fighter engines soon materialised as they tried to engage the bombers well away from the city centre.

'Where's the store of grenades?' he asked; if that was what she was doing, he would work with her.

'There are no more, *querido*. Me and my fellow *dinamiteros* are wearing the last of our supplies.'

'Ammunition?'

'Low,' she sighed, 'very low.'

'Then you should withdraw across the bridge and get behind the machine guns.'

Some of the fire he knew so well resurfaced then, as she spat out, '*Never.*'

The mortar fire had not ceased but the range was steadily dropping, and as it did so he saw some of the men present throw back a canvas cover to reveal lines of dark-green wine bottles, each with a bit of protruding rag.

'Petrol bombs, Cal,' murmured Alverson.

Never having seen them used, Jardine was thinking that fuel would have been better used laying a trap for what was coming: a shallow trench into which it could have been poured, then set alight once the enemy was over it. There was no point in that now, for it was obvious these worker fighters were not going to wait to be attacked – they intended to go forward first.

'Have the Regulares got automatic weapons, Florencia?'

'A few, not many.'

'Any spare rifles?'

She called to someone, another young woman, dark-skinned and just as weary, who came towards him with a Mauser and five rounds; even he understood the Spanish for 'that is all' . Tactical sense made what they were planning to do – not just stand and fight, but attack – utter madness.

It was made worse by there seeming to be no directing brain; the decision to move seemed like one arrived at by some collective osmosis. No order was given, but a mass of fighters, hundreds in number, armed with what weapons they had and many of these unreliable petrol bombs, began to move, not with haste but with a palpable and steely determination, several lit torches flaring in the line, this while Alverson's camera clicked.

'Do you come forward, Tyler?'

'No, Cal, this is as far as I go.'

A lone, young, male voice began to sing the anarchist song 'A las Barricadas', which Cal had heard in Barcelona, and it was soon taken up by others, rising to fill the woods through which they moved until it was being bellowed as they moved out into a large clearing, at the opposite side of which was the enemy, who, clearly under orders, fired off a rifle salvo. That it was effective made no difference; with a wild scream the mixed-sex militia just rushed forward.

Those with rifles were firing from the hip and shoulder on the move, those with bottles leaning into a torch-bearer to get lit their cloth fuses. As soon as they were aflame the run was at as much speed as they could muster, one or two crumpling at the knees as they were shot, others behind them picking up their dropped makeshift bombs, which had not broken on the soft uncut grass.

Seeking to stand still and aim, it was difficult for Cal Jardine to pick targets through a throng in front of him, that not made any easier by the dark-green uniforms of those he was seeking to kill, which in the trees made them indistinct. Five rounds did not go far even if they were effective and he had little choice but to go after Florencia, who had a grenade in one hand, with the other ready to pull the pin.

She had to be a target, so dropping the rifle he hauled out his pistol and began to fire at what lay right in front of her, his only hope in emptying it that he would disturb anyone aiming for what had to be one of their most dangerous opponents. At the same time, even if he thought her crazy, he had to admire the sheer fearless brio of her charge, not that she was alone in that, it was common to them all.

His curiosity as to why the bottles remained unthrown till the last possible moment was explained when they began to smash against the trees, the flames immediately spreading to the branches and the tinder-dry grass beneath, several inches long and untidy in clumps; they would not have broken otherwise. Florencia had thrown her first grenade, shouting as she did so to warn her comrades to duck down, immediately breaking the thread on another, and she hugged the ground.

Cal grabbed two off her, pulled the pins and threw them into the rapidly spreading flames of the burning petrol. These were sending up plumes of black smoke, which was working to obscure the anarchist fighters. It was also making life very uncomfortable for a unit whose attack had been forestalled, for with a slight easterly wind, the smoke and flames were being driven into their position. Shouted commands were coming out of the treeline and it was obvious the troopers were retiring.

Staying alongside Florencia, and after she had thrown another grenade, Cal was able to grab her and stop her entering the wood, where she would be isolated and a sitting duck – especially since her comrades' forward movement had petered out through a lack of both firepower and wine bottles – not that he got much thanks.

It was only when she struggled to get free that Cal realised she was in a state of such exhaustion she must be near to hallucinating; her eyes were like those of a wild animal, her kicking and screaming the act of a mad creature, both of which stopped abruptly when he slapped her hard. She stood stock-still, in shock, staring at him for several seconds, then burst into tears.

With the edge of the wood now ablaze and forming an impenetrable barrier, it was a peaceful withdrawal, for not even the most rabid militia fighter thought they could hold what they had taken. If their enemy did not advance as soon as the fire died down they would move to left or right to take them in flank. The real question was could they hold their original position?

What saved them was not their bravery but the arrival of what Alverson had predicted was needed. Unbeknown to those in the Casa de Campo, as they had been fighting the first troops of the International Brigades had come into the city, marching in disciplined columns up the wide boulevards to the cheers and tears of the populace. They did not stop; one brigade headed for the University area, the other straight for the Segovia Bridge and the Casa de Campo.

They heard the clumping boots first as they crept back to their start point, and that induced a frisson of fear; marching boots meant soldiers and that meant Nationalists. But the singing of the communist anthem, 'The Internationale', soon laid that to rest and, with a swaggering fellow at their head, in a cap with his communist red badge very evident, they passed four abreast, staring straight ahead, through the muddled crowd of anarchist fighters. They then began to deploy for battle.

The man at their head, later identified as Manfred Stern, alias General Kléber, stood to one side and began to shout orders to the militias to disperse, to go home and rest. That was when it finally came home to them that these brigades had come to their rescue, and rescue it was, because there was no doubt a Nationalist counter-attack was in preparation, and it was one they could not have withstood.

With Florencia between them in a state of near collapse, Cal Jardine and Tyler Alverson took her back to the hotel, where her lover got her up to their room, took off her filthy clothes, ran her a deep hot bath and lowered her in, then gently washed her body and hair. Having left her to soak for only a minute, he re-entered the bathroom to find her sound asleep, her blonde hair streaming out in the bathwater like the Burne-Jones painting of Ophelia.

Lifting her out was difficult, but when he had, Cal wrapped her in a towel and put her to bed.

The brigades had looked impressive, with their uniform dress and sloped arms, but it took little time to show that they were far from properly trained and nothing demonstrated that more than their losses. Knowing Florencia would sleep for an age, Cal went out to see if any of his boys were present in the other units, knowing he had not seen them at the Segovia Bridge.

He made his way to the University area, where he expected to find fierce fighting, and he found plenty. He also came, at a crawl, across Ernest Hemingway, well forward, right in the thick of a fierce firefight and too close for a non-combatant.

All he got was a nod of recognition and the American's attention went back to the battle before him; what Cal did not find was any of the Olympiad athletes, the men fighting being Italian communists, part of what was called, he discovered from those at the rear, the *Centuria Gastone* after their leader.

From what he could observe, the *Centuria* was attacking without much tactical nous; it was all frontal and fast up against a stout and well-organised defence made up, he suspected, of the hard elements of the Spanish Foreign Legion – odd that it should be non-Spaniards on both sides. Once back out of the fighting zone he noted the number of men being fetched back either as corpses or seriously wounded, and he also ran once more into Hemingway, he likewise observing the numbers.

'They're brave enough,' Hemingway said, as if he was damning with faint praise.

'They're taking casualties to no purpose.'

'Happens in a shooting war, friend.'

'The first people I would shoot are their commanders.'

That got a wry smile and a question. 'You figure you could do better?'

'They're not trained to the requisite standard for such an assault, anyone can see that, and you do not send forward men like that. You form them into a defence and get them to hold ground.'

'So how do you win a battle?'

'Attrition and on-the-job instruction in field tactics, not that those who command them seem to know how.'

'You a soldier, Mr Thomas?'

There was a moment when Cal wondered who he was talking to, until he recalled that was how Alverson had introduced him. 'I was once.'

'That does not surprise me.'

'Why?'

'You look like one, that's why.' Hemingway was staring, but not in an unfriendly way; in fact it was as if he was amused. 'So tell me where you soldiered?'

'Maybe over that drink,' Cal said, stalling, for no good reason he could think of; it just seemed right, or maybe it was habit.

In streets of some fairly smart apartment blocks, obviously the homes of well-heeled *madrileños*, they heard the sounds of echoed commotion, this explained as a small knot of black-clad men emerged from a doorway, dragging in their midst a struggling middle-aged fellow, clearly being arrested. Something he was seeing for the first time made it remarkable, but not so much as what followed next.

Out of the same doorway came Manfred Drecker, as usual smoking one of his long Russian cigarettes in between the wrong fingers, hand held aloft and full of that arrogance and righteousness that Cal recalled so well, while it was obvious, as he glanced in their direction, he immediately recognised him – not hard, he was dressed as Drecker had seen him last – the face screwing up with what looked like rage.

Cal rated that as a bit of an overreaction but he automatically put his hand to his pistol holster and the German's eyes followed it – Drecker would not know it was empty – a move also noticed by Hemingway.

'Friend of yours?'

'Bosom pal.'

The middle-aged captive had been set against the wall of the apartment block and was clearly pleading for mercy, not that it seemed to affect the men who had put him there; they merely stood back and unslung their rifles, shifting the bolts to put a bullet in the chamber.

'What's going on?' Cal yelled in German, which had everyone looking at him, not just Drecker.

'My, you are full of surprises,' Hemingway said laconically.

'What business is it of yours, Jardine?' Drecker demanded.

Aware that the American's thick black eyebrows had gone up in surprise, Cal ignored that and concentrated on what was obviously taking place in front of them, the clear prelude to an execution. Fighting to keep any anger out of his voice – Drecker was a dangerous man – he said slowly, again in German, 'This gentleman with me is an important American journalist. I do not think it will aid our cause for him to see what it is you are planning to carry out.'

'This man is a traitor, a class enemy and a fifth columnist.'

'Comrade Drecker, there is no such thing, it is a figment of General Mola's imagination.'

The use of the word 'comrade' caused Drecker some surprise; Cal had rarely been so polite in the past, but it was necessary to save the life of what could well be an innocent man, now sobbing and on his knees. And even if he was not innocent, the poor fellow was entitled to a trial, but it did not soften Drecker up as he had hoped.

'Then perhaps it is time the Americans, with their soft livers, saw what the revolution does with its traitors.'

'We are not the revolution, comrade, we are the legitimate government of Spain. Those in revolt are the people we are fighting.'

'*We*, Jardine?' Drecker spat.

The idea of being on the same side as the prize shit he was talking to was anathema, but with a life at stake it was worth it. 'You have seen me fight for the Republic.' Then he turned to Hemingway. 'Use your best Spanish, tell him you will let the world know that people are being shot out of hand.'

'I'll try.'

The language was not perfect, little better than Jardine's, but there was no doubting the sentiment or the fervour; what was worrying was the way it seemed to harden a countenance that was already an exercise in humourlessness. Drecker barked a set of orders and up came the rifles. As they did, Cal Jardine's hand went automatically once more to his holster.

'Whoa there, friend,' Hemingway hissed.

It was not that which stopped Cal, it was the look in Drecker's eye, one which promised he would be next against that wall; maybe if he could have dropped him he would have chanced it, then turned the weapon on his men, but his pistol was empty, the means to reload it not available, and somehow it was clear that a threat would not be enough.

At a second bark the rifles came up and took aim at a wailing fellow now with his head near his knees. Drecker gave the order to fire and the bullets slammed into the poor man's body, throwing it back. There was a gleam in Drecker's eye as he stepped forward, took out his pistol, aimed it, then looked at Cal Jardine as if to say 'this should be you'. Then he pulled the trigger, his final indignity the dropping of his used cigarette on the corpse.

The walk towards the pair who had observed this was slow, the words addressed to Cal, the blue eyes as hard as the lips. 'Have a care, Jardine; if you seek to interfere with revolutionary justice you may find that you are the next to be shot.' Drecker spun round, barked an order, and as he marched off his men fell in behind him.

'Nice guy,' said Hemingway.

'I don't see this as a time for irony.'

'I thought you were going to drop him.'

'What would you have done if I'd tried?'

'Knocked you out, what else? He would have had to kill me too.'

'Then you'll be glad to know that my gun has no bullets.'

Hemingway's shoulders were shaking with mirth. 'Now that would have been a dandy trick to pull off. Time, I think, for that drink.'

Cal pointed to the crumpled body, with a deep pool of blood seeping from the shattered head. 'What about him?'

'Number of bodies laying around Madrid on a day like this, one more won't make much difference, and the poor shmuck will never know we just left him to the crows. Besides, I have a pressing need. I want to know why it is Tyler Alverson introduced you by a name that's different from the one that communist guy used, given he seemed to know you real well. I don't know a heck of a lot of German but I take it your real name is Jardine?'

When Cal looked to demur, Hemingway added, 'A dollar bill gets me the hotel register.' It only needed a nod then. 'In my experience a reporter only does that when he's trying to hide a story from a rival.'

CHAPTER TWENTY-ONE

It did not take long to realise that summary executions were taking place all over Madrid, and as far as anyone could tell, all over Spain, if the reports were true. If it was not politics – and there was a lot of that – it would be, Cal thought, all the usual historical reasons that surface when society collapses: the settling of old scores, the avoidance of a due debt or even retaliation for an imagined slight long past. To try and stop it was dangerous and actually futile; it had its own dynamic.

For all they were still amateurs, the International Brigades had halted the Nationalist advance, albeit at a horrendous cost in men wounded and killed, and then began a successful counter-attack. The Foreign Legionnaires – Franco's best troops – were being pushed out of the University district and still the other columns could not breach the defences before the city centre.

There had been any number of crises, the whole defence a close-run thing, with aerial combat daily and the front ebbing to and fro. On one black day, the militias before the Toledo Bridge broke, only the prompt action of the top Spanish general stopping a rout, he rallying the fleeing fighters, then leading them personally back into battle with nothing but his pistol as a weapon.

Florencia, over the next few days, was in a state of emotional turmoil, a very changed person from the one Cal had known, given to sudden outbursts of tears during the day and nightmares later, and in no fit state to go back to the fight. There was no mystery to what he was observing, he had seen it too many times and had blessed his luck that though he could recall clearly the death and mutilation he had witnessed, he also had the capacity to contain it within himself.

She was seeing dead comrades, having visions of heads and limbs being blown off, of smashed bodies with staring eyes, while, on top of that, reliving every action of her own, every grenade thrown, the face of each enemy she had killed and many she had not, who would appear in her dreams like ravenous beasts ready to tear her apart. All he could do was hold her soaked-with-sweat body and comfort her with useless platitudes.

That meant he spent time in the hotel, his only action to acquire bullets for his pistol; he was waiting for Florencia to either recover or admit her problem so he could take her away from the front. If his days had their material comforts, they also brought forth a feeling he should really be on the way to Valencia to find out if the government were willing to buy arms from a source that would scare them rigid; they did not know old Zaharoff as he did – if he said it was safe to deal, that would be the case.

Then there was no avoiding Hemingway, or at least his probing. Tyler Alverson had been taken to task for his subterfuge and had come out fighting, telling his colleague, Ernie, in no uncertain terms that he would have done just the same, while admonishing Cal to stay shtum; not that 'Ernie', when not writing articles about what he was witnessing, failed to press.

'You know, Jardine, I work for one of the best-resourced news-gathering outfits in creation, which has a phenomenal library, and as for contacts, well, you can imagine. So if you have been a naughty boy, it is either in the collective memory or the files. You can save them some dollars by just telling me what I want to know.'

'There's nothing to tell.'

Hemingway then tried to get him drunk and, given he had hollow legs and a big swallow, it had been a challenge to stay sober, or, in truth, to stay quiet when not. For all that, as a companion he grew on Cal; he had a fund of scabrous tales, many of them in which he was the fool or victim, and he was very much a man's man, who promised that they would, one fine day, go hunting game in Wyoming and fish marlin together off the Florida coast.

'Any man that can drink like you, Cal, I call good company.'

Ernie had been an ambulance driver on the Italian Front in the Great War, had a medal for bravery for saving a man's life when wounded himself and, since publishing his first pieces, had covered as many wars as Tyler Alverson; he was a hard man not to respect, even if, when it came to bullfighting, a sport he extolled, Cal was on the side of the animal.

It was strange to observe these journalists; each day they would go out and seek a story, into the midst of a desperate battle, then come back to their reasonably safe haven – the city was still being bombed – and act as though it was just a normal day's work. Tyler and Ernie ribbed each other but it was clear there was mutual respect, and Cal took pleasure in both their company, while keeping a tight lid on his own history.

Hemingway had checked up on Manfred Drecker, now a member of the so-called Fifth Regiment, which, once the Civil Guard had been purged, was now responsible for security in the capital. Wholly communist, they were committed killers, and he also pointed out one thing Cal had not noticed: the correspondent of the Russian newspaper, *Pravda*, did not reside with the other journalists in the Florida Hotel – he was accommodated in the Soviet Embassy.

'Making up stories.'

'Lies more like.'

It was all very chummy, but then came the day of the file, produced and waved over a dry Martini by Ernest Hemingway, unusually having stayed in the hotel when everyone else had departed to the front.

'Cost an arm and a leg in cables, Jardine, but I have got you nailed.'

'Can I see?' Cal asked, nodding to the folder lying on the mahogany bar, hoping it did not contain too much.

'Hell no! If you do you'll find out who's spilling your beans. But I now know you are more than just an ex-soldier, so what are you up to?'

'I can't be up to much, Ernie, I have spent the past few days eating, drinking and nursing my woman.'

'Hell, I wish I was nursing mine. How is she?'

Cal looked into his drink. 'You know, Ernie, that's the first time you've asked.'

'Don't like to pry.'

'She'll recover, people do.'

'You?'

'Never had the problem, too callous probably.'

The folder was lifted and went to Hemingway's nose, as though he was sniffing the contents. 'What's it like shooting a guy in cold blood?'

'It's like shooting an animal, and it was not cold blood.'

'Kinda rough finding a guy in your own bed and with your wife.'

That image was one he saw more often than most: the terrified face of Lizzie's naked lover, her just as fearful, just as he put a bullet through his eye. He shook his head and lifted it as Ernie responded.

'Had a dame once who threw me over. Maybe I should have shot the bastard she married but, unlike you, I would not have been acquitted.'

The fact that Cal was now looking into the mirror behind the bar, and the expression on his face, made Ernie turn round, to see Florencia, still pale and drawn but nothing like she had been, standing a few feet away. Had she heard what Hemingway said, because it was not something Cal had ever told her about?

'Good news. Juan Luis is on the way from Saragossa and he is bringing with him the Barcelona militia.'

'I hope you're not planning to join them?'

She nodded towards Hemingway. 'This, what he said, is it true, *querido*?'

There was no point in denying it, so he nodded, unsure of her reaction given she turned and left. 'Thanks, Ernie.'

The reply showed that for a man not easily embarrassed it was still possible. 'I didn't shoot the poor guy, you did.'

* * *

Florencia neither immediately mentioned what she had overheard, nor allowed herself to be swayed when Cal found her changing into her fighting overalls. His assertion that she was unfit for combat was not met with her usual temper, but quietly rebuffed.

'*Querido*, sometimes you must just do things. These are my people coming to Madrid, men and women I have grown up with, and they are coming to drive the Nationalist pigs into a sewer, which is too good for them.'

'OK. But I will be with you at all times.'

'In battle?' she asked, with just a hint of her old coquettishness.

'No.'

The hand on his cheek was cool. 'That pleases me.'

'One promise: that once Mola's columns have been thrown back, you will come with me to Valencia. You know why and I will need your help.'

She smiled. 'For the cause, *querido*, as much as to be with you.'

'I can't marry you, much as I would like to. My wife is a Catholic and won't consider a divorce.'

For the first time since he had brought her back from the Casa de Campo she laughed. 'I am an anarchist, I don't believe in marriage. Tell me about what the American said.'

'How long before Juan Luis gets here?'

She accepted that he did not want to say. 'Not long, and I want to meet him on the Saragossa Road. Let me come into Madrid as a Catalan.'

If anything, Juan Luis Laporta, as well as his men, looked hardened by what they had been experiencing, leaner and fitter, not that their efforts had produced much in the way of an advance in Aragón; that had become a stalemate, thus, on paper, the reason for the shift to Madrid where they could be of more use.

It did not take long to establish the real reason – the communists were taking control and needed to be checked; three thousand Barcelona anarchists were just the people to do it, this extracted from their leader as Florencia went down the long line of trucks to say hello to many of her old comrades. It was plain he was now trusted.

'You must be careful, Juan Luis,' Cal said, having told him of what he had witnessed: not just that one execution but clear evidence of others, hard to miss with their bodies left in the street or hanging from lampposts with placards pinned on their chests detailing their supposed crimes. 'And don't think they won't suspect your reasons for coming here. I don't have to tell you they are suspicious of everyone.'

'Task number one, my friend, is to eject the Nationalists, then we can deal with Stalin's lackeys.' He had lost none of his bravado, Laporta, evidenced by what followed. 'And when we have cleansed Madrid, we can go back to Barcelona and shoot their Catalan cousins.'

'There's a couple of war correspondents I'd like you to meet. Americans.'

Laporta's eyes narrowed. 'To tell them what?'

'About yourself and the aims of your movement.'

'In America they execute anarchists.'

'They're not in America, they are here.'

'To the front first, let us see the eyes of Franco's pigs, then maybe I will talk with these *Yanquis*.'

The stop on the Saragossa Road had been to form up the column on foot; like the International Brigades, they would march through Madrid to the cheers of the locals, to bolster their morale. They already knew which part of the front they were going to – their job was to throw the Spanish Foreign Legion back over the San Fernando Bridge.

Invited, he declined to join in the march, at the head of which would be Juan Luis, and behind him each company, for they had formed themselves properly into a quasi-military unit, each led by a commander. Quite apart from it being Laporta's treat, he would have felt like a charlatan.

That Florencia was determined to take part was only natural, and it was a positive that in meeting some of her long-time companions she seemed to have regained some of her spirit. She entered Madrid just behind Laporta, her hand raised and fist clasped, singing, along with the others, all the best-known anarchist songs. And, as had the brigades, they went straight to the fighting front.

'So what happens now, Cal?'

Alverson asked this while not bothering to hide his disappointment; not only was his prime story not doing what he should, namely seeking out weapons and telling him how, but Laporta, the man of the moment, had declined to talk to him. They could see him now, moving around as if he were a great general, making encouraging remarks to his men.

'It's too late to launch any attacks today,' was the deliberately misunderstanding reply.

'You know that's not what I mean.'

'Tyler, I won't leave here without Florencia, and she won't go until the enemy have at least been sent back across the river, but she has promised me that once things are settled here she will help me.'

'And this Laporta guy?'

'Let me flatter him a little.'

'Up for that, is he?'

'And some.'

'Hello,' Alverson exclaimed. 'Here come reinforcements.'

There was no mistaking the provenance of the approaching column, some hundred men in their black uniforms, and with Drecker at their head it was clear here were members of the Fifth Regiment come to strut their stuff.

'Not to fight?' Alverson asked, when Cal mentioned that.

'They have done precious little fighting up till now. Killing yes, but not anybody who has a gun to point at them.'

The jeers from Laporta's men were quick to arise and they were sustained as the communists marched past them, accompanied by a raft of rude gestures. Surprisingly, they halted and about-turned before falling out, dispersing into the line of buildings that backed on to what was the present front line, part of the university. Only Drecker stayed in sight, lighting up once more.

'Maybe they are here to fight, Cal – to show the anarchists they are not the only hope.'

'Possible, I suppose. Let me go and talk to Napoleon over there and see if I can get him to give you an interview.'

In the gathering gloom, Laporta's men were lighting fires, and as he approached him, Cal was vaguely aware that the communists were forming up again – it had been, as he had guessed, no more than grandstanding. By the time he joined the man he had just nicknamed 'Napoleon' they were in the process of marching off back to the city centre.

Burly, still in his battered leather coat and hat, Laporta was playing the part Cal had assigned to him to perfection, hands on hips, spinning round, as though his eyes could encompass a battlefield he had not a chance of seeing properly without attracting sniper fire. Seeing Cal approach, he grinned and spoke in a loud voice.

'You examined the enemy position?' Cal nodded; he had done so through a periscope, which only gave a partial impression of what lay before them. 'In the morning we will take back the San Fernando Bridge.'

'Juan Luis, they have machine guns on fixed arcs of fire.' That got a dismissive shrug. *No change there,* thought Cal. 'It is what the Allies faced in the Great War and I think you know how many died.'

'Mr friend, we must show these communists our mettle.'

'That would make sense if they were showing theirs alongside you.'

It took some effort to get Florencia back to the Florida that night, but Cal insisted, not with foreboding – you cannot think like that – but people would die on the morrow and he wanted her to himself before they faced that. Awoken when it was still dark, it was a silent pair that dressed and made their way to rejoin what was now known as the 'Laporta Column'.

At least, this time, everyone had a weapon and the whole of Madrid had been resupplied with ammunition. Also, they were fighting over ground that had already seen much action, so there were lots of craters and dead ground. With what was a sort of bomb squad, he sought to lecture them on how to use that: to crawl from hole to hole until they could get close enough to throw their grenades.

The blowing of loud whistles launched the assault, which was not the only thing that made Cal think of the trenches of the Western Front; likewise the passionate yell as the militiamen and women left cover, the bayonets glinting in the sunlight. Then there came the steady rattle of the machine guns and death for some, terror for others.

The bombing team, the *dinamiteros*, under his guidance, crept out into the no man's land between the lines, seeking to stay below the raking fire that had obviously decimated their comrades, following Cal as he inched forward from crater to crater, then doing as he suggested, spreading right and left. It was only a hope that his call was heard, but crouched, he pulled the pin from his first grenade and set it flying forward, dropping down immediately as the ground before him spurted up displaced mud.

The explosions acted like a spring to those rifle-bearing fighters who had got stuck in dead ground; they leapt up and charged and paid a high price in getting to the enemy position. Cal was up and running too, pistol out, inside a series of entrenchments and sandbagged barricades, shooting until his gun was empty, then picking up a discarded rifle and working with the bayonet as he had been taught, all those years ago, in basic training.

The anarchists took the first position, only to find that their enemies had fallen back a second and prepared line of defence, and with their superior training they had taken their heavy weapons with them. Certainly they suffered – the position was full of the dead and dying of both sides – and as a victory it was only a partial one, for they were nowhere near the bridge.

It took all day to get the rest of the column forward and to make this one legionnaires' trench system their own, to get it ready for the next day's attack, and to also clear the intervening ground of the dead and wounded. For all they had suffered a hundred dead and five times that number with incapacitating wounds, their spirits were high.

As darkness fell, the main body moved back to the start point, where they could eat and sleep, only a strong piquet left behind. They were eating around the relit fires when they heard the sound of boots, and Drecker appeared once more at the head of his company. This time they stopped and shouldered arms, then listened as their commander read to them from the writing of Lenin, no easy task with the accompanying jeers and whistles. After twenty minutes they about-turned and marched off again.

The next three days were nothing short of a disaster, and nothing an exhausted Cal Jardine could say would get Laporta to call off his increasingly costly attacks. Even with wounded fighters returning they were down to a quarter strength and still the bridge eluded them; they were closer – through a periscope you could see the top of the roadway in the centre – they had forced back their enemies, but the cost, even if they were inflicting heavy losses, was disproportionate.

And, at the end of each day's fighting, Drecker would come up with his company of the Fifth Regiment, have a short parade, maybe harangue his men, smoke a fag, then march off again, and as he did this it was impossible to miss the reaction of Juan Luis's face; if he knew he was being goaded it made no difference, even if, on a headcount, there were fewer than four hundred effectives left out of his original three thousand.

The Fifth Company had just marched off, to a lower level of jeers than hitherto, in the main ignored through exhaustion. A near dead-on-his feet Cal Jardine was talking to Alverson and Hemingway, telling them the picture so they could report both on the attacks and the bravery being shown, when the rattle of an automatic weapon broke the stillness.

Cal spun round to see Juan Luis Laporta spin sideways. Worse, Florencia was beside him and she seemed to jerk, then shrink to the ground as he set off towards her as fast as he could. The feeling of the bullet hitting him was like a branding, not a pain, and as it turned him he was vaguely aware that just to his left, bullets were raking the ground; he looked to his right just as one of the firers was upset by panic, and found himself looking to the line of buildings. There was someone there, a vague shape that seemed familiar.

A second bullet took his shoulder, dropping him to his knees, and now he was crawling towards an inert Florencia and Laporta on his hands and knees, his head drooping. All around were cries and shouting, with people running in every direction to what seemed like little purpose. He did get to Florencia and he was sure he said her name, but there was no response and he passed out.

CHAPTER TWENTY-TWO

The antiseptic smell registered first and then, slowly, he opened his eyes. Above his head was a slow circulating ceiling fan and he knew he was in the Barcelona Ritz, yet when he reached out to touch Florencia, not only was she not there but the edge of the bed was too close to his hand. The stains on the ceiling where water had penetrated were wrong, not the sort of thing to be tolerated by the manager of a luxury hotel; but then, it came back to him, there had been fighting.

Turning his head he saw not blonde, tousled hair but another head swathed in bandages a few feet away, in a bed that was near to touching his own; the same on the other side, though the man in that was lying, eyes closed, in seeming contented sleep. That was when the first of the pain kicked in, a dull throb in his shoulder, and there was another, less significant, in his belly. Confused, the head of the nurse, leaning over him and smiling, was what finally told Callum Jardine he was in hospital, and one that was very crowded.

* * *

'You nearly didn't make it, old buddy; you lost a lot of blood and it was touch and go if they could get enough back into you to keep you alive. I couldn't carry you, and if I had not had Ernie Hemingway to help me you would be meat. He's a big strong guy and not too many people seemed to care about you – they were trying to save their own.'

Tyler Alverson said this to a patient now sitting in a state of some shock; the first question he asked the American got a slow and sad shake of the head – Florencia had been dead on arrival at the forward dressing station, and it took some time for that to sink in and to ask about Juan Luis Laporta. He had died on the operating table from a single bullet that had passed though his chest and lungs.

Both bodies had been taken back to Barcelona for burial in the cemetery at Montjuïc. The whole of the city did not turn out for Florencia, the great crowd came to bury Juan Luis Laporta, but she basked in the glory of every anarchist who could walk being at her graveside too, and many of the flowers were split between the two plots.

'The official story is it was accidental discharge, a weapon going off that shouldn't, some schmuck forgetting to put on his safety catch.'

'You believe that?'

'If I don't, Cal, I'm in no position to do anything about it.'

'You could tell the world.'

'And get thrown out of Spain for something I'm not sure of? No thanks. Besides, it might have just been someone who didn't want to die. You said yourself the attacks Laporta was pressing on with were crazy. OK, a lot of people would have been happy to see him dead, but there are too many conspiracies out there to go adding another one, and that would be about someone, I hate to remind you, the world knows nothing about.'

Cal knew he was in a rear area, the town of Tarancón, that he had been in a coma for three weeks and the doctor, a German socialist, had told him that the Battle for Madrid had fizzled out with neither side really able to claim victory. The city was still under threat but Franco had lost too many men to press home a new assault, especially in winter. The Republicans and the Nationalists were regrouping.

Alverson pulled a bottle of Johnnie Walker from his bag and handed it over. 'Ernie says to have this, it cures everything, and to remind you that you are due to go hunting and fishing with him as soon as the war is over.'

'Some pain in the ass, Tyler.'

'Yep, but then you don't compete with the big soft bastard.'

'Thank him for me, for everything. Tell him I'd give him another medal if I had one.'

'Look, I sent word to London, to Vince, and he got in contact with your wife.'

'Who rushed to my bedside,' Cal said bitterly, then regretted it. Lizzie hated blood, hated hospitals, and half the time probably hated him for all the grief he had caused her. The idea of a woman who jumped three feet when a balloon burst coming to a war zone was risible.

'Vince told some guy called Peter Lanchester, who I am asked to cable to say you are out of the woods, but I figure that's your call.'

'Doctor says I can try getting out of bed tomorrow.'

'What you should do is get out of Spain.'

'And ruin your scoop?'

'There will be others, Cal, and you . . .' Alverson did not finish that, but there was no doubting what he felt; going after those weapons could see him killed '. . . well, it ain't worth it.'

'Tell me what's happening, everything.'

'You planning to go home?'

'Just tell me,' Cal replied, so impatiently it supplied an answer to the previous question.

The truth was, not a lot was happening on the original front; it was trenches on both sides before Madrid – with Cal opining that at least they had learnt – the Nationalists holding nearly all of the western suburbs but unable to advance; likewise the defenders, who had dug in where they had no other method and erected near-impenetrable barricades in the working-class districts.

The city was being bombed daily and life was getting harder. A Nationalist assault to the north, an attempt to get across the Corunna Road, had ended up with another set of International Brigades being thrown into a mincing machine, but the enemy casualties were nearly as bad, and given the appalling weather conditions, it was no surprise the battle had descended into a stalemate.

Germany and Italy having recognised Franco's government the previous November, the Italians had sent ground troops in divisional strength, though they were billed as volunteers, and the supplies from the fascist dictators were pouring in through Portugal, despite a protest to the League of Nations. The democracies were still observing an embargo.

'The talk is we are in for a long haul.'

'Do Florencia's parents know?'

'No idea.'

'I need a pen and paper, Tyler, that's a letter I have to write.'

'You got it. I will try to stay in touch, but if the front moves so must I.'

'You forget, I always know how to find you.'

Writing his first letter was painful, a tacit admission that Florencia was no more, even if he knew it to be true. The reply came with a photograph of her on the day she had joined the *Mujeres Libres*, which for the first time produced tears, not many, it was not his way, but a reflection of the depth of his feelings of loss.

Replies came from other letters: from Lizzie, ordering him home, from Vince just wishing him well and from Peter Lanchester saying basically, but kindly, he had been asking for it and if there was anything he needed, etc. Monty Redfern, typically, offered to send a private ambulance all the way to Spain if he wanted one.

Recovery was slow, at first the mere act of walking a shuffling struggle, but as his strength began to return, Jardine began to exercise, gently at first, but with an incremental daily increase. The hospital he left as quickly as the doctor would allow, beds being at a premium, and he found a room in a house to rent, one abandoned by a supporter of the generals, though he did not ask if the family had got away or been shot, and it was there that Christmas passed and a new year arrived.

There was one other thing he could work on while he fought his way back to full physical fitness – his Spanish, which given he was surrounded by locals, began to seem competent, though he could never feel comfortable with the sibilant lisp, nor reach the degree of fluency he had with the French and German he had learnt as a child and youth.

Newspapers helped and it was from them, even this far from true civilisation, that he learnt in a week-old copy of *The Times* of the death of Sir Basil Zaharoff, which saddened him greatly. Naturally, he followed the course of the war, the battle in the winter snows in the mountains to the north-west of Madrid, as Franco tried to cut supplies to the city, again mostly a failure given it bled the Nationalists as much as the Republicans.

By the time Franco attacked and took Málaga he was running again, feeling no pain and ready to get back to what he saw now as a duty he owed to the memory of Florencia.

Barcelona was a city that, to a Briton, blossomed early, already in mid March full of flowers that, in the colour, seemed to mock the grey mood of the city, one that Cal Jardine had to fight in his own mind as certain vistas triggered painful memories. Unable to face his deceased lover's parents, he made straight for the headquarters of the POUM in Las Ramblas.

Getting to see Andreu Nin, even if he was no longer apparently a member of the Catalan government, was never going to be easy, alone even harder, and the offices of his Workers' Party were really the last place to talk with him – there were too many prying eyes – nor did he feel the telephone to be secure, even if the exchange which he had helped capture was still in anarchist hands.

So he dropped off a curt note, in Spanish, referring to their original meeting, hoping that the room number at the Ritz, as well as Florencia's name, would trigger his memory and asking that he make contact, then went back to the upper floors of the now much-depleted Ritz to wait for what was really the answer to a simple question – did he still want that for which he had asked and was he still prepared to fund it?

The reply took two frustrating days in coming and the sender had no idea how close Jardine had come to repacking his bags and seeking a way home, for to be here, staying in a room decorated exactly like the one they had shared, was to be constantly reminded of Florencia, and that, with no one to talk to, was agony.

In the end Nin showed the same level of precaution as he did; there was no call from a downstairs desk to tell him he had a visitor, just a discreet knock on the door, which when opened produced a thick envelope which was pressed into his hand. Opening it, he was surprised that what had been written was in English, though not of a very good standard, and ran over several pages.

The POUM leader was at pains to stress that matters vis-à-vis the communists had not improved, indeed they had deteriorated, this not aided by interim attempts to buy arms on the open market, and the reason the package was so thick was quite simply that Nin wanted him to know of what had been attempted and what failure they had suffered.

At every step, those with whom they dealt, usually foreign industrialists with little sympathy for the cause they were being asked to supply, demanded massive prices as well as huge bribes, first to sell any weapons at all, then to pay off the necessary officials to provide the End User Certificates that would allow the arms to be shipped to the Republic, people the Spanish negotiators never got to meet.

What followed turned the mounting difficulties into a farce, as the foreigners stalled on delivery, changed the terms of the agreements – always at the Republic's expense – then, when their goods finally arrived, they found them not to be what had been paid for and many were actually useless, while what could be employed was often dangerous.

Really he was telling Cal things he did not wish to know – they were finding out what he had told them, the arms trade was a dirty business – but he was obliged to read to get to the kernel of what was required. So he learnt that the Stalinists now controlled the Assault Guards, that their membership was nearing half a million and that their grip on the throat of the Republic had increased.

It was at the end he got to the nub: Nin, despite the difficulties his party faced in falling numbers, had transferred the sum of money originally mentioned to the account named and he wished the process discussed to be put into operation. He asked no questions, so the need to explain the source to which he was proposing to go – bound to be a problem of persuasion – never arose.

Cal had not expected that – he had anticipated some form of dialogue, certainly a heated discussion, and he would have told Nin, had that occurred, the provision of funds was unnecessary; he would have financed the first part himself. Yet it was an indication of the truth of what he had written that he could not risk a meeting, which meant his every move was being watched.

It made no odds; if he had the POUM funds he would use them and his business in Barcelona was finished. It was time to find his Greek, and the first step in that was to get back down to the Barcelona dock area and see if the smugglers he had used before were still operating. They were, and prospering.

Yet departing the waters off Catalonia was a lot more circumspect this time than last; there was no burst of powerful marine engines and a cresting bow wave, they left the harbour with the engines no more than idling, the ship securely dark, as was the harbour behind, and Cal had been told in no uncertain terms that silence was essential as they cleared the dredged channel.

The threat came from Italian submarines patrolling off the coast, though they were obliged to stay well out in deep water off a coastline that was noted for the long, shallow and sandy shelf, but they did put out boats full of armed men to seek the smugglers close inshore. It was a long time before the man at the wheel half-opened the throttle to increase speed and take them out in the deep Med.

In the myriad calculations Cal had to make, this one struck home. He was a long way from even having to worry about getting what he might purchase into the Republican harbours, but there was one salient fact that was obvious – they could not come in a Spanish vessel and he would have to be careful about the kind of ship used.

Once out at sea, with the coastline a distant memory, the captain could at last get up real speed, and it was exhilarating on two counts: not just the salt spray and wind on his face, but the feeling of leaving something behind, of the opening of a new page and closing a book on what had just gone before.

From Marseilles, a cable went off to Peter Lanchester asking for a meeting in Paris, and when a positive reply came he took the train north, having pre-booked a room in the Hôtel de Crillon, and that was where they met for dinner in the very formal and very grand restaurant *Les Ambassadeurs*, all gilt, a marble floor, mirrors and chandeliers in the style of Louis XV.

'Bit pricey this, old boy,' Lanchester said. 'Now I know why you told me to bring my dinner jacket.'

'It's just your kind of place, Peter, you being a sort of courtier.'

'Not sure I like *that* description, Cal, and I suspect all this grandeur is because you want something from me.'

'You don't think I'd ask you to come to Paris for your company.'

The response was waspish. 'I don't know for certain you'd cross the bloody road for my company.'

'In truth, there are a couple of things I need, but let me explain first.'

'As long as you include chapter and verse about your travails.'

'They are, Peter, intertwined.'

Peter Lanchester was a good listener when the need arose, eating his *soupe de poisson* and rarely interrupting as the last few months were explained, posing the odd question for clarification as he heard how Jardine had got involved because of the athletes, though when he came to the parting of the ways he could see his companion's brow furrow.

'But why did you stay on?'

Having made no mention of Florencia, his excuse was that he just wanted to see how it all panned out.

'Nothing to do with that anarchist floozie Vince Castellano told me about? He said she was a real lovely, if a bit of a handful.'

'Nothing at all.'

Cal was quick to continue, that being a place he did not want to go, and eventually got to the problems the Republic was having getting arms, which led to a general conversation about the actions of their own government.

'Not sure about Eden; bugger's an Old Etonian, of course, and when it comes to "shifty", they are taught that particular skill on arrival, but he might be doing the bidding of the cabinet, which, as you know, is full of a bunch of terrified old tarts, from Baldwin down.'

'Recovered from the abdication, has he?'

'Bloody nightmare that was, Cal, quite ruined everyone's Christmas.'

'Believe me, Peter, you are better off without him.'

'So, on with the motley; what is it you want from me?'

'I need a couple of false passports in different names, one because I might have to go to Germany.'

'Are you mad?'

'It's a big country, Peter, and if I am travelling under a false name I should be safe.'

'Why Hunland?'

The explanation did not make Lanchester feel any more comfortable, given Cal was talking about going right to the heart of the Nazi state, but there was no need for persuasion, given the cause, which, if it baulked at anarchism, was solidly anti-fascist. Once he was sure his fellow diner was determined to proceed, he concentrated on his food and they turned to what names should be on them.

'Lizzie's maiden name, Moncrief, will do for one. She has a brother, bit of a wastrel, but I know his background, so that gives me a ready-made legend. The other you decide, but I'd like a press pass too.'

'Explain.' The shake of Cal's head was vehement. 'If I take back a couple of photos it should be easily done.'

'Easily?'

'For a government minister, Cal, very much so, and the pass I will get forged.'

The exchanged look produced no name and that was no surprise. Peter Lanchester never let on who were members of his mysterious cabal.

'The other thing I need is a ship, British owned.'

'Can't the Dons provide one?'

'A Spanish-flagged vessel ups the odds of the nature of the cargo being discovered. Old Franco has a lot of sympathisers throughout

Europe, and besides, we will have to run the gauntlet of Italian submarines. Daft as they are, they won't dare put a torpedo into a ship carrying a red duster.'

'This all sounds fraught with peril, old boy.'

'It was ever thus. There's one other thing.'

Whatever else Peter Lanchester was, a bit of bigot perhaps, he was not a fool. 'I sense I am about to be asked to be active, which, in my past experience of you, makes "fraught with peril" seem like a picnic.'

'I might need you to oversee an exchange – just hand over some gold bars on my say-so – and it should be a piece of cake, but I hope it won't be necessary.'

'Are you staying here in Paris till I get your documents?'

'Paris in the spring, why not? My question?'

'We'll see, Cal, shall we?'

For all the beauty and gaiety of the French capital it was hard to be joyful. There was the heaviness of heart thinking how much better it would be with the company of Florencia, but added to that the politics of France were no better than anywhere else. The Marxist prime minister, Léon Blum, was struggling to keep his post, the unions were striking and madly agitating, but not as much as the zealots of the French right wing.

For all the flowers and the blossom on the trees, there was a palpable sense of doom in the air and he was glad when his passports and documents arrived and he could get back to his task, the first part of which was to take the train to Athens.

CHAPTER TWENTY-THREE

To travel through Greece was to enter another nation in political turmoil: it was in the middle of an election battle, in which fear of the communists mirrored that which Cal Jardine had left in Spain. They were expected to make great gains, and the taxi that took him from the main station of Athens down to the port of Piraeus, where Manousos Constantou-Georgiadis, the fellow he must see, had his factory, passed walls plastered with lurid posters, not one of which he could decipher.

What Ancient Greek he had learnt at school, not as much as he should since it was damned difficult, did not run to the understanding of modern political slogans, though it did make him reflect on what he had been taught about the glories of Athens and the Persian and Peloponnesian Wars, a reminder this was a country he had always wanted to visit.

You could not call on a man like Constantou-Georgiadis without first making contact in writing, which he did under the name Moncrief, by a cable he had translated into Greek, the day following Peter Lanchester's departure from Paris, using the Hôtel de Crillon as a very impressive postal address to which the man should reply.

That approach had to be circumspect, but the Greek was in the metal fabrication business, so it was not hard to come up with a reason to call, his claim to be a freelance industrial designer looking for a company to turn his drawings into products not requiring that he provide a registered business address that his contact could check up on.

On the outskirts of the port city, the factory, when they finally found it, was not impressive, more a tumbledown large workshop than industrial, like many of the buildings that surrounded it, in an area of dusty backstreets. When asked to wait, in itself a linguistic drama, his taxi driver looked uncomfortable; this was clearly known as a rough area.

Once inside, the reception area and the offices belied that first impression, being well furnished, bright and clean. Whatever the secretarial competence of the girl to whom he gave his name, sitting at the desk behind a large new-looking typewriter, she possessed striking attributes and that was before she stood up.

Blessed with long black hair, pale skin that obviously rarely saw the sun and a bosom the eye could not avoid being drawn to, she struggled with his name and his request, but gave him such a beautiful smile that he felt like an old and close friend. When she stood to enter the inner sanctum, she showed long legs in silk stockings, above high-heeled shoes, and a very becoming posterior that swayed deliciously when she walked.

Which made it all the harder to take seriously the walking syllabub that came out to greet him – Constantou-Georgiadis was not just short; he was all of five feet and shaped like a pear, with all his excess fat, and there was much of it, concentrated below his midriff, which made his walk a serious waddle. A pair of very thick-rimmed glasses set off his fleshy pasty face; this was a man who did not deserve his glamorous employee.

'English I no speak,' he said, in a way that made it sound as though he had spent all day rehearsing it.

The relief on his fat face when Cal replied in perfect German was palpable, and the flabby hand he produced to shake had a grip like a dead fish. Next he rattled off something in Greek to his secretary, before indicating they should both go into his office, where Cal was invited to sit, while the Greek went to occupy a chair on the opposite side that seemed twice the size he needed.

Cal had waited till this meeting to make up his mind as to what approach to use; he needed to form some view of whom he was dealing with – a sharp businessman or a mere front. Added to that, he was not in a position to negotiate the price he would have to pay – that would be decided by the seller, and so desperate was the Republic that it would cough up whatever was demanded.

This looked to be a bit of a fly-blown outfit, certainly from the outside, a facade more than a place of genuine manufacture, especially with such a beauty in the outer office and such a contrast before him. He saw no point in beating about the bush, so decided to avoid small talk and get straight to the point.

'I am in the market to buy a large quantity of arms and I believe you are in a position to help me do that.'

Manousos Constantou-Georgiadis, whom Cal had now decided to think of as MCG, sat so still and looked so shocked it was as if someone had hit him with a club; that was until his lower lip moved soundlessly several times before finally he could speak. 'I think you have made some mistake, mein Herr.'

'No mistake; those who had told me of your contacts do not make errors.'

'And who would these people be?'

'I believe if I said that, before he died, Sir Basil Zaharoff told me of your associations, you would not deny it.'

'I do not know Zaharoff.'

'But you know *of* him, and more importantly, he knew all about you; for instance, that you have a major shareholder called Rheinmetall-Borsig.'

'That is not hard to find out.'

'The nature of the association is not one I think you would broadcast – indeed I am sure you would wish to keep that very discreet – so it would take a man who knew both the arms trade and where the bodies are buried to set me on a trail that leads to your office. An office attached to what? Not a factory that could produce much.'

MCG stood up and waddled out of the door, returning with the cable that Cal had sent him and he had no doubt asked for, his face worried, looking at it as if it would provide either enlightenment or a route to credible evasion.

'Then you are not an industrial designer?'

'No, but I take it you are in the business of making a profit.'

'A man does not go into business for any other reason.'

'And if you were offered such a thing to an extreme degree, would it not be hard to resist? The client I represent has a difficulty of supply that is close to insurmountable. Any goods would have to be shipped without the usual documentation; for instance, there could be no End User Certificate and the whole matter would have to be so discreet as to be utterly and completely capable of being denied, and if not that, explained away.'

MCG's face was a picture; for all his features were too bloated to be interesting, Cal could almost see his mind working as his wetted lips were rubbed together. The glasses came off and went back on again, he sat forward in his chair, then pushed back, expelling air, which was all a bit excessive – if he was in the business, right at this moment there was only one client with those problems.

'Rifles?' he asked finally, a product easy to supply and relatively easy to both supply and ship with discretion.

'Yes.' Just as he began to look relieved, Cal added, 'And automatic weapons, light and heavy machine guns, mortars, both fifty and eighty millimetre, anti-tank and anti-personnel mines, and if possible, some light field artillery and the requisite ammunition to last for twelve months of combat.'

If he had had any blood in his face it would have drained out, Cal thought, as he reached into his pocket.

'Here is a list of the equipment I would like. In terms of quantity there is no limit, it is more what is able to be supplied, and I will undertake to ship from any port you name. I would, of course, be disappointed not to have the holds of that vessel full. As to payment, that will be made in gold to you and you must pay your principal, though I assume he will set the price.'

MCG's hand was shaking as he leant over and took the paper; if there had ever been any doubt as to where this was to be acquired, this inventory of the weapons removed that. Not only was their description listed, but also the names and numbers designated by the Wehrmacht.

'I will be staying at the Grande Bretagne. How long do you think it will be before you can provide me with an answer?'

'Tomorrow?' he suggested weakly.

'Good. Perhaps you will join me at the hotel for dinner and, if you wish, you may bring along your secretary for company.'

'She is not my secretary, mein Herr, she is my wife.'

Christ, Cal thought, *I must be getting old. Did I miss the ring?*

There was no chance to check on that on the way out, though he did try; he was escorted by MCG and his missus had her hands behind the typewriter.

There being no point in hanging about in the hotel, he had a chance to do a bit of sightseeing, naturally the Acropolis and the Parthenon, then the Temple of Olympian Zeus, where he was given to wonder at what the god would have to say about his games having been played in Berlin. He probably liked Plato, so he would approve, for if ever there was a proto-fascist it was the great Greek philosopher who so admired Sparta. If not, he would have cheered from the heavens for the feats of the black athlete Jesse Owens.

When he returned to the Grande Bretagne there was a message for Mr Moncrief at the desk, from MCG, which asked him to telephone. Put through, the call was answered by the unlikely Mrs MCG, who had a voice on the phone as silky as her stockings, albeit he could not understand a word she said, this while Cal tried to imagine the pair in bed, a congress so improbable he had to shake his head. Then he was put through.

'Herr Moncrief. I have been in touch with my principal and I have received from him permission to enter into discussions.'

'The first would be regarding quantities. Without that satisfied, the rest would be pointless.'

'I have been assured that there is sufficient produce to meet any needs you may have.'

'Then the invitation to dinner stands.'

'Forgive me for asking, Mr Moncrief, but is that your real name?'

Fishing, you fat little slob, but no doubt on instructions.

'It is the name on my passport, which I am happy to show to you.'

The silence at the end was telling; he did not believe him and why should he? This was not a trade at all – especially the one under discussion – for newcomers and amateurs. The real question was whether the Greek had the means to enquire and then the kind of sources of information to ferret out anything revealing. Never having been active in Greece, it was a reasonable assumption that he did not.

'Besides, I could be anyone. What matters is that I have the means to pay. Shall we say eight o'clock?'

'Yes.'

'And how many will we be?'

'Three.'

'Splendid.'

As he put the phone down he had a flash of memory and it was of a smiling Florencia, whose photograph lay in his suitcase. Alive, had he harboured the thoughts he was enjoying now, she would have gouged his eyes out. But she was not, and he knew, if she could speak from beyond the grave, she would be willing him to have a full life, but he did not entirely let himself off the hook.

'God, you're a callous bastard, Jardine,' he said out loud.

If they were improbable in his imagination, they were no better arm in arm. Cal was waiting to greet them at the hotel entrance, a courtesy he would not have extended for MCG if he had come on his own, and he certainly would not have lifted and kissed his hand as he did now hers, speaking in French, noting the gold band she wore, as well as a fairly substantial diamond engagement ring to accompany it.

The hand was elegant, with long fingers and painted nails, and proximity gave him a whiff of a very alluring perfume, before he was granted, as he lifted his head, another ravishing smile, while out of the corner of his eye he sought to see if her husband was annoyed. It was as if he did not even notice, seemingly too busy looking around at the well-appointed entrance, only moving when Cal did, following him through the held-open doors and into the lobby.

'Your wife speaks German?'

'No, only Greek, so we can discuss matters without her interference.'

'Is that not a strange word to use?'

'Women,' he spluttered, 'they do not know their place.'

He so nearly said, 'I hope so,' but stopped himself just in time, registering that if fatty had been fearful yesterday he was not that now; if anything he was being brusque, and that did nothing to make Cal feel they were going to have a pleasant evening.

Having chosen a private room, one with a view of the Acropolis in the moonlight, he had asked that it be provided with lots of flowers; it might be a serious business meeting but he wanted to impress her, which was not going to be easy given he had no idea of her name. In truth, he reckoned he was deluding himself, but it was pleasant to do so and added some interest to what was otherwise likely to be tedious.

The champagne he had ordered was already opened and the waiter poured three glasses as soon as they sat, the mood immediately spoilt by MCG snapping something at his wife, which brought from her a look of fury. In Greek, it might have been incomprehensible but for the way she downed the wine then glared at him. Clearly he was telling her not to drink too much, so Cal signalled for her glass to be refilled.

'To business,' he said as he turned to MCG, forcing his attention away from his wife.

'My principal doubts you will meet his terms.'

'I will answer that when you tell me what they are and what I am paying for.'

As MGC took a typed list from his pocket and passed it over, his eyes swivelled to his wife, who was having a third refill, which caused him to frown – clearly she liked a drink – but attention had to be paid to the business and Cal could not fault what he was being offered, for it was a gunrunner's dream. Everything he wanted and lots of it: 20 mm Flak cannons, Pak 36 anti-tank guns, MG 32 machine guns, machine pistols, Walther PP pistols and K98 rifles, all with ammunition and spares.

'The price?'

'Forty million Reichsmarks.'

It was hard not to blink; at the very roughest guess that was at least twice what the price should be, but he had to smile and make light of it.

'I am glad to see we are no longer pretending where these are coming from. Are you sure they can be delivered?'

'Herr Moncrief, you would not have come to me unless you knew more than I would wish, therefore I doubt you will need to guess at the power of the person who has agreed that what you have in your hand can be supplied. I, however, need to be sure you can pay.'

'Shall we order some food? If we do not, I think your wife risks spoiling her appetite.'

'You mentioned payment in gold. Is that here in Athens?'

'Not yet, but I do not see a problem, yet I must, as you understand, refer back to the source of funds and get their agreement to the price.'

'I do not think they have a choice.'

'There is always a choice, but I think they will accept.'

'Elena!'

The bark made MCG's cheeks wobble, but there was no mistaking the fury in the eyes and it got the same response as his earlier admonishment: she simply drained her glass, and that acted like a red rag. What followed was a furious exchange in Greek, not one word of which Cal understood, but he had engaged in enough marital quarrels of his own to be able to discern the gist.

She liked to drink, while he had not even touched his champagne, which indicated that she was a boozer and he was not. Good manners should have kept this under wraps, perhaps in a public space he would have been more circumspect, but with neither of those constraints

310

present, he went right off the deep end and was fully matched in response. For all she was a beauty, Elena also had the ability to look like a very angry crow with a voice to match.

The waiter had disappeared, Cal did not know why, but he had left the bottle in an ice bucket beside the table, which she grabbed by the neck and it looked as though she was about to crown her old man. That she did not was insufficient to calm him down and it was pretty obvious why – the damn thing was empty, which meant, they having had one glass each, she had drunk at least four. Then the waiter came in with another bottle – which Elena must have asked for – and things really took off.

Cal had to sit back; she still had that bottle in her hand and she looked like she was capable of using it on anyone. He had to admire the waiter, who, with what amounted to a full-blooded screaming match in progress, proceeded with his task – perhaps such screaming matches were common in Greece – the loud plop of the cork being ejected, that worldwide sign of celebration, just throwing fuel on an inferno.

MCG stood up and so did she, towering over him, which would have reduced Cal to tears of mirth if he had not worked so hard to keep his face straight; he needed this little twerp badly and, reluctantly, he would take his side if called upon to do so. Just then MCG smashed his fist on the table, spat out a final declaration and stormed out of the room. With a triumphant look, Elena sat down and calmly signalled for her glass to be filled.

With muttered 'excuse me's' Cal went out after him, to find him outside shaking with fury, literally like a jelly, his fists clenched and threatening the heavens with a punch. Sighting Cal, it was clear he had to fight to calm himself and it took several seconds. With a great effort he stilled his wobbly body and said, in a strained voice, 'I must leave, Herr Moncrief, but I ask for your indulgence.'

'My dear chap,' Cal said, lamely.

'As you will have seen, my wife and I do not see eye to eye. I have asked her to leave with me, and she has refused. I cannot stay, so I will await your response to what I have proposed to you until you are ready. I thank you for the invitation and apologise for spoiling your evening.'

'But your wife?'

'Let her have her food . . .' his voice rose a fraction '. . . and her drinks. Please oblige me by putting her in a taxi when she has had enough.'

'But—'

His voice was almost pleading. 'Please? Oblige me in this.'

'If you wish.'

'I shall go to my club tonight. I do not think I could spend tonight under the same roof as her.'

Cal was wondering if this little tub knew the expression 'all is fair in love and war'.

'Whatever you wish.'

He returned to another dazzling smile, to a woman who behaved as if nothing untoward had happened, and as well as that there was a bit of a look in her eye that was nothing less than a come-on. Seduction without words is hard but not impossible, and a willingness on both parts eases those inevitable moments of confusion.

MCG was right, his wife did not speak German, but she had maybe two dozen words of English and a few in French. So they ate slowly, they drank wine – in her case somewhat too quickly – and they stumbled through the steps that led inevitably to his room, where, once inside, conversation became redundant.

He did, as promised, put her in a taxi, outside that same magnificent entrance, but the sky was a dull morning grey at the time.

CHAPTER TWENTY-FOUR

The next weeks were a whirl of travel and activity, checking with Peter Lanchester in London that what he needed would be in place, dealing with the Greek to ensure both the terms of supply and the transfer of the money, once he had seen it shifted to a bank in Athens, none of that made any easier by events in Spain itself.

As for the war, the Republic was still mostly on the defensive. Franco had again failed to take Madrid in the first months of the year, while the last bastion of Republican resistance in the north-west, the Basque region, was under severe pressure from General Mola, who with the help of the German Condor Legion had ushered in a new phase with the bombing and utter destruction of the small town of Guernica, an act which shocked the world when news of the true number of deaths began to emerge.

For all the international protests it had another effect: it showed the power of aerial bombardment on built-up areas and brought home to many in the democracies what they might face should they engage in another war – in short, it strengthened the hand of the politicians keeping up the pretence of non-intervention, who could now ask those more bellicose if they were prepared to see their own cities reduced to rubble.

Regular Italian troops, in an operation sanctioned personally by Mussolini, with massed tanks, artillery and air support, had sought to capture the Guadalajara mountains which rose to the north of Madrid, their tactical aim to gain the heights and so roll down on the capital in conjunction with the Nationalists. It failed, with the Italians suffering heavy losses, not that the International Brigades fared any better.

Franco was not winning, but neither was he losing, yet when Cal Jardine got back to Barcelona, it was impossible to find a voice of the Republican side that even thought of stopping fighting; the problem was not a desire to go on, it was internal.

It was obvious matters had been seething uncomfortably since the death of Juan Luis Laporta, he being something of a local hero – there had even been a group set up to commemorate his name – with accusations flying about that he had been deliberately killed by his political foes, but that only poured oil onto the fires of endemic disputes that had raged for years.

On a hot day in May it came to a head when open conflict broke out in Barcelona between the anarchists and the communists. The latter, using their well-tried-and-trusted methods, had infiltrated and taken control of the Assault Guards in Barcelona too. This paramilitary body had grown in power, encouraged to do so by the Catalan government as a counter to the workers' militias who, since the generals' attempt to seize power, had policed the streets while ignoring not only orders to disperse, but any decree with which they did not agree.

The spark was an attempt, robustly repulsed, to try and take over the vital main telephone exchange, the very same building that Cal Jardine had helped to capture the previous July. Despite their superior weaponry, the Assault Guard found the workers impossible to dislodge.

The tocsin was sounded in the ranks of both the CNT-FAI and the POUM. Their members, with their weapons, poured onto the streets to do battle. It was an indication of how the power of the communists had increased in less than a year – they had been something of a fringe party in Barcelona before – now they had numbers and could contest those streets that had seen the regular army defeated.

Given the turmoil, getting a decision on such a vital matter had to be put on hold; Andreu Nin, Cal's main contact, was heavily embroiled in the fighting, for the very good reason that his party was still most at risk, while García Oliver, who had been despatched from Valencia to try and bring peace to the city, was weighed down by endless meetings and stormy negotiations.

These attempts were not aided by the rhetoric on both sides; the communists wheeled out their most potent propaganda weapon, Dolores Ibárruri, known as *La Pasionaria*, the woman who had coined the famous slogan during the battle for Madrid, *¡No pasarán!* Her views were outré and delivered with bile. They also lacked any grip on the truth, but that mattered less than that there were fools who believed what nonsense she spouted, which was that the internecine conflict was an anarcho-Trotskyist plot engineered on the orders of General Franco.

The counterclaims had more validity and went right to the heart of that in which Cal Jardine was involved, the fact that the Republican government was falling increasingly under communist control, politically, to add to their lock on military action. The workers' leaders were at pains to ensure their followers were not fooled by the lack of openly communist ministers – that was how the Stalinists operated: in the shadows, like rodents.

What brought matters to a peaceful compromise was not the endless talk, but raw military power, the arrival in the city of ten thousand heavily armed Assault Guards, enough men to drive any other force from the streets and with orders to show no mercy. That allowed García Oliver to knock heads together, though Andreu Nin, when he finally met with Callum Jardine, saw the eventual peace agreement as an outright defeat.

Able to communicate now without the need for an intermediary, Cal found the POUM leader resigned to his fate: Moscow would insist on the banning of his organisation and what would happen to him personally would be, he had no doubt, unpleasant. The notion that he should flee the country, a wise one, was politely declined.

'That would play into Stalin's hands, Señor Jardine.'

'Better that than Stalin's victim.'

'They are so skilled at lies, these Bolsheviks, I would be shown as a pawn of Franco, and as for my life, well, Trotsky was not safe from the ice pick that smashed his skull in Mexico.'

It was hard, looking at the scholarly Nin, to see him as heroic, he physically just did not fit the bill, yet he had a stoicism about his possible death that was very Spanish; if he was to be shot, he would face it with equanimity. But when it came to the most important point, he was no longer in a position to act to facilitate matters; his influence was now zero.

'Use García Oliver.'

'You trust a man who you believe has just thrown you and your people to the wolves?'

'I have no choice, señor, and neither do you if you wish to proceed with your plans.'

He did not like García Oliver and it was clear the feeling was mutual; it was not just lack of a spark of geniality, it was the feeling that, if things went wrong, here was a man who would somehow slip out of trouble while leaving Cal Jardine to face the consequences, very much like he had dealt with Nin.

The politician's instructions were to go to Valencia and wait until he had secured everything in Barcelona. Only then could he make an approach to Caballero, who would need to involve others now – he could not just send millions in gold out of the country on his own signature, though he would still keep it secret from the communists.

No sooner had he arrived than all his plans were thrown into turmoil when Largo Caballero resigned and was replaced by the one-time finance minister, and there was a new minister of war, Indalecio Prieto. Obliged to kick his heels for two weeks in Valencia, he found a room at the Hotel de Los Altos, a famous seaside spa hotel overlooking the Mediterranean, which had once been a favourite haunt of the European rich.

That was where Alverson found him and was able to bring him up to date on the politics, more than he had been able to glean from the newspapers and their screaming headlines that said the communists had got their way: the POUM had been disbanded, the offices and funds seized, their leaders arrested.

'Then slung,' Alverson added, gloomily, 'into a communist-run jail right in the heart of Madrid, and guess who's running it?'

'Who?'

'That Drecker guy you so love.'

'Is that a move up or down?'

'Definitely up.'

'Would you do me a favour, Tyler, and keep tabs on him?'

'Why?'

'His career interests me,' Cal replied gnomically.

The American shrugged. 'Whatever, but what about my scoop?'

Hungry for information on the progress of the arms buy, the American had to be content only with a part of the story; the arrest of Nin and his comrades made more insecure what was already a dangerously exposed position. He did tell Alverson that he had access to what was needed, but not the where and the how.

'So what about the when?' he demanded.

'It's not in my hands, Tyler, and if they don't get a move on, the deal I have arranged will fall through.'

'And the how much?' Alverson whistled when he was told; even he knew that was way over the going rate.

'Still, I guess they're used to it, Cal, even the Soviets are bilking them, big time, I hear. They have a real sweetheart deal: every time they despatch anything, they just take the Republic's gold out of their bank to pay for it.'

It was another week of thumb-twiddling before a message came from the new minister for war, asking for a meeting and giving an address which was not an official one, which meant a taxi to the main railway station, a wait and a check there was no tail, then another to the address. Prieto, a much more pleasant man with whom to deal, was keen that things should proceed and was there with a representative of the Spanish Central Bank, who could tell Cal the necessary gold had been shipped to Athens and was in a vault there under the control of the Republican ambassador.

It was necessary to agree certain codes and procedures, as well as settle some queries. The ambassador only had the right to make the payment; any communication with the Republican government had to be through him and it was essential that he was kept informed at every stage of the deal. Cal was relieved – Peter Lanchester would not be needed.

Yet the new man had his own ideas: would it be acceptable if the payment were released only when the vessel in which it was being carried cleared German territorial waters? Cal was of the opinion the best they could hope for was completion on it slipping its berth – not ideal, but better than paying for it prior to loading.

'My impression is that this is a trade they will want to repeat.' *And why not*, he thought, *given the profit margin?* 'So, they will not endanger the transaction by playing games.'

'I can guess why they are doing this, but why are *you* doing this, Señor Jardine?' Prieto asked, dropping his pleasant manner.

The Spanish bank official had the good grace to look embarrassed at the question, yet he too must have wondered why a non-Iberian was giving so much time and effort to aiding the Republic.

'García Oliver told me you have never mentioned a fee. Perhaps your payment is in the price you have given to us?'

It would have been easy to agree, to say yes, and to these men it would have made sense. That it was for the memory of Florencia he would keep to himself, for that would sound too sentimental, but given he did not like to be challenged in this way, it was much more to his taste to provide an answer that would do nothing to lessen any suspicions, so he said,

'You'll never know, will you? Now, if we are concluded here, I have to get back to Athens.'

MCG was not content to be told there was gold in the bank, he required to see it, and it had the same effect on him as any other human being, and Jardine knew that he was not immune to its allure either. It rested deep in the vaults of the Attica Bank, chosen for it being a relative newcomer to the Greek financial sector and eager for business in a country not overfriendly to Spain.

The sturdy boxes containing the ingots had been opened for inspection, and even in artificial light the precious metal had a shiny lustre that drew both the eye and the need to touch its cold surface. Looking at the Greek's face as he wetted his lips with anticipation, it was interesting to speculate how much of this prize would stick to his stubby little mitts. As his index finger stroked the mark of the Spanish mint, he gave an involuntary shudder.

Next they went to the boardroom, happily lent to them by a bank extracting a healthy fee for merely transferring the funds from one account to another with the required degree of discretion. Here the documents of sale were laid out, the formal contracts that he would take away for his scrutiny and the ambassadorial signature, one copy in German, the other in Spanish. It was while Cal was looking at them that MCG dropped his bombshell.

'It has proved impossible to move your goods without an End User Certificate, Herr Moncrief. Even in normal times that is a difficulty, but with the amount of international scrutiny at present it is too dangerous.'

'When did this come up?' Cal demanded, suspecting he was about to be asked for more money.

'Immediately the transaction was considered by those who advise my principal.'

That meant there was a lawyer involved, maybe more than one, which was not good for security.

'In this,' MCG continued, 'no one must be drawn into an international outcry. Merely shipping the goods without an EUC might do that – raise questions that would be embarrassing to have to deal with.'

Translated, that meant queries as to who had gained financially from the deal; not even someone as powerful as Hermann Göring could explain away the pocketing of payments that Cal suspected would never find their way into the coffers of the German finance ministry.

And if the Spanish Nationalists found out he was facilitating supplies to their foes, it would certainly get them going, albeit they would not make an excessive amount of fuss – they depended on the Nazis for too much – but they might just drop the kind of hints to Göring's rivals that would trigger an investigation.

The bloated little Greek had a strange look on his face – not a smile or a smirk – but one that not only hinted at his having the upper hand, but a deep degree of pleasure in being in that position.

'Difficult as it would be to accept, it is sometimes better to forgo a transaction than carry one through that throws up last-minute complications. It is to be hoped that you have a solution and one that does not affect the price.'

The message was plain and Jardine was sure the little bastard had got it: no more money, maybe none at all, and this for a man who had near-wet himself by just touching a gold bar. The pause was long, the hope that this British arms dealer, who must be making his own pile, might crack, one that fell on stony ground. The tub of lard was obliged to give in, which he did with a dismissive wave, as if it had never been a problem.

'Fortunately there is a way out of this impasse. I am friendly with a man who has the power to provide a solution. The certificate will say that the arms are being shipped to equip the Greek National Army. I think, given the political situation, no one will question the need.'

'And that man is?'

'Herr Moncrief!' MCG cried, to what was an absurd question.

Cal was thinking, did it matter? It was another link in a chain of people, and the more of those there were, the more likely information about the shipment and its destination could leak out, and he had no great faith in the highly voluble Greeks keeping a secret. But he soon realised he would just have to live with it, unpleasant as it was.

Did this little sod understand that the coast of Spain was blockaded and any illegal shipment would have to run the gauntlet, not only of Italian submarines who would sink them on sight if they had knowledge of the cargo and its destination, but also British warships, enforcing that democratic joke, the Non-Intervention Treaty? In a decade of doing clandestine deals this one had way too many people in the know, all of whom would drop him like a hot brick if exposure threatened.

Yet he was too close to completion to back away and there was also the knowledge that, on paper, this transaction was impossible. Maybe Sir Basil Zaharoff in his prime could have pulled it off, and there was, too, a slight glow in the thought that the old man would probably have entrusted the information he had passed over to very few people, indeed, he might be the only one.

Callum Jardine still had to make his way in his world, and if the deal needed to be kept secret now, these things had a way of filtering out to the wider arms-dealing community over time and his name would gain in reputation – if he was not making a money profit on this, it might translate into a healthy stream of income in the future.

He nodded and smiled, which made MCG smile too, and so pleased was he that a small and noisy joining of his hands in front of his snub nose was the result. Cal picked up the documents and transferred them to his attaché case.

'The meeting for the handover will take place here. I will cable the ambassador and I am sure you too will be informed that the contract has got to the point of finalising the payment.'

A nod.

'I will, of course, oversee the actual purchase, the transportation to the docks and the loading, at which point I will telephone to the Attica Bank and give them a code word which we have agreed between us. They will then put the ambassador on the phone for completion. Is that satisfactory?'

'Very satisfactory, Herr Moncrief. I must ask, how long has it been since you were in Germany?'

That made Cal Jardine stiffen, it being the kind of question that might have unpleasant undertones. His last departure, not that long past, had been a close-run thing and he knew there were people in Germany who would dearly love to get him in a cell with a couple of rubber truncheons in their hands and some bare electrical wiring. Yet looking at MCG and his bland expression, it seemed as if the question was an innocent one.

'Quite some time, but it is a country I am fond of.'

'You will find it much changed, Herr Moncrief, and for the better. I feel we could do with a dose of what the Führer has done in Germany here in Greece, particularly the way he has dealt with the communists.'

Not wanting to go there, Cal decided to change the subject. 'I forgot to ask you, Herr Constantou-Georgiadis, how is your lovely wife?'

MCG looked as if he had just been slapped, and as much as it was possible for the skin of his face to tighten it did just that. Did he know what had happened that night he stormed out of the Grande Bretagne?

'My wife,' he hissed, 'is where she should be, mein Herr, looking after my affairs.'

'She's very good at looking after affairs, I should think.'

CHAPTER TWENTY-FIVE

The train north was the Arlberg Orient Express, direct from Athens through Belgrade, Bucharest, then, after a change at Vienna, the journey north through Czechoslovakia to Germany and Berlin, where, once over the border, he was subjected to the usual continual checking of papers en route that went with the thorough Teutonic bureaucracy that existed in a country with more uniform per square metre than anywhere else in the world.

He spent a night in the Adlon Hotel, luxurious and central, but reputedly not much loved by the Berlin Nazis, who preferred the Kaiserhof. Even then, having checked in as Herr Moncrief, he ate in his room and had a careful look round the following morning before exiting to hail a taxi to take him to catch the train to Celle in Lower Saxony.

With eighty million Germans, the chances of running into anyone who knew his face were so slight as to be non-existent, but he had always been of the opinion that it would be a stupid mistake to ignore the risk, because you would feel a damn fool if it went wrong, and in his case, in this country, it could prove fatal.

Celle was a pretty place, very conscious of itself, once part of the electorate of Hanover which had produced the Georgian kings of England – a fact that was immediately mentioned to him as he checked into the Fürstenhof Hotel and they saw his British passport. Provincial in the extreme, it was miles away in time and thinking from Berlin, sharing only the very recognisable features of the totalitarian state: the ubiquitous swastika flags and banners, the exhorting posters, as well as the loudspeakers on lampposts and buildings which would play martial music as well as deliver messages from the propaganda ministry, just in case the populace did not know how great their country was.

From there it was another short journey to Unterlüss and the Rheinmetall-Borsig Werk. With three factories this was the one he had been told to go to; what they did not make here would be brought from the other plants in Kassel and Düsseldorf – the whole, once inspected and accepted, would be shipped up to the Free Port of Hamburg. Peter Lanchester had a cargo vessel on the way to dock there and wait, provided by one of his secretive backers, who was obviously in shipping.

Unterlüss was a typical small German town, dependent on the factory, with tall half-timbered buildings with steep sloping roofs and the serious-minded Saxon inhabitants. Reputedly the hardest workers in the country, their neighbours had a saying for them, that in a Saxon household 'even if Grandfather is dead he must work; put his ashes in the timer'.

327

The name he had been given was that of the factory manager, Herr Gessler, and having rung from Celle he was expected. Gessler was very correct, dressed in a grey suit that hugged his thin frame, with rimless glasses and his party badge on his lapel, an object he was given to frequently fingering. A tour of the factory was obligatory and it was something he would report back on, this being the manufacturing works for not only small arms and flak artillery, but for small-calibre naval guns.

Gessler had obviously been told to treat him as an honoured guest, an instruction which had no doubt come from above, but he was nervous in a way that made Jardine jumpy, given there seemed no reason for him to be. He was also a walking technical encyclopaedia who wanted to impart all his knowledge in a sort of breathless litany that left even a man with a professional interest in the subject wondering whether he would ever shut up.

The nerves had an explanation, which was provided as they approached the head office building having finished their tour. The Mercedes standing outside had a swastika pennant on its wheel arch and beside it, standing to attention, was a driver in the pale-blue uniform of the Luftwaffe.

Inside Gessler's office they met the passenger – a full colonel, sharp-featured and wearing a monocle, in a beautifully tailored uniform, boots so shiny you could have shaved in them, and a pair of grey gloves in one hand which he slapped into the other – who, having clicked his heels, introduced himself as *Oberst* Brauschitz.

'Herr Moncrief, I have come from *Oberbefehlshaber* Göring who wishes to meet with you. I am ordered to convey you to his hunting lodge at Carinhall.'

He did not want to go; it was like the lair of the wolf and he was aware that the excuse he offered was a feeble one. 'I daresay that will involve an overnight stay, Herr *Oberst*, and my luggage is at the Fürstenhof.'

Brauschitz responded with a thin smile. 'Please credit us with some sense, Herr Moncrief. Your luggage is in the back of the car. But I assure you, were it not, you would want for nothing, given the person who is going to be your host.'

'I cannot think I warrant the personal attention of the supreme commander of the Luftwaffe.'

For the first time the genial mask dropped and he almost barked. 'It is not for you to decide, it is for you to do as you are requested.'

There was no point in saying it did not sound like a request, even less in continuing to refuse. 'Herr Gessler, I thank you for my tour and I am sure I will be seeing you shortly in the near future.' That was followed by a keen look, to see if he agreed; if he did not, Cal knew he was in trouble. All he got was a sharp nod, which left him still guessing.

'Shall we go? My superior does not like to be kept waiting.'

That was an absurd thing to say; Cal did not know exactly where Carinhall was but it lay in a totally different region of Germany, further away even than Berlin. That was when he found out how they were going to get there.

'I take it you have no exception to flying?'

'None.'

The plane was a Fieseler-Storch, and once his case was in, there was not a lot of room. Brauschitz had replaced his service cap with a flying helmet and they were airborne very quickly. The noise inside the cramped cabin made talking extremely difficult, so Cal just sat back and admired the scenery as they flew fairly low over the countryside. On landing there was a second car waiting and now the colonel could talk.

If he was urbane, it was in a German way; correct and, in his case, slightly boastful. By the time they reached their destination Cal knew he was part of a military family that went back a long way, and that he was related to very many senior officers in the German army, including one on the General Staff. Fortunately, with it getting dark and the road being through thick forest, which shut out what light was left, he was unable to see the look of boredom on his passenger's face.

The so-called hunting lodge looked more like a low-lying Florida to Jardine; thatched roof, white walls and two storeys high. It stood in extensive grounds, proved by the time it took to travel past the steel-helmeted Luftwaffe guards at the stone-pillared gate and get to the house itself, which was lit up like a luxury hotel. Dominating the gravelled courtyard was a bronze statue of a huge wild boar. Inside, Cal's first impression was of overdecoration, not that he had long to look; a white-coated valet came in carrying his case and the colonel indicated he would take him to his room.

Once there, the man proceeded to unpack his things and hang them up, and that included his dinner jacket. 'Dinner will be served in an hour and dress is informal, mein Herr, shall I lay out what I think appropriate?'

'Please do.'

'With your permission, I will take the rest of your clothes when you have changed and have them sponged and pressed.'

'Thank you.'

The fellow was a perfect servant, except when he was finished and about to depart he gave Cal a crisp, full-armed, Nazi salute.

The two-fingered response was only produced when he had gone.

In a blazer and open-necked shirt, Callum Jardine still felt overdressed compared to his host, who was clad in a long, sleeveless hunting waistcoat of soft brown leather, green trousers and he too was in a white shirt and tieless. Never having seen Göring outside of newsreels, it was interesting to observe he was thinner than he looked on film, although still well built. The smile was the same, though, a full affair that pushed out his cheeks, rosy either from fresh air or the unnecessary fire in the huge grate.

'Herr Moncrief.'

'I don't quite know what to call you, sir.'

Göring went over to a table full of bottles and, having established that Cal would drink whisky and water, made it for him. Interesting that in a house full of servants, this conversation was not going to be overheard by anyone. The glass, crystal, weighed a ton but the whisky was a single malt.

Göring laughed and finally replied to the question. 'As long as you do not call me what they do in the part of Spain from which you have come. That, I do not think, would be flattering.'

'No. That would be rude.'

'Sit, Herr Moncrief, and tell me something of yourself.'

This was a situation in which Lizzie's brother's true story was no good. He was a lounge lizard who worried whether his tie matched his spats, never quite deciding, and letting his man do it for him after an hour of agonising. A life spent in the clubs of St James seeking to outbore the bores; that tale was not going to impress this man.

Added to that, Hermann Göring was no fool; he could not have got to his present position if he was. In the dog-eat-dog pit of Nazi politics he was a top man, and that also meant he was a ruthless killer. For all the smiles and the amiable expression he could have Cal taken out like a shot without blinking.

'I don't think it will surprise you to know that is not my real name.'

'No.' Göring waited, only speaking when Cal did not. 'Am I to be told what your real name is?'

'I rather suspect you might know already. You do, after all, have a great deal of resources with which to check up on people.'

'Captain Callum Jardine.'

'Not a serving captain and I never use that rank.'

'You're an interesting fellow, but I cannot see why you have become involved in this particular transaction. My information, which I will admit to you is limited, does not have you down as a fellow traveller of communists.'

'I do what I do for money.'

'The Republicans will be crushed.' Those words went with a hardening of the expression on his face, slight but noticeable. 'Germany will not allow them to triumph.'

'A man in my profession has no given right to supply the winning side.'

The thoughts that were spinning around in Cal Jardine's head made it hard to keep a poker face. How much did Göring know about what he had been up to in Hamburg? Was he familiar with his exploits in Romania? Was this all an elaborate trap, or would he go through with the agreed deal?

'And how are you to be paid, given what is stored in Athens is for what I am supposed to supply?'

That was responded to with a conspiratorial smile and a lie, which came easily. 'Naturally, there is more than one pot of gold. My trade, my fee, will be simultaneous with yours, but in a different location. I have no desire to trust my funds to a Greek bank, and before you ask, I will decline to tell you how high it is.'

Göring's chest heaved slightly. 'I have no concern about that, Herr Jardine, except that if it is too substantial it may be enough to allow you to retire.'

'People like you and I don't retire, we love the game too much.'

'It can be a deadly one.'

'That, if I may say so, is part of the thrill.'

'We shall eat together, and you will tell me about the places you have been and the things you have seen. Sadly, apart from Sweden and seeing the fields of France from the air, I have not been able to indulge in much travel.'

Göring was an engaging host and it was obvious that sitting at table being served fish from his lake and wild boar that he had shot himself, the one subject that was not to be discussed was arms sales, not with servants in the room. Cal was able to talk knowledgeably about hunting and fishing in Scotland, which he had done with his father, while his host listed the delights of the surrounding forests.

For a top Nazi he was remarkably free of the cant that generally peppered their speech – racial superiority, Aryan eugenics and the like – and, given he was an affable host, Cal had to keep reminding himself that this was an ex-fighter ace, a winner of the highest Imperial German decoration for bravery, *Pour le Mérite*, who had been with Adolf Hitler from the very earliest days.

In 1923, Göring had taken a bullet in the lower gut during the so-called Beer Hall Putsch, ending up in an Austrian hospital where he had become addicted to the morphine that they used to ease his pain. He had risen as Hitler had risen, not just because he was a close comrade, but also because he was a man who would do anything to achieve power and would certainly do the same to maintain it.

It was also clear that he had a degree of respect for his guest; it was one of those things that people who had fought in the Great War found quickly, a sort of shorthand route to understanding – both had seen the death and destruction, both had survived, and that meant they could talk almost like old comrades.

He was interested in Palestine, where Cal had helped some of the Zionist settlers to fight off their Arab neighbours, more as a place to which the Jews, a pest to him, could be despatched, than in anything else, and, of course, the war in the Peninsula was referred to, his opinion of Franco not a flattering one.

'I am glad you agree that Madrid is the key, Herr Jardine, but taking it by frontal assault is not the way to gain the prize. Talk to our generals and they will tell you that the way to win is to cut the capital off from its bases of supply.'

'Or to bomb them into submission.'

'A large city is a difficult target; not impossible, but the means to achieve that goal would have to be much more than the Condor Legion could put in the air.'

'You do not see it as barbaric, bombing civilians?'

'Herr Jardine, war has changed and will go on changing, but what you call "civilians" have never been safe from we warriors. Perhaps a few hundred years ago you and I might have met in the joust, but then it would not have troubled our chivalry to go and cut up a few peasants and perhaps rape their daughters. We would certainly have stolen anything they possessed. There is no good pretending that war can be fought with rules; best to forget any of that nonsense and get it over as quickly as possible.'

'Will we have another war?'

'It can be avoided.'

'How?'

'Give Germany back what she lost at Versailles. We have no objections to you ruling the waves, in fact the Führer admires the British Empire, but we are the land power to match your sea power. Let us look to our backyard and we will leave you to your oceans.'

'I think there are one or two nations that might object.'

'Nations? Is Poland a nation? No, like the rest it is the construct of a fool of an American president and men who were too supine to tell him to mind his own business.' That thought obviously angered him. 'The Americans do not understand Europe, and nothing proved that more than Woodrow Wilson's stupidity at Versailles.'

His voice dropped. 'We want peace, Herr Jardine; we *need* peace to restore Germany.'

'And once restored?'

'Then we can destroy the Bolsheviks and I hope and expect that is a crusade in which, instead of being enemies, the British Empire and the Greater German Reich will be allies.'

When Cal thought about what those same Bolsheviks were doing in Spain it was a tempting prospect, but he doubted it would ever come to pass. Göring barked an order and the dining room was cleared.

'You are a calm man, Herr Jardine, and I admire that. When I invited you here, I was not sure what to do with you.'

'Are you now?'

Göring stood up. 'I am going to retire. Sleep well.'

There was no sign of Göring in the morning, but he did hear the sound of distant gunfire, so he assumed he was hunting. There was plenty of other noise, made by workmen building, sawing and hammering, and a pre-breakfast walk showed that Carinhall was a construction site – if Göring needed money, this was where it was going.

On his walk he tried to sum up the man – he had a feeling if he got away from here, still questionable, he might be asked. Göring was a bit of an opportunist, which did not mean he did not believe in the German destiny of which he had spoken the previous night; in that he was passionate and perhaps that was why he was a Nazi, they being, to him, the only people who could restore the country to what it had been in his youth.

Yet for all his more open perspective and lack of humbug, he was as deluded as any of his comrades; he sincerely believed in an absolute impossibility, that Great Britain would let Germany have a free hand on the Continent. It was a chilling thought, and one he had harboured for many years, that there was going to be another war and maybe one that would be even more terrible than the last. Old Sir Basil saw it too, so did Peter Lanchester and his mysterious cabal of backers – why could not the politicians and the people who voted for them?

'It's not impossible,' he said out loud. 'It can be stopped and it must be stopped.'

'Herr Jardine.' It was Brauschitz. 'When you have breakfasted I will fly you back to Unterlüss.'

Well that answers one question, he thought. *He's not going to shoot me.*

CHAPTER TWENTY-SIX

Jardine had a lot of things he thought wrong with the Germans, and that came from growing up as a young schoolboy in Hamburg, having spent his formative years in a French *lycée*, which, it had to be said, made him exotic enough to avoid the bullying that might have come his way and very popular with the girls.

As a nation, never mind individuals, they were damned serious and too ready to take offence. Try being five minutes late for a meeting in a coffee bar and it was like the fall of the Roman Empire; what you say is what you mean – the exact opposite of the way the British behaved. A friendship declared was like a blood ceremony without a cut, and God help you if you failed to meet the obligations.

Yet you could not fault their efficiency: when they said his goods would be delivered on a set day, that was the day they would arrive in Hamburg, and he was there before them, in what was for him an old stamping ground. Gessler had assembled the agreed batch of weaponry, he had inspected everything and it was all proper; he had even tested random weapons and they worked.

There was a residual guilt from his last departure from the city, so hurriedly made, in which he had to go without saying goodbye to someone important: the lady who had not only occasionally shared a bed with him for several months, but also probably saved his life with a phone call. The walk he took around St Pauli, with a hat low on his eyes, took him past many of the places he had frequented and it was good to know the people who had been there before were still around.

They were doing what they had always done, selling the dream of a good time as long as you could pay, very likely purveying stuff you could buy for one mark for ten – twenty if you were a real idiot; the club hostesses were still pretending to drink what was supposed to be champagne and the heavies were still there to ensure the clients pay the excessive bills when they complained.

The sad bit missing was the bar of Fat Olaf, where Peter Lanchester had found him on that fateful day. That was closed and shuttered, and where was he? Had he paid a price for Cal Jardine getting away before the Brownshirt SA thugs arrived to beat his brains out? He hoped not, and the chances were good; Fat Olaf was a survivor, maybe he had opened up somewhere else.

He had walked the Reeperbahn, slipping into the Herbertstraße as darkness fell to make sure Gretl the great dominatrix was still plying her trade and her whips, glad to see her in a new costume of sparkling gold, glaring out with practised ferocity to the street, waiting for those players and payers who wanted to go home and tell a great story about their Hamburg adventure; it had never occurred to Cal that anyone really enjoyed the first part of Gretl's thing, it was the way she took the pain away that made her an institution.

He was sad that he dare not say hello, because he did not have a clue what had happened when he left; Lette might know and, if she still worked in the local party HQ, would be finished by now. She had an apartment in Trommelstraße, not a place with a telephone and not a good address, but one with neighbours who looked after her kids when she was working.

It was not easy to call without everyone knowing – it certainly had not been in the past, and many was the time he had been ribbed when he came of a night, doubly so if he was spotted by the old lady scrubbing the stone steps as he left in the morning, and in a sense he was breaking an agreed rule: she had always known if he went it would be sudden, he had an unspoken order that the break should be final.

It's damned difficult to be on the wrong side of a door when you worry about what might happen when you knock. Lette was a beautiful widow, good company, and there might be a new man in her life, which made Cal wish he could pretend to be some kind of door-to-door salesperson. That there was someone home, he knew – the radio was playing dance music.

He raised his hand to knock, then hesitated, thinking to walk away. This was all wrong, it went against the grain of everything he advised others to do, everything he thought right about how to behave – you cut the cord when it was life and death. Just then a neighbour came out to use the communal toilet and he had to hit the door to avoid suspicion.

It was heart-stopping the way the music diminished, the sound being turned down, and his heart was in his mouth as he waited, listening to the farting coming from the toilet. When the door was opened it was by Lette's daughter, Inge, no longer the gauche twelve-year-old he remembered, but a promising fourteen and looking like the beginnings of a real woman.

'Uncle Cal,' she cried, her eyes wide open with glad surprise; then she flung herself at him and her shout brought the two boys running. Christian and Günter, both younger than their sister. They were around his legs within seconds, shouting his name. Having ruffled their hair and said their names he looked up and there was Lette, in an apron and looking tired, in what passed for a hall; was she drying her hands, or was that hand-wringing fear?

'Hey,' was his feeble greeting.

She came forward, maternal in the way she shuffled the children inside so she could shut the door, this while he was subjected to a stream of questions asking where he had been, and as children do, the boys were telling him about what had happened to them in between now and the last time he had seen them, gabbling away in near incoherence.

She was clever, Lette, the way she shooed the children away so she herself could give him a kissed greeting, in truth the chance to whisper in his ear that he should say nothing incriminating, that the boys, particularly, could not be trusted.

'Say you have been at sea.' Then she turned and began to take off her apron. 'You take care of Uncle Cal, while I go and see if Old Ma Pieffer can look after you.'

Moans and groans ensued, the selfish cries of the boys contrasted with the self-possession of Inge as he was dragged to the table, covered in an oilskin cloth that had seen better times, to tell stories of South America, Spain, of creatures too fabulous to be real and to indulge in that visitor pastime, giving the children money.

'Are you coming back to stay, Uncle Cal?'

When he looked at Inge then, it nearly broke his heart; he knew she saw him like a parent and had done so from the very first day they had met. They had bonded as if it were predestined, she trusting him, he good with her, and if leaving Lette had been hard, leaving Inge, whom he thought of as a daughter, was worse.

'Boys, you have your bank still?' The yeses were larded with anticipation – he had always been generous, and Cal obliged by emptying his pockets of pfennigs and the odd mark, passing them over. Then they dashed into the only bedroom where, no doubt, they would boast one was richer than the other.

'Are you here to stay?'

He could not answer, but then he did not have to; his silence was sufficient. Looking at her, bonny but not yet fully formed, he wanted to take her in his arms and hold her as he had once done, maybe tell her the stories he had loved inventing. Somehow she was beyond that. It was a relief that Lette returned with the news that Old Ma Pieffer was on her way down.

'I can't, little one.'

Inge nodded and he knew that when he was gone she would cry. Lette had her coat on and was keen to get out of the door and there was just a flash of jealousy in Inge's eyes that her mother spotted and smothered with a kiss; if Cal was close to Inge, her mother was closer still. Then they were out on the landing, his nose twitching at the odour of the neighbour's noisy evacuation, down the stone stairs and into the street.

'What do you mean "We can't talk"?'

The laugh was hollow. 'What do you think will happen when Christian and Günter go to school tomorrow? Once they have sung a hymn to the damned Führer they will be asked if anything strange has happened and they will say Uncle Cal came back. Their good National Socialist teacher will ask who Uncle Cal is.'

'For the sake of Christ.'

'You do not know what they will say, what they will be asked, or the consequences, and that, my lost love, is life in the Third Reich; I cannot even talk in front of my own children, because if I do they will be encouraged to denounce me. So, do you think we could have talked in there about why you had to leave and the phone call I made to give you a chance to flee?'

'Is there somewhere we can go?'

'Cal, this is St Pauli, there are a hundred places we can go.'

'Am I allowed to say, Lette,' Cal said, leaning over her and looking down into her eyes, 'you look tired?'

'Two years nearly I don't see you and that is what you want to tell me? I have three children, a job I hate, surrounded by foul-mouthed bigots who should be taken out to sea and thrown overboard, and no one to tell.'

'Inge?'

'I cannot burden her.'

'I miss telling her stories.'

'She misses you more than she misses the stories.'

'What happened to the money I left for you?'

'It is still in the account you opened, I haven't touched it, and do I have to tell you why?'

'Questions would be asked if you were suddenly flush. But the idea was you could get a better apartment, one where Inge can have some privacy. She's of an age when she needs it.'

'I think we might have to use that money one day for something more serious than another bedroom.'

'I thought you might have found another man.'

'If I can find one I can trust, and who knows how to treat me right, then maybe I will, but all I meet are beery shits.'

The one thing never discussed, the reason she was trusted to work in the local Nazi party office, was her late husband, a rabid National Socialist who had been killed in street fighting prior to the 1932 elections. To the men she mixed with every day, Brownshirt thugs, he was a hero; to her a bully and wife beater she was glad was dead.

He had met Lette when out running – she was an ex-hundred-metre sprinter, and with no knowledge of her background they had begun to stop and chat while catching breath. She found release in talking to him, a man who hated the Nazis as much as she did, and said so, as well as being active in getting Jews out of Germany. Lette had become his lover; only later did he discover where she worked and how many times she had used her position to save those under threat herself.

It was no wonder she was tired, never mind the children and the job; she was living a double life, cursing Jews as diseased rats one minute, trying to warn them of the danger they were in without getting caught the next. He had suggested she get out before; Lette had refused while there was good to be done. When it came to being brave, Cal thought her ten times the person he was.

'Anyway, you have not told me why you came back.'

'It might have been for you.'

She punched him in the balls then, which given he was naked, had him out of the bed and hopping. 'Why did you do that?'

'You are a liar.'

Still rubbing hard, he acknowledged the truth. 'I know, and not a good one with you.'

It had been a strange relationship: he was fond of her without being in love, she, determined never to have another man rule her life. If there was sex between them, and there had just been that, and very enjoyable too, then it was based on deep friendship rather than passion, and if she knew that she was being used, it was a situation that troubled her not at all.

'Two years without a man in my life,' she said, her voice deep as she tugged him back into the bed. 'I hope you have not been too wounded – by that punch.'

She was asleep when he left, and when she awoke she found a thick wad of high-denomination Reichsmarks on the table and a one-line note, which read, '*For Inge's new clothes. Invent a rich relative XXX.*'

He was down at the docks before the line of railway trucks arrived, having used the papers he had to get through the main gate into the free port area and make sure the SS *Barhill* was at its berth, then getting back to the main gate to await the arrival. The way they took him was so professional that he did not see it coming at all: the van drew alongside, men in working gear appeared from nowhere, he was hit just hard enough to be stunned and then bundled into the back, thrown onto the metal floor with a knee digging into his back.

The command to stay still was backed up by a slap to the head and he knew his hands were being tied. He was thinking this did not make sense, unless Göring had had a change of mind; but why would he do that, because MCG in Athens would not get paid? Had there been a leak, with so many – far too many – people in on what was planned? There was nothing he could do but lie still and speculate.

The hollow sound when the van stopped told him he was in some kind of garage; there was the squeak of the door opening and he was hauled out, one man on each elbow hurrying him along through a doorway, then a couple of corridors, so he had trouble keeping his feet. He was taken into a bare room with a single chair in the middle, the sinister single light bulb above, then sat and tied down, realising as he moved that the legs were fixed to the floor. Then he saw the battered table against the wall with the rubber truncheons on it.

And then he was alone, but not for long, and the smiling blond fellow who entered gave him a shock, which he was not able to hide; this was bad, very bad, worse than Göring reneging. The last time he had seen Gottlieb Resnick had been on a Black Sea dockside, and the German had wanted to just shoot him then; he would want more now.

'Mr Jardine,' Resnick said in his accented, horribly ungrammatical English, 'you did not me believe when *auf Wiedersehen* I said, but here are we, once more with each other in company.'

'Are you still an *Oberstürmbannführer* or did you get busted to *Gefreiter* for that cock-up in Constanta?'

'It had on me no effect, but when you to hell get there is waiting a very damaged Romanian colonel to greet you.'

'He's dead.'

'Painfully so, but before he expired finally he express did the wish that you would as he did suffer.'

'Something you are looking forward to carrying out.'

'Tut, tut, Jardine. My rank allows that I watch others pain inflict, though in case yours I might an exception make, the payment for a fool making me look.'

'You really ought to do something about your English, it's bloody awful.'

Resnick came close and bent low, so his nose was nearly touching Jardine's.

'You joke now, but beg to die you will and listen I will not. If these walls could speak maybe Yiddish you would hear the voices of those before you gone, the shits who think that the Reich they can cheat and take elsewhere their stolen money.'

The laugh was more chilling than the words. 'They all think they their loot will keep hidden – that is the word, is it not? – but they tell, maybe when they have seen raped and sodomised their wife before their eyes by criminals diseased from the Hamburg jail, then to lie on the floor forced and clean Aryan piss drink. Even then some hold out, but when their pizzle is electric fried they talk.'

How long had they known he was in Hamburg? Did they know about Lette? Was there any point in even thinking about that?

'I have been away from Hamburg too long; anything I can tell you is long cold.'

'I from you want nothing of information. This is for my pleasure alone. You have out of me a fool made, I will make a wreck of you and maybe see how to die long it takes you.'

'I don't think I'm in a position to stop you, but there are people who know I am here in Hamburg.'

'But not in this room! First, a little bubble I puncture. You will wonder how you in Germany I know.' He went to the table and brought back a folder. 'When a certain fellow you approached, he was not sure if you were who you said, so he contacted German embassy.'

Resnick produce two photos, one showing blurred figures and

347

spots of light. 'Hard to get right in dark, but in morning light, look at this.'

The second picture was as clear as day, not surprising given it had been taken at dawn. It showed him smiling and waving at the taxi in which MCG's wife, Elena, was departing the Grande Bretagne Hotel.

'Makes a whore of his wife, does he?'

'She is not his wife, just secretary, and for extra pay, she plays a part.'

Clever little bastard, Cal thought, *I certainly underestimated him. How the hell had he managed it so smoothly?*

The door opened and the two men who came in looked like what they were: inflictors of pain, thick-necked, hairy forearms, muscles to spare and faces only a mother could love. One had a knuckleduster which he was keen Cal should see him play with, the other a long spike which he knew was soon going to be inside him and twisted.

You never know if you can stand this, all you can do is hope that somehow you keep a bit of your dignity. He had made a right chump out of Resnick in Romania and had enjoyed rubbing a little salt into his open wound. Positives? No mention or show of Lette or her children; she would have been bad enough, but if they started on Inge?

Was it better to plead for mercy quickly – appear to break early, scream and plead? Resnick was not after information but personal satisfaction. Too early and it would not work – maybe once they had his teeth out with that knuckleduster and had broken a few bones. Or was it the wires on his cock?

That the door burst open was not remarkable; that Colonel Brauschitz was standing there, looking as elegant as he had previously, seemed extraordinary. He held up a paper with a very large eagle on it.

'Resnick, I have an order here from the deputy Führer. This man is to be released immediately.'

'No.'

Brauschitz shook his head and gave a wan smile. 'You have a choice, Herr *Obersturmbannführer*. You can either obey this order, or rest assured you will yourself be tied to that chair before the day is out.'

Unable to obey, Resnick just stormed out.

'Be thankful we tap the telephones of those we do not trust, and also that General Göring has the power to frighten a man like Resnick.'

As well as having, Cal thought, *the certain knowledge that without me there would be no payment.*

'The railway trucks.'

'Are at the quayside.' Brauschitz looked at his watch. 'Nearly unloaded by now, I should think. The telephone connection has been set up in the harbour master's office, so you may make your call to Athens.'

'The arrangement was when she weighs.'

'If you wish to wait till that ship departs without you . . .'

The rest was left hanging in the air. Hamburg right now was not a good place to be left behind in.

'Harbour master's office it is.'

CHAPTER TWENTY-SEVEN

There was no feeling of relief even when the SS *Barhill* closed her hatches then cleared her berth. It was a long way to the mouth of the River Elbe and the North Sea, and even then, with the string of inshore islands that lined the coast, it took a request to the captain to get the ship directly out to sea, instead of hugging the shore, so Jardine could get out of German territorial waters. Even then he was not sure he was beyond the reach of the likes of Resnick – the Nazi state was a criminal enterprise and no respecter of anyone's laws.

It took time for him to calm down and stop his nerves jumping; facing death was one thing, what he had faced in that barren room was likely to be a recurring nightmare, but as of now, the sea air and the motion of the boat got to him, and after the tensions of the last few weeks, he fell into a long and deep slumber. From then on the days melded into a week in which he was in limbo.

On the high seas they were safe, it was when they came inshore that the trouble would surface. The master had to get the ship through the Straits without too deep an inspection and they were patrolled by the Royal Navy, a subject he was obliged to raise with the long-time seaman who, prior to a good dinner, poured him what he called a 'stiff one'.

'Are you aware, sir, of my instructions?'

'No. I was not party to the arrangements.'

'I have a manifest that says I am carrying agricultural machinery to Greece, but we both know that is not the case. My concern is for myself and my crew, for if we are caught breaking the embargo, as my destination suggests we will, then we will be in real trouble.'

'So?'

'So I need you to take full responsibility, as does the owner of the ship. With that in mind, I have a false manifest, naming you as the agent and shipper, a contract of hire for the vessel as well as a bill for same, and I need you to sign these papers so that I can, in all innocence, say I have been duped if we are subjected to a search.'

The folder was passed over and Cal opened it, and even if it did not make him happy, he had to admit the way it had been arranged was classy. These were things he had grown up surrounded by, shipping for profit being his father's business. There was headed notepaper for Jardine & Sons – oddly his old man had hoped for that at one time – several items of correspondence setting up the whole shipment, bills of lading naming the supposed cargo in detail, with quotes for prices as well as the invoice; everything, in fact, that got the ship owner, his master and crew off the hook and dumped any trouble squarely on him.

'I think you might need another stiff one, sir.'

Cal held out his glass. 'After what I faced in Hamburg, a jail sentence seems nothing to worry about.'

There was no attempt at dodging the Navy, trying things like taking the Straits in darkness, but Captain Roland had his own method of making this go smoothly and that was the contents of his drinks cabinet once more. Ordered to heave-to off Gibraltar for a cargo inspection, the naval officer who came aboard was taken straight to the cabin and given a pink gin and it was the Navy's own – Plymouth, and full strength.

After four of those the visitor was finally handed the false manifest, which he waved about. 'Damn it, old fellow, we're all Englishmen here, what? I take it all is in order?'

'Another gin?'

'Don't mind if I do.'

If an Italian submarine spotted them in the Mediterranean, as they chugged past the southern tip of the Balearics, they had no knowledge of it. Besides, there were Royal Navy destroyers about to ensure that a ship heading for Piraeus under a British flag was not interfered with in any way; the change of course, all lights doused, and the increase in speed to sail west past Minorca were done in darkness, but it was daylight when the *Barhill* berthed in Barcelona.

Indalecio Prieto came up from Valencia to inspect the now-landed cargo, which had lifted the spirits of more than just Barcelona – news had spread throughout Spain, though without his name being mentioned – given that those Italian submarines were taking a heavy toll of Soviet supply ships and severely choking off the provision of arms. He was happy to meet Cal Jardine's request for something

352

from the cargo in lieu of a cash payment, as well as providing very quickly a set of internal travel papers in his own name.

That night, he went down to the docks, to where the smugglers hung out, and using his contacts there bought another forged set in a different name, as well as some morphine and a syringe. The hardest thing was not getting hold of a car – they were cheap and plentiful – but the fuel required to make use of it, and that involved a little dealing on the black market.

Tank full and with a spare container in the boot, he loaded everything else he owned into it, leaving Barcelona for the last time and taking the road to Madrid.

The city was now very much a place under siege and was even more tightly controlled with checkpoints than he recalled. He was asked for his papers and passport time after time, though any search of his car was perfunctory. Inside the city perimeter, Madrid was subject to the intermittent barrage of artillery shells from the Nationalist front lines just over the river, which, when one came close, forced him to pull over. While he was stopped he could hear the rattle of machine guns to the north, in the still-contested University district, as well as what he thought might be a trench mortar.

Yet still people lived here, going about their daily lives, a lot of their clothing more rags than anything that could be called clothing, the faces pinched from lack of food, faces as grey as the stones in the piles of rubble which lay in every street and square, beside the deep craters which pitted the surfaces of both roads and pavements, ignoring the big signs which admonished them to get out of Madrid. Asked, they would no doubt have enquired where they were to go.

The Hotel Florida seemed to be very close to the front line now, but it made no difference; those shells from the bigger cannon could reach right to the eastern suburbs, so nowhere was safe. Many of the buildings close by were seriously damaged, yet once through the doors there was the concierge to greet him, who seemed not at all fazed by the thick coating of dust which covered everything and filled the air, catching the back of Cal's throat ever time he took a breath.

Welcomed as what he was, a returning customer, once his luggage was carried in he was shown up to a room at the back of the hotel, safer, as was explained, from shellfire, though he passed some rooms with just a sheet of wood where there had once been a door; the place had suffered.

An enquiry at the desk had informed him that the majority of the war correspondents still staying as guests were fully occupied trying to cover a Republican offensive at a place fifteen miles north of Madrid called Brunete. It was unlikely they would come back to their base overnight.

The shelling started while he was washing and shaving, which had him holding his razor away from his face and listening to the whining of their flight, as well as the crump as they landed. It went on for about ten minutes and stopped, so he went back to his ablutions, now that he would not suddenly cut himself in reacting to a nearby explosion.

The restaurant was still functioning, albeit with a severely diminished menu, but the food was wholesome if plain, and he sat there, sipping a beer, ignoring the occasional shelling, as darkness fell outside. Then he went upstairs and changed into the dark clothing he had bought before leaving Barcelona.

If they wondered at the desk why he wanted more food sent up to his room, they did not ask; guests were always odd, it did not need a war on your doorstep to make them act strangely.

Driving to his destination he was stopped twice and required to use the set of forged papers he had bought, which went with the press pass Peter Lanchester had provided him with; that was something he had learnt from his previous visit: no one moved around with greater ease than a foreign reporter – the Republicans saw anyone prepared to face their travails with them as friends.

He had parked and walked to where he now stood on a street corner just off the Calle de Atocha, a long avenue that bisected the city, in shadow, watching the arched, ecclesiastical doorway of a building as dark as every other in a city that feared to be bombed. Had this church been a place of torment during the Inquisition? It was possible, given its age. If so, it had been given a new lease of life to inflict misery for a different faith.

It was odd to think that a place where supposed enemies of the state were incarcerated, and very likely subjected to torture, had fixed hours of work, yet it just went to show how banal parts of what was happening in Spain could be. Guards worked in shifts and then went home, to wherever that was – in the case of the person he sought, an apartment he had taken over from a victim of one of his own purges, a short walk from the church.

He observed the new shift drifting in one by one, with a resigned gait; those going off for the night were more of a crowd – black-uniformed men who had turned the arrest, beating and starving of prisoners into a set of norms. No doubt it was sometimes thrown into turmoil by a sudden burst of suspicion, but on a day-to-day basis it was like clocking on and off in an office or factory.

The only person not doing that still had a fixed routine, and thanks to the rooting around of Tyler Alverson, Cal Jardine knew what that was. Somehow, being a creature of habit went with his personality, and right on cue, as the dial on Cal's luminous watch slipped past eight, he emerged onto the steps of the church, taking a cigarette case from his pocket, extracting one, tapping it on the metal, then slipping it between his two middle fingers, before lighting up.

Manfred Decker never went anywhere without two armed guards – was it necessary, or an affectation? Cal did not know, but judging by their lack of attention it seemed the latter. Most of those in Madrid who could be suspected of being class enemies had either already been shot, imprisoned, had fled, or were very circumspect when it came to dealing with authority. Thus, many months after the insurrection of the generals, life had settled for these non-combatants into monotony.

Cal moved as Drecker moved, glad there was enough starlight to keep him in view without coming too close. If the Calle de Atocha was not busy, neither was it empty. The early hours of darkness tended to be less dangerous; even the Nationalist artillerymen stopped feeding their guns to feed themselves, so people were scurrying along, head bent into their shoulders in a way that had no doubt become habitual.

There was arrogance in the communist's gait; he saw no need to hunch, instead he cast his eyes imperiously at those who passed him, in the imagination of the man following seeking to look into their souls for a hint of treachery. As people observed him getting close and took note of his garb – black leather coat, the pistol at the hip and that cap with the red star on his head – never mind the pair behind with slung rifles, they swayed away to avoid coming too close.

The door of the apartment block was deeply recessed, creating an area of Stygian darkness. Drecker had his lighter out, snapping it on to locate the keyhole, his two escorts waiting for the door to open. The flame went out, the key turned, and as Drecker stepped inside the darkened hallway, they followed. It was their job to shut the door, and it was as one turned to carry out his duty that the shadowy figure stepped forward and put a bullet from his Walther PP right in the centre of his forehead.

The phut of the silenced weapon barely registered; it was the door-closer being thrown backwards against his companion that made the second escort turn, what Cal could see of his face, really a pale blur, wondering what was going on. It was doubtful he had time to register it in his smashed brain.

That was when Drecker, switching the hall light on, heard the door slam and turned to see his two guards slumped on the hall floor and the assassin standing, feet apart with the pistol, the long barrel of the silencer too, pointing at his own head.

'On your knees, hands behind your head.'

The overhead light obscured Cal's face but Drecker's eyes registered he had recognised the German-speaking voice. A hand went automatically to the flap of his holster, but the third bullet hit his forearm and broke it, driving his hand well away from the gun as the instruction was repeated. A shocked Drecker sank to his knees as Cal darted forward and took his pistol, before resuming his shooting stance.

'I have come to make you pay for Florencia Gardiola.' Drecker, who had been holding his wounded arm with his head bowed, looked up, trying to compose his face for an automatic denial. 'As well as Juan Luis Laporta and, no doubt, hundreds of other innocents. You nearly had me killed too.'

'I did not kill them – they died, and you were wounded, by an accidental discharge.'

'No, you did not, but you gave the order, Drecker, to whoever fired that gun. Your mistake was to stay around in the shadows to ensure it was carried out. The first night after I met you, I saw you smoking a cigarette in the village square, and as you drew on it, the glow of the tip, because of the stupid way you hold it, lit up your cap badge. The night I was shot, I saw the same red star illuminated by a lit cigarette.'

'You are wrong.'

'No, Drecker, I am not. You waited to kill Laporta, and me too, marching up every night to keep his stupid attacks going and waiting till his own supporters were sick of it. Florencia was just a bystander, but what do you care?'

'A victim – how many victims have there been on this front?'

'Of their own side? You would know better than me. Now get on your feet.'

'If I am going to die, I prefer to die here.'

'You're going to stand trial first, Drecker, I want the world to know you are guilty.'

In pain as he undoubtedly was, Cal could see the flicker in the pale-blue eyes: hope, the prayer that his potential assassin might be stupid enough to seek judicial revenge in a city where it would not be him who would be the victim. Cal Jardine was holding his breath; he would kill him here if he had to, but give a man a chance of life and he should take it, even if it sounded crazy.

'Turn around. I am going to tie your hands, which will be painful. Do not make a sound.'

There was no gentility in what Cal did and he took pleasure in the whimpers of pain his actions caused, but the way Drecker did not cry out was promising; maybe he believed he was going to be handed over to a revolutionary court.

'My car is outside and ten metres to the left of your front door. It is unlocked, go to it and open the back door. If you try anything I will put a bullet in the back of your skull.'

The lit hallway, when the front door was open, was a risk, but it had to be taken and they were over the corpses and out in less than two seconds, now in the dark recess, with Cal's muzzle pressed against Drecker's neck.

'Walk at normal pace.'

That said, he dropped the weapon to run along his thigh, giving Drecker a slight shove to get him moving. The German did as he was asked, walked to the car, opened the back door and stood erect. With a quick glance to left and right to ensure no one was close, Cal hit him on the back of the head with the pistol butt, pushing him forward as he began to crumple, then leant down to heave in his legs. He had to close the door and go to the other side to drag him so he fell between the front and rear seats.

The syringe, already loaded with morphine, went into his backside and was emptied; it was not enough to kill him, but he would not be groaning if he came round. The blanket to cover his inert body was taken from the front seat.

Driving out of Madrid on the Valencia road proved easier than driving in from Barcelona. He was leaving the front line, and anyway, the checkpoints were less scrupulous in checking on a war correspondent, while the darkness concealed the comatose Drecker. Cal had to summon up all his reserves of calmness in a situation of real peril, but he had faced death enough times to smile a lot and trade pleasantries.

To do what he wanted to do he had to get clear of Madrid, and the risk of going through checkpoints just had to be faced, but tired men on a dark night reduced the chances of discovery. It also kept them alive, given, as well as the Walther PP, he had a machine pistol on the floor by his feet with a magazine clipped in, and he was ready to use it. If it came to the crunch and he could not get clear, Drecker and he would die within seconds of each other.

Out past those checkpoints he drove through Vaciamadrid and on in darkness to the next real junction at Villarejo de Salvanés, then took a left turn, heading for where, as far as he knew, lay the Nationalist front lines.

In open country, once dawn came, he stopped, topped up the car with petrol, ate the food he had brought from the Hotel Florida, then, sure the road was empty, uncovered Drecker so he could get a gag on him before putting the blanket back on top. As soon as the local bus went past him – he waved to the passengers – he got back in and followed it.

The front, away from the actual battle zones, was fluid and, with the limited resources on both sides, it was a case of roadside pickets rather than anything solid; there was no way they could afford the men to render it anything other than porous. The small town of Belmonte de Tajo was close by, and with his press credentials and less-than-perfect Spanish, he was taken for what he was, a foreign pressman in search of a background story.

In asking people how they were coping with the privations of war, he found that the actual demarcation line was no more than a kilometre down the road going west, and if those to whom he had spoken were surprised that he headed that way instead of the way he had come, well that was his business. The road he ended up on was a track, but his compass told him it was going in the right direction and a muffled groan from the rear indicated his prisoner had begun to stir. Time to talk to him.

'My first thought was just to put a bullet in your head.' Looking up from the floor, Drecker's eyes showed his confusion; Cal's voice was utterly without passion. 'But that would not have really given justice to Florencia, which is what you are going to pay for – her life, and my unhappiness at the loss. I have to tell you also, the notion of what I am about to do was inspired by a fellow countryman of yours.'

From inside his jacket Cal produced a large envelope.

'Inside here, in Spanish, is your name, rank and a description of your duties. I have taken your Communist Party membership card and wallet from your pocket. It also implies that you have information about the future plans of the Republican forces, which of course you do not. When they ask you for that information, you will deny that you have any and they will not believe you.'

The look had changed as had Cal's voice. 'They will kill you eventually, Drecker, for they are no more gentle than you have been to others, but not before they have done to you what you have inflicted on so many people, and when you are screaming in pain, I want you to think of this.'

Cal took the photograph of Florencia out of his pocket and held it before the terrified German's eyes. 'There's an expression we British use, it's called "poetic justice".'

He had to get off the track into the fields; there would be a Republican outpost somewhere and it was pure luck as he drove that he saw the two men that manned the gimcrack blockhouse waving to him to stop, while not far from where they were based stood the Nationalist equivalent, in this case a not very high watchtower.

Given they were defending the line, they were more proactive; whoever manned it loosed off a couple of shots at his car, more as a warning than an attempt to kill him. As soon as he was level with the watchtower he stopped, placed the things he needed as signs, got out and ducked behind the car, opening the back door.

'Goodbye, Drecker, enjoy your visit to the other half of Spain.'

Keeping the car between him and the Nationalists, he headed away, and sure he was beyond range, turned to regain the Republican area, coming round to the little blockhouse in a wide arc with fulsome apologies for being a stupid foreigner. He was with the two militiamen when the Nationalists finally and gingerly approached the abandoned car.

What they saw first was what Cal had left on top of the dashboard: a black cap, with a very prominent red star facing right forward, and standing beside that a card, bearing the crest of the *Partido Comunista de España*.

It was not long before one of them was running back to the watchtower, where there had to be a field telephone. Eventually one of them tried the engine, and when it fired it was driven well into the Nationalist zone. With many gestures that there was nothing they could do, the two Republican militiamen watched as the owner of the lost car, having accepted what had happened, began to walk back to the town, only using the finger to the finger-to-the-head gesture that he was mad when his back was to them.

From then on it was buses back to Madrid, where he met Tyler Alverson in the bar of the Hotel Florida and, to the sound of shelling and the rattle of gunfire, he told him the story he so badly wanted to hear.

'What now, brother?'

'Home.'

AUTHOR'S NOTE

One of the joys of writing fiction is the ability to not only imagine real and invented characters but to place them where and when you want. Facts are important but they, like the individuals who populate a novel, are there to facilitate the story not the other way round.

Of all the wars of the twentieth century, the Spanish Civil War must rank as the most complex, one in which the lines of battle between the Nationalists and the Republicans were clearly drawn, yet behind those fluid fronts, certainly in the case of the latter, other conflicts based on ideology raged and they were as bloody and unforgiving as anything that happened in battle.

Hindsight is a wonderful thing, but there were many voices at the time, and not all of them on the left, who pointed out that to stand back and plead the farce of non-intervention, while letting the fascist dictatorships supply Franco and his army, was a mistake for which we paid a high price in the subsequent decade.

It was a tragedy that the only friend to the Republic was the Soviet Union, made greater by an ideology – seemingly alien to us now – that the end justifies the means, even if it means killing those on your own side. In the end, that friend ensured the elected government of Spain would lose.

What I set out to do in this novel was to try and make sense of the aforementioned complexity. This is a story, not a history, though there is much of that laced through the narrative; where there are minor deviations, they are in place to facilitate and to entertain in a subject about which one could write a dozen books and still not cover it all.